THE GUNSLINGER'S COMPANION

MICHAEL DE STEFANO

I0653316

Night to Dawn

ISBN: 978-1-937769-30-7
Cover Illustration by Riaanvdb (Dreamstime Images)
Copy editor: Barbara Custer
Content editor: Robert Ruffo
All rights reserved.

Night to Dawn Magazine & Books LLC
P. O. Box 643
Abington, PA 19001
www.bloodredshadow.com

For Rose

TABLE OF CONTENTS

Chapter One: The Sacrifice.............................2

Chapter Two: Dolci and Uncle Joe......................14

Chapter Three: Blueberry Pie..........................34

Chapter Four: The First Anna Maria....................45

Chapter Five: Beautiful Hands.........................93

Chapter Six: The Art of Entitlement...................146

Chapter Seven: The Child Stays........................182

Chapter Eight: Reunions...............................217

Chapter Nine: The Secret of Cheerianna................232

Afterward...237

About the Author......................................238

PART ONE: PABLO

Chapter One
The Sacrifice

She was born Anna Maria Cordero. Has anyone ever been given a lovelier name? Those who knew her were of the opinion that her name, like a catchy song lyric, rolled ever so pleasingly from the tongue. However, Anna Maria's grandfather, Pablo Cordero, decided to sweeten the already melodious name by calling his granddaughter "Cheerianna." He thought *Cheerianna* was the sort of name that might be given to a squaw who in some way was exceptional. Also, being quite the doting grandfather Pablo Cordero was, he made the absurd claim that his one-day-old granddaughter actually flashed him a smile. Absurd as this was, Pablo believed it to be so. More than that, it was his hope that as Anna Maria grew, she would shower his life with all the sunshine that in one way or another went missing.

"Look, Martina, what a beauty she is!" the doting grandfather cried to his daughter. "And God bless her, she smiles just like your mama used to!"

Cradling her infant daughter, Martina Cordero looked up at her beaming father and cried, "Papa!" Overcome with joy and sorrow, she stammered and struggled to finish her words. When she did, tears fell from Pablo's eyes, for right there and then, Martina decided that her daughter would go through life bearing the same name as the mother the heavens denied her the chance to know.

At first, Pablo Cordero didn't intend to become a doting grandfather. For days he went about grumbling and crying after learning that his seventeen-year-old unwed daughter had gone and gotten herself pregnant. Pablo cursed Martina and the unborn child and the expectant

2

mother felt abandoned. Pablo himself was of the belief that his good name would go down in disgrace. He was ashamed for himself *and* Martina—a fact he had little difficulty making known. He went about his days sullenly, and when Martina began to show, he forbade her to leave the house.

"You'll remain here until I can figure out how to deal with the disgrace that you've brought upon us!" were his coarse and angry words.

Despite Pablo's irrationality, Martina dared not disobey. Times were getting tough, though, and Martina believed that they would suffer financially. She had cleaned for the well-to-do folks in Brownsville, but while locked away, she wouldn't be able to work. Her work yielded a modest income, but it did help in the difficult times. What's more, Pablo made Martina appear irresponsible by denying her the right to go and explain to her employers that she was forced into quitting. That alone should have told Pablo that locking away Martina was irrational, if not altogether cruel. For had it not also been his intention to lock away the eventual child until say…its thirteenth birthday, sooner or later he would have to reconcile what he referred to as a "disgrace" and explain how an infant showed up on his doorstep, and furthermore, why it was permitted to stay. Nevertheless, Pablo followed through with his threat.

"But Papa, how will we survive if I can't work!" cried Martina.

Pablo stormed off, ignoring his pleading daughter and never once looking back to witness the crushing effects of his angry silence.

"If Miss Lillie were here, *she* wouldn't turn her back on me!" Martina cried out. "She would still love me!" Pablo was gone. The expectant mother's desperate cries never reached his ears.

****

Martina was age seven when Pablo made his return to Brownsville. This he did after a seven year stint living and working on Edgar Trudeau's farm. Shortly after their arrival, Martina was befriended by a young girl named Marylou Kendry. It was Marylou Kendry with whom Martina cleaned houses. Unbeknownst to Pablo, Marylou Kendry took it upon herself to explain to their employers that it wasn't Martina's wish to quit, but was forced to do so by her "unreasonable father."

****

As time went by, Pablo became used to the idea of Martina pregnant. At last, he softened his position and had come to anticipate the arrival of his grandbaby with eagerness. Pablo's turnabout didn't come until Martina was too far along to resume her partnership with Marylou Kendry. By then it wouldn't have mattered, as the homes in Brownsville, Texas, owned by the wealthier protestants were too large to be cleaned by one person, therefore, Marylou Kendry had to recruit a new partner.

As time passed, Anna Maria—or, Cheerianna, as she was called by her grandfather, lived up to the pet name. Whenever Martina called to her daughter, she would stress the last two syllables singing, "Anna Mareeeeahhhh." Her melodious voice rang out beautifully. The doting grandfather, though, never called Anna Maria anything *but* Cheerianna. Anna Maria was a delight and the apple of her mother and grandfather's eyes. After the many struggles that Pablo had endured in his lifetime, he looked upon his *sweet Cheerianna* as God's way of rewarding him. After her birth, he never let a day pass without thanking God *and* Martina for giving him such a beautiful grandbaby.

As Anna Maria grew, Pablo and she would take long walks together on Sunday afternoons. As Anna Maria grew bigger, their walks became longer. They would walk hand-in-hand all over Brownsville, Texas. As they went along, Anna Maria would occasionally glance up at her grandfather with confidence that he was a man who knew and understood the world like no other.

"Look, my sweet Cheerianna," Pablo had said to his granddaughter, who was always eager for a story. "This is all that remains of Palmito Ranch."

"What happened to it, Grandfather?" asked Anna Maria—eager as ever for Pablo's knowledge.

This, Pablo enjoyed immensely—the enthusiasm with which Anna Maria called for an answer, and the doting grandfather never disappointed. He was thrilled when presented with the opportunity to engage his young hiking companion with whatever wisdom he had acquired in his time and travels.

"Palmito Ranch is where the last battle of the Civil War took place," Pablo told her. "It was also where my grandfather—your great-great-grandfather was killed while defending an outpost against the attacking Union Army."

"Were you sad, Grandfather?" asked Anna Maria.

"I was sad to learn that it happened," said Pablo. "But I never knew your great-great-grandfather. The Battle of Palmito Ranch happened before I was born."

"Why do we have to have wars?" asked the innocent child.

With a sigh, Pablo shrugged, for his granddaughter asked a most complicated question that would require a long and complicated answer.

"God only knows, my sweet Cheerianna," he began. "But this last war was the worst ever, I think. It seemed that every inch of the globe was

4

at war, if you can imagine such a thing." With more reflection than intended, he added, "War does strange things to people, Cheerianna. Strange things indeed. But for some reason that I can't seem to grasp, it seems that folks aren't happy unless they're fighting over something. Instead of learning about all the interesting things that make us different and celebrating them, we find it easier to go to war over them. I know what you're thinking; it doesn't make sense. But not everything about the world can be explained...not even by an old goat like me."

"You're not an old goat!" protested Anna Maria.

Pablo smiled warmly at his granddaughter—a gesture to reassure her that he would be around for years to come, and that there would be many more long walks to take and stories to tell. Then he added, "It used to be that in Brownsville, whites and Mexicans respected one another's customs and culture. But times are a changin', my sweet Cheerianna. Times surely are a-changin'."

"Grandfather, am I Mexican?" asked Anna Maria.

The question produced a hardy chuckle from Pablo, who knelt down in front of his granddaughter and assured her that she was indeed of the asked ethnicity.

"Then why is my skin so much lighter than yours and Mama's?" she wondered.

Hmmm, nothing like being set back on your heels by a child, thought Pablo. But just when he needed to, Pablo Cordero could be very creative—especially during those Sunday afternoon walks with his impressionable granddaughter at his side.

"The day that you were born was the bluest sky ever, and the sun never shone so bright," Pablo told Anna Maria, who at the time was age seven. "And just at the precise moment that you were born, the sun came down and peeked in the window. And do you know what happened after that?" Pablo gave Anna Maria no time to speculate, before gushing, "Your tender little body gathered up all that wonderful sunshine and you've been shining bright ever since!"

It wasn't often on those Sunday afternoon walks that Anna Maria shot her grandfather a skeptical look, but the fantastic explanation for her skin color, which she thought strangely lighter than her mother's and grandfather's, elicited such a look.

"Look, Cheerianna!" said Pablo on another of their Sunday walks. "There in the distance is the famous car bridge that I helped build back in 1910! Isn't it beautiful?"

"Sure, Grandfather," was Anna Maria's tempered reply, as she wasn't yet of an age when one can see beauty in something so commonplace as a bridge.

"The bridge connects Brownsville, Texas, and Matamoros, Mexico," Pablo told her. "After the bridge was finished, many of us walked all the way to Bagdad Beach in Matamoros and slept on the sand. When we woke, we saw the most beautiful sunrise ever! Nowhere on earth does the sun rise so beautifully as over the Gulf of Mexico, and the best place to see it is Bagdad Beach in Matamoros. Maybe sometime we'll sneak out and walk all through the night until we reach the beach. Then we can watch the sunrise and lie all day in the sand listening to the gulls and the water. Would you like that?"

"Oh yes, Grandfather," replied then nine-year-old Anna Maria. "I would love for us to see the sunrise together."

Indeed, the childhood of Anna Maria Cordero was more a delight than Pablo could have ever imagined. The days also passed happily for Anna Maria, who would wake particularly chirpy on Sunday mornings. After breakfast she would spring from her seat, grab Pablo by the hand, and off they would go walking, sometimes not returning until dusk. Who could be a cheerier soul than Anna Maria Cordero? But then Callahan would come by.

Callahan was an intimidating sort, always managing to come by when least expected. Though had his company been expected, there was no preparing for such an unwanted presence, less anticipate it. Callahan came whenever Pablo was away. He would stroll into the Cordero home as though having more right to the space than those living there; his presence loomed in such a way, it caused others to wilt.

This he enjoyed, and it prompted him to strut about with his superiority and smirk with a face filled with arrogance. Callahan lived for the opportunity to celebrate his affect. As a babe and toddler, Anna Maria took no notice of the menacing stranger. Later on she would run and hide whenever Callahan came by, and for the remainder of the day she wouldn't utter a word. Her silence troubled Pablo, who when returning home was accustomed to an enthused greeting. Martina pretended not to notice the uncustomary behavior. When questioned by Pablo, she would reply weakly, "She's probably just tired, Papa."

Now a bit older, Anna Maria met the smirking Callahan with a hard glare of her own. With her high cheekbones and proud chin pointed in his direction, she held her glare, refusing to back down. Callahan looked away from the unabashed child and directed his words at Martina. "You'd better teach that little lady of yours some manners, girly…you hear?" he warned. "Or I might have to teach her myself. I don't recon we'd want that, would we? Well…would we?"

Martina lowered her eyes. Callahan had a way of making her feel inadequate and more ashamed than her father ever did when first viewing her pregnancy as a disgrace. Anna Maria watched her mother's eyes travel to the floor—her posture slump like a school girl preparing to be scolded. Unable to understand why this man held such dominion over her mother, she became angry. It enraged her further, when witnessing the victorious grin that would come over Callahan whenever her mother assumed the stance of a guilty child. Martina went to Anna Maria and knelt before her. "Please, Anna Maria," she begged. "It's a nice day. Why don't you go out and play for a while."

It was of Anna Maria's proclivity to oppose her dismissal, but when she looked into her mother's pleading eyes, she did as asked. She didn't turn about and go running off as Martina had hoped. Instead, she walked backward carefully until reaching the door. She maintained her defiant glare, her eyes burning into Callahan. This she did despite the reprisal that could be in store for her mother. As Anna Maria backed her way toward the door, Callahan narrowed his eyes and began peering in at her. He took a step in her direction, giving her face a thorough examination as he went searching for a trace of resemblance.

Anna Maria took her leave without putting on her shoes and Martina was too out-of-sorts to remind her. The stones embedded in the hard clay road hurt her feet. She went along trying to remove Callahan, Martina, and the unfriendly road from her thoughts, in favor of conjuring images of what a sunrise would look like over the Gulf of Mexico while standing on the soft sands of Bagdad Beach in Matamoros. This, she imagined, not alone, but standing next to her adoring grandfather and holding onto his comforting hand. No doubt he would tell her some fantastic story such as, *My sweet Cheerianna, you must be akin to the sun, for only the earliest rays of light that sparkle on the gulf's waters are as beautiful as you.*

Callahan led Martina to her room. When he was through with her, he took a few bills from his fold and unceremoniously tossed then on the floor. From her knees, Martina stared at the bills, though she dared not gather them until after Callahan had gone.

"Whatcha lookin' at there, girly?" he asked with his familiar taunt that always managed to leave Martina feeling belittled. "Not enough, is it? Well, ain't you heard that times are tough—that there's a depression goin' on? Besides, you ain't no *real* whore, you see. But you are *my* whore. Now it'd be best for all concerned if you remember your place and not get all ungrateful on me. You hear?"

"Sir?" said Martina. *Sir* was the manner in which she addressed Callahan. "I got a job cleaning for a well-to-do protestant woman at the other end of town. The pay is very good."

"Well, is that so," said the haughty Callahan. "You tryin' to tell me you don't need my money anymore? Is that what you're tryin' to tell me? Cause if that's so, then maybe your old man needs to find out where all the extra coin has been comin' from for the past eleven years. And maybe that *'well-to-do'* protestant woman needs to find out just what kind of woman she has in her employment. So if I were you, girly, I wouldn't go lookin' to change our little arrangement. Are ya readin' me alright? Well, are ya?"

"Yes sir," was Martina's defeated reply, her eyes remaining fixed on the floor.

"Now, why don't you scrape up that cash and go and get that little lady of yours a decent pair of shoes," he said.

Later when Anna Maria returned, Martina ran to her side and begged, "Please Anna Maria, you mustn't tell your grandpapa about Mr. Callahan. If he found out about him, I'm afraid of what he might do. You must promise me, Anna Maria!"

It saddened Anna Maria that Callahan was able to reduce her mother to someone, who from her knees would plead for her silence. Begrudgingly, Anna Maria complied with her mother's wishes, though she went to her bed that night wishing Pablo could somehow find out about Callahan and chase him away...or worse. By then, Anna Maria was old enough to understand what Callahan wanted from her mother. What she couldn't understand, though, was why this man, who so clearly upset her mother, was never turned away. Martina, who otherwise was strong of spirit, hadn't the strength or will to stand up to Callahan, and this troubled Anna Maria as much as Callahan himself.

It was weeks before Callahan returned. On that day, Pablo came home and discovered Anna Maria sitting on the ground just outside the house. She didn't notice her grandfather approaching, nor did she look up, or respond when he called, "Hello, my sweet Cheerianna. How was your day?" Anna Maria seemed in a trance and was unable to be reached. She looked past Pablo as he approached.

"Cheerianna, what's wrong? What happened today?" the concerned grandfather asked. He then took his granddaughter's tender shoulders in his hands and gently shook her.

Anna Maria never looked up at Pablo, nor verbally responded to his plea. Instead, she took a stick, and with it she pried loose a stone from the hard clay that served as the Cordero's terrace. With the stone she scratched out words in the clay. Pablo looked on with foreboding curiosity as Anna Maria's delicate hand gripped the stone and began etching her cryptic message. No longer amused by the enigmatic behavior, he cried out, "What do you mean by these words, Cheerianna? I don't understand!"

Ignoring her grandfather, Anna Maria rose to her feet, tossed aside the stone, and walked away.

The bewildered man called after her, but not once did she bother looking back. Pablo, too, rose to his feet and was about to start after her, when he heard Martina call, "Let he go, Papa. She needs time to be alone. She will return."

"But I don't understand," cried Pablo. "What does this mean?" He pointed to the words *I fixed it* scratched out in the clay.

Martina took her father by the hand and led him inside. Kneeling by his side, she pressed one of his hard calloused hands to her face. Then as best she could, through pitiful tears, Martina Cordero began to explain with deep regret the past several years of her life. "Please don't be ashamed of me Papa," she pleaded. "For God's sake, don't despise me!"

"You're my child, Martina," said Pablo. "We've been through so much together. We helped each other to survive. No matter what, how could I not love you?"

"Please, Papa," begged Martina, "you must take Anna Maria away from here. This place is no longer good for her. Your precious Cheerianna can never know who Mr. Callahan really is! Please Papa—when she comes back, you must take her away from here at once!"

"But what about you, Martina?" cried Pablo. "How will you ever manage?"

"I'll survive, Papa," she said. "In my prayers I'll talk to Miss Lillie. She'll guide me. She'll tell me what to do, just like when I was a little girl."

"Martina, you're talking crazy," said Pablo. "Miss Lillie has been dead for years."

"No Papa!" Martina protested. "Miss Lillie has always been with me. She never left me. Oh, Papa…please tell Anna Maria that her mama loves her and that she tried. You'll do that for me, won't you, Papa?"

Pablo Cordero stood before his daughter. He ached from despair and all at once felt much older than his years. He tried to reconcile what Martina was asking of him. It broke his heart that his daughter, who grew up without a mother and who had already sacrificed too much was about to sacrifice herself. He began grasping for anything—*anyway* to keep his little family together. But in his heart he knew that Martina was right. It was time to take his granddaughter—his precious Cheerianna far away from Brownsville, Texas.

****

Stock prices dipped dramatically on September 4th, 1929. On October 29th, the market crashed as the United States lapsed into was would become known as The Great Depression. Meanwhile, the country was entering its tenth year of Prohibition. Brownsville, Texas, became a popular port of entry into Matamoros, Mexico for those wanting to drink *legally*. As for those not wanting to make the short trip and instead partake in recreational liquids right under the nose of the law? For those folks there was plenty of moonshine to be had. White lightning, rotgut, tiger's sweat, bush whiskey, skull cracker…call it want you wish; it was bought and sold just about everywhere and you didn't need to be well connected to get your hands on it. Some people made it, others sold it, and to varying degrees, still others who did both. Making it took a bit of skill— skill which, incidentally, wasn't unknown to Pablo Cordero.

Pablo learned the art of making moonshine back in 1902 from a man called Big George. Making moonshine wasn't Pablo's chief source of income, but during times when jobs were scarce and work was drying up, assisting in whipping up not only a few batches of moonshine, but Big George's highly sought after recipe enabled him to get by. Once Prohibition began, though, Pablo made certain that his moonshine making went undetected by the women in his life. He surely didn't want Martina or his *precious Cheerianna* to find out that he was breaking the law.

He would make what he thought was a plausible excuse for why he needed to disappear for awhile. Then off he would go, sneaking away to Edgar Trudeau's farm, where for years he had apprenticed under Big George.

The calendar turned 1930, and work was drying up everywhere at an alarming rate. Pablo was realistic—he understood that no employer was going to let go of a white worker in favor of a Mexican, no matter how skilled, or how many years he had been at a job. He figured it would only be a matter of time before he would have to hook up with Big George and call upon his skills as a moonshiner if he and his little family were to survive the times. Unfortunately, whipping up batches of Big George's recipe wouldn't be in Pablo's future. Separated from Martina, to whom he had given half his funds, and with his eleven-year-old granddaughter at his side, Pablo Cordero was down to his very last option.

It was May of 1930, when Pablo and Anna Maria Cordero boarded the Missouri Pacific Railroad. After their many Sunday walks together, Pablo was used to the curious way folks stared and the way others tilted their heads when glancing at his youthful sidekick. Anna Maria had prominent cheekbones and a proud chin—features certainly worthy of noticing. But it was her Mayan eyes that seemed to possess the wisdom of the ancients that caused folks to stare. Her cinnamon hair and fair complexion next to Pablo's dark and calloused figure was what caused them to look curious and to wonder. Nevertheless, with her hair, complexion, and features, it could be said of Anna Maria Cordero, that she was an exotic beauty. When they boarded the train, Pablo greeted the stares and curious glances with a contrived smile which most perceived as pleasant. Though, when moving along, he kept Anna Maria pressed to his side when making their way to the back of the car.

"Where are we going, Grandfather?" she asked, not sounding particularly hopeful that they were embarking on one of Pablo's promised adventures.

"Kentucky," he replied with more enthusiasm than was in his heart.

"What's in Kentucky?" wondered Anna Maria. Her mood seemed to brighten, figuring, why else travel to such a faraway place if not for reasons that would bring about good fortune?

"What's in Kentucky is a place called Crow's Farm and a good man named Cornelius," Pablo told his granddaughter. He could only hope that Crow's Farm *and* Cornelius were still around, and that he would be remembered. But those were thoughts he was wise not to share with his young traveling companion.

"Oh," said Anna Maria, unable to conceal her disappointment that they were traveling all the way to Kentucky only for the purpose of visiting a farm.

"It's a long trip, my Cheerianna," said Pablo. "Try and go to sleep."

"Okay, Grandfather, I'll go to sleep," she said. "And while I'm sleeping I'm going to dream that we're standing together on the shore of Bagdad Beach in Matamoros, Mexico, and watching the sunrise."

"You do that, my sweet Cheerianna," said Pablo. "And when you wake, you must remember to tell me all about it."

Pablo, too, was tired and wanting for sleep, but his heart, which was breaking for Martina, wasn't so accommodating. He took his satchel which was resting at his side and placed it on his lap. Through its soft, brown suede, he could feel the handle of a Colt Revolver—the famous 1873 single action it was—the same Colt model that was used by Theodore Roosevelt, Buffalo Bill Cody, Wyatt Earp, and Billy The Kid. The brown, suede satchel was a gift. As for the Colt Revolver? Call it a curious acquisition.

Pablo looked around the car and wondered how it must feel to be among the many eagerly anticipating their destinations. The happy chatter that surrounded him—the celebratory mood of the car's passengers—it all became a din that ripped away at his senses. Across the aisle sat two boys that Pablo determined were brothers. They were going on and on about Dizzy Dean, their beloved Saint Louis Cardinals, and that they couldn't wait to get back home. Once there, they would run straight away to Sportsman Park and try and sneak through the gate to watch their beloved ball team.

The eager and excited smiles—the happy chatter—the two brothers: Pablo Cordero was trapped in a moving train surrounded by many who served as glowing reminders of his failures.

Throughout the car was jollity and merriment—things that he could never provide Martina; though never missing was his effort. He noticed that Anna Maria's breathing had changed, for she had fallen asleep. He gave her head, which seemed to be resting comfortably on his shoulder, a gentle pat. He could have cried for how much his delicate, young traveling companion loved and trusted him. *I'll prove myself worthy of that love and trust, or die trying,* he thought. He laid back his head, closed his eyes, and listened to the chugging of the train—its unwavering repetition—an unrelenting repetition that seemed to mimic with irreverence his lasting struggles.

"You dream of that sunrise, my sweet Cheerianna," Pablo whispered to his sleeping granddaughter. "You keep dreaming and never give up hope."

When Anna Maria was born, Pablo pinned all his hopes on his granddaughter. All along it had been his belief that, together he and Martina could provide for Anna Maria all that he alone was unable provide for Martina. Now, as the Missouri Pacific Railroad chugged its way through Texas, Pablo Cordero was right back where he began—a man who once hoped that the world would show some kindness to a desperate soul journeying alone with his infant daughter.

Chapter Two
Dolci and Uncle Joe

Manuel Cordero fled from his native Mexico and headed east twenty-one years after the Texas Revolution—a conflict that began on October 2, 1835, and ended on April 21, 1836, and featured the famous Battle of the Alamo. The Mexican Reform movement, which began in the early 1850s, had prompted Manuel Cordero to cross over into territory belonging to the United States. The reform laws were polarizing Mexican society at a time when delegates were preparing the constitution of 1857. The purpose of the constitution was to reaffirm the abolition of slavery, secularize education, and uphold civil liberties. Manuel Cordero recognized that the Reform Laws and new constitution were politically dividing the country and setting the stage for a civil war. After Manuel settled in Brownsville, Texas, and began working at Palmito Ranch, he wrote several letters imploring his brother, Juan, to come and join him.

Please brother, Manuel wrote. *There's plenty of work here and the promise of a better life.* After his third attempt, Juan was persuaded. He packed up his family and meager belongings and headed for Brownville, Texas, and Palmito Ranch, where he worked alongside his brother. However, the world can provide all sorts of ironies, especially for those at its mercy. Not the least of its ironies saw Manuel and Juan Cordero flee their native Mexico, and narrowly escaping civil war—a civil war which began in 1858, and ended in 1861. This they did in favor of a country that, in 1861, was beginning a civil war of its own. In the beginning the move to Brownsville, Texas, proved beneficial to Manuel, Juan, and their young families. Then Palmito Ranch became a confederate outpost.

The American Civil War *officially* ended on April 9, 1865. However, not everyone received the memo. Despite an agreement that precluded

14

fighting between Union and Confederate forces on the Rio Grande on May 11, 1865, Colonel Barrett dispatched 250 men of the 62nd Colored Infantry Regiment and 50 men of the 2nd Texas Cavalry Regiment to attack reported rebel outposts and camps. After finding no one at White's Ranch, Lieutenant Colonel Branson, under the command of Colonel Barrett, repositioned the regiments for the purpose of launching an attack on a rebel outpost at Palmito Ranch. The Union Regiments managed to scatter the confederates, who later reemerged with a large cavalry force. Barrett, in turn, reinforced Branson with 200 men of the 34th Indiana Volunteer Infantry. The Volunteer Infantry torched all the rebel's supplies held at Palmito Ranch. Again, a large Confederate cavalry force, this time commanded by Colonel John S. "Rip" Ford, hammered the Union line with heavy artillery, forcing Barrett to call for a retreat.

That the Battle of Palmito Ranch occurred at all remains a mystery. Some believe Barrett was seeking a little battlefield glory for himself at the end of the war. Others claimed Barrett needed horses for the many among his cavalry who had been dismounted. Either way, the Battle of Palmito Ranch, no matter how unnecessary, cost Manuel and Juan Cordero their lives and left their young, vulnerable families alone to fend for themselves. The Cordero widows did all they could to hold their young families together. But it wasn't long after Manuel's death that his widow Nina, at the behest of her eldest brother Pedro, took her children and moved back to Mexico. Corina, Juan's widow, refused to be a burden on Nina's brother and so chose to remain.

Corina Cordero took her two sons, Juan Carlos and Cesar, and headed northeast into Louisiana. They settled in New Orleans, if you can call living on the streets *settling*. Corina figured the ethnic diversity of New Orleans would present a kinder scenario for three stray Mexicans than the less forgiving Texas—especially on the heels of a civil war. Juan Cordero hadn't much by the war's end. Just days before he was killed, as if though he'd foreseen his own death, he handed over to Corina what little he had for safekeeping.

With living on the streets, the days seemed to run together for the Corderos. Oddly enough, the nights seemed friendlier. Being as they were strangers in a strange place, they felt less conspicuous at night, and could remain hidden away from a society that at times gawked upon their lowly station. Despite the staring of the least compassionate, the vulnerable family never felt threatened. In spite of the challenges meeting their meager existence, Juan Carlos, despite his youth, swore to protect the younger Cesar and their mother.

By the time the family arrived in New Orleans, little remained in Corina's purse. They were starving and it was days before she managed to find work at a local market place. She made a meager wage, but enough to nourish her two boys with some left over for herself. Juan Carlos and Cesar remained nearby the marketplace while Corina worked. At night the three Corderos took to the streets, remaining in shadow or tucked away in the city's nooks and crannies until morning.

Bright and early they'd arrive at the marketplace. Again Juan Carlos and Cesar would remain nearby, while Corina unloaded wagon after wagon that came rolling in from the farms. She then filled baskets with a variety of fruits and vegetables to be sold. Throughout the day she lifted and carried hour after hour without any break. At the end of the day she cleaned fish counters until unceremoniously handed a broom. At week's end a marketplace merchant decided that he should have certain entitlements for being kind enough to employ one so desperate, and who, despite her trying circumstances, had youthful features and a supple figure. Juan Carlos tried to intervene but was beaten. Corina knew that she was in no position to refuse. She sent Juan Carlos away and allowed the brutish man to take her. She later explained to her sons that the man was kind and that he would give them money to buy better clothing.

By day, Corina labored until nearly dropping, and by night she was had by the marketplace merchants. This continued for weeks until she caught the eye of some women and joined up with them. Partly out of desperation, she decided to turn her youthful features and supple figure into a source of income. If she must be a whore, she figured, why allow herself to get passed around by uncouth market merchants for slave wages? Why not get paid her worth?

At first, Corina managed only a shack on the Bayou Lacombe. Still, it was shelter, a place to call home, and what's more, Juan Carlos and Cesar were able to attend school. Shortly after enrolling, Juan Carlos decided that school was not for him. To Corina's dismay, as she understood all too well the plight of the uneducated, he quit.

Following the Civil War came the great boom in railroad construction. Between 1866 and 1873, 56,000 miles of track were laid across the country. By 1872, although still a youth, Juan Carlos Cordero decided that he could serve his family *and* himself much better by laying track for a wage, instead of receiving what he established was "a useless education." Besides agriculture, the railroad industry was the nation's largest employer. Despite his youthful age, Juan Carlos Cordero had little difficulty acquiring employment with the railroad.

By that time, Corina Cordero's dubious profession was yielding quite an income, though her profession and its returns were unknown to Cesar and Juan Carlos. With that being the case, the industrious older brother sent nearly every penny he made home to his mother. It wasn't until the Great Railroad Strike of 1877 that Juan Carlos returned to New Orleans. When he arrived, he discovered that his mother and Cesar had moved from the swamps of the Bayou Lacombe into the city. Juan Carlos found the leap in his family's living standards curious. He also found the carnival atmosphere of New Orleans no less irksome than his days of having to sit still in a classroom. Perhaps it was the memory of having to survive on the streets that made the city seem so gloomy. While away he had developed a sense of worth by working for a young country building its infrastructure. This sense when juxtaposed, contrasted with *the laidback city* and its surrounding bayous. Either way, Juan Carlos Cordero looked unfavorably upon New Orleans, and he told Corina, "Mama, this place is no longer for me. I'm heading out west." Before he set out, Corina informed her older son, who unlike the younger Cesar came to understand her role in society, that it was no longer necessary to send home money.

****

Juan Carlos made it as far as to Oklahoma before falling in with a band of wheat belt migrants. Migrant farming was no less rigorous than laying track and paid far less, but he figured it wasn't a bad way to bide his time.

The wheat belt began in Texas, stretched through Oklahoma, and on up into the Dakotas before ending in Canada. It was toward the end of the harvest in Oklahoma that Juan Carlos got to know a shy orphaned girl named Dolci. By then the railroad strike had ended, but Dolci had become too great a source of fascination.

Dolci and Juan Carlos were approaching adulthood and traveled together as the migrants made their way north. When they reached the Dakotas, Juan Carlos and two others decided to stray from the band and make their way up into the Black Hills. The railroad wasn't enough motivation for Juan Carlos to stray from Dolci, but the prospect of finding gold was. Before the three adventurers broke away, Juan Carlos vowed to Dolci that he would return—if not by the time the band reached Canada, then sometime after they began their southern migration.

"I'll catch up with you. Don't you worry," he told her.

Inexperienced as she was, Dolci knew as much that, when a young man says not to worry and was about to go running off with other young men, and it was unclear who among them was wielding the influence…it was time to start worrying. Dolci and some of the older migrants warned Juan Carlos and his two companions that it was foolish for inexperienced young men who didn't understand the *"laws of the land"* to wander into the Black Hills—which essentially was Sioux country. But the prospect of finding gold deposits was too tempting. The young men didn't heed the warning. When Juan Carlos said goodbye to Dolci, neither knew that she was with child.

The United States government recognized the Black Hills of Dakota as belonging to the Sioux, although prospectors had found gold, albeit a small deposit in 1874. Two years later a larger deposit was found in the northern part on the Black Hills toward Deadwood and Whitewood Creek—its peak, though, was reached in 1877. By the time Juan Carlos and his companions headed into the Black Hills, it was already nearing the summer of 1878. Even for experienced prospectors the pickings would be slim. The best that the three could hope for, if they were lucky, was to unearth a few stray nuggets. But for three young men with hope, a dream, and an adventurous spirit, the likelihood of collecting only a few nuggets wasn't enough to deter them.

The wheat belt migrants finished with their work in the Dakotas and were on their way to Canada. All the while Dolci looked back over her shoulder hoping to see Juan Carlos Cordero running toward her. Before each look she wished hard, and with her spirit she tried to beckon to her side the only man with whom she had ever lain. But with each backward glance came a pang in her heart. When seeing Dolci's sorrowful eyes, Josiah Walton, an elder of the band, went to her side and tried to comfort her.

"He'll come back to me; won't he, Josiah?" Dolci asked the elder.

Josiah Walton reached out to Dolci with friendship and intentions that could only be regarded as honorable. "Juan Carlos seemed an honorable young fellow," he told her. "I'm sure he will *try."*

When the migrants reached Canada, Dolci realized that she was pregnant. This she disclosed only to Josiah Walton; although the perceptive elder had detected the subtle changes in her condition. Josiah kept Dolci by his side. Despite his advanced age of fifty-something Josiah managed to help Dolci with her share of the work.

The work in Canada ended and so began the southern migration. Still, Juan Carlos or his two companions failed to show. If the three young men had known anything of history and the Black Hills of the Dakotas, they might have learned what became of Ezra Kind and his six companions, and that the Sioux are not a people with whom anyone should trifle. Had Juan Carlos and his two companions not dismissed those among the band as old, discouraging fools, afraid of risk, and therefore condemned to harvest wheat all their lives, they might have been better prepared when setting off into the Black Hills.

The band of wheat belt migrants winded their way down through the Midwest returning to Oklahoma, where Dolci, while the kind and compassionate Josiah Walton held her hand, gave birth to a son she named Pablo Cordero. For Dolci, the birth of her son was bittersweet. Yes, she had delivered a healthy infant despite poor nutrition and the rigors of traveling with the band. But the absence of Juan Carlos cast a shadow on the early joys of motherhood. Josiah Walton did his best to keep up Dolci's spirits. Still, she tossed and turned every night for the likelihood that Juan Carlos and his two companions hadn't survived their ill-advised trek into the Black Hills—or, they *had* survived and had done quite well for themselves, and that the others convinced Juan Carlos that with his newly acquired wealth, it was foolish to return to an orphaned girl who had hitched herself to a band of migrants. To think that Juan Carlos could have been killed by the Sioux broke Dolci's heart. To think that he survived and journeyed on without her was no less painful. Josiah Walton tried to convince Dolci that if it was within Juan Carlos's power to return, he would have. The translation: Juan Carlos met up with an unfortunate end. That being the case, Dolci could go on believing that the father of the baby boy whom she carried in her womb while migrating up and down the dusty plains of the Midwest, and whom she now cradled close to her bosom, truly loved her.

Josiah Walton lost both his sons to the Civil War. "Strong young bucks they were. Hard working and God loving, for sure," he was fond of saying. Josiah didn't see his sons die, nor viewed their bodies before their burial. He learned of their deaths from afar and reconciled them as being part of God's plan, and that his sons had died for a cause in which they believed. Both Josiah's faith and sense of duty were steadfast. The vision of the strong valued family men he was certain his sons would have become had they lived helped him survive the loss. His wife's death, however, wasn't one to be reconciled.

One day Josiah Walton returned home to find his Annabelle tied to their front gate, her clothes torn, and throat slit—a warning to those who might be hiding any soldier considered an enemy of the state. Josiah understood the atrocities of war, but never imagined they would reach his front door. With his sons and Annabelle gone, and much of his land stripped away, Josiah Walton took what little coin he had and walked the earth. All he had was the clothes on his back, his faith, and a Bible given to him by his grandfather. He was a lost soul whose life was stripped bare and raped by a war.

For the next fifteen years he roamed up and down the dusty plains of the Midwest harvesting wheat. With all that he had lost, he was given to wonder "for what purpose is God keeping me on this earth." But as Pablo Cordero, who with his tiny infant hands took fistfuls of Josiah's beard and yanked, he knew for what purpose God kept him around.

Josiah Walton's beard color was a tattered mixture of gray and rust with a good bit of dust from the great plains of the Midwest permanently mixed in. To look at Josiah Walton at fifty-something, it was difficult to imagine him ever having had a youth or anything that could qualify as boyish features. Neither Josiah's gristly appearance nor hulking physique were in accordance with his calm demeanor and surprisingly soft voice—a voice which Dolci found reassuring.

"Pablo! Not so hard!" scolded Dolci, as her son with whatever infant strength he possessed yanked on Josiah's beard. But Josiah, to the delight of Pablo would laugh hardily, then encourage the little lad to try again. As Pablo grew to a young boy, with great affection he called Josiah Walton "Uncle Joe." It was a delight for Josiah in his waning years to be held in such high regard by a youngster. He never stopped mourning the loss of his family, but the childhood of Pablo Cordero took away some of the sting.

Most evenings when the work was finished and the band had settled in for the night, Josiah would take Pablo by the hand and together they would go wandering off. Not too far off they would go with lantern and Bible in hand, but far enough to be alone. Pablo would lie down in the soft, cool grass; and whether under an Oklahoma or Kansas moon, the God loving man whom Pablo called Uncle Joe, read aloud passages from the Bible. Some nights they would sneak off before dark to be alone and watch the remnants of the orangey Midwest sun as it dipped below the horizon. When every last bit of the sun was gone from sight, Josiah would light the lantern and open his Bible. This Pablo enjoyed—the day transitioning to night, and the orangey Midwest sun giving way to the moon. When away from the others and in wide open spaces as Josiah read from the Bible, Pablo would feel a remarkable sense of peace and calm. Whether it was the moonlight, lantern, cool grass, or the words from *the good book* read in the soft voice of one so well trusted, or everything in combination, Pablo could feel his spirit—his whole being lifted as though he were soaring high above the expanse of the Midwest plains.

Pablo never questioned the Bible. Like Josiah, he figured if it was written then it must be so. Whatever was good enough for Josiah Walton was good enough for Pablo Cordero.

Many among the wheat belt migrants were illiterate. Some were functionally illiterate, but most couldn't read at all. For Pablo, who thus far hadn't set foot in a classroom, nor would he ever get the opportunity, the Bible was his pathway to literacy. Night after night Pablo would listen as Josiah read passage after passage. Soon he could speak English not just well for a Mexican wheat belt migrant, but like a scholar. It wasn't long before it was Josiah laying down in the cool grass and gazing up at the vast Midwest sky and listening.

Teaching Pablo the value of literacy, the holy Bible, and the peacefulness of the moon and stars shining down on wide open spaces wasn't Josiah Walton's only motives for wandering off at night. Among the band there were few families. Mostly the band was comprised of solitary men without families—roughneck men, who at the end of the day could become quite rowdy and foul mouthed. It was the coarse behavior of these men that Josiah tried to shield from the young and impressionable Pablo.

Dolci was the only woman among the band not accounted for. At the end of the day when Josiah and Pablo went wandering off, others would settle into tents, shacks, bunkhouses, or whatever sufficed for accommodations. Always was it meager. Dolci did her best to stay clear of the men and would often attach herself to one of the families. This didn't always offer her ample protection, especially when the men went and got themselves good and drunk. When they *were* good and drunk, what would otherwise end up an evening of rude flirtation, resulted in her confronted by one, and sometimes more than one, who clumsily and with vulgarity attempted to have their way with her. Whenever that was the case, she would try her best to resist and to reason with them. There was one occasion, though, for the sake of keeping the peace *and* for the potential threat of violence, she relented and allowed herself to be taken aside by two of the men. None among the families faulted her. Nor did she mention the incident to Josiah Walton. She lived with it and prayed that it would never happen again. But she wasn't so fortunate.

One night after a hard day under a burning sun, the men went and got themselves plenty drunk. On that night, Dolci wasn't merely flirted with, rudely or otherwise. This time she was taken by force and raped

21

repeatedly by several among the band. The women of the band clung to their men as they listened to Dolci's muffled screams as she was carried off. The women cried silently, not wanting to upset their children. "It's just a silly adult game," some had said. "No one is *really* getting hurt." The few family men in the band dared not try and intercede. They turned away, pretending not to hear Dolci's desperate cries. Yes, the men felt cowardly, but never before had they witnessed the others so drunk and disorderly, and were afraid that any intervention would serve to put their own women at risk. For the wellbeing of their families they sacrificed Dolci.

It was 6:30 when Pablo and Josiah went wandering off and ten o'clock when they returned. Still, the drunken band was going hard at Dolci, who by then was only semi-conscious. The stench of sex and booze was nauseating. Josiah tried to push his way through the disorderly mob, but was knocked to the ground before he could reach Dolci.

"Wait your turn, old man!" one among the mob had barked.

Before Josiah could think to scramble to his feet and make a second attempt to free Dolci from the band of wild drunkards, he was savagely kicked in the face. Thirty years ago Josiah could have wrung the necks of these wild young men, but now at sixty-something, he was but a shadow of his former self and could only plead with them to stop.

A young and terrorized Pablo Cordero stood by and watched blood spout from the kicked-in face of Josiah Walton. It took one among the men rudely shouting, "Look, the little whore's son just showed up," for Pablo to realize what was happening to Dolci. He froze when observing the iniquitous scene of biblical proportions. The men turned and glanced back at Pablo, though with little regard. They hissed and their laughter was irreverent and hideous when considering the twelve-year-old might attempt to rise up against them. It was because of their disregard that Pablo was then able to weave his way unnoticed through the crowd. Before the men realized that he had altered his position and was making his way over to Dolci, he was already kneeling beside the man who was taking his turn mounting her from behind. Pablo placed a gentle hand on the man's shoulder. The gesture was strangely unfitting to the scene, and thus set off a chain reaction of bewildered gazes. The drunken band wondered if they were about to witness something incestuous— something so bizarre and deviant that not even they themselves could imagine. They settled into an odd sense of bemusement, not knowing what to anticipate. To Josiah Walton, who lay battered on the ground, Pablo appeared an angel subjugating an evildoer with benevolence.

Then Pablo seized upon the man whose shoulder he had gently placed a hand. With a forceful and mighty lunge, he wrapped his arms around the man's neck, and with his mouth engulfed his ear. Then with whatever strength he could summon, he began to bite.

Pablo's rage superseded any revulsion one could expect to feel when slicing through live human flesh with one's own teeth. The man bucked wildly, attempting to achieve separation between himself and Pablo's stranglehold and teeth. But Pablo managed to tighten his grip around the man's neck and didn't let go until his upper teeth met his bottom teeth, effectively severing the man's ear from his head.

Dolci, who was still unaware of Pablo's presence, scooted forward into a fetal position and buried her face in her hands. There she remained, naked, quivering and too exhausted to cry.

Pablo leapt to his feet and spit the bloody, mangled piece of flesh into his hand, before tossing it to the ground as though discarding something far too revolting to handle. From his hands and knees the man screamed and squealed like a tortured animal. His wild and agitated squeals served to frighten and sicken the others and caused them to look away. Some managed to look back with the intention of helping the man, but gagged once their eyes found the revolting body part that lay harmlessly in the dirt. Eventually the man's sickening squeals turned to throaty and husky sobs of, "My ear! My ear! He bit my fuckin' ear off!"

Josiah Walton managed to get to his feet. He walked through the stunned and silent crowd over to where the discarded ear lay. He stooped down and picked it up. He then gave it a thoughtful examination, as though since its severing it had become something other than a human ear—or, it *was* still a human ear that with a little ingenuity could somehow be repurposed. With a comical shrug, he ended his examination, as to conclude that the severing of an ear didn't merit such deliberation. He looked down at the man, who in his throaty and husky sobs continued to shout, "He bit my fuckin' ear off!"

These were the words of a man wholly unable to reconcile that reprisal for such deplorable actions was in any way imagined, expected, or deserved. Josiah then held the ear in his outstretched hand for all who dared to look. Glaring at the men, he uttered without any lack for irony, "I don't reckon Jesus will be coming by any time tonight...do *you?*"

Despite their illiteracy, some among the stunned group knew the story of Jesus and the soldier at Gethsemane—and that according to the Gospel, Jesus reattached a soldier's severed ear after Peter sliced it off with his sword.

"Well, do you?" shouted Josiah. No one said a word, or had anything to offer.

"Well, then, I guess that settles it," added Josiah. "You can't make a silk purse out of a pig's ear."

Then he unceremoniously tossed the useless ear aside, before going to aid the naked and quivering Dolci to gather herself.

The men were standing about with folded arms and were staring at the ground, when Josiah looked up and shouted, "The party's over, boys!" Josiah's angry shout caused Pablo, whose gaze was fixed on the discarded ear, to jolt and then straighten up. Pablo ran off, as it occurred to him the mortification that Dolci could suffer should she realize he had seen her naked body so egregiously compromised. By the time Josiah had gotten Dolci dressed and to her feet, her tormenters had also wandered away.

"Josiah, your face!" said Dolci. "You're bleeding!"

"I'll be fine," said Josiah in his usual calm manner. "It's only a few scratches."

When Josiah was through tending to Dolci, he noticed Pablo standing alone in the distance. He knew the boy was troubled by what he had just witnessed *and* by his own actions.

"Son, you know the Bible as well as anyone," Josiah said to Pablo. "And I know what you're thinking—that vengeance should only belong to the Lord. But sometimes the Lord works in strange ways. I'm thinking tonight he laid his vengeance in your hands. So don't you go giving it a second thought." Then Josiah took his brown, suede satchel and handed it to Pablo. "Here, I've been meanin' to give this to you. Inside you'll find a bit of money, the knife with the fancy handle that you've been eyeballin', and my grandfather's Bible."

"Uncle Joe, why are you giving me all your things?" asked Pablo.

"Well," said the elder, "there comes a time when a man needs to pass on whatever he has. I reckon that time has come. You just take particularly good care of that Bible, you hear?"

"Uncle Joe, you face is bleeding," said Pablo. Josiah had turned so that the full moon shed its light upon his wounds.

"It's just a few scratches," he said. "Not to worry." But that night, Josiah Walton laid down his head for the last time.

****

"Uncle Joe lived a good long life," Pablo cried to his mother the next morning. "And now he's finally at peace with his beloved Annabelle and his sons. I suppose we should be happy for him. I know you'll miss him, too, Mama."

24

Dolci burst into tears. It didn't occur to her until that very moment that her son was fast becoming a man and the person most responsible wouldn't be around to finish the job. She cried, believing that she was too inadequate to finish what Josiah Walton had started.

Pablo and Dolci spent the day working and praying. It was hard work, prayer, and grief that enabled Pablo, for the time being, to set aside his hatred for the men and their vile behavior, and his aversion for the others who sought not the courage to intervene. But Pablo knew if Josiah were standing beside him under the burning sun harvesting wheat, he would tell him, *"The only thing that hatin' is good for is for eatin' away at a man's insides. So you best get rid of it before there's nothing left of you."*

At the end of the day Josiah Walton was given a decent burial. Everyone among the band was feeling somber and filled with regret—so much so, that it was months before anyone went off to get drunk. The memory of a gangbang, a severed ear, and senseless death was enough, at least for the time being, to keep them in check. The unfortunate evening stayed in the forefront of everyone's mind, and for awhile the nights passed peacefully and without incident.

****

Pablo Cordero was fourteen-years-old by the late spring of 1894. It was then that the band arrived at Jeremiah Wright's farm on the Texas/Oklahoma border. Among the band, Pablo was the most well spoken. Since he sounded educated, he was appointed by the others to meet with land owners to negotiate wages. In the past, the responsibility belonged to Josiah Walton. Once a land owner himself, Josiah could speak their language and was able to gain a fair amount of respect. With him gone, the job fell initially onto the shoulders of illiterates, who at times were taken advantage. Most farmers offered what was considered a fair or customary wage, not that migrants possessed any real leverage when it came to negotiating. Sometimes, though, the band was lowballed. Once a farmer tried bartering with those who appointed themselves in charge by offering only one third the customary wage, along with a few gallons of his best moonshine, in exchange for labor. The farmer figured, once given their wages, the men usually headed on into town to get drunk and buy whores, so why not attempt to compensate them with one of their vices.

Before it ever had the chance to become confiscated, Jeremiah Wright sold his war ravaged land during the earliest days of Reconstruction, but at a devalued cost. He packed up his family and along with every ounce of his bitterness, moved, and settled on the Texas/Oklahoma border. Jeremiah Wright was bitterly opposed to entering into any sharecropping agreements with former slaves, but gladly offered tenancy farming agreements to disenfranchised whites.

"I'll have no niggers setting foot on my land," he proclaimed. I suppose one could think it ironic that shortly after Jeremiah Wright got his farm up and running, along with its *no niggers* policy, he went blind.

Enter Jed Wright, Jeremiah's son. Jed Wright never had any intention of taking over the farm, but hadn't the conscience to walk away from his sense of duty and loyalty. Jed's first order of business was to let go of his father's tenants. He cared not a lick what color his workers were. In his estimation, employing migrants gave him a bigger bottom line. Meanwhile, Jeremiah spent his waning years rocking away on the porch, drinking whisky, and longing for the scent of Carolina Jasmine. As he grew feeble, so vanished much of the bitterness he harbored over the war and his former land. But as Jeremiah's old bitterness's faded, his son Jed's grew. Jed felt trapped on the very farm where, as a young man, he dreamed of one day breaking free.

It was as fine a spring day as could be imagined, and Pablo and the others were toiling away on Wright's Farm. Even for a band of roughneck, wheat cutting migrants, there remained an appreciation for such a day. Despite that the earth is seldom kissed by such magnificence, as was the sky on that exceptional day, the only time the band bothered to look away from their work was when Jed Wright came trotting by on his fine Appaloosa horse. Jed named the horse Jasmine to please his father, whose days by then were numbered. Jasmine was a fine mare and it was Jed's custom to bring her out for an early morning run to stretch her legs. When he did, everyone among the band stopped for a moment to admire the impressive creature. In the later part of the morning, Jed and Jasmine came trotting by—this time to observe the workers. Jed wasn't necessarily a taskmaster, but he wanted his presence felt. He believed that was all that was needed for the work to get done in a timely fashion. Most often that was the case.

Jed trotted Jasmine over to where Pablo and Dolci were working. For awhile he sat tall and quiet, only bothering to look down his nose at the two toilers. Jed was an imposing figure when sitting atop Jasmine. Finally, when gaining Dolci's attention, he tipped his hat and then rode off. Later that afternoon he returned. From his imposing position in the saddle, he called, "Hello, Poco."

Without success, Pablo tried to omit any trace of indignation for being called Poco. His tone was sharp when he turned toward Jed Wright and said, "My name is Pablo." Pablo guessed correctly, that Jed Wright didn't forget his name, but instead, assumed that all Mexican men answered to *Poco* and were only too glad to do so.

"Whatever you say," said Jed Wright. The imposing man's manner had clearly suggested, *you're a migrant farm working Mexican! What difference does it make what your name is?* Then he added while gesturing at Dolci, "So how much would you want for her?"

"Sir?" said Pablo.

"Money, Poco!" barked Jed Wright. "I beg your pardon…*Pablo*. How much *dinero* do you want for the woman?"

The forty-year-old rider of the fine Appaloosa Horse wasn't aware that the fit and attractive thirty-one-year-old woman whom he was trying to purchase was Pablo's mother. Although, had Jed Wright understood the situation, it's doubtful that he would have used a more tactful approach.

"She's not for sale!" protested Pablo, after momentarily disarmed by Jed Wright and his absurd request. No longer was Pablo attempting to omit any indignation.

"Is that so?" The imposing man uttered this as though the sale of Dolci was a foregone conclusion, and that the only remaining issue was price. Meanwhile, Dolci went right on working, pretending not to understand a word that was exchanged between her son and Jed Wright.

"Yes!" said Pablo. "It *is* so! And will remain so!"

"Well, we'll see about that, Poco," threatened Jed Wright.

"There's nothing to see," Pablo continued to protest. "She's not for sale!"

"You know, Poco, I was under the impression that you were a smart boy," Jed Wright continued to threaten. "Now I don't know how kindly these men would take to knowin' that they could've had a little extra coin in their purse—and that the only thing preventing that from happening was the sale of a woman."

Jed gestured to the others across the way. Pablo's eyes traveled until resting on the backs and shoulders of weary men toiling under an unforgiving sun. Jed paused, before adding with mock concern, and to the point of taunting Pablo for the impossible position into which he was placing him, "No, Poco, I don't reckon they'd take too kindly to that at all. Now you be a good boy and you think about that. And meanwhile try not to work too hard."

Jed took one last dig while tipping his hat to Dolci. "Be a *smart* boy, Poco. Come up with a price. I'll be back sooner than you think."

As Jed Wright rode off, Dolci laid down her tool and held firm to Pablo's arm. She was unable to conceal any misgiving Jed Wright caused her to feel.

"Don't worry, Mama," Pablo told her with whatever reassurance he could summon. "I won't let anything happen to you."

Pablo did his best to put Dolci's fears to rest, but he knew there was going to be trouble. Jed Wright *had* put him in an impossible predicament. It was either sell his mother to be used as a sex slave, or answer to an angry mob. Evil or insurgence—there were no friendly options. He knew what Jesus would do and what Josiah would want him to do, but he was yet a boy and not a strong one at that. He also knew that it was pointless to go before a band of poor, illiterate migrants and make an appeal for loyalty, compassion, and humanity. Were he to stand with an opened Bible in hand, and with fury, deliver the word of God, even the more superstitious among them would be hard to win over. The fear of God would not work. These poor, woe begotten migrants would rather risk being struck down than to go without the provisions a little extra coin could provide.

The arrival at Wright's Farm marked two years since Dolci's gang rape. During that time Pablo learned to forgive the men—many whom which still travel with the band. But he could not, nor would he ever forget the image of Dolci on her hands and knees surrounded by men who had already taken their turn and were cheering wildly. The imposing Jed Wright sitting atop his fine Appaloosa horse brought back that night with a vengeance—the image, the hate…the vileness. Unwittingly, Pablo's jaw began to tighten, his teeth were clenching. He shuddered after allowing himself to fill with rage old *and* new, and to the point where he could once again experience the sensation of his teeth piercing through human flesh. For a moment the sensation gave him a perverse sense of satisfaction. But the moment passed, and with a start he turned away and spat out what he thought was blood and the gruesomeness of mangled flesh.

"Pablo!" cried Dolci. She had never seen such a grim look come over her son's face and it frightened her.

"It's all right, Mama," Pablo told her. "I'm fine. Everything will be all right." Though he hadn't any idea how to make things right. He would dread the sight of the fine Appaloosa horse trotting toward him when Jed Wright made his late afternoon rounds. His heart would sink watching Jasmine's elegant gait—her proud and majestic prance. He looked skyward with the notion that Josiah Walton, his Uncle Joe, could somehow hand down an answer.

28

Later that day when the sun was setting, Pablo and Dolci wandered away from the band. Just as Pablo and Josiah had done on countless nights, they laid themselves down in the cool grass and watched the sun give way to the moon. When the day finished surrendering, Pablo read from the Bible. He interrupted a passage to glance over at Dolci, whom he had suspected was no longer listening.

"Mama, what's wrong?" he asked.

"I was just thinking," said Dolci, "how different things might have been if my Juan Carlos, your father, were still here."

It was often that Dolci spoke of Juan Carlos to her infant son. Cradling him, she would tell stories of the "brave adventurer" who went journeying off into the Black Hills and who would "one day return." Then a year went by, then five. As the years flew by, she thought less and less of Juan Carlos Cordero. Dolci had only known Juan Carlos less than a year before he set out to seek his fortune. At the time she was a young girl in love, and therefore was in love with the idea that the world was a place that held for her possibilities. But no longer was she that young girl.

"I'm tired, son," she told Pablo. "And I'm getting more tired by the day. I can't do what I used to and you're havin' to work harder all the time." Smiling warmly at Pablo she added, "These fields and dusty old plains have taken a good bit of the life out of me. I'm thinkin' maybe a change'll do me good."

Being a mother, it was instinctive for Dolci to be selfless; though right away Pablo recognized her transparent attempt to get him off the impossible hook from which he was dangling.

"You're talking crazy, Mama!" he cried. "I would never sell you! I would never leave you behind, especially with a man like Mr. Wright."

Pablo's words brought a tear to Dolci's eye. She thought to herself, *if only Juan Carlos had once upon a time felt so strongly.* She reached out and with a gentle hand touched Pablo's face. "You sound good when you read, Pablo," she said. "I like listening to your voice." She lay her head back down in the cool grass, and while gazing up at the stars, she allowed herself to become lost in her son's voice as it spoke the words of the holy Bible. For awhile she felt unburdened and able to pretend that all was right with the world.

When Pablo and Dolci returned to camp it was unusually quiet and subdued. The only evidence that there might have been any rallying or commotion, was the embers of a bonfire around which three men remained gathered. Their conversation ceased when they noticed Pablo and Dolci approaching. Pablo had good reason to be suspicious of the men, and was of the notion that their sudden silence wasn't a coincidence. He regarded them with misgiving; their glaring eyes, he concluded, were a warning of things to come.

"Everything all right with you tonight, Pablo?" one asked. Though missing was even the slightest trace of what could pass for genuine concern.

"Everything is fine," Pablo told the man. He attempted to sound bright in his reply, but their disingenuous concern caused him to wince and to sound guarded.

Just as Dolci and Pablo were about to enter their canvas enclosure, the men gave a menacing laugh. *They know,* Pablo thought. *Mr. Wright must have come looking for me tonight and then told them.* Pablo sat perfectly still with an ear pointed in the direction of the men. He listened to their crude conversation, hoping for a clue—any sign as to what he could expect from the men had they indeed learned of his predicament.

Not a word was mentioned, and like the dying embers of the bonfire the men disappeared.

It had been a long and trying day, and when Pablo lay down his weary head, all he could see in his mind's eye was Jasmine, the magnificent Appaloosa horse. How he dreaded the morning and the thought of seeing that horse. He prayed that sometime during the night Jed Wright would have an attack of conscience and wake up with a changed mind. But Pablo knew it was frivolous to have such hope. He cringed knowing that sometime before the sun was overhead, he would have to choose between evil and insurgence. The festering thought was such that, despite his weariness, he was unable to sleep. When he sat up and opened his eyes, it startled him to discover the silhouette of a man standing outside the canvas enclosure. He positioned himself in front of the sleeping Dolci and waited.

The man held a lantern in one hand and a bottle in the other—the shadows of each Pablo could easily recognize. The man tilted his head back and emptied the last few swallows from the bottle into his mouth. He gargled, swallowed, then tossed the bottle aside. The bottle inadvertently found a stone and shattered, causing Dolci to stir. Pablo then listened as the uncouth man proceeded to urinate just outside of what passed for their dwelling. Pablo figured that one of the men who earlier was standing beside the dwindling bonfire had come to forewarn him, or perhaps *enlighten* him with a little persuasion. Moments later, the man pulled open the canvas flap which served as a door to the enclosure and stumbled inside, bringing along with him the stench of urine and whiskey.

"Hello, Poco," he said. "Nice evening. Don't you think?"

"It's very late, Mr. Wright," said Pablo.

"Not for what I've got in mind, Poco," said Jed Wright. His hideous laughter burned in Pablo's ears. "My old man always said, it's never too late for doin' business, and in his day he was a pretty shrewd businessman."

"But I haven't yet come up with a price," pleaded Pablo. His weak and predictable stall tactic was obvious even to one so drunk.

"Well, like I said, Poco, it's a nice evening, and with a full moon," said Jed Wright. "Maybe after a nice moonlit stroll you'll get it all figured out. Meanwhile, I'd like to sample the merchandise…if you catch my drift."

Pablo leapt to his feet as though he had every intention of rising up against Jed Wright, but Dolci alertly grabbed hold of his arm.

"Please, Pablo," she whispered. "It's no use. We can't win. All we can do is to try and survive."

"Be a good boy, Poco, and listen to your mama," said Jed Wright, with a victorious grin. "You know what they say; Mama knows best." Pablo grabbed his lantern and brown, suede satchel and went storming off. "You best come up with a price, Poco…that is before I'm all through here," Jed shouted at Pablo's back.

Once upon a time Jed Wright had a sweetheart, but that was many years ago. The blind, belligerent, and overbearing Jeremiah scared her off. Jed blamed the poor girl more than his embittered father and never again got that close to a woman, regardless of the fact that Jeremiah Wright had long since mellowed. As the years passed, Jed grew lonely and miserable—not the sort of man a woman would want. His misery drove him to become foul and take by force what no longer could be earned.

Pablo Cordero sat restlessly in the cool grass. With his lantern by his side, he flipped through the pages of his Bible. He searched wildly, believing that somewhere in the text was an answer to his impossible predicament. Then in a fit of rage, he threw *the good book* to the ground and cried, "There's nothing here, Uncle Joe!"

It was at that precise moment, when rebuking the holy Bible that Pablo realized that his hand had been resting on the answer. However, there are truths and solutions that, although effective, can cause one to shudder instead of bringing forth serenity. Nevertheless, he rose to his feet, and with grim determination he made his way back to the canvas enclosure. As he came upon the camp with its band of sleeping migrants, his nostrils filled with the stale and burnt remains of what earlier was a roaring bonfire. He froze for an instant, when noticing the muted illumination coming from Jed Wright's lantern—its warm glow was filtering through the canvas. He set down his own lantern before he crept toward the light. With much greater finesse than Jed Wright had earlier, Pablo pulled open the flap which served as a door to the meager accommodation. With agility that was both deft and silent, he slipped inside.

To Pablo's surprise *and* disgust, Jed Wright appeared a man in direct contrast with the imposing figure that earlier sat regally atop Jasmine, the fine Appaloosa horse. Jed Wright's nakedness made him seem far less than ordinary, along with being awkward and unattractive. With unsightly tufts of hair indiscriminately attached to loose, tumbling rolls of flesh, Jed appeared remarkably unimpressive next to Dolci's beauty and tautness, though Pablo's eyes somehow managed to remove Dolci from the scene. (It would be years before the blotted out image of Jed Wright slapping her buttocks and the degrading manner in which he pushed down on her head while mounting her from behind would surface in his mind.)

For Pablo, tonight seemed altogether different than the night of the drunken gangbang. Then, in somewhat of a trancelike state, Pablo weaved his way through the drunken lot as they shouted their encouragement to the one taking his turn. The next thing Pablo knew, he was spitting up foul tasting blood mixed with mangled flesh. Later that night, Josiah Walton convinced him that, while vengeance may belong to the Lord, "Sometimes the Lord works in strange ways. I'm thinking tonight He laid his vengeance in your hands." But tonight Pablo was in control and fully aware of each silent step that advanced him nearer to the vulgar Jed Wright. There was no sense of an omnipresent being working through him. Tonight's vengeance was his and his alone. His hand squeezed the hilt of a knife used a thousand times in the past throughout long laborious days under an unforgiving sun. Like most laborers, the tools of the trade became an extension of his hand. Then, with a deft flick of his wrist, the life was instantaneously gone from Jed Wright's body.

Pablo looked away, not wanting to bear witness to his mother's nakedness. He hastened her to dress, but Dolci's gaze was fixed on the blood that was dripping from the blade of a knife once belonging to Josiah Walton.

"Mama," Pablo said sharply. No longer in the throes of her stupor, Dolci began dressing.

Meanwhile, Pablo reached into Jed Wright's purse and stripped him of his cash.

"You won't be needing this anymore," he said to the dead man. Then he stripped Jed Wright of his Colt Revolver—a 1873 single action model—the same model used by Buffalo Bill Cody, Wyatt Earp, Billy the Kid, and Theodore Roosevelt.

"Mama," said Pablo, "it's not good for us stay here. It won't be safe. We should leave long before the others wake up."

Other than far away from Wright's Farm, Pablo had no idea where they should go, or in which direction it would be best to head.

"Pablo," said Dolci, taking firm hold of her son's hands. "Many years ago your father once told me of a special place in Matamoros, Mexico called Bagdad Beach. He said 'Nowhere on earth does the sun rise so beautifully.'"

Pablo took Dolci into his arms. "I'm sorry for all that you've had to suffer in your life," he said. "I'll try from now on to make it better for you."

Pablo took a moment to clean the blood from Josiah Walton's knife. Then he placed it in his brown, suede satchel, along with the dead man's cash, Colt, and the Bible that once belonged to Josiah Walton's grandfather. An unlikely, though very effective array of articles. Then Pablo knelt down and prayed for the soul of Jed Wright, that in death he should be free from the demons that afflicted him when living. When he was through praying, he and Dolci slipped into the night.

Chapter Three
Blueberry Pie

"All aboarrrrd! All aboarrrd! Next stop Saint Louis, Missouri! Next stop Saint Louis, Missouri!" barked the conductor, as the train was resting at the station in Little Rock, Arkansas.

Passengers noisily shuffled on and off the Missouri Pacific Railroad, as porters were loading and unloading their baggage. One porter needed every bit of his agility to scoot around a woman, whose hat brim was wide to the point of being absurd. Meanwhile, the two brothers from Saint Louis were all wound up at the mere thought of catching a glimpse of Sportsman Park. They cheered when hearing the conductor announce the name of their hometown. Then at once with ardent enthusiasm, they jumped into the aisle of the car. The older boy, who Pablo heard called Maxwell, mimicked Dizzy Dean's pitching wind-up. As he did, the younger Jackson mimicked Frankie Frisch's batting stance.

"Come on, fire it in there, Diz," yelled Frankie Frisch's imitator.

Pablo had several hours over several hundred miles which to observe the two youngsters. He found their playfulness and chatter refreshing—unlike the woman in the absurd hat, who when observing the energetic pair, made a sour face to indicate her displeasure.

Occasionally Pablo would catch the older Maxwell paying little attention to the chattering Jackson. The reason being, he was busy stealing glances at the slumbering Anna Maria, whose cinnamon hair and exotic features at rest had become quite the source of fascination for the boy. Maxwell's fascination drew smiles from Pablo. In turn, Maxwell would blush. Afterward, each would return their attention to their respective traveling companions.

"So tell me my sweet Cheerianna," Pablo asked his waking companion as the Missouri Pacific Railroad rolled through Arkansas, "did you dream of Bagdad Beach and of the sun rising over the Gulf of Mexico?"

"Oh yes, Grandfather," chirped Anna Maria while stretching out her limbs. "I dreamed we walked all through the night and the sun rose just as we arrived at the beach. You should have seen the way the sun sparkled in the water."

"If you dreamed that I was there with you, then I must have seen it, too," said Pablo.

"We saw it together," said Anna Maria, as she snuggled closer to Pablo. "And I liked the way you looked, Grandfather, when the sunlight hit your silver hair."

In an exaggerated display, Pablo put his hands to his head, as though it were unimaginable to be so old as to have silver hair.

"Don't worry, Grandfather," said Anna Maria, "you'll never be old."

"Ah, maybe so," said Pablo. "But now you must tell me how your dream ended."

"We lay down in the sand and slept until the tide came in and washed over us," Anna Maria told him.

"I guess we had to walk all the way home in our soaking wet clothes?" said Pablo. Then he sank into his seat thinking, *home…what home?* The mention of the word made him grimace.

"It was a beautiful dream, my sweet Cheerianna," said Pablo, forcing a smile. Then he closed his eyes and listened to the monotony of the chugging train. Occasionally he glanced over at Maxwell and Jackson. The two were poring over their baseball cards and trying to determine who between them had the best collection.

"Grandfather," said Anna Maria, "tell me that story again—the one of how you met my grandmother."

"Ah, you like that one, do you?" remarked Pablo. He then smiled before beginning his soliloquy:

"Well, it happened way back when I was working for *The Brownsville Herald.*" He paused as he usually did at this point in the story. As always, he squeezed his chin when trying to remember the newspaper's former name. The contemplative look was Anna Maria's cue to chime in with, "It used to be called *The Cosmopolitan,* but then Jesse O. Wheeler bought the newspaper and renamed it *The Brownsville Herald.*"

As always, this produced a chuckle from Pablo, who said, "I think you can tell the story better than I." He glanced once again over at Maxwell and Jackson. The two were still poring over their baseball cards. He also stole a quick peek at the woman with the absurd hat, who thus far managed to maintain her unpleasant expression.

Pablo couldn't imagine anyone finding youth and the exuberance it often brought as a nuisance. Briefly he felt sympathetic, when it occurred to him the notion that perhaps the woman had always wanted children but was unable have them, and therefore acted bitter whenever in their presence. *Or,* he thought, *maybe she's just a miserable old hag*...never mind that the woman was ten years Pablo Cordero's junior. Nevertheless, Pablo flashed a mischievous smile when thinking, *the latter was the more accurate scenario.*

"Every morning I would wake up extra early," Pablo continued. "That way I would have time to go by Hutchinson's Pastry Shop. It was a mile out of my way and I didn't want to be late for work. Not that I could afford to buy anything—Mama and I had to be careful, you understand. But I loved to walk by that pastry shop first thing in the morning. It always smelled so good! I use to stand right outside and inhale as hard as I could. Then I'd try to imagine how all those wonderful smelling pastries tasted. Sometimes I'd peek in the window and watch Mr. Hutchinson putting the pastries and pies in the glass case. Even though I never bought anything, he never shooed me away. Anyway, I remember Mama once telling me that when she was a little girl, she tasted blueberry pie and thought it was the most wonderful thing in the world.

"Well, early one Sunday morning, I crept out of bed, and as fast as I could, I ran to Hutchinson's Pastry Shop. I had put some money aside, you see, and was gonna surprise Mama with a blueberry pie. I ran like the wind because I didn't want to be late for church. Well, as it turned out, on the way home I decided to take a shortcut...at least I thought it was a shortcut. I ended up walking through an unfamiliar field. I started to get nervous because I knew Mama didn't like being late for church, but I kept right on going. Because I was nervous, it seemed the field went on forever before ending at the back of this great, big farmhouse. Was it ever big? It was like our house times five!"

"I thought it was times ten," Anna Maria chimed in.

"You're right, my sweet Cheerianna," said Pablo. "It *was* times ten. I guess I'm getting a little old and forgetful. It's a good thing that I have you around to remind me of things."

"Not a chance, Grandfather!" scolded Anna Maria. "You're not getting old."

Pablo smiled before reaching to stroke his granddaughter's cinnamon hair. "Well, when I reached the farmhouse," he continued, "I looked up at one of the second-story windows. And there she was—your grandmother—the most beautiful woman ever! I stood there in the field

36

and watched as she brushed her long black hair. I forgot all about the blueberry pie, Mama, *and* church! Then your grandmother sensed that someone was staring at her. She looked out the window, and when she saw me, she got startled and closed the curtain. I waited hoping that she would reappear. I wanted just one more glimpse of her. I wanted to be sure that my eyes weren't playing tricks on me and that I really did see her. You know, it's not every day that you see the most beautiful woman ever. I waited an hour before I realized that I was getting good and hungry. I don't have to tell you that Mama's blueberry pie was in serious jeopardy. I paced around the field trying to ignore my growling stomach. It wasn't for another two hours that your grandmother finally reappeared."

"I thought it was five hours," Anna Maria chimed in.

"You see, there I go again, forgetting all the important details," said Pablo. "You're right, it *was* five hours. Well, anyway, she looked down at me from the same second story window and asked, 'What are you still doing here? Are you crazy?' My tongue was so tied, and I was so nervous I couldn't think of what to say. So, like an idiot, I ended up saying 'I have pie' and then raised it up to show her. She asked me 'what kind is it?' I told her 'blueberry.' She said, 'I don't care very much for blueberry, come back when you have apple.' And just like that, she disappeared. So, as fast as I could, I ran back to Hutchinson's Pastry Shop and explained to Mr. Hutchinson my predicament. And do you know what he did?"

"He gave you an apple pie?" replied Anna Maria.

"That's right," said Pablo. "Mr. Hutchinson said that he remembered what it was like to be a young man in love, but that he never heard of anyone ever trying to woo a girl with pie. He said that I could pay him back whenever I had the money, but that I shouldn't forget the real reason that I came by earlier this morning. I assured him that I wouldn't and ran home and presented Mama with a blueberry pie. Before I made it to the door, she called out to me, 'Where are you off to so fast?' That's when I told her that I just met the girl that I'm going to marry.

"The sun was already setting when your grandmother finally reappeared. 'You don't give up easily, do you?' she said. I told her, 'I'll never give up.' And that was the very first time I saw your grandmother's beautiful smile."

****

It's some story that Pablo Cordero tells—vivid, romantic, not to mention enormously fanciful. For years he would sit and tell the colorful tale to an enamored Martina. Then Anna Maria came along. On their Sunday walks he would regale his equally enamored granddaughter with the same vivid, romantic, and fanciful tale. But only a shred of the story was true. Pablo did work for *The Brownsville Herald*, but not in the capacity that he allowed his daughter and granddaughter to believe.

Every morning at the crack of dawn, Pablo would make his way over to East Van Buren Street. Once there, he would fill his newspaper bag. Then off he would go to deliver the news to the citizens of Brownsville, Texas. At the end of his route there was always a few extra newspapers— one which he kept for himself. Pablo had all but memorized the Bible, which served him well during his transitory life on the wheat belt. But if he were to settle anywhere, he figured it best to start learning about the *real* world and *The Brownsville Herald* was as good a place as any to start.

As one might imagine, Pablo made only a meager wage delivering the newspaper; although the tips, which most handed over gladly, some begrudgingly, helped. Nevertheless, he was glad to be away from the dusty plains of the Midwest, the wheat belt, and especially the unruly band of migrants. But he missed Dolci terribly. She didn't survive the journey.

After fleeing from the band, the two made it as far as Madisonville, Texas, before Pablo realized that Dolci had taken ill. Throughout the day as they were coming upon Madisonville, Dolci was burning with fever—a fact that she never revealed to a son determined to get as far away from Wright's Farm as he possibly could. They journeyed swiftly and Dolci did her best not to become a liability.

Dolci spoke little to Pablo that day. Whenever she gathered the strength to talk, it was to mention, or to wonder aloud at times, incoherently, about Bagdad Beach in Matamoros, Mexico.

Pablo paid little attention to Dolci's ramblings. Throughout their journey he wore the grim expression of a man much more concerned with the lifeless body of Jed Wright, who might discover it, and how much distance they had put between themselves and the Texas/Oklahoma border and Wright's Farm. He wasn't particularly concerned with a destination whose only promise was that of scenic beauty.

Later that night Dolci grew cold and clammy and began to shiver violently. Pablo tried o remain calm, but was helpless. It was already past nightfall and he didn't know the roads, less could he see them, and so he was unable to run off to seek help. Besides, he didn't want to leave Dolci to shiver alone in the dark. What if he lost his way and never made it back to her? He wrapped her in his shirt and held her tight, making every effort to keep her cold, shivering body warm and prayed that she would hang on until morning.

At times throughout the night, Dolci rambled on about Juan Carlos and that Pablo had a grandmother named Corina and also an Uncle Cesar, and that they lived in New Orleans. This was the first Pablo heard of a grandmother and uncle, but he was inclined to believe that Dolci was either dreaming aloud, or that it was the fever concocting an imaginary family. Toward morning Dolci's shivering had lessened. As this happened, she spoke clearly words of love to a son who cradled her.

"With all my heart I love you," she said. "And for every day of your life I've been thankful and proud."

"Stay with me, Mama," Pablo pleaded. "Just stay with me and before we know it, it'll be morning and I'll go and get help."

Before the earliest rays of sunlight had the chance to illuminate the tiny town of Madisonville, Texas, Pablo was off and running. The first place he came by, which happened to be the only place open so early in the morning, was Hutchinson's Pastry Shop.

"Whoa, whoa, whoa! What's the big hurry there, young fellow?" asked Ben Hutchinson. "Where's the fire?"

After Pablo finished huffing and puffing his way through his agitated explanation, Ben Hutchinson right away put in a call to Doc Crandall, who, in a town the size of Madisonville, Texas, save for the seldom middle of the night labor pain, wasn't used to his sleep being disturbed. Nevertheless, Doc Crandall, with as much agility as he sixty years would allow, sprang into action.

"Don't you worry, son," Ben Hutchinson assured Pablo. "Doc'll be here in a flash. He's one of the good ones. This town is lucky to have him."

It seemed that no sooner Ben Hutchinson had finished with his reassuring words, Doc Crandall had arrived and in a flash they were off.

"She's over there." Pablo pointed to the area where Dolci lay in the tall grass. "She was speaking to me right as I was leaving." This he added disquietingly, though without allowing himself to rationalize why the morning sun or the noise from an approaching carriage hadn't caused Dolci to stir. Doc Crandall nimbly stepped down from the carriage and was first at Dolci's side. He shielded Dolci from the onrushing Pablo just long enough to close her eyes.

"I'm sorry, son," he said.

Pablo fell to his knees and buried his face in Dolci's bosom. "Mama!" he cried.

Ben Hutchinson and Doc Crandall backed away in order to let Pablo have a few moments to grieve privately.

"What a pity," Ben Hutchinson said to Doc Crandall. "And so young."

"And such a pretty thing, too," said Doc Crandall. "It's a shame to come to such an end."

Doc Crandall went and knelt beside Pablo. Placing a gentle hand on his quivering shoulder, he asked, "What was your mama's name, son?"

"Dolci. Dolci Cordero," cried Pablo.

From the first moment Dolci held her infant son in her arms, who was to go forth in life bearing his father's surname, in her mind, she, too, was a Cordero. She never referred to herself by any other name. Pablo was her validation. Although Pablo suspected that Dolci and Juan Carlos were never wedded, he elected not to spoil the fantasy. It never occurred to him until the moment when Doc Crandall asked him his mother's name, that, he never knew her *maiden* name. Dolci never spoke of parents, when she was born, or where she grew up. It was as though she was born right out of the dust of the Midwest plains, or spawn from the wheat which she spent her life planting and harvesting. Dolci Whoever, a woman with no known origins, came to an early and unfortunate end.

"Now, don't you worry, son," said Doc Crandall. "You're in Madisonville, Texas, and we do right by folks. We're gonna give your mama a decent Christian burial."

Doc Crandall and Ben Hutchinson placed Dolci's body in the carriage. Then off they rode back to Hutchinson's Pastry Shop.

"Now son," Doc Crandall told Pablo when they arrived at the pastry shop, "you stay right here and let Ol' Ben take care of you. I'll go and make the arrangements."

Doc Crandall's first stop was to drag Somerset Evans, the pastor of the Methodist Church, from his bed. Then it was off to Kirby's Farm to see if Dutch Kirby could spare his two sons, Clay and Carl, for a little grave digging. Meanwhile, Ben Hutchinson tried to be of some comfort to a grieving young man.

"When's the last time you ate anything?" asked Ben Hutchinson. Pablo could only manage a weak shrug. He couldn't remember if it was yesterday, the day before, or last week.

"Well," said Ben Hutchinson, "I hope you don't mind blueberry pie. Always been a favorite of Mrs. Hutchinson's, you know. And boy does she ever give me the business if I come home at the end of the day without a fresh one tucked under my arm. You see, she grew up on a farm in Kentucky, Mrs. Hutchinson did. As a young girl it was her job to pick the blueberries. Off course, for every two she picked she ate one. Crow's

Farm it was called…and still is, by the way. Anyway, her younger brother Cornelius grew up and took over the old farm. But my Betsy…she grew up and took over me."

Ben Hutchinson's last remark came with a chuckle. Pablo forced a smile at the baker's banal attempt at humor, though not since Josiah Walton had Pablo known such an easy acquaintance as Ben Hutchinson. That, along with the pie, Pablo decided, was worth a smile. But Ben met Pablo's forced effort with a frown and said, "Gee, I'm sorry to go on like this, son. I guess sometimes I get a little carried away…don't know when to stop running my mouth…or so I've been told."

"Sir," said Pablo, "I've never had blueberry pie before. It's delicious."

"Well, I'm glad you're enjoying it," said Ben Hutchinson. "And by the way, the name's Ben, not *Sir*. I don't like being too formal, you know."

"My name's Pablo," the grieving young man told the baker of the delicious pie. He elected not to add, not *son*, for it gave him a spark of warmth that Ben Hutchinson and Doc Crandall referred to him in such a way.

"You know, son, about the toughest thing that anyone can go through in life is losing their mama," said Ben Hutchinson. "I know. Been over ten years now that my mama is gone. But I can tell you, as hard as it may seem, it'd be ten times harder for your mama if it were the other way around. And I know right now it don't seem possible, but one day a girl'll come around—someone just like your mama, and she'll take most of that sting out of that your heart of yours."

Ben Hutchinson finished with his words of comfort, and Pablo his pie, just as Doc Crandall came pulling up in his carriage.

"I guess it's time to go," said Ben Hutchinson. But no sooner Ben spoke, Doc Crandall stepped down from his carriage.

"I heard a rumor there's baked goods in this place," he said.

"Doc won't admit it, but he gets a bit ornery when his stomach is empty," Ben Hutchinson told Pablo with a wink.

"Nonsense," said Doc Crandall, who then made quick work of a slice of blueberry pie.

The three rode in silence, save for Doc Crandall mentioning the niceness of the weather Madisonville had been enjoying of late and Ben Hutchinson muttering his agreement. They pulled up alongside the Methodist Church, and from there walked around back to where the fallen citizens of Madisonville's past were laid to rest. There, as Doc Crandall was expecting, stood the strong and youthful figures of Clay and Carl Kirby. Both had each worked up quite a lather and were now leaning on

41

their shovels to indicate their exertion. However, Dutch Kirby looked fresh as a daisy, as he was only there for the purpose of supervising his sons. Doc Crandall's wife, Alice, and Ben Hutchinson's wife, Betsy, was also there. Somerset Evans, who was holding firm to his prayer book, was ready to begin.

As Pastor Evans read from his prayer book, Pablo gazed into the faces of eight people, who either helped orchestrate, execute, or in the case of the Kirby boys, labored so that his mother could have, as Doc Crandall put it, "A decent Christian burial."

Eight people, all perfect strangers, never having exchanged a single word, nor knew a thing of the life and times of Dolci Cordero were gathered quietly and respectfully at her final resting place. Pablo found this pleasantly odd. He and Dolci had done nothing to touch the lives of these fine citizens from Madisonville, Texas, and yet here they were, strangers carrying out what they believed to be their civic duty. They had no way of knowing that Pablo and Dolci were lowly migrants gone astray. It was Pablo's belief, though, had the fact been known it wouldn't have mattered. Also, it mattered not to Pablo whether it was civic duty or the fear of God that motivated these good folks. He was grateful that Dolci wasn't destined to remain off to the side of the road where she perished, but was laid to rest with dignity. Despite stumbling upon Madisonville from the wheat belt following the slaying of a ruthless landowner, dignity was deserved, and this Pablo truly believed. If not so, why else would God have aligned him with Ben Hutchinson and Doc Crandall? *Yes,* he thought, *thank God for Ben Hutchinson and Doc Crandall.* He couldn't imagine journeying on having left Dolci right where she lay.

Pablo tried to cling to Somerset Evans' fine words as he read from his prayer book. However, his own thoughts kept drowning out the good pastor. *How evil and good and unpredictable is the world?* He tried to reconcile that Josiah Walton and the eight who stood with him today were of the same god that gave to the world the unfortunate Jed Wright and the men who gang raped his mother. He couldn't imagine God creating the world only to fill it with tyranny and evil to entrap men, or to better determine whether *that* which He created was corruptible. But there was always Josiah Walton—a man who symbolized that tyranny and evil were the choosing of the weak, and weren't to be tiptoed around for fear that one was easily corruptible, but instead, confronted and soundly defeated.

In Pablo's judgment, Josiah Walton was a man amongst men— Job incarnate. How else could it be explained that after losing both his sons to a war, and his beloved wife as a result of that same war, he was able to journey on—never allowing his heart to be consumed with hate and bitterness, or allowing evil to corrupt his soul. Conversely, Jeremiah Wright merely had his land devalued. Thereafter, they each made a choice.

Pablo watched as Betsy Hutchinson put a handkerchief to her eye. He wondered, *who are these people?* But no sooner had he asked the question, he knew in his heart that these eight citizens from Madisonville, Texas were proof that Josiah Walton was watching over him—that his Uncle Joe had made certain that Dolci didn't leave this world unceremoniously from the dusty plains of the Midwest, or from the side of a lonely road, but surrounded by souls that, like her own, were kind and gentle.

"Don't worry, Mama," Pablo whispered to himself. "Uncle Joe's waiting for you and he's gonna welcome you into his family."

Pablo returned his full attention to Somerset Evans, and the good pastor read eloquently from his prayer book. The sun was comfortably warm on Pablo's back, and if possible, it would have been his wish to linger for longer than it would take for the pastor to finish the service. For when through, these eight fine citizens of Madisonville, Texas would return to their lives...leaving Pablo to do what? He was a solitary young man without kin, friends, or ties of any kind in a big world that just got bigger.

When Somerset Evans had finished, Alice Crandall and Betsy Hutchinson introduced themselves to Pablo and offered him their "deepest condolences." The two women left together with the good pastor as their escort. Dutch Kirby and his two sons nodded to Pablo and then respectively tipped their caps.

"Come son," said Doc Crandall. "It's time for us to go and let the Kirby boys finish their job. Pablo reluctantly walked away with Doc Crandall and Ben Hutchinson. The three headed for Doc's carriage. As they went along, Pablo glanced back several times at the Kirby boys, but they waited until Pablo was clear out of sight before shoveling the earth into Dolci's grave.

"So which part of Texas are you and your mama from?" asked Doc Crandall, when they reached the carriage.

"Ahh...we're not from Texas," replied Pablo.

Pablo was momentarily disarmed. He found Doc Crandall's question strange and perplexing.

"Not from Texas, are ya?" said Doc Crandall.

Doc's manner was suggesting, *all the best people come from Texas, you know.* Then with a chuckle, he added, "Actually, I'm Pennsylvania Dutch. And Ol' Ben here is from Kentucky." Then he placed a firm and friendly hand on Pablo's shoulder and asked, "So, where *are* you from?"

Again, the strange and perplexing question, to which Pablo painfully squeezed out, "I'm not from any particular place."

"Aw, come now, son" said Doc Crandall as they boarded the carriage. "There's no need to be embarrassed about where you're from. Folks around these parts don't have an uppity bone in their body. *That* you can be sure of."

"Doc's right about that," Ben Hutchinson chimed in. "Nothing but good simple folk around here."

"Well," remarked Doc Crandall, "judging by the look of those hands of yours, wherever it is you're from, you were no stranger to hard work." Doc Crandall looked at Ben Hutchinson and nodded with emphasis as if adding an exclamation point to his perceptive observation. "And if I might add, Dutch Kirby's always looking for an extra pair of hands—and he's not the only one. Why, Ben's brother-in-law, Cornelius, is always griping that he can't get good help."

"Boy, ain't that the truth," chimed in Ben Hutchinson. "Cornelius still hasn't forgiven me for marrying his best picker. Yeah, son, if you don't mind settling way up there in Kentucky, there's plenty of work to be done at Crow's Farm. And I'll be sure to put in a good word for you."

"I'm grateful for all that you've done," said Pablo, acknowledging both Ben Hutchinson and Doc Crandall. "But the truth is, I have a date with a sunrise."

"Well, every man has got to follow his own star," said Ben Hutchinson, just as the carriage stopped in front of the pastry shop.

Doc Crandall raised an eyebrow as to scoff at the idea of following stars, dates with sunrises, or chasing rainbows. Then he turned toward Pablo and said, "Those hands may say hard work, but behind those eyes I'm seeing something else—maybe someone too smart to be a common laborer. I'll bet you have quite a story to tell, Pablo Cordero. Quite a story indeed. When you're all through with your sunrise, if you wanna come back and tell it, ol' Ben and me wouldn't mind listening."

Before Pablo made his way through Madisonville, he stopped by the Methodist Church. He peeked around back just as Dutch Kirby was pounding a wooden cross into the ground.

"Rest in peace, Mama," he said. "Rest in peace."

Chapter Four
The First Anna Maria

Alone, Pablo Cordero stood on the sands of Bagdad Beach in Matamoros, Mexico and waited for the sun to make its appearance. Slow but sure the world turned and the sun began casting its early morning rays on the calm gulf waters, making them shimmer with brilliance, along with enlivening an otherwise weary young man who journeyed through the night. As the minutes ticked away, and as Pablo watched the sun rising with his feet pressing into the sand, the grief over losing Dolci no longer enshrouded him. His soul began to stir. He had a strange but thrilling sense of isolation and of being at one with nature or his maker. For that reason, he sensed that something great could happen—something spiritual and wondrous that would surge and pass through him like an impromptu gust of wind—illuminating and inspiring, before returning to stillness, but leaving him imbued.

He looked to the sky with the hope of seeing amid the many clouds his mother's face or his Uncle Joe. Perhaps God might allow him a peek into the heavens to see the father he never knew. He stood with arms outstretched and face pointed skyward, expecting *something*. But there were no faces amid the clouds. Nor were there any previews of Heaven. The sun, just as it had on a million mornings past, rose and did so without any impromptu gust of wind or any sort of omnipresent moment. Pablo reached for his brown, suede satchel and departed Bagdad Beach feeling hollow and alone; he wondered why he bothered making the trip. He laughed with self-deprecation and derision, thinking how he anticipated something spiritual and wondrous—a biblical moment like the many he had read about, then cried for his emptiness.

****

When arriving in Brownsville, Pablo lived as a squatter. Not that he needed to, nor was it a conscious choice—but after years of a migratory existence he knew no other way. As chief negotiator for the migrants, he understood the value of a dollar. It was within his means to live not in squalor, but to afford what some considered the basics or fundamentals; he simply didn't deem such things necessary.

In Pablo's brown, suede satchel, along with the Bible and knife that he inherited from Josiah Walton, and the Colt Pistol looted from Jed Wright, was what those of a low station considered a small fortune. However, Pablo spent money only on the necessary provisions he needed to survive. When doing so, he used only the money he earned delivering *The Brownsville Herald.* Thus far he hadn't touched a dime of the money left to him by Josiah Walton. Those funds, he didn't feel entitled to use, nor did he know how, or for what means they should be used. In his heart, Pablo felt that should he part with them, he would be parting with what little remained in the world of his Uncle Joe. Conversely, Pablo had no sentiment for the Colt or cash that he lifted from Jed Wright, and felt perfectly entitled to sell the Colt and squander the cash. Nevertheless, he chose to horde those items along with his cherished possessions.

It was most unusual for a man like Josiah Walton to end up a migrant marching up and down the dusty plains of the Midwest. But for a man who once existed wholly for the joys of home and hearth, and then having that aspect of his life stripped away, life thereafter seemed of little consequence. He saw no point in rerooting himself or starting anew. Josiah saw no chance of home without hearth—without the family that once surrounded him, so he walked and worked until he died. Pablo was far too young to adopt such a philosophy, but that's precisely what he was doing…although unwittingly. And although never having anything that could qualify as a home, in his mother and Josiah Walton there was hearth…or at least an adequate representation. For the time being, he was a lonely young man with no means to an end and no goal.

After rising early and delivering *The Brownsville Herald,* Pablo walked the streets of town, stopping occasionally to read the extra copy that he kept for himself. After awhile, he began recognizing folks—and they, him. He walked the same route every day and the cordial nods of passersby gave Pablo, if not a warm spark, at least some sense of belonging. He may have been a wandering soul dangling on the very fringe of society, but society seemed a place within his reach.

At the end of each day, Pablo ended up at the Brownsville-Matamoros Ferry. A boardwalk was being constructed there along the Rio Grande River. The ferry came in handy when confederates needed to transport cotton to Mexico when southern ports were blockaded by the Union Army. Not that Pablo concerned himself with the ferry's history—but taking ferry rides was the one frivolity that he allowed himself.

Besides the occasional ferry ride to Matamoros—a town which for Pablo, held a certain measure of lure, for its existence was passed on to him by Dolci, who learned of it from Juan Carlos, (Juan Carlos Cordero had only *vaguely* remembered the town of Matamoros and Bagdad Beach. His remembrances came mostly from conversations between Juan and Manuel Cordero. Later the recollections of Corina fed his memory) it was the construction of the boardwalk that attracted Pablo to the river. When there, he would watch with interest as the men applied their industry to the Brownsville side of the Rio Grande. He soon became a familiar presence down by the river and one day was offered a job. Pablo Cordero: a small fortune in his brown, suede satchel and now not *one*, but *two* jobs. He was doubtless the richest squatter in America!

In the early morning, Pablo raced through the town of Brownsville, Texas. With alarming speed and efficiency, he delivered *The Herald* to every doorstep along his route. Then it was off to the ferry and the river for a day of hammering nails and sawing wood. There wouldn't be time during the busy day to read his extra copy of *The Herald*. Most often, there wasn't enough daylight less concentration remaining in his weary eyes when the workday was through. So each day he stashed his extra copy in his brown, suede satchel and waited for Sunday. After delivering the Sunday edition at a more leisurely pace, it was off to the river for a day of relaxation.

Working on the boardwalk, as Pablo was learning, was no less strenuous then migrant farming. However, he found the work far more satisfying and with that satisfaction came motivation. Whenever he stepped back and examined the progress, he would delight in the notion that he was contributing something to a town and its people. Not to suggest that there wasn't honor in planting and harvesting wheat. In Pablo's estimation, though, it fell short of the satisfaction one gets watching the many stages of an edifice during its construction. Besides, Pablo wasn't just grateful for work every day, but for work every day in the same locale. He was hoping that at last and for good, his migratory life was behind him.

At the end of each workday, those of the boardwalk construct who didn't have family to which to go home, or a sweetheart waiting on them, stayed around for the nightly bonfire and booze fest, which took place near the landing of the ferry launch. Just as the sun was about to disappear below the Rio Grande, and the ferry had deposited its last passengers on the Matamoros side of the river and was set for its return trip to Brownsville, the fire was lit and the spirits were poured.

"Hey Poco," one of the workers called to Pablo, "why don't you stick around and join us tonight? You worked hard; you deserve a little celebrating."

Ordinarily, Pablo would take exception to being called *Poco* and be quick to remind the offender of his birth name, as well as pointing out that it was ignorant to think that all Mexican men answer to the same name. Unlike Jed Wright, though, the man seemed good natured enough and clearly meant no disrespect. Pablo elected to let the harmless invitation go unchallenged. He simply gave the man an indecisive shrug, to which the man replied with a chuckle, "Come on, young fella. The worst that'll happen is we'll make a man out of ya."

The comment drew a smile from Pablo. After which, followed the introductions of some very colorful characters, such as: Dirty Jack Doyle, Frankie "The Prick" Donato, Smokey Bones, Lucky Kaminski, Fat Fuck McGinn, and Lefty Carson. (Lefty, not because he was a southpaw, but because he was born without a right testicle.) Incidentally, the introducer of the colorful crew and inviter of Pablo, referred to himself only as "Mick."

"Here kid," said Mick with a twinkle and a smirk. "Take a swig of this. It'll do ya some good. Might put a few hairs where ya don't want any—but it'll still do ya some good."

"Yeah kid," said Dirty Jack Doyle. "It'll loosen up them ol' bones and muscles, for sure."

"To say the least," said Lefty Carson.

"Yeah, especially after swingin' hammers and pushin' and pullin' saws all day," chimed in Smokey Bones.

Guardedly, Pablo took the bottle in his hands and was poised to take what Mick called *a swig*. He could tell by the way the men were all gathering around that it was some sort of initiation. He wanted to first put his nose to the bottle in order to warn his mouth of the punishment that it was about to receive, but knew such action would be frowned upon and seen as a sign of cowardice, and no doubt would produce jeering from the men. So in one swift motion, Pablo threw back his head and poured the harsh liquid into his mouth.

The liquid burned to the high heavens when it hit the back of Pablo's mouth. He thought his heart would surely explode if he permitted the liquid to advance as far as his throat, then slide down through his esophagus and on to wherever such an ungodly liquid sought to go. He wanted badly to spit out the dreadful liquid, but he refused to give the men the satisfaction that their awful potion had overpowered him, though his twisted and distorted face revealed otherwise.

"First sip burns like a son-of-a-bitch, don't it?" said Lucky Kaminski.

"Welcome to the club," laughed Lefty Carson.

Pablo could clearly remember the bonfires on the wheat belt and how foul and threatening the men became when they drank. When dowsing their miseries and hardened souls with spirits, they effectively became evil-incarnate. But as Pablo stood among Mick and his colorful friends, he felt perfectly safe. Sure, these men of the boardwalk construction were not well educated, but they were far from illiterate, and when they drank it was to celebrate their camaraderie and friendship at the end of a good day's work—and as Pablo was finding out, there was plenty of humor and merriment to go around.

"I'll tell you what," said Mick. "No one...I mean no one can whip up a brew like Big George!"

"Best damn moonshine this side of the Mississippi!" said Dirty Jack Doyle.

"This side of heaven!" said Smokey Bones. "Them bastards over in 'Bama and Tennessee don't know shit about good hooch!"

"I can vouch for that," said Lucky Kaminski. "I grew up in Lynchburg."

"God bless Big George," said Fat Fuck McGinn. "He can get Lefty's one nut to dance a tango in his ball bag."

"Who's Big George?" Pablo asked.

Pablo didn't have any real interest in who Big George was, but figured it was a good cue to interject himself into the conversation. He had to repeat the question, as it was initially drowned out by the laughter created by Fat Fuck McGinn's ball bag joke.

"Big George is a colored fella that works over there a ways on Edgar Trudeau's farm," said Mick. "That's a few miles west of here in case you don't know." Mick followed up his words by pointing in the general direction. Then after a long swig he added, "Moonshiners come a dime a dozen down here in these parts. But it's worth the trip over to Trudeau's farm when word gets out that Big George whipped up one of his special batches. He's as big and black as they come, is Big George, but good God A 'mighty can he make some moonshine!"

"Big George tries to tell Mick, here, that he's just plum lucky— that it's just the way that the sorghum and corn grows over there on Trudeau's farm," said Smokey Bones. "But Mick thinks that that's all just a bunch of bullshit, and that Big George is addin' some secret ingredient… and he ain't tellin'."

"Whatever it is," said Lefty Carson, "he better not take the secret to his grave." Then they all threw back their heads and poured Big George's secret potion into their mouths, including Pablo, who afterward agreed that the second swig was decidedly less abrasive than the first.

"So what's you got there in your little bag of tricks, Poco?" asked Mick. He pointed to Pablo's brown, suede satchel.

Mick's innocent curiosity caught Pablo off guard, as there were items in the bag he wanted kept secret. He stammered before blurting out, "The Bible."

"You're kidding…right?" asked Mick.

"I'm not," replied Pablo. He couldn't understand why Mick thought it was so odd that someone would carry around the Bible.

"Just look at him, Mick," said Lucky Kaminski. "He ain't kidding."

"Well I'll be a son-of-a-bitch," said Smokey Bones. "All this time we been drinkin' and cussin', and with a holy man right here in our midst?"

"Let's have a look," said Mick.

Mick wasn't convinced that Pablo was truthful regarding the bag's contents. Pablo didn't *want* to deny Mick a peek at his Bible. It was a simple enough request. Unwillingness to produce such a harmless item could spark suspicion, something Pablo didn't want to do.

For the first time since the bonfire was lit he was nervous. He looked into the eyes of the men and misread their curiosity as anger toward his reluctance. Nevertheless, he in no way wanted to expose his other possessions—least of all, his cash. The thought crossed his mind that he should pay a visit to the Brownsville National Bank. It was no longer prudent to manage his affairs from a bag.

Pablo managed to set aside his misgivings and unbuckled his satchel. Tilting the opening toward him, he carefully sifted through the knife, Colt, cash, and old copies of *The Brownsville Herald* awaiting his attention, until his fingers were resting on the Bible. Once the *good book* was securely in hand, he eased it from its hiding place.

The men were so preoccupied with the idea that Pablo had a copy of the holy Bible in his possession, they weren't the slightest bit curious of what else the *bag of tricks* might contain. Despite the darkness which had already fallen, no one bothered to try and steal a peek. To a man, they held their ground.

"That's the Bible, alright," said Lefty Carson, as Pablo handed the good book over to Mick.

"For sure, you're not the original owner," said Mick. "This book's been around, hasn't it? I'll bet it's a hundred years old, if not more."

"If it is that old," said Dirty Jack Doyle, "then maybe it's worth something."

"You'd better keep your hands off it, Jack," warned Lucky Kaminski. "You're liable to burst into flames if you touch it, beings you ain't ever been inside a church before."

Frankie "The Prick" Donato and Fat Fuck McGinn looked at one another and wondered when each had last made an appearance in a place of worship. It was too long ago for either to remember. Incidentally, Frankie Donato got his nickname "The Prick" because he was known in his earlier days to have been handy with a knife—not that he ever used a knife to cut wheat or to kill...unlike Pablo. He whittled, among other things, and his knife *was* and still *is* a handy source of reassurance.

"It *is* that old, Jack," said Mick. "But its only true worth is in the pages if someone cares enough to read 'em." And with a wink, Mick handed the Bible back to Pablo.

"Jeez, Mick, does this mean we have to start walking the path of the righteous?" asked Dirty Jack Doyle. "I mean, now that we have a holy man in our midst…"

"Jack, you dirty bastard," Smokey Bones chimed in, "you wouldn't know the path of the righteous if they built your damn house on it!"

The party started to breakup once Big George's spirits were consumed and the bonfire was reduced to smoldering embers. When Pablo began walking away, he felt a firm hand on his shoulder.

"These boys, Poco, they can get plenty rowdy; there's no doubt about it," said Mick. "But they work hard and there ain't a mean bone in a one of their bodies. I guess what I'm tryin' to say is, I don't know how closely you follow that book; but believe me, you can do a lot worse than these here fellas."

What Mick didn't know, nor could know, was that Pablo knew worse—far worse than Mick or any of the other fellas of the boardwalk construction could imagine. But those were thoughts that he kept to himself.

"Thanks," said Pablo. "I'm looking forward to tomorrow."

****

In the spring of 1898, Pablo Cordero moved in with Smokey Bones. Until then, Pablo had been living with Lefty and Linda Carson. The Carsons were married in the autumn of 1896. That same year the couple invited Pablo for Christmas dinner. The invitation eventually led to Pablo being offered the newlyweds' spare bedroom. But, wouldn't you know, Lefty, despite being minus a testicle, was not only able to knock up his new bride, but saddled her with twins!

"Heaven forbid Lefty had a complete set in that ball bag of his," said Smokey Bones, "or poor Linda would surely be done for!"

Pablo knew that Lefty and Linda would feel awful asking him to leave. He never let it get that far. He took his brown, suede satchel and walked a few blocks east, where he split the rent with Smokey Bones. The apartment was only one room with a bath. Smokey slept in the bed while Pablo slept on a secondhand couch he purchased from a neighbor. The arrangement worked well enough for awhile. Such arrangements, though, are inclined to become a bit too cozy. This would become true of Smokey Bones and Pablo Cordero, especially should one or the other decide that they had charm enough to land a sweetheart, and Smokey was the first to hit pay dirt.

There were no hard feelings on Pablo's part. It was Smokey's place to begin with, and besides, the two weren't destined to remain roommates forever. Hard working and not altogether bad looking young men that they were, it was only a matter of time before they showed up on the radar of some woman. The way Pablo saw it—it had been four years since elevating himself to a place folks refer to as *society*. Not that he had gotten even a whiff of society's more well-to-do—but that *he*, a former migrant farm worker, had reached society at all was remarkable. Now it was time for a place of his own, and he had plenty of cash stashed at The Brownsville National Bank. Besides, Brownsville was a growing city where there was plenty of work.

****

One by one the bonfire boys married off. Even Fat Fuck McGinn found himself a nice girl to deem him a worthy catch. Only Mick remained a bachelor, as well as the agent between the others and Big George's moonshine. For the sake of the wives and the babies that seemed to come along every season, though, the bonfire/booze fests weren't as frequent as they had been in the past—or, as Lucky Kaminski put it: "In the good old days."

Pablo gave up delivering *The Brownsville Herald*, but continued with its reading. He didn't bother having it delivered, but preferred to pick up a copy on the way home from work at Abercrombie's Drugstore on Elizabeth Street. Mr. Abercrombie always saved him a copy. Now that he had a place of his own, he preferred reading the paper after work, as it helped to pass the increasing number of nights not aided by a bonfire and Big George's moonshine. On Sundays, he still opted for a comfortable spot down by the river.

One particularly hot and humid Sunday morning, that was where he was headed, when he found himself fascinated by the folks shuffling into the Blessed Juan Diego de Guadalupe Roman Catholic Church.

Pablo stumbled upon this scene on many a Sunday morning; although, this morning one family in particular garnered most, if not all of his attention. There was nothing extraordinary or exceptional about this family—only a husband and wife with their three children. Neither were they typical. Despite the bustling crowd, Pablo managed to examine them without a moment's digression as they made their way to the church. He sensed that he knew the family well. As for the father; he had seen this man's face a thousand times over the span of thousands of days, and yet they had never met—not even a passing glance on the street. It was only the image that the man portrayed that Pablo recognized—an image of desperation and of the hopelessness that accompanies the endless toil in the life of a migrant—the image of a trapped man in an unforgiving world and whose spirit was long ago crushed. The man's legs were still sturdy, his hands strong, but for how much longer? As Pablo observed, deep within the man's dark brooding eyes was the look of one who long ago surrendered. Pablo grew up toiling right alongside men just like this—the look in their eyes was irrevocably etched in his memory. This man had that same look. Pablo suspected that he and his family were migrants—or worse, were among the woe begotten that society pretends not to see— the ones who prefer to remain in shadow, but on Sunday morning, for the love of God, will come forth.

The man's wife was typical of a woman of her circumstance, in that, for the sake of her children, she smiled and pretended. Inside, though, was where she hid all her suffering, as the daily ritual of survival had all but worn away her once abundant resolve. The two boys, who Pablo placed at age six and eight, walked with a lilt—their youth served as an effective shield to deflect any misery launched in their direction. As for the girl; she was too old to lose herself in ignorance, and yet too young to lose all hope. She was stuck somewhere between the heart that her father wore on his sleeve and the smile that her mother routinely learned to force. One thing was for certain; Anna Maria Lopez was the most beautiful creature that Pablo Cordero had ever laid his eyes upon. With a luxurious sea of shiny, black hair ending at the small of her back, and the warm, radiant glow of skin that belied the harshness of her days, Anna Maria Lopez walked with poise—her willowy form seemed to glide amid the others who merely stepped their way toward the church. To his surprise, Pablo discovered that he was standing inside the Blessed Juan Diego de Guadalupe Roman Catholic Church as he unwittingly followed the glorious creature.

Never before had Pablo set foot inside a house of worship. Although he considered himself to be a man of God and of the Bible, he never sought a specific religious denomination. He had no idea what it meant to be Catholic, Protestant, or any other religion. His pathway to God was without distinction.

Pablo sat in the pew right behind the Lopezes. He took his eyes away from Anna Maria long enough to gaze upon the impressive architecture of the grand Roman Catholic structure. In the past four years, Pablo worked on one edifice after another in the town of Brownsville. In doing so, he gained a fair amount of knowledge of materials, what they cost, and how they were acquired. However, he had never worked with materials of the likes with which the church was comprised. This left him wondering, with whose dime was the ornate palace built?

Pablo sat behind Jorge Lopez to better gaze upon the profile of his beautiful daughter—the slope of her delicate nose, the corner of a soft and remarkable eye—an eye which thus far hadn't noticed its captive admirer.

Despite his fascination, Pablo made every attempt to hone in on the priest, whose voice was bouncing off the walls and raining down from the dome. He found the acoustics anomalous and took some getting used to. At last, he allowed the priest's words to reverberate throughout the church without any effort to try and bring them to his ears. While the words washed over him, he allowed himself to become lost in the face of one so beautiful. He wished to remain in perpetual reverie, conjuring thought after thought of how he and the glorious creature could spend a warm Sunday afternoon. However, in the course of his reverie, his eyes drifted away from Anna Maria, traveling to Jorge Lopez, before resting on his wife, Martina. It was while observing the woebegone couple that Pablo was transported back to the dusty plains of the Midwest and wheat belt, where he planted and harvested under an unforgiving sun for what amounted to slave wages. He shuddered to contemplate circumstances that would send him back to those hot, dusty plains. At once, he shifted his eyes to revisit the lovely Anna Maria.

Along with her impeccable posture and her proud chin, there was an elegance to Anna Maria Lopez that made her standout from all others—including those, who according to their attire were of a much higher station. Pablo couldn't imagine Jorge or Martina Lopez possessing such traits, even before their spirits were broken. Like Dolci Cordero, Anna Maria Lopez was a delicate stem at the end of which bloomed an exquisite flower trying to survive in a harsh and barren land. When gazing at Anna Maria, Pablo conjured images of his mother—the lustful way men ogled her—their vulgar advances. He wondered what might have this magnificent creature, who sat between her pretending mother and slumping father in a house of worship, been forced to do against her will. He dismissed the abhorrent thought before it ever had the chance to fester into something he couldn't bear.

Pablo was jolted from his reverie when realizing that the priest's voice ceased reverberating off the walls and ceiling. All went quiet, save for the soft murmuring that ran throughout the church, along with the shuffling of feet. He looked away from Anna Maria to view a congregation, which began shaking hands with one another. "Peace be with you," they were all saying when shaking hands with those within their immediate proximity. Pablo found the ritual curious, but pleasing. Then Jorge Lopez turned toward Pablo and offered a hand. Jorge didn't notice Pablo's brief hesitation, during which, and with some reflection, he examined the man's knurly appendage. When the two brought their hands together, Pablo was surprised to discover that his own hand was equally rough and calloused. "Peace be with you," said Jorge Lopez.

Pablo returned the sentiment, though Jorge's eyes remained downcast throughout their brief exchange.

To Pablo's delight, Anna Maria, too, offered him her hand. He was embarrassed about his hand's condition and prayed that the girl wouldn't be too repulsed by his touch. Should she in any way recoil, he feared the dream of a tender touch and affectionate words spoken on a warm Sunday afternoon would be over before it could begin. He received Anna Maria's hand as if it were a delicate flower whose petals he dare not bend. "Peace be with you," she said, smiling demurely at one who looked back with admiration.

Pablo Cordero tried to imagine a day in the life of Anna Maria Lopez, whose demure smile launched him into a hyper-romantic notion that he already knew her, and furthermore, would one day soon and to her delight, swoop down from up on high and rescue her from a life of endless toil. Pablo and Anna Maria would stroll the town of Brownsville at sunset before wandering into Abercrombie's Drugstore for a bag of hard candy. Just as Pablo had on many a days past, Anna Maria would find the candy a delight. Next they would stroll along the river on the boardwalk. There, Pablo would mention with a hint of pride, that he and his friends had built the strong and sturdy structure on which aspiring young lovers walked hand-in-hand along the Rio Grande on moonlit nights. It would only be natural for Anna Maria to be curious about Pablo's friends. He would oblige, naturally, but would omit the "Dirty" in Jack Doyle, the "The Prick" in Frankie Donato, the "Fat Fuck" in McGinn, and that Lefty Carson was simply another lefthander. At dusk they would board the last ferry for Matamoros on their way to Bagdad Beach. There they would share their first kiss and remain in a warm and loving embrace until the tip of the rising sun cast its first rays on the Gulf of Mexico.

Seemingly out of nowhere appeared four men. Two were making their way down the center aisle of the church—the other two the side aisles. Each was holding firm to a long stick which fastened to a basket. To Pablo's astonishment, the men stopped at each pew and dangled the baskets in the laps of folks, some of whom Pablo could easily determine were Brownsville's less fortunate citizens. Pablo raised a curious brow. This wasn't the God of which Josiah Walton spoke. Yet, people were reaching for their purses for whatever they could spare, or for whatever was expected—Pablo had no way of knowing which. Finally the basket arrived at the pew where sat the Lopezes. Before the basket made it to where it dangled in Jorge Lopez's lap, Pablo alertly seized his hand.

"Sir," he said, "I respectfully ask that you allow me."

Jorge Lopez glared at Pablo. *How dare you assume that I need your charity,* was the message that flashed in the man's otherwise brooding eyes. For a moment, Pablo thought he had made a huge miscalculation in his judgment and that Jorge Lopez was about to make a scene. Then he looked once again into Jorge's eyes. There was no mistake. Pablo had seen those eyes too many times in the past.

"Sir." Pablo leaned forward to whisper into Jorge Lopez's' ear. "I have no one in this world. No one to look after. No family to feed."

It wasn't Pablo's intention to make Jorge Lopez feel inadequate, or himself to appear heroic in the presence the man's beautiful daughter. His motive was pure—the gesture discreet, yet it didn't escape Anna Maria, who in turn flashed the same demure smile as when Pablo earlier took hold of her hand. Meanwhile, Martina Lopez pretended not to notice the subtleness that transpired.

Mass ended and the parishioners of the Blessed Juan Diego de Guadalupe Roman Catholic Church spilled into the street. With eyes dissecting the crowd, Pablo kept the Lopezes in sight and followed them, but at a distance. Occasionally Anna Maria glanced back. When doing so, evident was her same demure smile and a twinkle in her eye. Charmed beyond hope, Pablo smiled in return, pretending to mosey along *incidentally* in the same direction. All at once he was feeling clumsy, inspired, and foolish. When seeing Anna Maria's twinkling eye, he was Pablo Cordero…heroic lover. In the seconds that elapsed between the backward glances, he was a stalker lurking in shadow, and whose intentions were clear to all those whom he passed along the way. He wondered where and when the journey would end, but more importantly, how.

Jorge Lopez trudged onward with downcast eyes, while Martina Lopez pretended not to notice her daughter's backward glances at the young man who she knew was following her. When at the northwest limits on town, Pablo found it most odd that the Lopezes walked such a distance to attend a church service. It was there that Anna Maria once again glanced back at Pablo. This time her smile and the twinkle were gone. In their stead was a look that portrayed sorrow and regret. Step after step after block after mile, Pablo followed the Lopezes, only to have his spirit crushed by one telling glance. It came quite unexpected and he wanted to run up to Anna Maria, seize her by her arms, and cry, *"What did that look mean? Why, after all this, did you dash all hope?"* In his own hyper-romantic mind, Pablo had gone far beyond the point of hello. Though, crushed as his spirit might have been, he continued trailing after the Lopezes.

Soon the road turned to dirt, and along with the journey it ended at Mortimer's farm—a farm whose chief cash crop was cotton. Anna Maria turned back for what she knew in her heart would be the last look at a young man who thought so much as to follow her. Her downcast eyes were more telling than mere words. *Now you know, my dear Prince, the squalor in which I live—the truth of my wretched existence. Before no one else could I feel so ashamed. It would be my wish to see you again, but I know that I never will.* That was the message that Anna Maria sent Pablo, which he received loud and clear.

Then Pablo watched as the Lopezes disappeared into their ramshackle dwelling.

Jorge Lopez had entered into a binding sharecropping agreement that overwhelmingly favored the land owner, Clive Mortimer. To make matters worse, a few years ago, Clive Mortimer charged Jorge exorbitant prices for seed and tools against next season's crop, which underperformed. This left the Lopezes in financial ruins.

Pablo walked away from Mortimer's farm with a heavy heart. The following day he was quiet and pensive, and at times appeared to be daydreaming. He didn't partake in the usual banter that occurred throughout the work day.

"Looks like our boy here is at long last in love," chirped Smokey Bones.

"Yep, I'd say the ol' love bug took a good size bite out of 'im for sure," teased Lefty Carson.

"Is this true?" asked Mick. "Are you in love?"

All Pablo could do was answer with an indecisive shrug.

"So what's her name?" asked Lucky Kaminski.

Again, Pablo answered with a shrug—this time to indicate that the subject wasn't up for discussion.

"Aw, for cryin' out loud," said Dirty Jack Doyle, "it's safe to tell us her name! The only one here you have to worry about is Mick. The rest of us poor bastards are *already* married!"

Pablo stammered, twisted, and winced before finally admitting that he had yet to learn the name of the girl responsible for his dramatic change in mood. He hadn't gotten that far, but was "working on it." The awkward confession caused Frankie "The Prick" Donato and Fat Fuck McGinn to double over in a fit of laughter. (A doubled over Fat Fuck McGinn was quite a sight.) Then poor Pablo had to endure further laughter and ridicule when explaining that he was charmed beyond all hope with mere smiles and glances from a nameless girl.

"Jeez, Pablo, what'd she do, mind fuck ya?" wondered Dirty Jack Doyle.

"Now just a minute, Jack," said Mick with a hard glare. "The way a woman looks at you can say a lot more than her words. So let's give our young friend here the benefit of the doubt."

"Jeez, Mick," asked Dirty Jack, "when'd you get to be such a romantic?"

"You *do* know where she lives, don't you...so you can call on her?" asked Smokey Bones.

The question sent Pablo tap dancing through a rather unconvincing *kinda-sorta* reply. This he managed, though without ever revealing that the girl of his dreams lived only one step above a squatter.

"Well, when ya do call on her," advised Lefty Carson, "leave the Bible on top of your nightstand. You don't want her thinkin' you're aimin' to become a priest. A nice long stem rose'll do the trick. But make sure it's a red one, though. Girls like red roses."

"Yeah, look how it worked for you," laughed Smokey Bones. "You ended up with twins!"

Bright and early on the following Sunday morning, Pablo, plus a rose, but minus the Bible as Lefty Carson had advised, positioned himself adjacent to the front door of the Blessed Juan Diego de Guadalupe Roman Catholic Church and awaited the girl of his dreams. He tossed and turned for hours trying to think of something to say when he saw the willowy Anna Maria Lopez making her way to church. Yet there he stood, unarmed, unprepared, and without a single word or phrase resting on his lips.

After much tossing and turning that only resulted in frustration, Pablo decided that it was fruitless to try and sleep, as the thought of a girl whose name he had yet to learn caused him great restlessness. So out he went well before dawn to walk the quiet, lonely streets of Brownsville. The town was tranquil and strangely still in the dark a.m., so quiet that his footsteps seemed amplified and at first distracted his thoughts. He found the air thick and heavy at that hour. Stranger yet, it smelled different than it did in the daytime.

The only soul Pablo wandered upon in the sleepy town was a lamplighter, who was snuffing out the light in front of Abercrombie's Drugstore. Even the prostitutes were scarce at such an hour. Despite the stale air, the darkness, and desolate streets, Brownsville in the eerie morning seemed friendlier than the kindest day on the dusty plains of the Midwest.

Pablo liked the lamplights. They made the night seem cozy, more alive, and he less alone. He wanted to call to the lamplighter, *"Could you please wait awhile longer before snuffing out the lights?"* Instead he called "Good morning" quietly, so as not to disturb anyone's slumber. As he went along, he peeked in familiar store windows hoping to see a sign of life—an early welcome to a new day, but all was dark and quiet. *How nice a fellow is Mr. Abercrombie,* he thought. *Always saving me a newspaper and throwing a few extra pieces of hard candy in the bag.* Pablo liked sucking on hard candy when reading *The Brownsville Herald* in the quietude of his home during the evenings when absent was Big George's moonshine and bonfires.

Folks like Mr. Abercrombie made the wheat belt, the unruly band of migrants, and the men who gang raped Dolci seem millions of miles away. Migratory living and the world of Jed Wright was long behind—but come morning, he would once again see the dark brooding eyes of Jorge Lopez, and it would all come rushing back. The very notion of Jorge Lopez was all too unsettling and caused him to second guess an involvement he spent a week imagining, but the vision in his mind's eye of the man's daughter overpowered any lingering doubts.

Pablo waved to the lamplighter, who returned the greeting with a quick nod, then took his ladder and scurried to the next post. Pablo followed the man from post to post until every last light in the sleeping town was snuffed out. The man seemed to enjoy the service he provided for the town. As Pablo observed, he was remarkably nimble when scurrying along with his ladder, and equally nimble when climbing. He considered how many nights he lay in slumber, while this man, who he presumed was a volunteer, scurried about town with a ladder tucked under his arm. He considered the many roles that needed filling to form a society, and this nimble fellow was doing his part. Lastly, he thought of ruthless landowners and men so callous that they seem not to possess souls. But like Mr. Abercrombie, the lamplighter was a reminder that those days were behind. When the agile fellow snuffed out the last light, Pablo thanked him. His gratitude, though, was more for his quiet company that served as a comfort on a sleepless night, than for a service that most often went unnoticed.

The dark, misty hours became a qualified morning, and the town of Brownsville came alive. At sunrise, Pablo stood in front of the Blessed Juan Diego de Guadalupe Roman Catholic Church. The light of a brand new day stung his weary, sleep divested eyes—his stomach was empty and nervous. After the passing of a restless-turned-peaceful and contemplative night came a morning that saw him feeling out-of-sorts. Wanting to escape the harshness of the morning light, he headed for the dimness of the church, only to tug on a locked door. In his weary mind, he perceived a locked door as an ominous sign—one causing him to doubt all that he had read, or believed existed in the demure smiles and twinkling eyes of Anna Maria Lopez, before it all turned to gloom at the end of the road.

Throughout the long and languorous morning, Pablo's demeanor rose and fell with each passing minute. He began to pace fretfully as the eight o'clock hour neared. When arriving, the hour brought along folks by the dozens and from every direction all flocking toward the church. Pablo tilted his head and shifted his eyes to better dissect the advancing crowd as he went in search of a girl, whose feet when she walked seemed to glide just above the ground. His stance remained fixed, his eyes busy, as the crowd went bustling by from all angles. Some paused and scowled to indicate of their displeasure, as Pablo's presence obstructed their path to the church. He wanted to shout, *"How can you all be so obtuse! Can't you see I'm looking for the most beautiful girl in the world?"* Despite all the unfriendly frowns and glares, he remained undaunted as he continued with his search.

Soon the crowd thinned and was reduced to a few stragglers. Still there was no sight of the man once perceived a migrant, or his beautiful daughter. At last, all that remained was a solitary soul clutching the stem of a red rose. A whole week's worth of hope and expectation had gone up in flames. It was only fitting that the sun should disappear, storm clouds roll in, and for Pablo to sit alone on the church steps holding a rose in the pouring rain. He began to wonder whether last Saturday night he drank too much of Big George's moonshine, and that there *was* no man perceived a migrant and whose eyes were filled with Pablo's past; and that there was *never* a lovely young woman who charmed him with demure smiles and twinkling eyes. Maybe it was all a hallucination or dream, and that last Sunday he never left his bed.

Pablo entertained the unlikely notion, but not for long. Then, like a man on a mission, he set aside his weariness and went trudging through the pouring rain. He needn't tell his feet where to go, as he knew every step—every turn. He walked with purpose and all the while ignoring the downpour and the passersby scampering for shelter. It wasn't until well beyond the northwest limits of town, where the road turned to dirt and he found himself sloshing through puddles and slipping in mud, that he became mindful of the conditions. Moments later he entered the acreage of Mortimer's farm and positioned himself directly in front of the same ramshackle dwelling into which a week ago he watched the Lopezes disappear.

"It was no hallucination," he muttered to himself. "No dream."

Pablo stood sinking into the mud while hanging onto a soggy red rose. The rain continued to pour down on him. When first facing the ramshackle dwelling, he felt both bold and foolish. This was an odd combination, he realized, and it caused him to wonder, *what sort of fellow stands in front of a ramshackle hut in the pouring rain holding a rose?* Despite his boldness and foolishness providing him an odd sense of exhilaration, he was uncertain whether to knock, or to remain ankle deep in mud waiting until someone noticed him. During this time of deliberation, one of the boys appeared in a window. At such a distance, Pablo was uncertain whether it was the one thought to be the six years old or the eight-year-old. The boy smiled at Pablo and waved—amused that anyone would allow themselves to be drenched by a downpour while standing ankle deep in mud without any attempt to gain shelter. Pablo engaged the boy by smiling rather idiotically, then returned his wave. There they remained—Pablo in the rain while sinking in the mud, and the boy in the window, exchanging funny faces. Some time had gone by, when Pablo took his eyes from the window and rested them at the door, which at last was being pushed open. The boy had remained in the window, leaving Pablo to assume that he must have alerted someone of the strange man standing in the rain clutching to a limp rose. From behind the door and out into the downpour stepped Jorge Lopez. He advanced toward Pablo with the same downcast eyes that the drenched man remembered from a week ago.

"You're that young fella from the church, aren't you?" asked Jorge Lopez, once he and Pablo were face to face.

"Yes sir, I am," replied Pablo. "But I didn't see your family at church this morning."

"Mrs. Lopez wasn't feeling well this morning," said Jorge Lopez. "But I'm sure you didn't walk all this way in the pouring rain to learn why we weren't at church."

"With all due respect, no sir, I did not," said Pablo. "The reason I'm came was to ask permission to call on your daughter."

"I see," said Jorge Lopez, though the confession came as no great surprise. "I had a feeling we would see you again." Then after a brief, but thoughtful pause, which saw Jorge wipe the rain from his eyes, he added, "It's hard to deny someone who has come all this distance and in these conditions. Therefore I will not. Come by next Saturday at four."

"Sir?" asked Pablo. "What is your daughter's name?"

"Anna Maria," replied Jorge Lopez.

"Would you please give this to Anna Maria?" begged Pablo, and he handed Jorge the soggy rose. "Tell her it's from the boy who followed her home from church."

Jorge Lopez reached out and took careful hold of the soggy flower, then tipped his hat to Pablo.

Pablo started to turn away, and then added, "Sir, give my regards to Mrs. Lopez, that I hope she is feeling better."

Again Jorge Lopez tipped his hat. Pablo watched as he began his plodding walk back to his home, unhurried, despite the rain. He raised his eyes above Jorge Lopez's shoulder and once again discovered the young lad, who all along had remained in the window. The youngster smiled when regarding the soggy flower his father was about to bring into their home. Then he made a funny face. Pablo returned the gesture.

The following morning he waltzed into work whistling a tune that no one recognized, or was able to distinguish, other than it was unmistakably happy.

"Uh oh, looks like our Don Juan, here, got himself a name," teased Smoke Bones.

"And a date," said Pablo, unable to cease from grinning. "Next Saturday at four." The favorable news prompted Frankie "The Prick" Donato and Fat Fuck McGinn to break into a chorus of "When You Were Sweet Sixteen."

I love you as I never lov'd before,
since first I met you on the village green
Come to me, or my dream of you is o'vr
I love you as I lov'd you
When you were sweet, when you were sweet Sixteen.

"Good God A, mighty that was awful!" cried Lefty Carson. "My one nut coulda sung it better!"

"A pack of hyenas coulda *howled* it better!" said Lucky Kaminski. "Just by dumb luck they'd a hit *one* right note!" (The suggestion of course being that Donato and McGinn hit none, but their rendition of the popular song wasn't nearly as awful as their friends would have them believe.)

"Don't pay 'em any mind, Frankie," said Fat Fuck McGinn, when seeing a hint of indignation flash in the eyes of his crooning partner following the unfavorable critique. "These lousy bastards just don't appreciate good music, that's all."

McGinn's indignation was apparent, too. He wasn't the slightest bit sensitive about "Fat Fuck," and as a younger man took it in stride when called "The McGinnest" to his middle brother's "McGinner" and youngest brother's "McGinn," but like Donato, he believed that he could sing and didn't appreciate being told that he couldn't.

"Looks like I'd better get on my horse," said Mick, as he gave Pablo a congratulatory pat on the back, "or pretty soon I'll be the only bachelor in town."

64

All wound up and unable to contain himself, Pablo went running from his home. In doing so, he arrived at Clive Mortimer's farm an hour earlier than expected and paced about in an area where he could remain inconspicuous. He allowed his hyper-romantic imagination, which of late had little or no limitation, to run wild as he wore out the ground. Once again, he did as Lefty Carson advised and left the Bible home in his brown, suede satchel. He also remembered to bring along another single long stem red rose. This time he would present it to Anna Maria personally.

Anna Maria blushed when receiving the elegant blossom. Decorously staid she remained while in the presence of her father, who made every effort to bring a smile to his mouth, and her mother, who appeared happier and less restrained than she intended. When seeing the effect the presentation of a rose had on its receiver and four onlookers, particularly Martina Lopez, Pablo tried to resist a triumphant grin, but failed. He did, however, remember to inquire about Martina Lopez's health. The two youngsters rushed to the window and looked on as Pablo and their sister made their way to the road.

When winding their way into town, Pablo spoke not a word of his past, for it was too akin to Anna Maria's present. Tonight and hopefully beyond, as was his intention, he wished for Anna Maria to escape her dismal presence—to shed her unpleasant reality, and together they would look toward a bright future.

There was an elegance to Anna Maria Lopez—a sense of decorum that is often lacking in those of lower stations. As Pablo would acknowledge, it must have been by some cruel trick of nature or the way the stars happened to align, that she ended up not only the daughter of a sharecropper, but one so unsuccessful. Pablo didn't look down on Jorge Lopez, but instead felt empathy. Like so many others Pablo had known in the past, Jorge was a victim of his own illiteracy and therefore was easily taken advantage.

"Do you like the hard candy?" Pablo asked Anna Maria, as they were exiting Abercrombie's Drugstore in favor of a stroll by the river. Before their departure, Mr. Abercrombie gave Pablo a congratulatory tip of his cap for landing such a stunning beauty. The drugstore owner was also thoughtful enough to have complimented Anna Maria on her "lovely dress" which Martina Lopez busied herself making the very next day after Jorge agreed to allow Pablo to call on their daughter.

"I like things that are sweet," she told Pablo. When she looked into his eyes, it then occurred to Pablo that Anna Maria wasn't merely taller than he remembered, but taller than him. (Not that Pablo was a particularly tall man. He was only five feet six inches.)

"I've never been as far as the river, before," said Anna Maria when they were strolling the boardwalk. No sooner had she made the fact known, Pablo began guiding her toward the ferry, which had just completed its return trip from Matamoros and was again preparing to launch.

"It's exciting," she said, as they looked out over the water.

Pablo made certain that they were back at the dock for the last returning ferry to Brownsville. This was a major alteration from his original script. His hyper-romantic vision of Anna Maria and him embracing on Bagdad Beach until the sun rose over the gulf would have to wait. For the remainder of the evening he would need to improvise.

To a passenger, most of whom were couples in want of romance, everyone was gazing up at the full moon, which shone splendidly over the Rio Grande. Once the ferry docked, everyone scattered in every direction—some were heading home, others were off to their next romantic destination, leaving Pablo and Anna Maria alone and to linger.

"I've never seen the city at night before," Anna Maria said with a sense of wonder. "The river, the streets, the lamplights—it all looks so beautiful."

"For more than a thousand nights I've seen the city and the river," said Pablo. "But I've never seen them look as beautiful as tonight. They must've been saving their best for you."

Before Anna Maria could blush, Pablo took her into his arms and kissed her. When their lips parted, he reached up with a gentle hand and touched her face. He wanted to fall to his knees and plead, *let me rescue you and love you and take care of you forever!* Although he never said a word, Anna Maria looked into his eyes and then let her willowy form fall into his rescuing arms.

****

In the spring of 1899, Lucky Kaminski ran out of luck. Poor Lucky slipped from scaffolding and plunged three stories to his death. On the day following Lucky's funeral, a deeply saddened and agitated Frankie "The Prick" Donato got shit-faced drunk (a term used by Smokey Bones) in a local saloon, where a brawl happened to break out. The brawl was no fault of Frankie's, but it resulted in him pulling a knife. Frankie mistakenly believed that the threat of a knife would calm the fray. And although the wounds that Frankie administered to a couple of drunken roustabouts were of the non-fatal variety, it led to his arrest. Afterward, Dirty Jack Doyle, Fat Fuck McGinn, Smokey Bones, Lefty Carson, Mick, and Pablo all put up money for Frankie's bail, then stood before the judge as character witnesses.

In the autumn of the same year, Lefty Carson said farewell to the city of Brownsville and all his friends, in favor of his Uncle Lou's cement company in Saint Louis, Missouri.

"Times sure are a-changin'," said Mick, at an early December bonfire which saw plenty of Big George's moonshine consumed. Then on May 5, 1900, seventeen-year-old Anna Maria Lopez became Mrs. Pablo Cordero.

****

Since settling in Brownsville, Pablo hadn't let a year go by without traveling north to Madisonville, Texas to visit Ben Hutchinson and Doc Crandall. Pablo was always invited for Thanksgiving and Christmas dinner, but seldom was he able to make both. Sometimes during the winter, work slowed, and he was able to visit for several days. During these visits, he would tell Doc and Ben of his humble beginnings. When doing so, he always remembered to give thanks to Josiah Walton, a man who lost his family to a war—a lost soul who had just enough love remaining in his heart to look after a young boy. Before leaving Madisonville, Pablo, along with the Crandalls and Hutchinsons, would visit Dolci's grave.

"So what's in Madisonville?" asked Anna Maria, as she and Pablo were preparing to travel north for the Christmas holiday.

"Blueberry pie," replied Pablo. "Have you ever had any?"

"I've only ever had apple pie," replied Anna Maria. "Mama used to make it for my birthday. But I imagine blueberry pie is also delicious." After musing over the virtues of pie, she shot Pablo a curious look, then asked, "Doesn't anyone in *Brownville* make blueberry pie?"

The droll remark drew a chuckle from Pablo. Then he began to tell Anna Maria all about his fine friends from the north, and that blueberry pie was but a bonus.

"It wouldn't matter even if we *were* just going for pie," said Anna Maria. "It will be exciting to travel to another town." The newlyweds threw together a few belongings, wished their friends a Merry Christmas, and headed north.

Anna Maria Cordero stood agape and watched as dish after dish was paraded from the kitchen into the dining room, where, with fine presentation they were laid on the Crandalls' twelve-foot-long mahogany table.

"I didn't think there was this much food in the whole world," she whispered to Pablo.

Indeed, it was an impressive spread that Alice Crandall and Betsy Hutchinson had prepared. Turkey, stuffing, potato mash, sweet potatoes with a glaze, corn, asparagus, cranberry puree, rib roast with horseradish and mushrooms, and a spiked punch bowl, which Doc Crandall was rather glib when warning, "Could be a bit heavy handed, so we best watch out."

"He's getting old," said Alice Crandall. "His hand shakes."

"Nonsense!" said Doc, as he gave Somerset Evans a conspiratorial wink. "Our good pastor here accidentally hit my elbow just when I was mixing in the hooch. Imagine that?"

"A likely story, Doc," said Dutch Kirby. "But next time have our *'good pastor'* hit your elbow a little harder."

There was laughter throughout the room, then everyone raised a glass. After several toasts and Merry Christmases were exchanged, Ben Hutchinson cornered Pablo and congratulated him on his marriage. Then the two recalled their conversation six years ago, when Ben told Pablo that one day someone special would come along and take most of the sting out of his heart.

The grieving young man had listened politely to Ben's words, but at the time he couldn't imagine that such a day would ever come to pass. Gazing at Anna Maria, he considered the unlikelihood of a squatter without a single relation one day becoming the world's luckiest man.

Then he set his eyes on the bountiful table and those with whom he was about to feast, and who once provided a heartbroken young man a sense of belonging and have continued to do so ever since. *How wonderful the world can be,* he thought. It was almost too much to imagine. But Pablo was of the belief that every person of faith experiences a moment, an hour, or perhaps even a day feeling the luckiest soul alive and possessing a spirit without any grasp of boundaries. To feel this at all is remarkable. To know it every day is a gift.

"So, my good young friend, what are your plans?" Doc Crandall asked Pablo. "I mean, now that you've already gone and married the prettiest gal in all of Texas." This, Doc added while nodding admiringly at the blushing Anna Maria, just as everyone sat down and was preparing to dig in to the glorious feast. Before Pablo answered, the always charming Doc winked at his wife—a subtle gesture to remind Alice Crandall, that in matters of beauty, she was number one and all others were a distant second.

"Well Doc," said Pablo, "as you know, I have plenty of farming experience—my wife, too. We were thinking about saving up to buy a few acres of our own."

"I see," said Doc Crandall.

The old doctor's tone had implied that farming was below someone of Pablo's intellect. Doc was always after Pablo to move to Madisonville, where he could help his young friend to pursue a formal education. At one time Pablo was keen for the idea, but since setting foot in the Blessed Juan Diego de Guadalupe Roman Catholic Church, all he wanted was to provide for Anna Maria. Still, Doc held to the belief that Pablo was keen for a formal education, and therefore suspected that the idea of saving to buy a few acres belonging to his new bride.

"Farming—an invaluable labor—an honorable profession," proclaimed Dutch Kirby.

"Easy for you to say, Dutch," said Betsy Hutchinson. "Why, with a manageable amount of land and two strong sons at your disposal. But my poor brother, Cornelius, up there in Kentucky, with the biggest farm in the state…why, he's always cryin' that he can't find enough good help."

"Yeah, it's poor old Cornelius alright," chimed in Ben Hutchinson. "And he still hasn't forgiven me for marrying his best picker."

"It's not your fault, Ben, for knowing a good catch when you saw one," said Alice Crandall.

"Anyway, here's to the land and all that can come from it," said Dutch Kirby. To those sentiments they all raised a glass.

Following a dinner that produced full bellies and many sighs of delight, Pablo sought out Somerset Evans. Together the two went walking in the cool December air.

"I love spending Christmas in Madisonville," said Pablo. "It gets better every year."

"Can't argue with you there," said Somerset Evans. "Alice and Betsy sure put out some spread, they do." Then the good pastor patted his bloated belly.

"For sure they do," agreed Pablo. "But the real reason I came north this Christmas was to see you, Pastor."

"I'm flattered, Pablo," said Somerset Evans. "But why so formal?"

"Because I came to see you as a pastor…for counsel," was Pablo's reply.

"Oh?" said Somerset Evans; his curiosity peaked.

"I have a confession that I need to make," Pablo told the good pastor.

"I see," said Somerset Evans, wary of what could follow. Then he was quick to point out, "But in the Methodist religion, it's perfectly acceptable to confess your sins directly to God."

"I know that," said Pablo. "And I've tried."

Pablo hadn't suggested that talking to God left him unsatisfied, or lacking fulfillment. Although, he did manage to painstakingly illustrate, there were instances requiring judgment by one's own peers, and that such judgment could carry the hope of reassurance regarding one's transgressions.

The first night the newlyweds slept together, Pablo began to stir before letting out a quiet moan. Moments later he became restless, then agitated, until finally he sprang into a sitting position. He let out a cry...then another and another. Although his cries were scarcely audible, they managed to awaken Anna Maria. Though able sense the depth of torment in those faint cries, she couldn't imagine the horrors that caused them. She tried to comfort her husband. Several times she called out his name, but then concluded he was sleeping. Anna Maria looked warily at one presumed terrorized. Despite her trepidation, she put her ear to Pablo's lips and listened to his faint cries, but heard nothing distinguishable. She wrapped her arms around Pablo and lowered his head to the pillow, pressing his face to her bosom. She held him until his trembling body went limp and had returned its peaceful slumber. Anna Maria spent the remainder of the night awake watching her husband sleep.

As any woman might have, Anna Maria found her first night of matrimony unsettling. Come morning, she woke and asked politely, "How are you feeling this morning?"

Pablo replied, "Never better," and did so wearing a smile indicative of a man who couldn't have been happier with his place in the world. Anna Maria elected not to mention the reason for the innocuous question until the following morning after the episode reoccurred and has been reoccurring every night of their young marriage.

Pablo was aware of his dreams, but not of the faint, tormented cries and trembling that accompanied them. It wasn't until Anna Maria and he were wed that he had shared his bed. Although Pablo and Smokey Bones slept within close proximity of one another, the episodes went unnoticed because of Smokey's thunderous snoring.

Many nights Pablo dreamed of his teeth piercing human flesh. He could feel them traveling swiftly through warm, living tissue, then like a

70

cold-blooded carnivore, he would violently shake his jaw, ripping the last fiber of flesh and severing a mangled, necrotic body part from his prey. The warm trickle of blood in his mouth caused him to spring upward while choking and spitting. At this point, Anna Maria would coddle him until his trembling subsided.

Other nights, Pablo found himself back on the dusty plains of the Midwest and wheat belt. There, dozens of migrant men stood about cheering wildly—their eyes glazed over with evil. Through the shouts of the unruly mob, Pablo could hear poor Dolci's desperate cries. Frantically, he began pushing his way through the mob. He tried to call out to Dolci, that she should have every confidence that he was coming to her rescue. "I'm coming Mama," he tried to call out, but his words wouldn't travel beyond his own mind. He called her name again, but the result was the same. At last, he pushed aside the last man in his path. To his horror, he discovered Jed Wright—his fat, thrusting body eclipsing Dolci's slim, delicate form. Pablo grabbed a fistful of Jed Wright's hair and yanked. The evil man's head snapped back. Then with great swiftness and might, Pablo ran the blade of his knife across Jed's neck, thus, rendering him lifeless. He then turned toward the unruly mob with a mixture of fear and vengeance, and with the notion of daring any among them to step forward. To his surprise, he discovered that the mob had disappeared.

Pablo was shocked when first learning of his night terrors. But what bothered him was the distress that it was causing his new bride; although, Anna Maria did her best to conceal any anxiety that she was feeling.

"I'm sure it'll pass," she told him.

But what wouldn't pass, to the point of haunting Pablo, was the dilemma of whether or not to tell his new bride the reasons behind the reoccurring nightmares. As time went by, Pablo concluded that, by letting go of his secret—by intimating his sin to another mortal soul, he might unburden himself and attain absolution. However, this was not a theory that he was willing to try out on his new bride. Therefore, he turned to Somerset Evans for judgment and the reassurance of a forgiving God, and with the hope of vanquishing his nightmares.

"I do hope everyone saved room for dessert," chirped Betsy Hutchinson, as the dining room table was supplied with blueberry pies, bowls of whipped cream, and decanters of freshly brewed coffee. The dreamy look that came over Pablo whenever he gorged himself on blueberry pie never failed to produce smiles from both Alice Crandall and Betsy Hutchinson.

"My dear, please don't hesitate," Alice Crandall told Anna Maria. "Help yourself to seconds before you husband devours every morsel in sight."

"I never tasted anything so scrumptious," said Anna Maria. "But I couldn't eat another bite."

"Do keep in mind, though, my dear," warned Alice Crandall, but in a friendly tone, "you're now eating for two."

Pablo was about to shovel another forkful of blueberry pie into his awaiting mouth when the utensil slipped from his fingers and onto the plate, producing an awful clanking noise.

"What would you say, Betsy?" asked Alice Crandall. "Six weeks?"

"Oh, I'd say you've hit the nail right on the head," said Betsy Hutchinson.

Doc Crandall took off his eyeglasses and tossed them on the table. The manner in which he did so suggested, *how could I, a Doctor of nearly forty years, have missed that which was so painfully obvious to my wife and Betsy Hutchinson?*

"Looks like the old Doctor's losing his touch," teased Alice Crandall.

"Just blame it on the punch, Doc," said Ben Hutchinson. "After all, you drank darn near half the bowl!"

"Well, I guess this calls for a toast," said Somerset Evans. "But Ben's right, Doc; you did quite a number on the punch bowl. There's nothing left to toast with except coffee." This well known fact supplied Doc only mild embarrassment, which he quickly and easily shook off.

Everyone stood and raised their coffee cups. "To the newlyweds," said Somerset Evans. "God has blessed Anna Maria with child, and Pablo—a *most* deserving man, with a family."

Everyone sipped from their cups, then applauded. During the applause, Pastor Evan managed to gain Pablo's attention. He nodded subtly and mouthed the words, "May peace be with you."

****

"It's strange Grandfather," said Anna Maria, "but somehow I feel that I know her, and not just through all the stories that you've told. I've always felt connected to my grandmother; that somehow she's been with me all along." Then she added, but with a frown, "I guess it sounds kinda crazy, huh? To feel so close to someone who died so long before I was born?"

"No my dear Cheerianna, it's not crazy at all," said Pablo. "In fact, I once heard that, when someone dies before their time and their soul is gentle and beautiful, as was the case with your grandmother, it remains in limbo searching the whole world over for the right soul with whom to connect."

"Uh huh! So my grandfather believes in reincarnation, I see," said Anna Maria, displaying genuine surprise despite long since accustomed to Pablo's whimsical ideas.

"Surely you're not suggesting that I'm too old and cynical to believe in such things?" asked Pablo.

"You... cynical and old..." cried Anna Maria. "Never!"

"Well, you do have your grandmother's proud chin and understated elegance. In fact, there's much of her I see in you," Pablo told his granddaughter.

Anna Maria was well aware that the comparison to her grandmother was Pablo's loftiest form of praise.

"Do you still miss her, Grandfather?" asked Anna Maria.

"Miss her *and* still love her...every day," he said. "Every day I talk to her. And every day, like it or not, I'm one step closer to her."

Pablo grew misty eyed and turned toward the window. When he was confident that his voice wouldn't quiver, nor would he shed a tear, he turned and faced Anna Maria. "It still seems only like yesterday," he said. "I can remember the morning in every detail—what we did—the words we spoke. As always, I was sitting at the table having my coffee and reading the newspaper. Your grandmother stood behind me with her head on my shoulder. She would remain there until I finally put down the newspaper and paid attention to her. It was kind of a game, you see—a silly contest to see if she could keep her head on my shoulder longer than I could ignore her."

"I'll bet you caved first," teased Anna Maria.

"And you would be right," Pablo happily admitted. "I was always the first to cave, and that morning was no different. I threw down my newspaper in defeat, and your grandmother smiled victoriously. Except for her swollen belly, she looked just as she did the day we were married, if not more beautiful.

"That day, your grandmother was planning to visit her mother, who had been sick with a dreadful summer cold. I didn't think it was a good idea for her to walk such a distance, especially in her condition. But your grandmother loved to walk. We'd go out walking together every night. She loved to walk in town just as the lamplighters were coming

73

around, and she especially loved strolling down by the river."

"Lamplighters?" said Anna Maria.

"Why sure," said Pablo. "The world didn't always have electricity, you know." He continued, but not until after a thoughtful pause and sigh to better compose himself. "Anyway, she made it only half of the way to see her mother that morning when she collapsed in the street. I had no recollection of who told me, or how I arrived at the hospital. The next thing I knew, they were handing me your mother. I never even had the chance to say goodbye."

"End of the line! Arriving at destination Saint Louis, Missouri!" barked the conductor. "Arriving at destination Saint Louis Missouri!"

As the train chugged into the station, Maxwell and Jackson leapt to their feet, giddy to be back in Saint Louis, where their beloved Cardinals played baseball. Unfortunately, during their celebration, the younger Jackson brushed up against the back brim of the snooty woman's absurd hat, knocking the front brim over her eyes and onto the bridge of her nose.

Seeing this, Anna Maria let out a giggle that was alertly thwarted by a squeeze from Pablo's hand. Maxwell and Jackson held their collective breaths. Then, with an exaggerated display, the snooty woman repositioned her absurd hat, glared disapprovingly at Anna Maria, Maxwell, and Jackson, then went storming from the train. When she was no longer in plain sight, Anna Maria and the two brothers erupted into a chorus of laughter. Pablo, who never made a habit of laughing at the expense of others, could no longer help himself and joined in the fun.

"It was nice riding with you boys," he said.

"Yeah, same here," said Maxwell. Then he added rather awkwardly while looking in Anna Maria's direction, "Well...see ya around." Anna Maria smiled demurely at Maxwell, whose arm was being tugged on by his overly excited brother.

Pablo and Anna Maria would have a two hour layover before the train was to leave Saint Louis, Missouri for Louisville, Kentucky and Crow's Farm. They went walking, but were careful not to stray too far from the station.

"Come, my sweet Cheerianna, let's do a little sightseeing," said Pablo. The agreeable granddaughter held onto her grandfather's arm and together they strolled along and talked just as if it had been a typical Sunday in Brownsville. As was the case on those many Sundays, Anna Maria drew several stares from passersby, who found her Mayan features and cinnamon hair a striking combination.

"Did you know *your* grandmother?" wondered Anna Maria.

"I didn't know her when I was growing up," replied Pablo. "After my grandfather was killed in The Battle of Palmito Ranch, my grandmother took my father and Uncle Cesar and settled in New Orleans. My father didn't care much for New Orleans…or so the story goes. He left home as a young man and never returned. It wasn't until much later that I discovered I had a grandmother. I met her, but only briefly. Her name was Corina, but the people of New Orleans knew her as, *"The Saint."*

"The Saint?" said Anna Maria.

"Yes my sweet Cheerianna," said Pablo. "You see, from what I was told, she ran a boarding house…or school, you might say, for orphaned, abandoned, and wayward girls. She gave them shelter, fed them, clothed them, and taught then the importance of generosity. She also taught them that the good Lord gave us two hands—one for the giving—the other for the taking. 'Always be a friend to mankind' was her motto."

"It sounds like she was an interesting person," said Anna Maria.

"At the very least she was…*interesting*," said Pablo. His tone was subtly caustic. Anna Maria was either adrift and didn't catch her grandfather's subtle intonation, or *had* caught it and elected to let the remark go unchallenged. Pablo believed that it was the latter, as his astute, young traveling companion wasn't in the habit of missing things.

****

A steady stream of people shuffled in and out the newly opened Ernie's Café on Peters Street. At an adjacent street corner seated at an unbalanced table covered by a threadbare tablecloth was a Gypsy fortuneteller from Romania. "Carpathian Catharsis" is what her crudely fashioned sign read—the calligraphy on her sign was almost as unbalanced as the table on which it sat. The outlandish service appeared in demand, as there sat a young woman mesmerized by the Romanian. Two others were seated nearby and waiting their turn. After all, this was no ordinary fortune telling, but genuine Carpathian Catharsis—whatever that meant—and the Gypsy's clientele expected a much deeper and comprehensive look into their pasts and futures, and spiritual liberation as a result. Most often, those wandering away from the Gypsy's table did so feeling as though they got a bit of their money's worth.

Alexandra was her name, though her accent caused her to gloss over the "x" and so she pronounced her name "Alee-sandra." She wore magnificent robes which were brought from overseas. When performing her Carpathian Catharsis, she spoke in the third person. "Alee-sandra must now meditate…Alee-sandra will now call upon the spirits as only she can…"

75

For someone born and raised on the wheat belt, and then later spent their early adulthood in Brownsville, where the most exciting attractions were the river, ferry, and hard candy from Abercrombie's Drugstore, New Orleans, Louisiana was a heavy dose of culture shock. Cradling his infant daughter, the wide-eyed Pablo Cordero looked at streets that were lined with legitimate theaters, vaudeville theaters, music publishing houses, and night clubs. Live music came pouring in on him from everywhere…and it was still daytime! With everything that he had thus far seen since arriving in the *eclectic* city, though, Alexandra, the Gypsy fortune teller from Romania, as they say, took the cake.

Shortly after Martina was born, Pablo decided to take the chance that it wasn't just Dolci's delirium that spoke of a grandmother named Corina and an uncle named Cesar, who years ago settled in New Orleans—that these people truly existed and could help look after his infant daughter…*their* kin. Briefly, but only briefly, Pablo entertained the idea of leaving his infant daughter in the care of Jorge and Martina Lopez; but Jorge labored long and hard, and these days, Martina was frequently ill. Besides, the Lopezes were poor, getting along in years, and still had two boys to look after. They did, however, make a genuine offer to look after the infant Martina while Pablo applied his industry, but Pablo didn't have the heart to burden those already so well burdened. He believed this to be a wise decision, but the journey to Louisiana proved more difficult than expected, and New Orleans was more eclectic than he imagined. Like many decisions, this one was second-guessed, as there was plenty of hours and miles which to do so.

On his way to New Orleans, a broken hearted Pablo had thought, *if only Lefty Carson had stayed in Brownsville.* Lefty's wife Linda had taken quite a shine to Pablo. Linda Carson loved children and perhaps wouldn't have minded looking after one more, but thanks to Lefty's Uncle Lou and his cement company, the Carsons resided in Saint Louis. Moreover, Pablo didn't want to move to Madisonville and impose on Betsy Hutchinson, or Alice Crandall, neither of which were spring chickens. So, along with his brown, suede satchel and the infant Martina, Pablo Cordero came to New Orleans in search of the only family he had—if indeed they existed.

Occasionally, Alexandra would look away from the young girl whose fortune she was attempting to tell, and glanced in Pablo's direction. He was honing in on what the Romanian Gypsy had to say about the girl's past and future. It was clear to Pablo, when Alexandra looked his way, lacking was any friendliness and welcome. Martina, who was resting peacefully in his arms, made not a sound. This left Pablo to assume that he was standing too close to the fortuneteller's table and perhaps was running interference with the spirit world. It also occurred to him that the cause for the unwelcomed glances were the oddity of a man never seen before in New Orleans holding an infant in public without the presence of a woman by his side. Whatever the reason, Pablo stepped back to what he deemed a suitable distance. Despite his new position, he could still hear the outlandishly clad Romanian state, "It was the influenza that killed your grandmother from Pennsylvania, not her weak heart." At once the young girl's eyes flared. Then she praised the Gypsy for her remarkable insight.

Despite the distance from which Pablo now observed the unusual craft, Alexandra still appeared preoccupied with his presence. This time, when diverting her attention away from the young girl and onto Pablo, she narrowed her eyes into a glare that could only be perceived as threatening.

Pablo had no idea why, but he sensed that he was a great distraction to the Romanian. Surely he had given the spirits plenty of room to maneuver…or so he thought? Nevertheless, he further distanced himself from the street corner. Moving off to the side, he positioned himself to Alexandra's back. Still, the Gypsy seemed preoccupied. Soon she grew agitated. When seeing this, Pablo turned to leave. He figured whatever curiosity he might have had regarding Carpathian Catharsis was not destined to be fulfilled. As he turned to leave, Alexandra slammed her palms down on the unbalanced table, rose to her feet, and shouted in her native tongue, "Trebuie s-a dus, pentu ca nu este nimic nu poate face pentu!"

Pablo froze when he heard the foreign words. Despite having his back turned to Alexandra, he knew at once that the angry, unfamiliar words were directed toward him. He turned toward the Gypsy just as she was dismissing the young girl along with the two others who had been waiting.

"I'm sorry, but you'll have to come back another time," was Alexandra's terse dismissal. The three girls looked at one another and shrugged. Between them there wasn't a shred of comprehension. It finally occurred to the agitated Gypsy that she was still speaking in her native Romanian. She repeated herself in English and the girls walked away muttering their disappointment.

Already having shouted her unfriendly words in her native Romanian, this time Alexandra shouted to Pablo in English, "I already told you, there is nothing I can do for you!"

"I wasn't looking for help," Pablo calmly replied. "I was just fascinated how you knew about the girl's grandmother." When noticing the perplexing look that came over the Gypsy, Pablo added, "Remember? Pennsylvania? The influenza?

"Oh, that. She told me about it, herself," the fortuneteller admitted.

"She was a prop?" Pablo asked, sounding disillusioned.

"No, not a prop," said Alexandra. "But you would be amazed at all that comes from the mouths of chatty young women that they themselves don't realize."

"So you're a fraud?" asked Pablo. Though, no sooner the words flew from his lips, he regretted the accusation. Besides, what did it matter to him that a fortuneteller from Romania trying to scratch out a living in New Orleans was a fraud?

"Think what you like," said the Gypsy. She gave a dismissive wave of her hand and Pablo turned to leave. He hadn't gone but a few paces, though, when Alexandra added, "It's a show, you understand. A novelty. But I'm no fraud!"

"Really?" said Pablo, with more haughtiness than was intended.

"Don't pretend to know me!" snapped Alexandra. "Don't you dare pretend to know me!" Then she began flailing her arms as though Pablo was an evil spirit that she was attempting to ward off. Pablo cradled Martina high against his chest—a purposeful display to demonstrate for the irrational loon he figured he was now dealing with, that a man journeying alone with his infant daughter was hardly a threat—not to her—not to anyone. The maneuver worked. After composing herself the Gypsy added, "Most come to Alee-sandra with only a passing interest; they wish only for their silly fortunes to be told. But there are those among us who give off energy—energy and signs that only the few who are able to hover between the world of men and the world of spirits can see." This the Romanian said with an unmistakable tone of warning, before further adding, "The weight of the world can be seen in their sad eyes—their stories are imprinted on their faces." As she spoke, she leaned closer to Pablo. "You are one such person, my friend. That much Alee-sandra can see."

Without success, Pablo tried to resist a cynical grin. Though, his grin lasted only until the Gypsy added gravely, "In your eyes, my friend, Alee-sandra can see you once killed a man."

The Gypsy's tone wasn't accusatory. She simply stated it as a matter of fact—a fact that caused Pablo's legs to sway as though any second they might give way under his own weight. Alexandra went scampering for a chair to set under him should they do so.

Pablo knew with certainty that the killing of Jed Wright wasn't information that he let slip out, or that the Gypsy somehow made a lucky guess. Sure, Alexandra was a novelty—even a carnival-like curiosity—a girl has to make a living. Though whatever Carpathian Catharsis *was* or *meant*, Pablo knew this Romanian Gypsy who called herself "*Alee-sandra*" had special insights.

"Here, drink this," she told Pablo, then handed him a cup. "Go on," she added, "it'll make you feel better."

Pablo didn't refuse, but at first looked hesitantly at the Romanian Gypsy's potion before raising the cup to his lips. A blend of sweet and tart nectars, it was, with an aromatic spice unfamiliar to Pablo. It may or may not have been laced with alcohol—he couldn't tell. It was sweet in his mouth, but burned in his throat—its taste could only be described as foreign. It made him smile, though, as it brought back the memory of Mick and the bonfire gang and his initiation to Big George's moonshine.

Pablo's smile vanished as fast as it came when he wondered whether Alexandra knew of the method in which Jed Wright was killed. Thus far she hadn't said and Pablo wasn't about to go asking, nor would he offer. Pablo searched the Romanian's eyes, but saw no evidence—no twinkle revealing that she had unearthed the secret. Martina let out a soft cry, as Pablo had unwittingly tightened his cradle and clenched his teeth, as he was envisioning his hand gripping the knife that was used to deftly flick across the throat of Jed Wright. Noticing Pablo shudder, Alexandra urged him to drink more of her curious concoction. Pablo did as the Gypsy urged, this time throwing back his head and taking a longer sip. The burn in his throat was sobering.

Afterward, Alexandra reached over and placed a gentle hand on the infant Martina. She smiled when stroking a tender cheek.

"A parting gift from one so well beloved?" she asked; though it was meant more as a factual statement, rather than a question.

"Or a curse," muttered Pablo.

"There are few…very few indeed…but there *are* those among us whose hearts are so pure and whose souls are so gentle that they were never meant for this world," said Alexandra. "Those of whom I speak are God's messengers. They are angels sent from heaven, and God allows them to live among us but only for so long. Then He must call them back."

It was a simple deduction to make, that an unfamiliar man wandering alone the streets of New Orleans cradling an infant was a widower. One wouldn't necessarily need to be steeped in the art of Carpathian Catharsis to arrive as such a conclusion. But it was the Romanian Gypsy's accurate assessment of Anna Maria's spirit and character that brought a tear to Pablo's eye.

"She was a beauty of the rarest kind, was she not?" asked Alexandra. "A delicate flower in a harsh world. When someone like that touches us, we are never again the same. But my friend, we never really lose them. They are always with us."

Pablo took the last swallow of the Gypsy's potion and firmly placed the cup on the table—a gesture to signal that he was all through and now ready to move on.

"Be careful, my friend," warned Alexandra. "This town is not for everyone."

"Oh?" said Pablo—his manner suggesting that the Gypsy elaborate.

"Those whom you seek may not wish to be found," warned Alexandra. "And those whom you may find, you may end up wishing that you hadn't."

"Do you always speak in such riddles?" Pablo wondered; though he wasn't nearly so annoyed as the question might have suggested. Alexandra smiled and said, "Sometimes I forget that I'm not working. A bad habit, I suppose." Then she grabbed Pablo's arm and said, "Come, my friend. Follow me."

Alexandra invited Pablo to her "dwelling" as she called it. Along the way, he told her where he was from and why he had journeyed to New Orleans.

"I have reason to believe that I have family living here in New Orleans." Then he asked, figuring Alexandra's profession had given her access to many people, and mainly women, "You wouldn't happen to know a woman named Corina Cordero, would you?"

"I know of only one woman in town with the name Corina, but she calls herself Corina LaSalle," said Alexandra.

"LaSalle?" said Pablo.

"Yes, after Rene`-Robert Cavelier, Sieur de LaSalle, the French explorer who discovered Louisiana," said Alexandra, attempting to impress Pablo with her sense of history and of the world.

"Oh, right, of course," said Pablo; though he never heard of the French explorer.

Not without an effort, Pablo succeeded in not acting the slightest bit taken aback when entering a dwelling that was every bit as eccentric as its sole inhabitant. Never had he seen such an eclectic menagerie of furniture, unusual objects, and assortment of outlandish fabrics. But what he found most peculiar was the darkness in which Alexandra lived. Her dwelling amounted only to a cubby with little exposure, and the only two existing windows were heavily dressed.

Additional fabric was also hung alongside the drapery. More was hung at the center, where the drapery met to form a slight separation. All this overlaying of fabric was to prevent any penetration of daylight. Once inside, Alexandra struck a matchstick, then scurried about to light her many candles. Once the area was amply illuminated, it was painfully clear that house cleaning was not a skill that the Gypsy fortuneteller from Romania had thus far acquired. From within the refuge of her tiny dwelling, Alexandra may have shunned daylight, but dust was apparently welcome.

Her lack of housekeeping skills notwithstanding, Alexandra was nothing less than warm and hospitable. She invited Pablo to "sink" into her couch. A worn, faded, and in some areas threadbare couch it was. When Pablo made contact with the relic, he smiled thinking Alexandra meant *sink* literally, as the couch all but swallowed him.

"So where might I find Corina LaSalle?" he asked.

"She's very important, you understand," said Alexandra. "She won't see you without an appointment."

"So how do I go about making an appointment?" asked Pablo.

"You must first go to ahh…a *place,*" said Alexandra. "Yes, that's right…a *place*. I believe it's called…let me think…S-Serendipity." Alexandra managed to squeeze out the one word name of the establishment where Corina LaSalle could be found. Her frazzled state hadn't escaped Pablo, though he couldn't imagine why all the hemming and hawing, or why the subject of Corina LaSalle caused such a noticeable shift in temperament.

"So where is this *place* called Serendipity?" asked Pablo.

"It's at the corner of Canal and Rampart Streets," said the Gypsy. "Inside you'll find a gentleman barkeeper. He will help you. But I must warn you, my friend. Beware of the bend in the river; because of it the streets are laid out at all sorts of odd angles. A stranger could get lost and wander about for hours…perhaps even longer. And you must also remember, my friend, that once you cross Canal Street the names of the streets change. For example, Bourbon Street becomes Carondelet Street. It's very complicated, you see."

Alexandra tried to be subtle in discouraging Pablo from his search, but failed on both counts.

"So tell me, my friend," the Gypsy asked with only a slight hint of hostility, "who is this Corina LaSalle to you, anyway?"

"I have reason to believe that she's my grandmother," replied Pablo.

"I see," said Alexandra.

Lapsing into her work voice the Gypsy continued on, while pretending that Pablo's suspicion about Corina LaSalle was news to her, and that it was unlikely that this woman who named herself after a French explorer was his grandmother. At this, too, Alexandra failed, as subtlety clearly wasn't her strong suit.

"You don't want me to find her, do you?" Pablo asked with a note of accusation. "Or is it that you don't believe that she's my grandmother? Which is it?"

All Alexandra could manage was an ineffectual nod.

Pablo lurched forward on a couch that didn't seem to want to let go of him. "You know her, don't you?"

"Yes, I do know her," Alexandra at last admitted. "Or, I should say, I *knew* her. Our paths crossed many years ago when I first came to New Orleans. But I haven't seen or spoken to her in some time...years, in fact."

"I should get going," said Pablo. But before he could manage to hoist himself up from the sunken in couch, Alexandra was quick to remind him of his long journey.

"You look tired, my friend," she said. "Perhaps you should rest up awhile before you run off."

Alexandra was right—Pablo was near exhaustion and the mere mention of weariness and rest caused his shoulders to slump and his eyes to droop. He wasn't sure if it was the length of his journey, Alexandra's curious potion, or the dimness of her dwelling, but all at once he began fading and spiraling, and at last was succumbing to the Gypsy's suggestion. He stared into the flickering flame of a candle and imagined the warmth of a bonfire, cozy nights surrounded with friends by the river, and Big George's moonshine—a time before Martina and his first ever glimpse of Anna Maria. He felt his feet being lifted from the floor and placed on the couch. His last cognitive sensation before drifting off, was feeling the weight of the tender Martina lifted from his chest. He wanted to object, but hadn't the strength.

Later when he woke, before he could emerge through his grogginess and focus his eyes, he hoped to discover himself seated at his kitchen table with newspaper in hand and with Anna Maria's head resting on his shoulder—how lovely it used to feel. He would toss aside the paper and with great joy celebrate her victorious smile. Instead, he found himself in a dimly lit room with the infant Martina resting on the lap of a Romanian Gypsy he had only known a few short hours. Despairing, he closed his eyes.

"A broken heart can bring about more exhaustion than any amount of labor, my friend," said Alexandra. Before Pablo could concur, she asked, "So who is Uncle Joe?" Pablo looked curiously at the Gypsy, for the question seemed to come from out of nowhere.

"You must forgive my curiosity, but when you were sleeping you called out to someone named Uncle Joe," said Alexandra. "It sounded as if you were asking him for guidance. At one time, he must have been a very important person in your life."

"He was…at one time," said Pablo; his manner indicated a time long past. Then he added as though no amount of discouragement would work, "I must get going."

"Very well," said Alexandra. "I suppose if you must go, it's best to do so before nightfall."

Gently running her fingertips over Martina's tender infant skin, she added, "Good luck, my friend. We'll be here…right where you left us. And remember, the names of the streets change once you cross Canal Street."

Pablo walked away feeling out of sorts and wondered if he hadn't lost his mind. Perhaps Alexandra put him under some Old World Carpathian spell while he was asleep. Not since Martina was born had she been out of his sight, and now he was leaving her with a stranger.

****

Miles Gordon came strolling into Serendipity at five o'clock sharp, just as he had every day since he began playing at the establishment. As was often the case at that time of day, there were only a few men seated in the lounge. Serendipity wasn't an establishment that catered to the after work roughneck or common laborer—a fact made certain by its exquisite ambience and high prices. It opened for business at three o'clock, but the kind of business that provided Serendipity with its considerable stream of revenue didn't begin until seven. When Miles Gordon arrived, he would sit at the piano and work on music of the likes which Serendipity's patrons hadn't much appreciation. Then at a few minutes before seven o'clock, he would allow his fingertips to skillfully transition from classical music to the more popular themes of the day. But from five to seven it was Miles Gordon's time—his favorite time of the day. It was also Sam Ott's favorite time of day. Sam would stand behind the bar polishing glasses and lining up the correct bottles for the evening's expected patrons. When doing so, he listened to Miles' remarkable command over eighty-eight keys.

Sam Ott was by no means a patron of the arts: Miles Gordon was the barkeeper's only window into the world of classical music; but what a window it was, and for two hours a day. If there was a piece that caught Sam's ear, and most had, he would ask the name and then would write it down in order to make a future request. Sam was always disappointed when learning that such profound music had unimaginative titles such as Sonata in B minor. "That doesn't describe anything," Sam would complain, but he had always said that Miles Gordon was wasting his talent playing in a brothel, albeit the classiest brothel in town, and that he was meant for much greater things. For a dark-skinned boy who grew up near the bayou, the sophisticated New York theaters and concert halls seemed a galaxy away. The world's loss was Sam Ott's gain.

Upstairs in her boudoir, Corina LaSalle was enjoying her customary late afternoon pampering. She sat slouched in her chair wearing a satin blindfold trimmed with lace, on which was embroidered the cursive letters, *C L*. Kneeling on the floor at Corina's feet was her eager to please "valet" as she liked to call her. Corina found the terms *page* or *slave girl* demeaning, lacking appeal, and not at all in accordance with what was perceived as an important station at Serendipity. The young girl (valet) was busying herself with an application of fresh polish to Corina's fingernails and toenails, when Corina sighed with delight, as the romantic and haunting melody of Chopin's opus 9 Nocturne #1 in b-minor had crept its way up the stairs, settled into her room, and filled her ears.

"I feel like an angel floating away on a cloud," she cooed.

At age sixty, Corina LaSalle was still attractive, and in the estimation of many, cut an impressive figure. She was no stranger to the luxuries her dubious profession afforded her, but it was the beautiful sounds that Miles Gordon produced on the ivory that transported her and helped her to forget the horrors of Palmito Ranch, the son who left home, and whose return she still awaited. It has been some twenty-five years now that Corina has waited to hear word of Juan-Carlos Cordero. Her repose was disturbed by heavy footsteps on the stairs. A moment later there came a rapping at her door.

"Ms. LaSalle?" called Sam Ott.

"Just shoot me, Cassandra," said Corina, as she playfully petted her valet on the head. "Do me a favor and please just shoot me now."

Cassandra let out a giggle when Sam Ott rapped once again on the door.

"You've got me, Sam. There's nowhere for me to run—nowhere to hide," Corina called out, clearly mocking whatever importance Serendipity's gentle barkeeper thought his unexpected visit might have had.

"Does that mean I can come in?" asked Sam Ott. His question produced another giggle from Corina's attentive valet.

"By all means, Sam, please do," was Corina's disingenuous reply.

Sam Ott was tall, well built, had a beautiful handle-bar mustache, and eyes that twinkled. But his best trait, as Corina LaSalle many times acknowledged, was that Sam Ott had no idea just how truly handsome he was. Aside from his abundant good looks, he was a true gentleman barkeeper.

"Ms. LaSalle, there's a young man downstairs to see you," said Sam.

"Really? A *young* man?" said Corina, overly stressing her surprise. "I can't remember the last time a *young* man came to call on me." The remark caused the kneeling Cassandra to let out another giggle.

"He says it's important, and that he'd like to speak with you in private if he could," said Sam.

"Speak to me? In private? A presumptuous young fellow, I see," said Corina. "Does this insolent man have a name?"

"He called himself Pablo…Pablo Cordero," said Sam.

Sam Ott was just about to add, *he seems like a nice enough chap,* when Corina straightened up. When she did so, her foot knocked the bottle of nail polish from Cassandra's hand, sending it clear across the room. Cassandra shrieked, then went scampering to retrieve the bottle before any of its contents had a chance to leak out and spoil Corina's Persian rug. Sam Ott took a step back. His eyes ceased from twinkling as he waited for his employer to regain her composure. Then he appeared to brace himself before he asked, "So what shall I tell him?"

"Tell him…he can wait if he wishes," said Corina. Glancing over at her clock, she added, "But don't send him up to me until six."

Sam Ott disappeared to carry out Corina LaSalle's wishes. When Sam had gone, she slumped in her chair. Cassandra, who was always eager to please, peeped, "Shall I finish polishing your nails?"

"Perhaps later," said Corina. Then with a subtle wave of her hand, she dismissed her valet.

****

Pablo inched his way closer to Miles Gordon. He wanted a closer view of the pianist's talented hands. The once migrant was curious as to how Miles went about executing such wonderful sounds and with such swift and seemingly effortless precision. Thus far, Pablo hadn't been exposed to the world of performing arts. In fact, before arriving in New Orleans, the only musical exposure he had came by way of the vocal variety, which, sadly, was the singing of "When You Were Sweet Sixteen," among other popular songs, by Frankie "The Prick" Donato and Fat Fuck McGinn. Pablo smiled remembering when Lucky Kaminski said of the crooning duo, *"a pack of hyenas coulda howled it better."* Then he shed a tear for poor old Lucky. Sam Ott came by and whispered Corina's instructions in Pablo's ear, but by then, he had all but forgotten his purpose for venturing through the streets of the eclectic city. He was in reverie—his soul wide open and allowing the strains of Chopin to find their way in.

****

For more than ten-thousand nights, Corina Cordero, or LaSalle, as she called herself, went to bed with the gunfire of Palmito Ranch ringing in her ears. Night after night, like an artist, she lay with men, pleasuring them in the way she had her husband, Juan. This, she did with the hope of seeing a glimmer in an eye, or to hear an endearing word from a mouth— a sign that somehow through the bodies of other men, the spirit of Juan Cordero had manifested. But at the end of the night there was only Corina, alone and once again to sense the terror that she felt when Nina and she huddled together with their young children and prayed that the gunfire wouldn't find its way to the bodies of Juan and Manuel Cordero.

The Corina Cordero who once fled Mexico with her husband, while cradling the infant Juan Carlos, in order to escape the atrocity of civil war, could never have imagined herself the owner of such a place as Serendipity. However, when one is forced to reinvent oneself, one can never be certain of the result. Corina LaSalle: businesswoman, establishment owner…prostitute? She sat alone in her room staring at the hands of a clock—all at once anxious, thrilled, and terrified of the young man who waited below, and who any minute would come knocking at her door. It was 5:59 when Sam Ott pried Pablo from the rapture of Miles Gordon's musical spell. Corina's heart sank when the expected knock came at precisely six o'clock.

"Come in," she called weakly.

When the door was pushed open, there stood Sam Ott, his moustache turned up, his eyes twinkling as always. Corina let out a sigh thinking that the young man who shared her namesake grew tired of waiting—the indignation of being told to wait around until six o'clock got the better of him. She felt an odd mixture of relief and disappointment. She was curious about this person who called himself Pablo Cordero, but wary of why he sought her out. What did he want to know? What news might he bring? A moment later, Pablo emerged. Stepping around the much taller and broader shouldered Sam Ott, he entered the room.

Pablo tried to channel all his attention in Corina's direction, but his eyes went roving all around a room than was filled with more extravagance and finery than one could hope to see in a lifetime. Corina herself was attired such that she was in concert with the room's luxurious ensemble. And unlike Alexandra, who while within the refuge her dwelling shunned the daylight, Corina kept her drapery pulled back, allowing the early evening's setting sun to flood the room with warmth and light that accentuated the lines of her still handsome face.

"Please have a seat," was her cordial invitation to Pablo.

"I came all the way from Brownsville, Texas hoping to meet you…hoping that you actually existed," said Pablo. When he took his seat, he tried to continue in his fascination and interest regarding Corina's luxurious surroundings. Instead, and what he hoped was with subtlety, he began to size her up and to formulate certain notions, before arriving at one in particular.

"I don't know who you think I am," said Corina. "but I find it most curious that someone would travel such a distance based on an uncertainty, then sit before me with such judging eyes."

Pablo aborted his *subtle* critique of the prostitute. His eyes traveled to the floor where, while being chastised, he began to decipher the pattern in Corina's Persian carpet.

"Now you look here, my curious young friend," she continued firmly, "Serendipity is no different than any other business. We provide a service—we expect a return—and we're more a friend to mankind than most. Of that you can be sure."

Pablo wasn't aware of the obvious manner in which he examined the once active prostitute, now current and defensive owner of Serendipity. After receiving an earful, he lifted his eyes from the carpet until they met Corina's. He was about to beg her forgiveness and explain that it made no difference to him how she, who calls herself *Corina LaSalle* made a living, but he had a clear sense that Corina wasn't interested in his approval and thus elected to remain quiet.

"But it's quite alright, my friend," Corina continued. "You're not the first man ever to look at me disapprovingly."

Corina stood and sauntered over to the window. Turning from Pablo, she leaned on the sill, inviting the warmth of the sun's rays to permeate through the pane and drench her aging face.

"My younger son, Cesar," she went on. "As a boy he would lose himself in books, studies, and childhood friends—not for a second did he consider how I was providing for him. All he knew was that his mama loved him and that she was giving him a good life. Nothing else mattered. But my older son, Juan Carlos? Ahh…now he was different. He never said a word—never once confronted me, but he knew. I could always see it in his eyes that he knew. Then one day he up and left. Oh, he had his excuses, for wanting to leave, but I knew better." With a sigh, she added, though more to herself, "That was twenty-five long years ago."

After sighing, her shoulders slumped as if she suddenly had to bear the weight of all those years, and on her face there formed the sort of expression that often occurs when all hope has gone. Then she looked over her shoulder and down her nose at Pablo, who remained seated— his posture, rigid. Reasserting herself, she said, "The eyes don't lie, my friend. They never do. And a mama knows her son."

Corina turned and took a step toward Pablo, with the hope of seeing a vestige of her first born.

"You know my Juan Carlos?" she asked. Her voice was ringing with hope, and for the first time she abandoned her aristocratic tone in favor of her long suppressed Mexican accent.

"I never got the chance to know him," said Pablo. "He was…*gone* before I came along."

Pablo tried to be delicate by using the broader term "gone" with the hope that Corina, who was starting to swell with emotion, would interpret *gone* simply as *went away*. She wasn't fooled by Pablo's attempt at delicacy.

"In what year were you born?" she demanded to know.

"1879," replied Pablo.

"No!" shouted Corina. "It is not possible! It's just not possible! He would have only been twenty-one years old! My Juan Carlos was much too strong to have died so young!"

Corina turned away from Pablo and again she faced the window. "You are mistaken, my friend," she cried. "Yes, you must be mistaken. There are so many Corderos. There must be hundreds, in fact, even thousands who through the years traveled from America to Mexico, and

Mexico to America, and all because of these GODFORSAKEN WARS! What makes you so certain that we are talking about the same person?"

Pablo rose up from his chair and made his way over to Corina, who had burst into tears and was pounding her fists on the windowsill. He placed a gentle hand on her shoulder. Not that he expected the gesture to be much comfort, though he knew not what else to do.

"How did you know where to find me?" she cried.

Pablo began recounting Dolci's waning hours—the fever induced ramblings in which he decided to have faith.

"Even if it were so, that I am your grandmother, as you can plainly see, I'm terribly unsuitable," admitted Corina. Reaching back, she took Pablo's hand. "I know that you have come a long way, but I would like to be alone for now if you don't mind."

As Pablo released his grip on Corina's shoulder, she said, "I'm sorry about your mother. I'm sure it must have been difficult."

"Yeah, I'm sorry, too," said Pablo.

Pablo stepped away from Corina and made for the door. He began to regret his journey to New Orleans, for thus far it only served to crush what little hope remained for an aging prostitute. He opened the door; then before leaving, he turned toward Corina and said, "You have a great-granddaughter. Her name is Martina and she is beautiful."

"I'm sure she is," said Corina as she stared at the window and the reflection of her tears.

"I really am sorry," said Pablo. "I'm no stranger to loss. God took my beloved Anna Maria the very day our daughter was born."

"We Corderos surely are a cursed lot, are we not?" said Corina.

"Maybe so," said Pablo.

It was just a few minutes before seven. The once quiet lounge of Serendipity had become quite a gathering. Miles Gordon was now beginning his skillful transition from the music that gave him great joy and satisfaction to the more popular themes of the day—the kind of songs that Frankie "The Prick" Donato and Fat Fuck McGinn would sing by the bonfire. Pablo slipped through the lounge and exited Serendipity unnoticed. From the street he glanced up at Corina's window, but she was no longer there. Like the setting sun, she disappeared and would remain hidden away all night in her room.

It was Pablo's hope that Corina, a woman in the twilight of her years, if not overjoyed, would have been receptive to learn that she had a grandson and great-granddaughter—lineage from her ill-fated son, and that he would fit in with what remained of his long lost family.

It was not to be, though, and as he went along, the noisy streets of New Orleans seemed to be telling him just that.

His heart ached for the quiet strolls Anna Maria and he used to take in the early evenings.

Through the town of Brownsville they would go, and they remembered to stop at Abercrombie's Drugstore for hard candy, before ending up at the river. If they started out early enough, they would ride the ferry to Matamoros. If not, they were satisfied with the river from the Brownsville side. On the way home they would watch the lamplighters.

The sound and flavor of New Orleans was more than a small town man with a broken heart could bear. So, too, was the dimly lit dwelling of the Romanian Gypsy fortune teller. Pablo wished that he could be gone without again having to experience Alexandra's morbid little cloister.

"You see, my friend" said Alexandra. "We're right here where you left us."

Pablo guessed that *"my friend"* was a catch-phrase that stuck with Alexandra and one which she learned from Corina, as he had been called such all day by both women.

"Did you work for her?" wondered Pablo.

Alexandra lowered her eyes. "You must understand, it's not something I'm proud of," she said. "I was young and she was so beautiful and seemed so sophisticated. I looked up to her. I—I did whatever she asked of me."

"Forgive me, it wasn't my place to ask," said Pablo. "And believe me, I'm not judging you. I was just curious, that's all." Then he reached down and took hold of Martina.

"I suppose it would be useless for me to extend my hospitality, for Alee-sandra knows it is your wish to leave," said the Gypsy. "But remember, my friend, wherever you go in this world, you have an angel on your shoulder. Your Anna Maria is always with you."

Pablo was grateful that Alexandra didn't make a fuss and insist that he spend the night. Despite not caring much for New Orleans, a hotel room with a view seemed more welcoming than Alexandra's dark, dusty dwelling.

The following morning at the station, a man unknown to Pablo accosted him. The unknown man smiled and handed Pablo an envelope.

"For you," he said.

Pablo, rather guardedly, reached for the envelope.

"Go on," the man urged. "Look inside; it won't explode."

Pablo almost let Martina slip through his arms when he saw the amount of cash that the envelope contained.

"B-but I don't understand," he stammered.

"She may not be the ideal grandmother," the man said, "but she *can* be very generous."

Folded up alongside the cash was a note that read:

Dear Senor Cordero,

There are holes so deep and so terribly empty that they cannot possibly be filled. I will pray that you have better luck than I.

Most sincerely,
Corina Cordero

"Come nephew," said the man. "Before you return to Texas, allow me buy you lunch at my favorite café. And while we are there, I will tell you the history of our family. You should find it most interesting. By the way, I am your Uncle Cesar."

PART TWO:
MARTINA

Chapter Five
Beautiful Hands

Upon returning to Brownsville, Pablo was greeted with good news from both Mick and Smokey Bones. After New Orleans—a trip that was profitable, informative, revealing, emotional, but ultimately empty, good news from friends was certainly welcome.

Despite departing the city with a nice sum of cash in his brown, suede satchel, Pablo hoped to establish a relationship with Corina. Although Uncle Cesar was nice enough to buy lunch and had taken the time to get Pablo up to speed on the family history, beyond that, he showed little interest in the way of a long lost nephew traveling with his infant daughter. Pablo departed New Orleans feeling un-tethered to those who were his kin.

"You'll never believe it," Smokey Bones said to Pablo, "but our good ol' friend Lefty Carson just had himself a lucky number four! But this time, he and Linda finally got the baby girl they always wanted. Boy I'll tell ya, that ol' Lefty sure has got himself one perdeegous nut."

"Prodigious, too," said Pablo, winking at Mick.

"You betcha," said Smokey Bones.

Pablo was thrilled for the Carsons. He cared for Lefty and Linda and never forgot their generosity. Everyone from the old bonfire crowd was happy whenever news or well wishes came floating in from Saint Louis. But Pablo was especially thrilled with the news that Mick had to tell.

Realizing that Pablo couldn't drag the infant Martina to and from a construction site each day, Mick put in a good word for his friend at Trudeau's Farm. Mick explained to Edgar Trudeau that he had a friend in need, and that this friend had a daughter that "might need a little looking after." What Mick omitted was the fact that the said friend's daughter wasn't yet an able bodied child prepared to pull his or her weight, but an infant.

"Gee, I guess the joke's on me," said Edgar Trudeau, as Pablo with babe in arms stood before the frowning man.

Edgar Trudeau and Mick were raised together from the time that they were three-years-old. Their fathers were best friends and fought together in General Lee's army. They grew up a couple of farm boys who didn't care for the cause one way or the other, but were pressed into duty.

Mick's father came home alive but wounded. His wounds were more than he could bear, and soon after Mick was born, his mind started going. Then one day without a word to anyone, he upped and disappeared. They found him, but not until days later, miles from home and with a hole in his head made from a bullet.

"It was a hunting accident," Edgar's father declared, and no one dared to dispute it. Afterward, the Trudeaus took in Mick and his mother, but the poor woman grew more despondent by the day and didn't live long enough to see Mick become a man.

"It pays to have friends in high places," Mick told Pablo. "Edgar's good people—he'll be fair with you."

Mick playfully patted Pablo on the back and added, "Now remember, keep a sharp eye on Big George and see if you can find out what his secret ingredient is."

"You took the trouble of getting me a job so that you could turn me into a spy?" said Pablo.

"Hell no; we don't wanna cut into Big George's business; it's not like that at all," Mick assured his friend. "For years we all been dying to know what the hell he puts in the stuff to give it its kick and makes it taste so good...you included."

"It'd be a real son-of-a-bitch if Big George's brew turned out to be the Fountain of Youth and that we're all gonna live forever," said Smokey Bones.

****

Pablo looked over Edgar Trudeau's shoulder. Off into the distance he saw a man splitting logs. The man was as dark as night and as big as a mountain and Pablo knew at once that it must be Big George. Meanwhile, Edgar Trudeau kept glancing down at Martina as if to say, *"This is certainly an interesting situation—Lord knows how it's going to work out."*

"We don't do any sharecropping or tenant farming around here. I only use hired hands," Edgar told Pablo. "But you're welcome to the bunkhouse next to Big George's and Miss Lillie's place. It's yours to do whatever you want."

Pablo didn't remember Mick saying anything about a Miss Lillie. *Probably thought it wasn't important enough to mention,* he concluded to himself. He continued looking on with fascination as Big George split logs with the greatest of ease.

The bunkhouse was a far cry from his home in Brownsville. Whatever the accommodations, he hadn't expected them to be otherwise. Besides, after having been born on, and for years survived the harshness and rigors of life on the wheat belt, he shouldn't feel too badly about Martina having to survive life on one farm, where her father was always within close proximity. Indeed, thanks to Mick, Pablo landed where he could work, rest, and look after Martina until she was old enough to go off to school. By then, to some extent, she would be able to look after herself, enabling him to return to his life in the town and place where he and Anna Maria shared many lovely days and splendid nights.

"Mick tells me that you've done some wheat farming in the past," said Edgar.

"Yes sir, I've surely done my share of wheat farming," said Pablo, although, the infant resting in his arms caused Edgar Trudeau to maintain a skeptical expression.

"Harvesting sorghum is a little different, but I imagine you'll get the hang of it quick enough," said Edgar. "Jim, Tex, and Big George will teach you the ropes. And believe me, you couldn't find three better fellows with whom to work."

Still in the throes of fascination with Big George's effortless log splitting, Pablo never saw Edgar's wife, Leila, nor their four-year-old daughter, Laura, approaching. It wasn't until Edgar announced their presence that Pablo took his eyes away from the massive log splitter.

"Is that a real baby?" asked Laura.

"Oh, yes, she is quite real," Pablo informed the four-year-old.

"How old is she?" asked Laura, getting up on her toes to peek in at Martina's infant face.

"Right now she is still zero," said Pablo.

"Zero? She can't be zero! She has to be something!" cried Laura.

Pablo looked down and smiled at Laura. "She'll be one before you know it," he told her.

"Well, when she turns one," said Laura, "I'll play Happy Birthday for her on the piano."

Laura signaled for Pablo to bend down so that she could whisper in his ear. "I like watching Big George splitting logs, too," was her cryptic message. Then she winked at Pablo before she and Leila turned to walk back to the house. Before they went inside, Laura stopped and called, "Hey mister, what's your baby's name?"

"Martina," Pablo called back.

"That's a pretty name," replied Laura. Then she sang, "Happy birthday Martin…happy birthday to you." Then she and Leila disappeared inside.

When Pablo returned his attention to Edgar, he noticed that Leila and Laura weren't the only ones to disappear; so, too, had Big George. A moment later, though, not too far off from where Big George was splitting logs, Pablo saw a door being pushed open by an arm that seemed too thin and weak to perform such a task. Soon a figure that Pablo established to be that of an old woman, and therefore assumed was the aforementioned Miss Lillie, carefully stepped outside. She put a hand to her eyes to shield the bright midday sun and squinted in the general direction of Pablo and Edgar Trudeau. She was a scrawny and knurly old woman, and her age and diminutive stature made her look darker then Big George, though she was not. As she walked, her old bones uncoiled one at a time before her gait smoothened. To Pablo's surprise, for it was only a moment that he glanced back at the door through which Laura and Leila had disappeared, Miss Lillie was already within the vicinity of Martina's cooing.

"Well now, what have we got here?" she asked, alluding of course to Martina. Directing her words at Edgar Trudeau, she added cheerily, "Been a while since ol' Miss Lillie, here, had a young'un to look after." Winking at Pablo, she further added, "Everyone that's ever come through this ol' farm has had their turn on Miss Lillie's lap." The scrawny old woman then clasped her hands together as though relishing the idea of yet another child pressed to her bosom.

"Indeed they have," said Edgar Trudeau. He tipped his hat to Miss Lillie to indicate that he had been the first of many. "And Mick and me still remember every word to all those songs you use to sing to us."

Before Pablo could realize it, the stealthy Miss Lillie had stolen up to him, and with a deft maneuver, she lightened him of his tender load. Cradling Martina, she said, "Well, ain't you just the lil' love bug. No, Mr. Trudeau, this lil' missy, here…she won't be no trouble at all." After a playful nuzzle she added, "You's just a lil' angel sent here to keep ol' Miss Lillie good and young, you is. Yes sir, Mr. Trudeau, I believe we's gonna get along just fine. Just fine indeed."

Edgar could never get used to the idea Miss Lillie calling him *Mr. Trudeau.* Until his father's death, he had always been *Edgar.* But Miss Lillie was a firm believer in decorum. "A man of your station needs to be addressed in a certain manner," she often told Edgar, who had since given up arguing the point.

Pablo looked on as Miss Lillie gazed adoringly down at Martina, who lay peacefully in the old woman's coal black and bony hands. He then looked skyward, for he thought he heard the voice of Josiah Walton saying, "*No one said the hands of God would be beautiful.*"

"But they *are* perfect," Pablo unconsciously blurted aloud. The odd remark produced curious glances from Miss Lillie and Edgar Trudeau.

"Come child," said Miss Lillie, walking off with Martina in arms, "the day's a gettin' on, it is; but there's still plenty to celebrate." Then she began singing, "*Joshua fit the battle of Jericho, Jericho, Jericho. Joshua fit the battle of Jericho, and the walls came a tumblin' down . . .*"

The song was no more familiar to Pablo than a Chopin Nocturne. He found its rhythm strangely fascinating, though, and Miss Lillie's voice pleasing. Then he chuckled to himself when imagining the mess that Frankie "The Prick" Donato and Fat Fuck McGinn would have made of the unfamiliar tune.

"I'd say your Martina is in good hands...wouldn't you?" asked Edgar Trudeau.

Edgar's question was sobering and momentarily caused Pablo to stiffen and to feel enshrouded with desolation. He watched the chirpy Miss Lillie waltz away. Nestled in her arms was what Anna Maria had carried in her womb, but never got the chance to hold. But there was no disagreeing with Edgar Trudeau; Martina was in good hands.

"You might as well go and rest up for tomorrow," said Edgar.

Pablo agreed and went and did as suggested. He sat on the edge of what would serve as his bed—a bed that lacked both the size and comfort of the one that he and Anna Maria had so joyously shared. Though, for him it made no difference—the cot was only a place on which to lay and rest between long laborious days—to remember the past and to ponder the future, but never to explore a woman. He reached into his brown, suede satchel for his possessions. He carefully laid them out on the cot. First was the Colt revolver, then the knife. Next came the Bible, which lately hadn't received much attention. Last was Anna Maria's hairbrush— the only article that he bothered to salvage from his life and home in Brownsville. He examined each article, remembering how he came by them, but mostly what they represented: A rape, a killing, God, and love, all carefully placed side by side on a cot. Thus far the pendulum of fortune and misfortune had swung dramatically in the life of Pablo Cordero.

Pablo figured it was just as well that things hadn't worked out in New Orleans. He was much better suited for life on a quiet farm surrounded with good folks, rather than the eccentricities of a big city. Despite the well mannered Sam Ott and the virtuosity of Miles Gordon, Serendipity wasn't his kind of scene. He took his odd array of items from the cot and returned them to his satchel, then laid back his weary head. Before a single thought of his home in Brownsville and Anna Maria could creep their way into his head to stir him up, he was fast asleep. Later that evening, Miss Lillie came wandering into the bunk house with Martina cradled in one arm and a lantern in her free hand. She set the lantern down beside Pablo and watched its light flicker across his peaceful face. No longer did the carnivorous and murderous nightmares find their way into his sleep.

"That's your daddy, there, lil' missy; sleepin' peacefully, he is," whispered Miss Lillie to the infant. Then she took the back of Martina's tiny hand and caressed it against Pablo's cheek.

"May God bless you," said Miss Lillie to the sleeping Pablo Cordero. "And believe me, you's gonna need all the blessins he can send ya. Lord knows, ol' Miss Lillie, here, she done walked a thousand miles in your shoes. But they say the good Lord...why, he don't give nobody nothin' they can't handle. So you just rest for now." Then she took her boney, coal black fingers and gently ran them through Pablo's hair. "Okay lil' missy," she said. "It's best now we said goodnight to your daddy."

****

When morning came and Pablo opened his eyes, his first thought was that he might have woken up in Heaven. Whether the morning of a Christmas spent in Madisonville, Texas, or as fine a spring morning as was ever woken up to on the seemingly endless wheat belt, never had a morning smelled so delicious, and with great satisfaction he tried to inhale every bit of it; though before he could exhale, he rose with a start, for missing against his chest was the warmth of an infant to which he had grown so accustomed. In wasn't but a moment that passed, though, before he regained his senses and remembered his whereabouts. When he peeked outside, he discovered that Big George's talents didn't end with log splitting. The big man was busily going about the task of grilling eggs, cornbread, and juicy slices of beef and ham. The early morning sunshine and the sound of a sizzling grill helped Pablo to put any lingering thoughts of the dark little worlds of Corina Cordero and Alexandra the Romanian Gypsy behind. The aroma coming from Big George's grill was a sign that, if nothing else, the day would have a glorious beginning.

"This is some surprise," said Pablo, as he approached Big George, whose size was much more imposing up close and under the early morning sun.

"Git use to it," said Big George, with a broad grin. "This is how we start off every day."

"Maybe this is Heaven after all," Pablo thought aloud. The remark was intended for himself, but it was loud enough for Big George to hear. Big George laughed in his usual manner, which was suppressing a belly laugh, which in turn caused his massive shoulders to shake with vigor. Whenever Big George smiled, everyone smiled. Whenever he laughed, everyone laughed right along with him.

"I take it you're Big George?" asked Pablo.

"That's just who I be," replied Big George, again with a broad grin. Then in a guarded manner he added, "And I take it you's that fellow Mick sent here to try and steal my moonshine recipe." Seeing how easily Pablo was unnerved by the accusatory remark, Big George again let loose with his customary laugh—his massive shoulders shaking more dramatically than before.

"He a good fella, Mick is," said Big George. "A body can do a lot worse for a friend—that's the gods honest truth."

"I was reared on your moonshine," said Pablo. "I can still remember my first sip. Strange, but I feel like I know you."

Pablo was just about to assure Big George that his recipe was perfectly safe, when Miss Lillie with Martina in arms, Jim Ambrose, and Tex Billingsly all converged at the table.

"Hey there, fella," said Tex Billingsly to Pablo. Offering his hand, he added, "Jim and me just come from yonder." Tex pointed to the right of the bunkhouse.

"Yep, just a lick to the west," said Jim Ambrose.

"By a lick, he means 'bout a mile or so," Miss Lillie chimed in.

"And we could smell the cornbread the whole way over here," sighed Tex Billingsly, his dreamy eyes all a flutter.

After everyone got acquainted, Big George piled the food and all the fixings on the table. But before Miss Lillie allowed it to be passed around, she prayed: "Lord, from the bottom of our hearts we thank ya for all this good food, for all this good land to work on, and for one another...especially for one another. And Lord, if ya don't mind me bein' so bold as to ask for a few extra blessins; I'd like to ask that ya keep our friend Pablo, here, good and strong so he can work...and ol' Miss Lillie, here, good an' young so she can look after our lil' missy. And at last, I ask

99

that ya help this sweet child, here, to grow up to be a fine young woman. Amen."

"Well, everybody dig in!" said Big George. Then he laughed his familiar laugh, and everyone joined in. Then he added with delight, "Good gosh a mighty, are we gonna have us a harvest today!"

"Ya sure it's time?" asked Tex Billingsly, though Tex knew better than to doubt Big George about whether or not it was the right time for a harvest.

"I ain't never been wrong yet," said Big George. "I was up d'smornin' with the cock crowin'—up that end, I was." He pointed toward the northeast acres of the farm. "Them seeds is nice an' doughy—just the way I like 'em."

"Doughy?" said Pablo.

"You see, with sorghum, it all has to do with the seeds," said Tex Billingsly. "Stalks can take anywheres from three to four months till harvest time, and size don't matter none. A stalk can grow six feet tall and sometimes twelve, but it's the seeds that'll tell ya when it's time for a harvest. And Big George…why he's an expert at knowin' just how them seeds should feel."

"You ever had sorghum so fresh it ain't even been jarred yet?" Miss Lillie chirped brightly.

"No, I haven't," replied Pablo.

"Well, then you's in for a real treat," said Miss Lillie.

"I'll say," said Jim Ambrose. "And if you think this cornbread is somethin' else, just wait'll ya taste fresh sorghum poured over Miss Lillie's biscuits!"

"You got you a good workin' knife?" asked Big George, just as the last remaining morsels of what had been a superb breakfast were being devoured.

Pablo couldn't imagine that cutting sorghum was much different than cutting wheat. His knife, as he remembered, was more than sufficient. Nevertheless, he went digging into his brown, suede satchel so that Big George could critique a tool of the trade that had been idle now for the better part of a decade.

"My, I'd say that's a good workin' knife, alright," said Big George, marveling at the well crafted specimen.

"Holy Toledo!" said Tex Billingsly. "Would ya look at the workmanship on that there handle!"

"I'll bet that's really worth somethin'," said Jim Ambrose.

"How'd ya come by such a fine piece as that?" wondered Big George.

"A dear friend gave it to me on the very night before he died," said Pablo. He then added reflectively, "It's hard to believe it's been eleven years already that he's gone." For a brief moment the others respectfully lowered their eyes and were silent. Then Miss Lillie stood up to get a closer look at the fine knife. Running her boney fingers over the handle, she said, "Must've been a real good friend. A real good friend indeed, I'd say."

"His name was Josiah Walton," said Pablo. "By the end of the war he had no family left. What little he did have in this world, he gave to me."

With full bellies, knives in hand, and with Big George leading the way, the men started out for the northeast acreage of the farm. It wouldn't be long before Tex Billingsly's two nephews would join them in the harvest.

The northeast and southeast sections of the farm are a combine fourteen acres on which grows the sorghum. On the acres to the northwest stand groves of orange, grapefruit, lemon, and lime trees. On the southwest acreage Edgar Trudeau keeps chickens and cows for his own purposes, but also to supply a few local merchants from whom he derives a modest income. He also grows just enough hay to feed the draft horses which he uses to pull the tillers and plows.

Anything extra is used for bartering with other farmers in the region. On the southern most acres to the west is where corn is grown. The corn has a specific purpose, and Big George looks after those acres as if they were his children. A portion of the corn is harvested and sold, and from what remains comes the best moonshine in all of Texas!

"Ya just run that fine blade of yers down that stalk until all the leaves are off," Tex Billingsly told Pablo. "Then cut the stalk about five inches or so from the ground. Next, ya whack off then seed heads."

Big George made the work look easy—effortless in fact—no one could keep up with him. When it came to using a knife, Tex Billingsly could match Big George in skill, but certainly not in strength. Tex's nephews weren't too shabby, either, despite them not being adults and therefore working at a slightly lower rate. Then there was Jim Ambrose. Tex Billingsly would often refer to Jim Ambrose's poor battered hands as "Ham hocks."

"For cryin' out loud, no wonder Kid Gleason knocked ya out in the second round!" barked Tex.

"Aw, come on," complained Jim Ambrose, "if I were sober, I coulda taken The Kid that night. You know I coulda."

"Pablo, do you realize that yer in the presence of a genuine legend," said Tex Billingsly. "Yes-sir-e, Mr. Cordero, this here is none other than Pawtucket Jim, the most dangerous pair of hands on the East Coast." And with that, they all followed Big George in a chorus of laughter.

"You're a fighter?" Pablo asked.

"*Was* a fighter, a few years back," explained Pawtucket Jim.

Tex Billingsly and Big George had gotten into the habit of calling Jim Ambrose by his fighting name, or *Pawtucket* for short.

"He sure was, was our Pawtucket, and a pretty darn good one, too," Tex Billingsly chimed in.

"Yep," said Pawtucket Jim, "I was undefeated back east, I was. And by the time I got to Chicago I was 40 – 2 and makin' quite a name for myself. But that's when all my troubles started. Ya see, I was fightin' in this club in Chicago back in '93, when I took Buster O'Keefe all the way to the twenty-first round before I knocked 'im out. But that's not the half of it. I broke the pinky finger on my left hand in the fifteenth round. So, ya see, I couldn't use my jab anymore—all I could do was try an' fake out ol' Buster by bobbin' and weavin'. But I knew if I didn't plant one on him soon, I'd run out of gas and he'd end up plantin' one on me. Finally I caught 'im leanin' an' planted one right under his chin. After the fight I taped up my hand an' went an' had me a double shot of whiskey to try and deaden the pain. That's when these two fellas came over to me. 'Hey, ain't you Pawtucket Jim?' the one says. 'You looked real good out there tonight.' So I says, 'Thanks fellas.' Well, we got to talkin' an' they brought me another whiskey. Then they brought me another, an' another, an' another, until I got so shitfaced drunk, I fell off the damn stool. I mean, how in the hell was I supposed to know them two hustlers were Kid Gleason's handlers, an' were aimin' to bet darn near the whole house on 'im!"

There came another chorus of laughter led by Big George, who said, "No matter how many times he tells it, it always be a funny story."

"Anyway," said Pawtucket Jim, "the next morning I woke up all hung over. That night when I got to the club, I was swingin' at air. Hell, they coulda felt the breeze all the way back east, I bet. I couldn't have hit The Kid that night with a damn paddle! Well, the next thing I knew, I woke up, an' there's Tex standin' over me. 'Ya dumb bastard,' he yells down at me, 'that ain't the way ya done it last night!' An' when seein' how The Kid was gettin' all the glory an' I was all alone, Tex kinda stuck by me. After he innerduced his-self, I asked 'im where he was from, 'cause I could tell he wasn't from Chicago, ya see. 'I'm from Texas,' he says. 'Tex...Texas...get it?' So I says, 'I got knocked *out*, not knocked *senseless*.'

102

Anyway, that night Tex an' me both decided that Chicago was too big and too fast for our likin'. Tex said he was headin' back home. So I came taggin' along."

"It took us darn near two years to get on down here to Texas," said Tex Billingsly. "I think we had at least one job in every state along the way. We tried whisky in six different states, including Tennessee, and I'm tellin' ya, no one can top Big George!" Hearing that, Big George beamed with pride as he always did whenever someone sang his praises as the best moonshiner around.

At noontime, Edgar Trudeau came by with a trailer hitched to his draft horses. "Miss Lillie's got lunch ready," he called to the others. As the men started off, Edgar began collecting all the cut stalks and started loading them onto his trailer. He would do this several times over the next few days. Once he was all loaded up, he would transport the stalks back to the barn where they were stored until pressing time. Big George insisted on two days of harvesting and one day of pressing—he didn't like the stalks lying around for too long. He would convert one acre at a time into syrup. An acre usually yielded one hundred gallons, give or take.

As the others turned and began walking away, Pablo spotted a woman wandering about in the field well beyond the sorghum. She appeared aimless and confused, and Pablo thought she might be in need of some help. He called out to her, but the woman didn't look his way. Pablo was certain that she must have heard his call, that his voice had traveled far enough to have reached her ears. Nevertheless, he called to her again, after which, Edgar Trudeau said sharply, "I said Miss Lillie's got lunch. I'd be best to do her the honor of being on time."

There was no mistaking the edge in Edgar's tone. Pablo could sense that it had far less to do with Miss Lillie and getting back for lunch in a timely manner, and much more to do with the strange woman in the field, but he couldn't hazard a guess as to why. He also had a keen sense which told him that it wasn't the right time to go asking. He did as Edgar urged and joined the others for a lunch that was every bit as impressive as breakfast.

To Pablo's surprise, the strange woman was still in the field when he and the men returned to their work, but now was much further away. Like a child without a care in the world, she walked in circles, as if playing a game that required imagination. Even at such a distance, Pablo was able to determine that the woman was no child.

"Do you see that?" he asked Tex Billingsly.

"See what?" Tex asked.

"There's a woman out there twirling around in the field," said Pablo. "Do you see her?"

"Nah...don't see no woman," said Tex.

"Sure you do, she's right over there," said Pablo. He pointed to better guide Tex's eyes.

"Can't see no woman," insisted Tex.

"Well, then, maybe Big George can see her," said Pablo.

Before Pablo had the chance to gain Big George's attention, Tex Billingsly took firm hold of his arm. "Nah," he said. "Big George can't see her neither...you understand? So let's just forget it."

"Yeah...sure," said Pablo, recoiling, as Tex Billingsly's tone wasn't much unlike Edgar's had been earlier. Then a mystified Pablo Cordero and a glaring Tex Billingsly returned to their work.

Pablo couldn't imagine why this strange woman, who wandered and twirled about in open fields, sparked such strong reactions among the men of Trudeau's Farm. Judging from the reactions, he figured today wasn't the first time that the strange woman made an appearance. Though, when glancing down at the impression Tex left on his arm, and remembering Edgar's abrupt tone, he wisely decided not to ask again...at least not yet.

Pablo tried, though with little success, to put the strange woman from his mind and not allow her to become a distraction, while he, along with the others, labored. He was only half listening to the anecdotes of Tex Billingsly and Pawtucket Jim, but got his cue to laugh, when seeing the massive shoulders of Big George pumping up and down. For Pablo, the strange woman was an enigma to which he desired a resolution, but none was forthcoming. She appeared vague and had an elusiveness that gave him the impression of someone possessing an otherworldly presence. Then he remembered Mick saying during one of the bonfire evenings, *"There are folks in this world so dawg gone crazy that, they don't know they're crazy."* Pablo was much younger then, and, in fact, was still a boy. At the time he wasn't sure what Mick meant, nor did he remember to whom he was referring, but the comment drew quite a laugh from the others. What Pablo *did* remember, and rather fondly, was that bonfire nights in their odd and colorful way could be every bit as educational as the Bible and *The Brownsville Herald*, and often that education came in handy. Right or wrong, he concluded that the woman's body was searching for a mind that had long since gone astray.

One last time Pablo glanced out into the open field. By then the woman was at a much greater distance, though he could still see her twirling about as she went on her way. "Too crazy to know she's crazy," he mumbled to himself. Still, he wondered why the men of Trudeau's Farm shunned this poor woman or perhaps even feared her, as the sane are often wary of the crazy.

****

"Grandfather, I'm really worried about Mama," cried Anna Maria. "Maybe it wasn't such a good idea to leave her all alone. I think we should go back."

"My sweet Cheerianna, your mama...she's very strong and resourceful." This, Pablo said with more conviction than was in his heart. Still, he failed to spark confidence in his young traveling companion as evidenced by her downcast eyes.

"You must believe me," he continued. "In fact, when she was a young girl, she had to be responsible...like an adult, you see." Then he added with a chuckle and with the hope of creating a lighthearted moment, "By the time your mama was eight-years-old, she was already running the household. She was telling *me* what to do! That's the truth."

Hand in hand, grandfather and granddaughter continued on their stroll, taking in all the sights and sounds of Saint Louis, passing the time until their train was ready to depart for Louisville, Kentucky and Crow's Farm. Despite Pablo's efforts, he couldn't yet erase his young traveling companion's doubt, nor eclipse her sense of foreboding.

"Is anything going to happen to Mama because of Mr. Callahan?" she wondered.

"It's a fine spring day," said Pablo. "The sun is warm on our shoulders and the sky is clear. Let us not waste any of it thinking about Mr. Callahan." He knew any discussion of the *terrible man* would only serve to further upset his young traveling companion.

"When will Mama be able to come to Kentucky?" Anna Maria wondered.

Pablo stopped in the middle of the sidewalk and knelt down in front of his granddaughter. Taking hold of her hands, he said, "It's going to take some time, my sweet Cheerianna. There are some things that your mama must take care of before she can leave Brownsville. Very important things. I know it's hard, but please try and understand."

"Last night I stood outside Mama's bedroom door," said Anna Maria. "She didn't know that I was there and was listening. I heard her talking to Miss Lillie. She was asking her for strength."

"I heard her, too," admitted Pablo. "We must all find strength wherever we can. Miss Lillie was very strong and had a heart of gold. You mama and me would never have survived in this world if not for her. When your mama was a little girl, Miss Lillie taught her many things. In fact, Miss Lillie taught us all many things."

"I know," said Anna Maria. "Whenever I would ask Mama how she knew something, she would always say, 'Miss Lillie taught me.' And I can still remember all those songs she sang to me. Mama said she learned them all from Miss Lillie."

"Some of us really do leave the world a better place when passing, and Miss Lillie surely was such a person," said Pablo. When seeing Anna Maria smile, Pablo got to his feet and they continued along on their stroll. After awhile Pablo mentioned, "I remember those songs, too, you know. Maybe whenever you're feeling sad and missing your mama, I can sing them to you."

With a pained expression, Anna Maria looked up at Pablo and said, "I love you, Grandfather, but you sound terrible when you try to sing."

"Is that so?" said Pablo. He laughed remembering the indignation that Frankie "The Prick" Donato and Fat Fuck McGinn would suffer whenever criticized for his lack of vocal art. "Well then," he said, "maybe I can just whistle while *you* do all the singing, and together we'll know that somewhere out there, Miss Lillie and your mama are smiling. Now, how would that be?"

Before Anna Maria could answer, he took her into his arms. He pressed her to his chest and held her there for some time. He didn't want her to see his own doubt and foreboding which was far greater.

****

As the men returned from the field with aching muscles and empty stomachs, the aroma from Miss Lillie's stove reached their noses, sending them into a swoon.

"Our lil' missy here had herself a good day," said Miss Lillie. "Hardly fussed at all. But now she'll be needin' a hug from her daddy," and she handed Martina over to Pablo. After everyone filled their bellies, Pawtucket Jim, along with Tex Billingsly and his two nephews, headed for home.

"We'll be here bright an' early," said Pawtucket Jim, as though already anticipating the smell of cornbread and Big George grilling up breakfast. Then he gave Big George a firm pat on one of his massive shoulders. In turn, Big George broke into his customary laugh, which produced good humor all around. Moments later, Big George excused himself from the table and headed for the southwestern-most acres, leaving Miss Lillie, Pablo, and Martina alone to enjoy the quietude and warmth of a late summer evening. The sun was hanging low, but still managed to set ablaze the southwest acreage. Big George strolled through his cornfield, taking his time to examine each row as he went along.

"I hope ya don't mind me sayin' so, but you's a bit of a mystery to me," remarked Miss Lillie.

"How so?" Pablo wondered.

"Well," replied Miss Lillie, "anybody can tell that you's an educated man. But we farmin' folk don't usually bother much about learnin' how to talk so good. An' believe me, I ain't sayin' you's uppity, 'cause you ain't. Miss Lillie can spot an uppity fella a mile away, she can."

"Uppity I'm not and have no cause to be," said Pablo.

"Pardon me for being a curious old woman, but how did ya end up here with us farmin' folk?" wondered Miss Lillie.

"First let me say, I'm not too proud to be here; that, you can be sure of," Pablo told her. With a good deal of contemplation, he added, "Where we start out in this world can be just as difficult to overcome as the color of our skin."

"I reckon there's plenty of truth in that," Miss Lillie said with a sigh. "Plenty of truth, indeed."

She was about to excuse herself from the table, when Pablo said, "I saw the strangest thing today out there in the field." He pointed toward the acres where the stalks of sorghum stood tall. "It was a woman, and she was all alone and twirling around in the field like she didn't have a care in the world. She was behaving like a child, but I could tell she was along in years. I called after her, but she acted like she didn't hear me. And what was stranger yet, I was scolded when trying to talk about her."

"Yep, I imagine you was," said Miss Lillie. Then she leaned toward Pablo as if about to divulge some big secret. "Ya see, that woman you saw out there in the field; her name is Golda…and she's Big George's mama."

"His mama?" said Pablo, incredulously. Then he tilted his head and began to examine Miss Lillie with the belief that she must be mistaken. "But I… "

Before Pablo could to finish his thought, he was interrupted by Miss Lillie, who said brightly, "Oh, you thought *I's* Big George's mama?" She laughed and thanked Pablo for the compliment before adding, "Oh no, I's Big George's grandma."

"Still, I don't understand," said Pablo, who was beginning to find the woman from the field a more perplexing matter than was originally believed.

"Well, as you can rightly tell, poor Golda's as crazy as a loon," said Miss Lillie. "And Big George…why he don't like it when she comes around. Ya see, he's got this idea in his head that one day he's gonna end up just like his mama. So whenever he sees her, he gets all foul tempered, he does. Big George can be as gentle as a lamb, he can, but when he get his-self all worked up, sometimes it can take the rest of the day to talk sense into 'im. That's why when the men see Golda, they do all they can to make sure Big George don't see her, too."

"But…how…did…Golda ever get to be Big George's mama?" Pablo wondered. He clumsily squeezed out the question, figuring that, the woman who twirled about in open fields was either a wandering soul or village idiot to whom Miss Lillie's son had once foolishly helped himself.

"She wasn't always crazy, was Golda," said Miss Lillie. "She was a fine woman at one time. That's the truth."

"So what happened?" asked Pablo.

"My boy…my Ezekiel? why, he was a tanner, an' a good one, too," said Miss Lillie. "He learned the trade from his daddy, he did. Anyways, back then when we was livin' in Alabama, Ezekiel says, 'Mama, we's free now. I's gonna start my own business.' I told him…I says, 'Ezekiel, we ain't nearly so free as you like to think.' Especially down there in Alabama, we wasn't, an' that was the gods honest truth. I can still remember my husband's last words 'fore he went off to fight in that terrible war. He said, 'Lillie, if I don't make it home, I'll be awaitin' for ya up there in Heaven. An' when ya gets there, ya can tell me what it was like to live free.' I wanted to tell 'im, 'If you don't make it back home, you's gonna find out what freedom is long before I ever will.' But I didn't say a word. I just let my man walk away, and that's the last I ever saw of 'im."

Pablo straightened up, as Miss Lillie's thoughts on freedom struck a chord.

"None of us is truly free," she said. "For as long as we down here, we's all beholden to somethin'. But on Judgment Day the good Lord's gonna hold me in the palm of His hands an' say 'Miss Lillie, you done some good down there, or at least you tried.' An' only then will I truly be free.

"Anyways," she continued, her tone growing solemn, "it seems that whenever white folks get all worked up, they gots to go and find themselves a colored man. Well, they found them one, alright. My Ezekiel wasn't in business but a month 'fore they came an' dragged 'im from his shop. Then they went to his home an' told poor Golda where she could find 'im. She stood there, did poor Golda, lookin' up at her man…her Ezekiel, who she was so proud of…hung, beaten, and burned. That was

108

back in '75, twenty-seven years ago, and poor Golda ain't been able to utter a word since. Well, it weren't long after that, that I packed up myself, Big George, who wasn't even three-years-old at the time, and Golda. I figured it was time for us to be movin' on away from Alabama."

Our lil' missy, here, had herself a good day. Those were the words Miss Lilly spoke as they all sat down for dinner. The words echoed in Pablo's head, and this caused him to wonder, *how resilient must this woman be to have walked such a road and to have it in her heart to care for my child.* He looked down at Martina resting in the old woman's arms. He then smiled when thinking, *how wonderful is God. My dear child, you've found your Josiah Walton.*

"When I came over here to Texas, I wasn't here but a day, when someone said, 'I knows a man down the road who could surely use a hand.' Well, when I knocked on the door, Edgar's daddy said, 'Miss Lillie, you's heaven sent!' 'Cause, ya see, back then in those days, Edgar's mama—Miss Laura was her name—she worked just as hard as Edgar's daddy. So Miss Lillie, here, she cooked all the meals and looked after Edgar, Mick, and Big George. I even tried to be a friend to Mick's mama, but she would just sit an' stare out the window, the poor thing. I couldn't hardly get a word out of her. I guess losin' her man the way she did done her in for this world. Edgar's daddy said it was a huntin' accident, but everyone else seemed to know different. Anyway, the boys 'id be playin' right outside her window, but I don't think she ever saw 'em. She'd be lookin' straight ahead with that same blank stare hour after hour, day after day. And as for Golda? Why, she'd go runnin' off every day and not come home 'til dark. I didn't wanna go an' tell Edgar's daddy, 'cause I didn't want 'im thinkin' I brought 'im a whole mess of trouble, ya see. So I set some food aside for whenever she came wanderin' home. But one time…"

When she paused, a sorrowful look came over Miss Lillie, as though the incident happened only yesterday. "…she came back later than usual, and with her clothes all tore up. I said, 'Please dear Lord, have mercy and look after this child.' But then I took matters in my own hands. I locked Golda in her room, I did. It was a week that went by before she got good and brave and went climbin' out the window, and she ain't been back to live with us since. But every night I leave a plate out on the porch, an' first thing I do each mornin' is go an' check. Before Big George even opens his eyes, I go sneakin' out the door. Sometimes that plate's all cleaned up. Other times I look out an' see the birds peckin' away at it."

It broke Miss Lillie's heart to think that Golda—Ezekiel's wife and the mother of Big George was somewhere out there in the world living like an animal—a stray, who only came sneaking around when she was good and hungry.

"She's in her own lil' world, she is," said Miss Lillie. "Crazy as a loon an' happy as a lark, an' not knowin' a damn thing. I suppose that be the good Lord's way of takin' care of her. But I pray real hard He has mercy an' takes her 'fore anything happens to me." Then she added, as though making peace with God and herself, "These old hands have raised babies, cooked meals, and worked fields, and I don't begrudge none of it…not for one second. I reckon the good Lord knew just where to put ol' Miss Lillie. And now I has me a new purpose."

Miss Lillie's last remark drew a smile from Pablo. Then he gazed down at Martina resting in the old woman's arms.

"I bet you has you some story, yourself, ya do. But that'll be for another time," said Miss Lillie. "Best now to get some sleep. The mornin' comes on quick, it does."

Miss Lillie walked away cradling Martina and humming a song unfamiliar to Pablo. When she reached her door, he called out to her, "Did you ever read the Bible?"

"I's been a God fearin' woman all my life," she said. "An' I know plenty a what's in the good book." Then she added regretfully, "but I ain't never been much for readin', ya see. Ain't never learned it proper-like, I suppose." Then she disappeared into her dwelling. A moment later, in the distance, Pablo saw the massive silhouette of Big George coming toward him.

"Got all the ways to the last row a corn 'fore I can't see no more," said Big George when he came to within an earshot of Pablo. Before he went inside, he turned to Pablo, tipped his hat, then said as he flashed his infectious grin, "That be one fine lookin' lil' lady ya got there. God bless ya." Then he removed his hat before the necessary ducking it took for him to pass through the door.

Big George—a mountain of a man and a true gentle giant—the maker of moonshine and sweet sorghum and happy to be a hired hand working on Edgar's Trudeau's Farm. Pablo thought, *the good Lord knew just where to put Big George, it seems…and Miss Lillie…and most everyone else..except me, that is.* He looked up at the stars and considered the unlikelihood of having not only Josiah Walton, but also Doc Crandall, along with all his friends from Madisonville, and now Miss Lillie come into his life, and each had done so right at his hour of need. Pablo was a man of faith, not

110

chance and coincidence, and so he saw Miss Lillie as one more confirmation of his faith along the pathway to Anna Maria. He also knew better than anyone that *the Lord giveth, and the Lord taketh away*. However, in his case, it was the other way around. He laughed to himself thinking, *I've got to be the most fortunate unfortunate man on the face of the earth!*

From the wheat belt to Brownsville and now Trudeau's Farm; the road of Pablo Cordero has surely come with its own unique set of circumstances. But tonight Pablo vowed to do his best for Martina, work hard for Edgar, and make the most of his days on Trudeau's Farm for however long it was necessary to be there. With Anna Maria never far from his thoughts, he would walk his road for however long God intended.

Pablo went to the bunk house with the notion that he would retire for the night. As he stood inside the door, the moonlight shone through a window, making conspicuous his brown, suede satchel. He went fishing in the satchel for his Bible, then went creeping next door. "I hope I'm not interrupting," he said to Miss Lillie. Then he set the lantern down on a table and the Bible on his lap. He flipped through the book until he found his page. "The Book of Ezekiel," he said. Then he read: *In the thirtieth year, on the fifth day of the fourth month, while I was among the exiles by the river Chebar, the heavens opened, and I saw divine visions. On the fifth day of the month, the fifth year, that is, of King Jehoiachin's exile, the word of the Lord came to the priest Ezekiel, the son of Buzi, in the land of the Chaldeans by the river Chebar. There the hand of the Lord came upon me...*

Like children receiving their bedtime story, Miss Lillie and Big George nestled together and listened. Occasionally Pablo would glance up. When he did, he saw the same wonder in their eyes that all those years ago Josiah Walton must have seen in his; and so born was the nightly ritual of Bible reading.

"That same man who give ya the knife, he give ya this here Bible, didn't he?" asked Big George.

Pablo responded to Big George's perceptiveness with a warm smile. Later when he laid down his head, he imagined the cool grass under his back, a million stars in a Midwest summer sky, and Josiah Walton's soft voice in his ear. On the outside, Josiah Walton and Miss Lillie were as different as night and day. But in their souls, just as Pablo knew there was a God and a Heaven, he knew they were kindred spirits. They each had looked on helplessly as an unforgiving world raped them. Yet, along with the strength of their faith, they carried on with the willingness to give.

****

The following day was much of the same, including a brief Golda sighting, along with Tex Billingsly and Pawtucket Jim regaling Pablo with stories of their Illinois to Texas odyssey.

"I didn't have no handlers, ya see," said Pawtucket Jim. "So Tex here...he convinced me to take my purse from the Kid Gleason fight an' bet it all on 'The Kid.' The way he figured, why should them two hustlers in Kid's corner rake in all the dough; we can play at that game, too. Well, it was even money on 'The Kid' and he knocked out Cannonball Williams in the eighteenth round. It sure was nice to rake in some dough, but I still wished it were me in there against Cannonball. I had a wicked right cross, ya see, and Cannonball had a habit of dropping his left hand. I think I coulda taken 'im, and it wouldn't a taken me no eighteen rounds to do it in, neither!"

"Water under the bridge," said Tex Billingsly. "Besides, only three losses in nearly fifty fights ain't nothing to be sneezein'at. So consider yourself lucky. Most fighters your age don't have any wits left at all. At least you still have a couple."

Big George never minded when Tex and Pawtucket told their stories. He could have listened to them over and over. True or false, they were always amusing, and if he heard them every day it would have been fine. It was through those embellished stories with all their colorful anecdotes and zesty hyperbole that Big George was able to travel beyond the friendly confines of Trudeau's Farm and its neighboring town. There was a time when he wished he had the freedom of spirit that Pawtucket had when traveling west, and Tex, when traveling north; they each got to see a bit of the country before finding themselves grounded on a farm. Not to suggest that Big George was a man filled with regret. He loved Trudeau's Farm, and with good reason was fiercely loyal to Edgar's father. On the other hand, Tex Billingsly's two nephews would roll their eyes whenever their uncle and Pawtucket Jim would relive their glory days. They would have one another in stitches when silently mimicking their uncle and Pawtucket Jim, who were too wrapped up in their own legend to notice that they were being mocked. Pablo found the two boys' pantomime even more amusing than the two storytellers.

By the day's end the barn was stocked with sorghum stalks all waiting to be pressed. Edgar had held on to the #12 cane mill that his father bought from the Chattanooga Plow Co. twenty years ago. "It's sentimental," he would often say.

The #12 cane mill was powered by a horse hitched to a pole. The horse would walk in circles as stalks were hand-fed through the mill, producing about forty gallons of cane juice per hour. The #45 Chattanooga cane mill, which every so often came up in conversation, was powered by a seven horsepower hit-and-miss engine that was belted to the mill and produced about 120 gallons per hour.

"We's doin' just fine with your daddy's old mill," Big George would often say. Edgar couldn't tell if Big George was just telling him what he wanted to hear, or if he truly meant it. Big George wouldn't have minded a more powerful mill, but he was the only one at Trudeau's Farm who had the perfect knack for turning all that green juice from the stalks into delicious syrup. And although he could handle a bit more, he was going along just fine with the extraction of forty gallons of juice per hour.

When they were youngsters, Edgar's father had Edgar, Mick, and Big George all pulling their weight and then some. But mostly it was Big George who hung onto every word whenever Edgar's father discussed the farm, the work that needed to be done, and how it was to be carried out.

"With the right preparation and planting, ya oughta get eight-hundred gallons of juice out of an acre, and from that, a hundred gallons of syrup," Edgar's father would say. When it came time for converting all the extracted juice from the stalks into syrup, Big George would watch Edgar's father like a hawk. From the lighting of the firewood, until the last batch of juice reached the last compartment of the evaporation pan, Big George would observe the entire process. Then one day Edgar's father turned to Big George and said, "Alright son, I think it's time ya give her a go."

That was Big George's defining moment, and he passed with flying colors. From that moment forward, he no longer felt like "the poor colored boy" that Mr. Trudeau magnanimously took in, but a strong and sturdy young man who had as much worth as any of the hired hands. At the end of the day, Mr. Trudeau put his arm around Big George and said proudly, "Son, if I die tomorrow, I'll do it knowin' that this old farm will still produce the best sorghum in all of south Texas!"

As was the case with Mick, Big George barely had the chance to know his father, nor did he remember him. When they turned eighteen, Edgar went off to school, Mick left the farm for work in Brownsville, and Big George, as expected, became Mr. Trudeau's right hand man. It was the saddest day in the lives of all three men, when seven years ago, Mr. Trudeau passed away.

"I's all ready for another batch," Big George called to the others from inside the screened enclosure.

The purpose of the screened enclosure was to keep bugs and debris from landing in the juice, while allowing the steam to escape. Big George worked all day long transferring cane juice from one compartment of the evaporation bin to the next. All the while he stirred and skimmed until each batch had reached its final phase. Then, at just the precise moment that a batch was removed, all the green cane juice was transformed into delicious sweet sorghum!

"Another batch comin' right up," yelled Pawtucket Jim.

Tex, Pawtucket and Pablo spent the day at the #12 Chattanooga cane mill, pressing, collecting and straining juice. Every hour or so they would brake just long enough to hitch a fresh draft horse to the pole. By day's end they had collected half an acre's worth of juice, which Big George skillfully converted into fifty gallons of sweet sorghum. Once the last batch of the day was collected, strained, and delivered, Pablo remained inside the screened enclosure and watched Big George at work. Pablo was curious to see how the thin green juice that he had spent the day collecting became syrup; although it was Big George's massive arms and shoulders while at work that garnered most of his attention.

"Ya know, this here ain't no moonshine I be whippin' up," Big George told Pablo. "Mick don't care none 'bout how syrup's made."

"I already told you, I'm not a spy," said Pablo. Big George laughed with his massive shoulders pumping up and down.

By the end of the following day, Big George had whipped up a total of one hundred gallons of sweet sorghum to be sold. As always, he somehow managed to squeeze out an extra half gallon, with a quart each going to Leila Trudeau and Miss Lillie.

After the first and last harvest, Miss Lillie would bake biscuits and everyone was invited up to the main house. Like a family who owned a vineyard, anticipating the first sip of wine, they all sat around the dining room table awaiting Edgar's response as he dipped his spoon into the jar.

"Here's to Big George," he said. "And another successful harvest!"

The applause that followed put a sparking grin on Big George's face. Then everyone's attention turned to the middle of the table, where sat Miss Lillie's biscuits waiting to be dowsed with heaping tablespoons of delicious syrup and then devoured. Martina was sitting on Miss Lillie's lap and appeared to be observing the joyous scene, when young Laura Trudeau took a bit of syrup on the tip of her pinky finger and smeared it on her lips. To the delight of the gathering, Martina's wide eyes appeared to grow even wider. Then she clumsily tried to draw the syrup into her mouth.

"Our lil' Miss Laura, here, done gave you a real treat, she did," said Miss Lillie. Turning toward Pablo, she added with a chuckle: "Just wait 'til our lil' missy here gets a few teeth in her mouth. She gonna just love chompin' down on Miss Lillie's biscuits…won't you child?"

There's an angel on my shoulder, Pablo thought, as he began remembering what Alexandra the Romanian Gypsy fortune teller had told him. *How else could this be explained?* He let his eyes travel around a room in which he witnessed festivity brought about by the simple pleasure of biscuits with syrup. But he knew it was much more than that: He knew this celebration represented weeks of planning, preparation, and labor—and that big, or small, everyone in the room made a contribution to what went into the jar that was now being passed around the table. Pablo began to feel warm and very much at home.

Later that night, after reading chapters ten through twelve from The Book of Ezekiel to Miss Lillie and Big George from the solitude of the bunk house, Pablo composed a letter to Doc Crandall and Ben Hutchinson. He hadn't written them since his return from New Orleans, and wanted to let them know that he was fine and that he and Martina should be expected for Thanksgiving. *P.S. Tell Dutch Kirby that he was right when he said farming is an honorable profession.*

The sorghum harvest continued until mid-November. Thanksgiving came and went, as did Christmas, but not before Mick came by for a visit. To Pablo's delight, he brought along a pound of hard candy and a copy of *The Brownsville Herald* from Abercrombie's Drugstore. "Merry Christmas," he said.

"Thanks Mick. I sure miss this," said Pablo. "And be sure to give Mr. Abercrombie my regards."

Off course it was the need for spirits as much as Yuletide cheer that prompted Mick's visit, though Pablo was no less grateful.

"Anymore, I always seem to be waitin' 'til I'm down to my very last swallow before I bother trekking out here," grumbled Mick. "I guess these days I'm lazier than I am thirsty."

"You'll be staying for Christmas dinner, I hope," said Edgar.

"Wouldn't miss it," said Mick.

Mick had no clear memory of his father. After his father was through putting a bullet in his head, Mick's mother wasn't much of a factor in his life and had remained such until dying in his thirteenth year, leaving him an orphan. Through Mr. Trudeau's strong and steady influence, always filling Mick with self-worth, he never felt much like an orphan, and Christmas was always a joyous occasion. Then Mr. Trudeau passed away. Shortly thereafter, Edgar married and had a family of his own. As the years went by, for Mick, Trudeau's Farm seemed more a place of fond memories than home. It was all in his head, though; no one made him feel that way—least of all Leila. Nevertheless, it was always right before Christmas when Mick ran low on moonshine. And although he was never without offers from those of the old bonfire gang, Edgar, Big George, and Miss Lillie were the only real family that he had.

By the time the New Year was rung in at Trudeau's Farm, the citrus harvest was in full swing. Before the last orange was plucked from its tree, Martina was starting to crawl. By the time she turned a year old, she was walking. True to her word, Laura Trudeau had everyone up to the main house, where she played *Happy Birthday*, and there was plenty of cake and celebrating.

"Our lil' missy's sure comin' up in the world," said Miss Lillie.

The summer flew by as it often does. Before anyone realized that it had passed, Big George was right there to remind everyone that the seed heads atop the stalks of sorghum "are nice and doughy." The beginning of the sorghum harvest was once again upon them, and that was right about the time that Martina was running circles around everyone at Trudeau's Farm.

The infancy of Martina Cordero had been an ongoing source of fascination for Laura Trudeau. So, too, was Martina's first year as a toddler. Everyday Laura would come down from the main house to visit. Often she would stroll Martina out into the fields where the men were working. Despite Martina's capable legs, whenever Laura wasn't strolling her around, she would insist on carrying her.

"She's not a doll, ya know," Miss Lillie would often remind Laura. Other times she would say, "She ain't never gonna get no use outa those shoes her daddy bought her if ya keep carryin' her everywhere."

Eventually, Laura Trudeau went off to school. There, naturally, she met and mingled with girls her own age. The toddlerhood of Martina Cordero no longer provided her with the same fascination it once had. Laura's visits became less frequent until they stopped altogether.

****

Five-year-old Martina Cordero stood motionless as she watched a Model R Ford drive up to the main house. It wasn't everyday that an automobile drove up to the farm. A moment later there appeared a woman dressed handsomely and carrying books that the youngster concluded

116

were too big for novels, or any sort of children's story books. With her arms wrapped around the books, the woman held them pressed to her chest as she made her way to the front door. Both her style of dress and manner of walking were foreign to Martina. This prompted her to conclude that the woman must be someone terribly important. Once the fastidiously looking woman disappeared inside the house, Martina continued to swell with fascination over the woman's means of transportation. It was only moments ago that Miss Lillie warned Martina, "I's got work to do, child, so you best not go wanderin' off today. Stay right where I can keep a good eye on you." Martina heard Miss Lillie loud and clear, but the fine looking Model R Ford had its own gravitational pull, easily overpowering one so youthful and curious. Martina went wandering off, remembering not a single word of Miss Lillie's warning.

Miss Lillie didn't have to do much scolding when dealing with Martina. Usually a sharp clearing of the throat, followed by glaring down her nose was sufficient enough to launch Martina into standing at attention. Any words that may have followed were redundant. Miss Lillie didn't mind Martina wandering off, but only when she wasn't too busy and had the time to lag behind while keeping a sharp eye out for the youngster.

Like an adventurer, or explorer, Martina enjoyed wandering off into the farthest reaches of the farm. Not wanting to spoil a young girl's sensation that she was braving her way through what was believed to be uncharted territory, Miss Lillie would try to remain out of sight until it was time to rein in the five-year-old.

Often times, Martina enjoyed getting lost in Big George's cornfield, or zigzagging her way through the groves of citrus trees. Like any child, she longed to be bigger than she was, and would measure her progress by launching herself upward, hoping her fingertips would at last find the underneath orb of a dangling orange. Once when wandering off alone, she ended up in the field where the men were working. For sweating, laboring men, the sight of a sweet, overly curious five-year-old girl can be every bit as refreshing as a cool drink. And as Marina Cordero would learn all too well, sweet, overly curious five-year-old girls can easily wrap grown men around their fingers. Although, by the nine-hundred and ninety-ninth question it was unanimous among the men that Martina had reached and surpassed the point of annoying. At that point, she heard the sharp clearing of a throat. Martina needn't turn around to know that it was Miss Lillie standing behind her. Nevertheless, she made a sharp about-face, then was swiftly escorted home.

Along with pretending to be an adventurer or explorer, Martina enjoyed playing hide-and-seek in the cornfield—especially when she got the chance to play with Big George. Pablo and Pawtucket Jim were fine for fun and games, but with Big George, somehow fun and games always became more fun. Big George would turn his back to the cornfield and then count to fifty. When he went in search of Martina, he would always allude to her diminutive size in such a large place as a cornfield, and that it would surely take hours, if not days to find her. Big George would then say the silliest things to get Martina to giggle and give up her position. "Ya see that big ol' sun hangin' up there," he would say. "Well, he ain't just hangin' around, ya know, an' doin' nothin' like some folks are want to do on Sundays. He's lookin' down and spyin' on folks, he is. An' he done bent down an' told a ol' fox, who done ran off an' told a rabbit, who done hopped away an' told a squirrel, who done just whispered in my ear that he just seen a lil' girl as cute as a bug's ear an' sweeeeter than a Georgia peach—and she's right overrrrrrrrr there!"

Martina would feel the giggle rumbling in her belly and then moving on up into her throat where she tried with all her might to keep it stuck. But a five-year-old girl can only keep a giggle stuck in her throat for so long before having to let it go. Afterward, Big George would come marching out of the cornfield grinning beautifully with Martina sitting high atop one of his massive shoulders.

Just as Martina reached the Model R Ford and started poking around, she heard clusters of musical notes pouring out of an open window. Abandoning her fascination for the automobile, she scattered dust and pebbles as she went scampering off in the direction from which the music came. Inside, and seated at her piano next to the owner of the Model R Ford, was Laura Trudeau. Her fingers were dexterously racing across the keys, as she executed scale after harmonic scale to perfection. Her teacher looked on stoically, but with approval. Outside, Martina was leaping with all her might to try and latch on to the windowsill and pull herself up in order to look inside, but her diminutive stature would not accommodate her ambition.

"What on earth is making all that racket?" the owner of the fine Model R demanded to know.

The woman's hostile tone put a swift end to Martina's attempt to achieve the windowsill. Martina pressed her slight figure flat against the house when she heard angry footsteps pounding their way across the hardwood floor in the direction of the window—a window which the owner of the Model R aimed to close. Martina remained perfectly still and held her breath. She heard Laura say to her teacher, "Please don't. I like the fresh air when I play."

"Fresh air isn't any good for a piano," the woman insisted. "It can warp the cabinetry and distort the sound."

"But it isn't damp outside today," pleaded Laura.

"Very well," said the fastidious woman, "but fresh air or no fresh air, any more disturbances, and the window will have to be shut. I can't very well concentrate on your playing if I have to contend with outside noise."

Martina exhaled quietly into the palms of her hands and sank to the ground, where, after already having disturbed a piano lesson, she remained, afraid to move. Inside, Laura Trudeau was agonizing through one of Clemente's Sonatinas. Not that she didn't play it with a fair degree of proficiency, but was bored with the piece and wanted to move on to something more pleasing to her ear.

The five-year-old who sat crouched below the window sill was no more enamored with the sonatina. In Martina's estimation, the piece had no discernible melody, and she couldn't imagine why poor Laura was forced to painstakingly play it over and over. Nevertheless, she chose to remain crouched and motionless below the windowsill throughout the lesson. It wasn't until hearing the roar of the Model R Ford's engine, that she realized that she had fallen asleep—unwittingly lulled into slumber, no doubt, by the repetition of a piece that fell far short of inspiring its youthful performer and even more youthful listener. Remembering Miss Lillie's warning about wandering off, Martina leapt to her feet. She was about to launch herself into a desperate sprint, when once again she fell captive to the musical notes that came pouring out of the window. However, this time, absent were the harmonic scales attacked with vigor, or the indiscernible phrases played dispassionately. Instead, there came a lovely strain with a fiery undercurrent that stroked Martina Cordero's youthful imagination.

Beethoven's Fur Elise was a favorite of nine-year-old Laura Trudeau. She played it beautifully and often—or, whenever she wasn't practicing the material that her teacher set before her. She began playing through it a second time, when once again, Martina began her quest for the windowsill. In her determination to gain the sill, Martina hadn't realized that Laura stopped playing, had exited the house, and was already standing behind her with arms folded and wondering, *what is this idiotic little girl trying to do?*

"What on earth are you doing?" Laura demanded to know—her tone quite sharp.

The shriek the Martina let out was heard acres away by the men. They stopped working only long enough to wonder "what on earth could have made such an awful sound?" However, Miss Lillie knew exactly what produced the awful sound and stopped her work to go in search of the source.

"For Heaven's sake, you'll wake the dead!" cried Laura. Martina was quick to put her hands to her mouth with the idea of blocking any further sound that might escape.

"You're Martina, aren't you?" asked Laura. With her hands still pressed to her mouth, Martina answered with a nod.

"You've grown up a bit since the last harvest, I see," said Laura.

"But you didn't celebrate with us," said Martina; her tone suggesting the older girl explain herself.

"I had to practice," Laura told her. "Besides, I don't care much for syrup."

Martina reacted predictably to Laura's dislike for syrup by crying, "But it's everybody's favorite! How could you not like it?"

"I *do* like Miss Lillie's biscuits, though, but only with butter," said Laura.

"Do you like bugs?" asked Martina, searching for something that they might have in common.

"Don't be silly. I hate bugs!" cried Laura. Then she added rather haughtily, "And I suppose *you* like them?"

"They're alright, I guess," replied Martina; her enthusiasm tempered once the older and more sophisticated girl was through expressing her feelings. Her perkiness quickly returned and she grabbed Laura's hand and said, "Come on, I wanna show you something."

"Alright, alright, you can show me, but you don't have to pull my arm off," cried Laura.

"Sorry," said Martina.

"So where are you dragging me off to?" wondered Laura.

"You'll see," replied Martina. Along the pathway she held on to Laura's hand and occasionally skipped.

"I didn't mean to scare you back there," said Laura.

"I didn't mean to scream," said Martina. "But I like listening to you play."

"My teacher said that I have perfect pitch and that it's my duty to become a pianist," said Laura. "You know…like a prodigy."

Martina knew nothing of what it meant to have perfect pitch, or to be a prodigy. So while Laura was going on about such things, Martina reached up and touched her hair. Laura shot her a quizzical look, to which Martina responded, "It's so light and pretty. And how do you have all those curls?"

"I inherited my mother's pretty blonde hair," said Laura, proudly. "She makes me these curls every day—barrel curls she calls them. They're okay, I suppose, but I have to sit very still while she sets my hair. She says that I should wear my hair a certain way and wear certain dresses, and that I have to look like a future pianist, not a farmer's daughter. Well, after all," she added, as to concede Leila's position on such matters, "she *is* my mother, so I guess she knows what's best."

"Yeah, I guess so," said Martina, but with only halfhearted agreement.

"I'm sorry," said Laura. "I didn't mean to go on like that. I forgot…"

"That's okay," Martina chimed in. "Papa says that my mother wasn't a real person, like you or me. He said that she was an angel, and that God let her come down from Heaven just to give birth to me. Well, we're here now."

"Where?" asked Laura.

"Here," replied Martina, and she pointed at the cornfield.

"It's just an old cornfield, silly," said Laura. "What's the big deal about an old cornfield?"

"It's where we play hide and seek," explained Martina.

"That's a childish game," said Laura. Then with a hint of superiority, she added, "I sorry. I forgot. You *are* a child."

Ignoring the budding pianist's superior tone, Martina said excitedly, "Now *you* count to fifty, while *I* go and hide. And remember, no peeking!"

"Whatever," said Laura. She rolled her eyes as Martina went sprinting off to lose herself in the cornfield.

"I can't hear you counting," shouted Martina from within the cluster of stalks.

"27, 28, 29," said Laura with mock emphasis, as though having long since lost her patience for what she determined was a silly game.

"You're not peeking, are you?" Martina called to the prodigy.

"I wouldn't dream of it," said Laura. "48, 49 and 50! Alright, I'm coming in after you. But I better not see any bugs in there. If I do, they had better be on the ground so I can step on them."

"Don't worry," whispered Martina to a ladybug that she cupped in her hands. "I won't let anything happen to you."

It had been several minutes that Martina hadn't heard Laura complaining bitterly about the bugs or the possibility that her dress might become soiled. She wondered whether she hid herself so well that Laura abandoned the search and had gone home.

"I think we're all alone, ladybug," she whispered. Then she carefully placed the ladybug on the leaf of a cornstalk. Without making a sound, she rose to her feet. She hadn't taken but a step, though, when from behind she heard a sharp clearing of a throat. She needn't turn around to see that it wasn't an aspiring young pianist with barrel curls in a pretty dress who didn't care much for bugs.

"Child, you best run your narrow behind on home 'fore I put a good whoppin' on it," scolded Miss Lillie. Before you could say *Jack Robinson,* Martina Cordero was off to the races.

When Miss Lillie made it home, she handed Martina a broom. "Here," she scolded. "This floor could surely use a good sweepin'. And when you're all through, you best be settin' the table. The men 'ill be comin' outa the fields soon."

Miss Lillie glared down her nose at Martina. But even a five-year-old knew Miss Lillie couldn't stay angry for more than a minute or so. Martina went about the business of sweeping the floor with the strains of Beethoven's Fur Elise going round in her head.

"I don't know…it seems somebody awfully happy to be sweepin'," said Miss Lillie.

"Laura's real pretty, isn't she?" asked Martina, as though placing the young prodigy's beauty in a realm that she herself couldn't dream of attaining.

"Child, you's just as pretty as anyone," said Miss Lillie. "An' prettier than most, I'd say."

"But Laura has real light hair," said Martina.

"And you have real dark hair, and it ain't no less pretty to look at." This, Miss Lillie stated as a matter of fact and was quite emphatic when pointing it out.

Shortly after they resumed their chores, Miss Lillie wondered aloud, "What's that I hear ya hummin', child?"

"Just something I heard Laura playing on her piano," replied Martina.

"She plays real nice, our lil' Miss Laura, she does," said Miss Lillie. "I can't says I understand all that she plays. It sure ain't what I grew up singin'." Then Miss Lillie called Martina to her side. "Ain't no harm in lookin' up to Laura Trudeau," she told her. "After all, she's four year older than you. But child, don't you never go thinkin' that anyone's better than you. In the eyes of the Lord we's all equal. Some of us come into this world a lil' luckier than others, but somewheres down the road we all gots to leave—even the ones with pretty light hair." Then Miss Lillie knelt down beside Martina and began singing, "*Joshua fit the battle of Jericho, Jericho, Jericho. Joshua fit the battle of Jericho…*" Then with gusto, Martina raised her broom and shouted, "*And the walls came tumblin' down!*"

****

When Pablo took his last swallow of whiskey, he was feeling painfully enveloped by the high spirited room. Unlike Big George's moonshine, which became smoother and more pleasing with each swallow, the cheap liquor which he regrettably consumed became less forgiving. Clearly nervous, he set down his glass on the table, then allowed himself to be led through the raucous room of men and up the stairs of The Inn. Along the way he refused to meet even a single pair of eyes. He didn't wish to bear witness to the celebration of baseness and corruption. *What has happened to me?* he wondered. *Where is my soul?*

Each step on the stairs creaked, as if announcing to all others in the room that he was next—that it was now his turn to be led away. With his tentative ascension of the stairs, there came a coarse jeering that assaulted his ears. He mistakenly thought the jeering was intended for him, but discovered it was over a dart game which, when he was drinking his glass of whiskey, he'd given some of his attention. Once upstairs, he was led down a long and narrow hallway.

The floor was terribly uneven—each step gave him the sensation of either going up a hill or over a cliff. At the moment, Pablo was wishing for the latter. He was glad to be away from The Inn's raucous and at times ill-mannered patrons, but wasn't any happier with his new environment and circumstances upstairs. With much trepidation, he stared at the door at the end of the hallway. He knew behind that door must be his destination, for it was the only door in the hall that had been left ajar. As the woman was pulling him along, he glanced down at his hand, which felt strangely detached from the rest of his person. *Surely she must sense my rigidness and apprehension*, he thought.

Pablo had been dreading this moment from the time that he had arrived at The Inn. As he sat grimacing, while allowing cheap liquor to trickle down his throat, he prayed for something to happen that would change his circumstances, or alter the game plan, including zealous lawmen entering the disreputable establishment. He would have gladly traded the door at the end of the hallway for a night in the local jail. But the activity that occurred behind that door and all the other doors wasn't something with which the local lawmen concerned themselves.

The Inn, as Pablo had painfully observed, was a far cry from Serendipity. It was lacking top shelf liquor doled out by a gentleman barkeeper (Sam Ott), and a musician with any degree of virtuosity (Miles Gordon). It paled wholly in comparison with Corina LaSalle's luxurious love nest.

Earlier, when Pablo's eyes were traveling over the room, he had wondered how many of these men, all of whom were common laborers, thought enough to bathe before coming. With that in mind, the women upstairs, whom life had no doubt *kicked to the curb*, as they say, (else how would they have ended up in such a place as The Inn) had garnered his sympathy. As he was being led through the narrow hallway to the slightly ajar door, he wanted to point out, *I'm not like those other men downstairs, you know. I'm different. Surely you can see that, can't you?*

No sooner had the thought entered his head, it occurred to him that, to this woman, *or girl*, he was nothing more than a stalk of sorghum waiting to be stripped, cut, and pressed. It mattered not a lick that he had a young daughter that every day finds ways to steal his heart, or a deceased wife with whom he still speaks when alone at night. It was useless to point out that he had a Bible that he read regularly to less literate friends, or that he thought enough to bathe before coming. All that mattered was that at the end of the night he paid for services rendered. The Inn was not an establishment where folks came displaying the loftier side of their character.

"That's what Sunday mornin' church is for," said Pawtucket Jim. The former fighter's earlier remark made Pablo grimace more so than the cheap liquor.

Once a month on a Saturday night after setting some money aside, Tex Billingsly and Pawtucket Jim would go heading into town. For the past five years, without success, they've tried to persuade Pablo to join them.

"Not this time," Pablo would tell them. He would usually cite needing to spend time with Martina, or having to resume his Bible reading to Miss Lillie and Big George as his handy excuses.

"No need to make such a big fuss over goin' into town," Miss Lillie told Pablo when together in a private moment. "The Lord knows that in your heart you's a virtuous man. Besides, folks ain't usually in the habit a makin' saints outa farmers."

"God sees our action," said Pablo.

"Sure He does," said Miss Lillie. "But you's here five years, already, and you ain't been off this here farm 'cept once or twice a year to go see your friends up north in Madisonville. The only other time you leave is to go to the post office, and even then you won't take Edgar's horse when he offers it to ya. For one measly lil' night at The Inn, I think God 'ill look the other way."

Pablo shrugged to indicate that he was still indecisive on the matter of going into town on Saturday night, but then realized that Miss Lillie had a valid point: Self denial only leads to self denial, and that while here on earth, there wouldn't be anyone looking to reward or congratulate him for his *priestly* lifestyle. He made whatever peace he thought necessary with God. In prayer, he explained that he was convinced by others that he was entitled *one* indiscretion, if for no other reason than to prove that he was human. The exercise was farcical, Pablo knew, but he went through with it, nevertheless.

"To err is to be human. Ain't that what they say?" asked Pawtucket Jim.

"That's right," agreed Tex Billingsly, "but the Lord most likely won't see it that way; 'specially if ya already know ahead a time that yer gonna be errin'. Prayin' beforehand is like covering yer bets and the Lord don't care much for gambling."

"What's ya tryin' to say, then, Tex, that we're goin' to hell?" asked Pawtucket Jim.

"Yep, I recon that's about where we're all headed," said Tex Billingsly.

The two hired hands began to grapple over which, if any of the Commandments they were breaking by going to a whorehouse, but neither knew their Commandments well enough to judge how they might pertain to their monthly transgression. This was one of those conversations (and Tex and Pawtucket had many) that Pablo pretended not to hear, and that Miss Lillie tolerated to a point before scolding the two.

The day that Pablo arrived at Trudeau's Farm, he laid down his weary body and prayed that by the time morning came around and he had opened his eyes, Martina would already be old enough to go off to school and to look after herself, so that he could return to Brownsville and grieve among people and surroundings that were both comfortable and familiar. He never imagined that in conversations with Miss Lillie, watching Big George turn cane juice into syrup, and toiling away on the acres of Trudeau's Farm, he would find salvation. But that's exactly what he found.

Salvation notwithstanding, it occurred to Pablo, one day when he observed Martina, who by then learned to feed chickens, milk cows, and churn butter, that it wasn't just the hands of *her* clock that were ticking away—that he hadn't been placed in storage or preserved until the time was right to resume his life in Brownsville. For the past five years Pablo had worked and saved, and with one eye always on the horizon. Admittedly, he was growing weary.

"Only thing I know 'bout horizons is, they don't never seem to be gettin' any closer," said Miss Lillie. "But ol' Miss Lillie sure does know a thing or two 'bout the here an' now; an' that is, the good Lord...He done give us two hands—one for the givin' and the other for the takin'; an' He for darn sure knows what's truly in a man's heart. So you go on into town with Tex and Pawtucket. And while you're gone, if it makes ya any happier, I'll pray for ya."

Pablo thought Miss Lillie's logic seemed a bit skewed. *A man who ordinarily shuns weakness and carries around in his heart the best of intentions was more entitled to the occasional sin? What would Josiah Walton think?* he wondered. *What would God think?*

Pablo was fully aware of God's purpose for a man having two hands. Despite what was in his heart, in his own estimation he had done his share of taking: An ear, a life, Josiah Walton's possessions, kindness from the folks of Madisonville, and money from a grandmother who tried to deny him, to name only a few. As he walked into town with Tex Billingsly and Pawtucket Jim, he couldn't help but to wonder, *who on earth ever benefitted from my existence?*

While pondering to himself the validity of his existence, he began glowering with disgust over the tone of Tex's and Pawtucket's conversation. Not that he didn't understand the point of the evening, but he preferred that it wasn't described to him in such crude detail.

"No need to get so uptight, Pablo," protested Pawtucket Jim. "Even whores gotta eat, ya know."

"Yeah," added Tex Billingsly. "If them girls had someone to teach 'em how to be a seamstress, or a school teacher, they wouldn't be workin' at The Inn. But a lot a folks ain't so lucky, ya see. So let's just have some fun tonight and not think too hard about things."

Even whores gotta eat. The philosophy of one Pawtucket Jim. The world according a to a man who may have taken one too many hits to the head. *Even whores gotta eat.* Pablo's first inclination was to display revulsion for Pawtucket Jim's crude remark. But then quite unexpectedly a light went off in his head. *Of course, even whores gotta eat,* he knew. *Everyone must eat.* It also occurred to Pablo that, Pawtucket Jim's philosophy rang true and was relevant to most walks of life the whole world over. In most political and religious doctrines, more or less, there can be found a passage stating, though with much greater eloquence: *Even whores gotta eat.* All Men Are Created Equal…And The Meek Shall Inherit The Earth…Even Whores Gotta Eat. Pawtucket Jim, in his own crude way summed up the entire human race and managed to effectively do so with only four simple words. Good for Pawtucket Jim; the most concise philosopher in human history! However, all this simplification of philosophy didn't give Pablo any more stomach for what he could end up doing before the night's end, though it did help him to better reconcile the company he was keeping. But then he saw The Inn in the distance, and so came a pang in his heart, and with that pang, what came to mind was the angel on his shoulder—the same angel whom which Alexandra the Romanian Gypsy fortune teller had spoken. Miss Lillie insisted that for one measly night at The Inn, God would look the other way. He could only pray that so, too, would Anna Maria.

The prostitute pushed open the slightly ajar door at the end of the hallway just far enough for her and Pablo to slip inside. Then she turned about and pushed the door closed—the latch clicking in place caused Pablo to gulp nervously. The prostitute smiled sweetly at Pablo. Then with the agility of a cat, she threw herself onto the bed. Her shapely legs were clad in fishnet stockings, which she rubbed together as though wanting to keep them nice and warm for whenever Pablo was ready to explore her womanhood. She tossed her head back, causing all her hair to tumble to one side, where it danced and shimmered beautifully just above the mattress. Then with a impish grin she said, "Well, Poco, why don't you tell Juliet what your pleasure is."

"My name isn't Poco!" Pablo shouted in anger. "It's Pablo! It's not that much harder to say, even for a…" Pablo was thankful that he was able to catch himself before completing the harsh remark. After all, *even whores gotta eat.* He turned away from the prostitute and went to the window, where he hoped to compose himself.

"I'm sorry mister," she cried. "I didn't mean nothing by it…honest. I was just tryin' to be friendly-like…that's all."

"I know," whispered Pablo, though without bothering to look the prostitute's way.

"Mister, please don't tell my boss that I got you all upset," she cried, "'cause if he finds out he'll..."

"It's okay, it's not your fault," Pablo softly interjected. Mumbling more to himself, he added, "Some wounds just don't seem to want to close all the way."

As Pablo stared at the window, his own reflection began to fade. In its stead came the image of Jed Wright—his unsightly nakedness draped sloppily over the delicacy and loveliness of Dolci Cordero. In the window Pablo watched with mounting hatred and helplessness the disturbing image of Jed Wright pushing down on Dolci's head and then slapping her buttocks. "Like an animal he treated her," was his whisper through clenched teeth. "Like an animal."

"Mister, are you all right?" the prostitute wondered. Her voice rang with trepidation, but served to bring Pablo back into the present.

"I'm fine." Pablo wiped the moisture from his cheeks. He stared back at the window, but all that could be seen was his own reflection.

"Do you still want me to do anything for you?" the prostitute peeped. She squeezed out her words, hoping they wouldn't further upset her customer who already appeared distressed. After Pablo replied with a mere gesture to indicate that he rather she not, the prostitute added, "Well, you still have the room for another fifty minutes. I suppose we could just talk, if you want to."

"No offense, but I would prefer to just talk," Pablo told her; although it pained him when considering fifty minutes of conversation with someone whom he assumed was incapable of holding up her end with only the benefit of words. He didn't hint as much, but he would have rather the prostitute disappear altogether so that he could lie down in peace and allow the unsuitable liquor he had earlier consumed to finish wreaking its havoc on his innards.

"I don't know if this is a real good time to bring it up," the prostitute again peeped, "but as far as conversations go, it'll be a real expensive one. So if you change your mind..."

The remark drew a chuckle from Pablo, which served put the girl at ease. *Even whores gotta eat,* he thought, and somewhere down the hall, Pawtucket Jim was making darn sure of it.

"So what's your name?" Pablo asked.

"Juliet," the prostitute replied. Beaming with pride, she added, "You know, like as in Romeo and Juliet."

"I'm sure Shakespeare would be proud," said Pablo, whose tongue-in-cheek humor had gotten lost on the prostitute. "But what's your *real* name?" he asked, figuring that, although *Juliet* was plausible and a much more common a name than Corina LaSalle's valet, Cassandra, it was still unlikely. Juliet flashed Pablo a bashful smile and peeped, "Marcie. Marcie Cooper."

"So how old is Marcie Cooper?" Pablo asked.

"She's twenty-one," replied Marcie, with unshakable confidence.

"Really? Well, what do you know; me too!" exclaimed Pablo, mocking the false coincidence with great exaggeration. "So when's your birthday? Wait, don't tell me…let me guess…"

"Alright, you got me," Marcie Cooper chimed in. Lowering her eyes, she shamefully admitted, "I'll be seventeen this September." The confession prompted Pablo to fetch Marcie's robe which was draped over a chair beside the window. He took the robe and placed it over Marcie's shoulders, then went and moved the chair alongside the bed.

"Uh oh, I feel a speech comin' on," said Marcie. She checked the clock and saw that she still owed Pablo another forty minutes.

"No speech," said Pablo. Then he unzipped his brown, suede satchel.

"What's you got in that bag, Mister?" Marcie asked guardedly.

"Just a copy of the Bible," replied Pablo.

"Holy Toledo!" cried Marcie. "I mean, you're kiddin' me… right? You done brought a Bible to a whorehouse!"

"Can you think of a more fitting place?" was Pablo's ironical reply, before unveiling the *good book.*

"Well, I'll be damned to hell in a hand basket!" cried Marcie Cooper. "You're gonna read me the Bible, aren't you? I got forty minutes of Mary Magdalene due me, don't I?" Then she threw herself down on the bed and groaned as though in agony. "I guess I should make myself comfortable, huh?" Though before her head had the chance to hit the pillow, she bounced up and added playfully, "But I bet if I took all my clothes off, I could getcha to leave, couldn't I?"

Pablo smiled as Marcie Cooper, despite her fishnet stockings and tumbling hair, had became irresistibly mischievous and to the point of being childlike.

"I'm not going to read you anything," Pablo told her. Then Marcie watched with a mixture of anticipation and unease, a man who was in essence a stranger, reach into a brown, suede satchel for what had been resting buried beneath the Bible. When Pablo produced what that

129

something was, he placed it in the palm of Marcie's hand, then folded her fingers around it. In a flash, Marcie sprang to her feet. Losing her balance, she fell backward on the bed.

"That's an awful lot of money, Mister," she said with a note of suspicion. "I mean, you're not crazy or something…are ya? 'Cause I heard of folks doin' things like this, and then the next thing ya know, they're cartin' them off to the loony bin."

"The loony bin may very well be in my future, but that day hasn't yet arrived," Pablo assured the young prostitute. "You see, I've been keeping myself stuck away on a farm for the past five years. I've done plenty of saving and now I have more than I can use."

"I guess what you're sayin' is, this is my lucky day," said Marcie, as she stared disbelievingly at her hand.

"You can make it your lucky *life*, not just your lucky day. That is, if you choose to," Pablo told her. "But most often we're afraid to make the right choice. Maybe, Marcie Cooper, you'll be the exception. Anyway, there's enough there to get you far away from this place and then some. I know a man named Mr. Abercrombie—a real nice fellow. He has a drugstore over in Brownsville. He sells lots of nice things, and I'm betting he can use a pretty girl with a real nice smile to help move his merchandise. Just tell him Pablo Cordero sent you. I'll write to let him know that he should be expecting you."

"Gee, thanks a lot, Mister," said Marcie, whose eyes were no longer in accordance with her attire, as they were expressing the hopefulness of a child.

"Well, goodbye Marcie Cooper," said Pablo. "And good luck."

Pablo would have preferred jumping out of the window instead of having to wind his way through the hardcore, raucous crowd below. The men who patronized The Inn were men who labored hard, day after day, week after week, and now they have come for their *just reward*. After all, *even whores gotta eat*. Pablo respected these men and begrudged them nothing, but in such multitudes, he found them foul and ill-mannered.

"When Tex and Pawtucket come down, tell them I'm already on my way," Pablo said to the man keeping bar. He said this as though he was being pulled in the direction of the door. The fellow keeping bar sneered at Pablo, for he had portrayed, however unintentionally, a man too high of moral standard for a place such as The Inn. Pablo made his swift exit, never bothering to glance at the highly animated crowd that was still gathered around the dartboard. He walked away wondering whether later on the other prostitutes would share a good laugh over his magnanimous gesture or whether he indeed helped a young woman to buy back her soul.

At the farm, he noticed that the screened enclosure in which Big George turned cane juice into syrup was well illuminated. He knew at once that Big George must be whipping up batches of his special potion, which meant any day now Mick would be coming by.

"You home kinda early, ain't ya?" asked Big George.

"You're up kinda late," said Pablo.

It was in late summer, when waiting for the sorghum to mature, that Big George made the largest batch of his famous moonshine.

"You can come in if you want," said Big George. "But I's almost done."

"You're not afraid I'll steal you secret?" said Pablo.

"Oh, I's much too far along for anybody to be stealin' anything," said Big George. Then he laughed his customary laugh before adding, "I guess it didn't go so good tonight."

"I guess not," said Pablo. "Not all of us are cut out for The Inn, I suppose." Then he patted Big George on one of his massive shoulders, before handing him a towel to wipe the beads of moisture that had built up on his face from the steam.

"Sounds like you got a bit on your mind," said Big George.

"When I was back in Brownsville, it didn't matter how hard I worked," said Pablo, "it always felt like play, because I knew at the end of the day my Anna Maria would be there. God, what a great feeling that was. I would grin all the way home just knowing she was there. Just the thought of her gave me such joy. But no matter how much I still love her or cherish her memory, I can't replace the feeling I used to get whenever I knew that I was about to see her. I'll never know that kind of thrill again, I don't think. God, how I miss it; and there doesn't seem to be anything else on earth that can replace it."

"Sound like she was some fine woman," said Big George. "An' a woman like that don't come 'round but once. But at least ya git to watch Martina grow up."

"Yeah," Pablo said with a halfhearted sigh, "I guess that's my consolation prize."

"Oh, but she's much more than that," said Big George. "She's *so* much more."

"I know she is," said Pablo. "But when I lost my Anna Maria, I had to reinvent myself. And because of that, there are days that I feel like only a copy of a man—that I'm watching Martina through a glass window—or like a specter whose in the scene, but can't be part of it." He sighed again when realizing, from the dusty plains of the Midwest and wheat belt, to Brownsville, and now Trudeau's Farm, his life has been a series of reinventions. Then he looked up at Big George and asked, "So how about you?"

"Oh, I had me a sweetheart once," said Big George. "Met her at the church just across the way, I did." He pointed in the direction of the cornfield. "I come home one Sunday an' told Edgar and Mick, I done just see'd the prettiest gal anywhere. But when they ax me what her name was, I couldn't tell 'em. I said, 'I ain't learned it yet.' Well, they both hollered at me and told me that I's as dumb as an ox, an' that I oughta get on into town an' try an' find her 'fore someone else does. Well, I done just what they told me."

"I had a similar experience," Pablo chimed in, remembering when Mick and the others gave him a ribbing for falling hopelessly in love with a girl whose name he had yet to learn.

"Anyways," said Big George, "we started courtin' on Saturday afternoons, and then I'd see her at church on Sundays, too. Sarah Jane Patterson was her name, and she could smile like the sunrise, she could. So I know what ya mean 'bout work not seemin' much like work."

"So what happened?" asked Pablo.

"Her daddy...he worked for the railroad, he did, an' they done sent him up north to Ohio," said Big George. "That was back in '89. Mr. Patterson...he told me I could come along if I wanted. He said 'George, maybe I can find you some work up north.' But Mr. Trudeau...he treated me like a son, he did, and there weren't no *maybes* 'bout this here farm. Well, for a long time Sarah Jane wrote me every week. I weren't much for writin', so Edgar...he helped me with the letters. After a year the letters didn't come but once a month. Then they didn't come at all. I bet she got herself a real nice fella and she raised up some fine babies, she did."

"Maybe so," said Pablo, "but I'll bet there isn't a day that goes by that you don't cross her mind."

"That's a mighty fine thought," said Big George. Then turning toward Pablo, he added, "When folks is raised on farms, it seems like some can't wait 'til they's all growed up so that they can get away. But this here farm..." The famous moonshiner paused and pointed to the ground. "It ain't no different than the blood that runs through my veins." Then he held out his massive arms for Pablo to examine. "The sunset over the cornfield—the smell of citrus in winter. I owe my life to this farm."

****

Two years later: Just as she did every day during the summer months when all through with her chores, which consisted of feeding chickens, collecting eggs, milking cows, and churning butter, Martina went dashing for the main house. Once there, she would lie on the hardwood floor underneath the grand piano as Laura Trudeau displayed her virtuosity. Martina always enjoyed Laura's playing, but especially liked the vibrations that the strings sent to the floor, which in turn were transferred to her body. Often, to satisfy Martina, Laura would play passages louder than the composer intended. Occasionally, and usually when right in the middle of a piece, or climax of a phrase, she would loudly strike a dissonant chord when noticing Martina looking a bit too relaxed. Martina would then spring into a sitting position as if doused in the face with a cold glass of water. Besides ruining Martina's repose, which always gave Laura a chuckle, it was also the young pianist's way of saying that she was tired of playing and in need of fresh air.

It was the summer of '09, and the girls had grown quite close since the day Martina tried to launch herself up to the windowsill and then afterward dragged Laura off to the cornfield. It was during that same summer when Pablo first spent any length of time away from Trudeau's Farm.

"There's this fellow I know up in Kentucky and he's got a farm ten times this size," Edgar told Pablo. "He's an old friend of the family, you might say. I only met him once, but my dad seemed to know him real well. Anyway, he says there's been a strain of influenza going around, and that he's lost more than half his manpower. He's been calling everyone he knows hoping they can spare a man or two. I'm thinking maybe a change of scenery will do you some good."

"Maybe," said Pablo, though his body language said otherwise.

"It would only be for about a month or so," Edgar told him. "Maybe not even that long. He assured me you'd be back in plenty of time for the sorghum harvest, if that's what you're worried about. And he'll pay your travel expenses, too. The man's name is Crow, by the way."

"Cornelius Crow?" wondered Pablo—his interest suddenly peaked.

"You heard of him?" asked Edgar—his face filled with surprise.

"I know his sister, Betsy—Betsy Hutchinson. She's an old and dear friend," replied Pablo.

"Didn't even know he had a sister," said Edgar. "Well, hallelujah, what a small world!"

"I'll say," said Pablo.

"And no need to worry about Martina. There's plenty of eyes around here. You can bet as sure as the world is spinnin' that she'll be well looked after," said Edgar.

The next day Pablo placed whatever provisions he thought he might need in his brown, suede satchel and was off. He made it only as far as the road leading to the farm, when Edgar rode up alongside him.

"I might've known you'd try and hike all the way to the train station," he said. "Now climb on in."

****

"That was the ugliest sound I ever heard!" cried Martina after she sprang up from the floor.

"It wasn't meant to be pretty, you know," said Laura. Then Martina attempted to make a face to match the dissonant chord that Laura loudly and unexpectedly struck. Her efforts launched both girls into fits of laughter.

"It's a nice day," Laura managed to say through her laughter. "Let's go outside."

"Let's run through the fields!" Martina clamored.

As always, the prospect of running wild through the fields and the excitement that it would bring flashed in the younger girl's eyes.

"Why don't we sit outside in the sun and watch Big George split logs," suggested Laura. "Then when he's all done, we can help stack them."

"We did that last time," complained Martina. "Today I wanna run through the fields!"

"Fine," grumbled Laura, "we'll run through the fields. But honestly, do we have to look for bugs?"

"Only the interesting ones," said Martina.

"I don't see what's so interesting about ladybugs and grasshoppers," Laura sneered. "If you ask me, I think they're ugly. And besides, they give me the willies."

"You should've never been born a farm girl," said Martina.

"It was just my luck," said Laura. "But one day when I'm older, I'll live in a city. And when that day comes, I'll get to look at tall buildings and fine lady shops, and there'll be no bugs—not even the interesting ones."

Despite all the complaining and cajoling, Martina exploded through the door with Laura trailing a few paces behind. Together they went tearing through the farm, while waving and hollering hello to Big George and Miss Lillie. Big George rested his ax at his side and delighted in the girls' youthful energy with his usual shoulder pumping laughter.

"That Martina sure can run, can't she?" he said with a gleam, when turning to Miss Lillie.

"Like a lil' whippet, she is," replied Miss Lillie. "Anymore she's gettin' to where she's too fast for my eyes to keep track of her."

"She makes us all seem a lil' older than we is," said Big George. "But she sure makes this old farm a lively place, she does…like back when me, Mick, and Edgar were young'uns."

"You both best be back in time for supper," Miss Lillie called out, but her warning never reached the ears of the young sprinters. The girls sprinted until they reached the wide open field beyond the acres of sorghum. Martina mercifully stopped to allow Laura to catch her breath.

"Let's go all the way to the creek this time!" she cried, unable to contain her enthusiasm. Her restless legs were clamoring to unleash their untapped energy. Before Laura had the chance to regard her unsuitable clothing for such a journey, (during their last creek adventure she spoiled her dress) Martina was already pulling her along. "Come on," she cried. "Maybe we'll spot some critters!"

"Gee, I can't wait." Her drollness notwithstanding, Laura allowed herself to be pulled along by her younger overzealous sidekick. However, before they made it halfway through the field that led to the woods, through which ran the aforementioned creek, Laura came to an abrupt stop.

"Your feet aren't hurting you already, are they?" asked the rough and tumble Martina, who at times would lose patience when Laura displayed too much daintiness.

"My feet are just fine," replied Laura with a hint of indignation.

"Then what?" asked Martina.

"That!" snapped Laura. She pointed in the direction where she wanted Martina to look.

Neither Martina, during any of her solo adventures and explorations to the furthest reaches of the farm, nor her and Laura together on their numerous hikes into the woods had even caught a glimpse of Golda. Furthermore, neither had any knowledge of her existence. Whenever Edgar was about to mention, or in some way allude to Golda, Leila would always signal, or make some sound to suggest, *not in front of Laura*. Leila didn't want their young prodigy getting all curious about a crazy woman who occasionally came dancing through the fields. Of course, no one dared mention Golda's name in front of Big George. Nor had anyone deemed it necessary to forewarn Martina about the crazy woman, who from time to time came dancing through the field like someone who had escaped an asylum for the insane.

"Hey, lady," Martina called out to Golda. Golda acted as though she didn't hear the youngster, or perhaps was unable.

"Shhh," scolded Laura. "She might be crazy, ya know. I heard those crazy people can be dangerous."

"She looks happy to me," said Martina.

"That's how they look, crazy people...like they're too crazy to know any better," Laura pointed out.

"Let's follow her," Martina boldly suggested.

"Are you crazy?" said Laura. "She might lead us to a whole village of crazy people. We could end up being barbecued...or worse!"

"That's the silliest thing I ever heard," said Martina, and she rolled her eyes at Laura's outlandish notion. "She's probably headed for the creek, which is where we're headed." She grabbed Laura's hand and once again began pulling her along.

Martina directed her steps toward Golda. Golda continued to meander about, appearing to have no sense of purpose or any knowledge that she was being trailed after by two young girls. Ignoring Laura's warning, the fearless Martina quickened her steps. Laura was still holding Martina's hand, but remained a half pace behind. At last sensing the girl's presence, Golda abandoned her childlike gyrating in favor of a more purposeful march. She began heading in the direction of the woods—a place to where she often escaped and where she hoped to be left alone. Martina pressed onward, though, her short choppy steps quickening. Despite Laura's trepidation, she remained only a half pace behind, still clinging to Martina's hand. Golda glanced back, as she sensed that the gap between the girls and her was narrowing.

The sun's position was impeding Martina's ability to make out Golda's expression of fear. However, it allowed Golda to clearly see Martina's determination. As Golda's fear and Laura's apprehension swelled, so emboldened became Martina. Just as the young girl was about to call out to Golda, the terrified woman began running through the field with abandon.

Golda knew every path—every nook and cranny of the vast woods that she so desperately tried to gain. For years the woods had been her haven. Once there, she would locate one of her many hiding places and remain safe from the world and all its cruelty.

Martina broke free from Laura's hand and began chasing after Golda. Laura didn't share nor understand Martina's curiosity and determination. Martina didn't understand it herself. If asked, she wouldn't have known whether she was chasing after Golda to make a closer
136

examination of someone Laura perceived as crazy, or if the strange woman, who appeared to be running for her life, needed help. Whatever the reason, Laura felt compelled to join in the chase and was now running stride for stride with her young companion.

For thirty years Golda had lived like an animal. She had been beaten, sodomized, and used in the most dehumanizing ways imaginable. There were men, who, for a short while had taken her in. In those rare instances, she was used as a slave and was shown less regard than a barnyard animal before the men thoughtlessly tossed her back into the world.

Night after night without fail, Miss Lillie would set a plate of food out for Golda. There were stretches that went on for days and sometimes weeks when the plates remained untouched. No sooner Miss Lillie had sighed, thinking that the good Lord had showed mercy and had finally taken Golda, she would wake and find an empty plate licked clean.

With all that Golda, for decades had consciously or otherwise endured, she had never been chased after. Without having any clear understanding of why, she was moving with purpose, and that purpose was urgency. With each stride influenced by urgency, feelings which for years had remained dormant were now beginning to awaken and were inching her closer to reality. She stumbled, but only momentarily, when glancing backward to see the young, determined legs of Martina and Laura gaining on her. She reached down deep, hoping to find the necessary strength to outrun her pursuers. Despite her being overcome with fear, her strides remained swift and true. Still, her pursuers continued to gain ground.

On and on went the chase—the hunted desperately trying to gain the woods, where stood the chance of hiding herself away—the unyielding hunters in pursuit. On a summer's day and sundrenched field, it was young versus old—discovery versus fear. At last, and with the woods only a hundred yards away, Golda's distressed lungs began to falter—her gait, which all along had been steady, began to unravel. At the point where the field met the woods, she was overtaken—the youthful legs of Martina and Laura had proven too much. At that spot, Golda went tumbling hard to the ground—her bony, undernourished body rolling forward several times before coming to a stop. Martina and Laura stood at what each concluded was a safe distance.

They watched, as Golda, while prostrate on the ground gasped for air. The girls held their collected breaths waiting for Golda to say something, or to make some sort of move. They took an apprehensive step backward, when Golda, despite the effort that it took, rose to her feet. Unsteadily, the frightened woman began backing her way into the woods. She had only gone a few paces, though, when she found her back resting against a tree which impeded her progress. From there, she sent her arms flailing outward in wild gesticulations, as a haunted animal would when attempting to ward off those perceived as predators.

"You see, I told you that she was crazy," whispered Laura.

Ignoring Laura, Martina called, "Are you okay, Miss?"

"Of course she isn't okay," was Laura's snippy remark. "Just look at her, for crying out loud. Crazy people *aren't* okay."

"Please, Ma'am, let us help you," pleaded Martina.

Martina's entreaty caused Laura to roll her eyes and to believe that she was no longer in the company of one, but perhaps *two* crazy people. Though when further witnessing her young friend's compassion and uncompromising willingness to reach out to a stranger, albeit one perceived as crazy, Laura began to feel ashamed.

In the past, despite much complaining, Laura Trudeau delighted in Martina Cordero's energy, and celebrated her unabashed ways. Now, although in the presence of one believed to be lacking any understanding, she was feeling overshadowed and saw herself as weak and ineffectual. She stood motionless and silent and watched Martina boldly step forward and again try to reach Golda, and through means of compassion gain her trust. With all her youthful beauty and talent, inadequacy was not a feeling to which Laura Trudeau was accustomed. Finally, but while remaining a step behind Martina, she managed to peep, "You don't have to be afraid of us. We won't do you any arm."

"I don't think she's afraid of *us*," said Martina, though her notion was unfounded.

"Then who?" snapped Laura, as though, right or wrong, she was bothered by the alleged perceptiveness of one four years her junior.

"I don't know," replied Martina. "I can't explain it. I just know it's not *us* she's afraid of.*"*

"That's not much help," said Laura.

Nevertheless, Martina was correct; it wasn't the girls themselves that Golda feared. It was reality piercing through her cocoon of insanity that she found so threatening. It was reality that Golda feared; not the threat of being beaten, or sodomized. Somehow being chased down by two young girls brought her to that threshold.

Finally Golda's arms began to relax—her posture became less defensive.

"What's your name?" asked Martina.

All Golda could do was to stare at the ground and tremble in response to the simple question.

"If you come back to the farm with us, we can get you help," Martina told her.

"She's right," Laura chimed in. "My dad and my mom, and Miss Lillie and Big George will surely know what to do."

As if struck forcefully by something unseen, Golda dropped to her knees. There came upon her face only a vestige of unspeakable and long suppressed torment, yet it caused Martina and Laura to shudder. Golda tried to cry, but could only manage strange, throaty groans that sounded less than human, but not quite animal. The sounds came deep from within. An agony that had been buried for decades, with all its strength, was trying to surface and at last find its voice.

Martina went and knelt down beside Golda. "What's wrong?" she asked, not raising her voice much above a hush.

Golda pointed to herself, then folded her arms to mimic a cradle. She rocked them back and forth, and while she did so, tears trailed down her cheeks.

"I think she's trying to tell us she's someone's mama," said Laura.

No sooner had Laura finished her accurate interpretation of Golda's pantomime, she and Martina looked at one another as if struck by the same realization.

"Are you Big George's mama?" asked Martina. The question caused both Martina and Laura's eyes to swell with wonder. Then like a lake whose dam has at last failed, thirty years of suppressed anguish, along with the blotted out image of Ezekiel's hanged and burned body came gushing to the surface.

****

"Them two young'uns have been gone for quite awhile now, I'd say," said Miss Lillie. "Too long, in fact."

"Most likely they's down by the creek," said Big George. "An' our Martina...I bet she tryin' to get poor lil' Miss Laura good an' brave enough to cross it." Then he added after swiftly bringing down his ax on a log, "Either that, or she's showin' her all the holes where the rabbits and moles be hidin'."

"All's I know is, if that lil' Miss Laura comes home with one more of them pretty dresses of hers all spoiled, Leila's gonna get plenty angry, she is," said Miss Lillie. "She gonna take both them girls and ship 'em on out. That's for damn..."

Miss Lillie had a pail of water in one hand and a scrub brush in the other, both of which she dropped before staggering. She hadn't much agility remaining in her old, frail body, but what little there was allowed her to stagger forward just far enough to successfully reach the very table which she was preparing to clean, before finding herself on the ground.

"Dear God in heaven!" she cried. "Praise sweet Jesus, it's a miracle!"

Big George laid down his ax and alertly went to Miss Lillie's side. He held onto her until he was confident that her legs were squarely beneath her. It hadn't occurred to Big George until then, when looking down at his massive hands holding Miss Lillie's frail body, how old she had gotten.

"The good Lord done put everything right, like only He can!" exalted Miss Lillie.

Big George thought it most peculiar for Miss Lillie to praise the heavens with such zeal over a well placed table. Then out of the corner of his eye, on the path that divides the northeast and southeast acres of sorghum, he spotted Martina and Laura. Their return was much more subdued than their exuberant departure. There was no running, skipping, or hollering hello, though their spirits appeared to soar high above the tallest stalks of sorghum. On their faces was much more than the expected happiness that often accompanies childhood in summertime. In fact, it could be said that, two young girls ventured off into the fields as mere children and returned with a greater understanding of what God expected of humankind. Indeed, that's what could be said.

In between Martina and Laura and walking hand in hand with both girls was Golda. Her steps reflected apprehension. On her face was a measure of both sadness and fear. However, if one was to look very hard, one would also discover a glimmer of peace, and therefore, hope.

"Tex, will ya come an' look at this!" exclaimed Pawtucket Jim.

"Well, I'll be a son-of-a-bitch," said Tex Billingsly. "Now I seen everything."

"Them two gals are really somethin' else," said Pawtucket Jim.

Leila, who by then had been keeping an eye out for Laura, was quite bemused as she held onto the railing when she stepped down from the porch. Edgar had abandoned the task of unhooking his draft horses from the plow in order to observe what Miss Lillie had described as, *a miracle.*

"I didn't think I'd live long enough to see this day," cried Miss Lillie.

Big George released the grip he had all along maintained on Miss Lillie and dutifully returned to his ax. He wasn't filled with the same sense of wonder as the others. It would take *some* effort and getting used to on his part, but Golda had at long last returned.

****

In a letter to Edgar, Pablo wrote:

> *You were right; the change of scenery has done me a world of good. I can't imagine anything more beautiful than summer in Kentucky. And like you, Cornelius Crow is a good man to work for.*
>
> *P.S. Kindly pass along to Big George that his artistry has been well appreciated up here at Crow's Farm.*

What Pablo omitted, for he didn't feel it necessary to mention: harvesting summer fruit wasn't as labor intensive as harvesting sorghum. Cornelius Crow left the care of horses, swine, and cattle, along with the harvesting of hay and tobacco, and the milling of corn and wheat in the experienced hands of his workers not affected by the influenza. The last minute recruits, who were organized by a man named Gabriel, a long time hand of the farm, were awarded the less strenuous task of harvesting the many acres of various fruits and berries.

Pablo spent most of his days working right alongside fifteen-year-old Cornelius Crow Jr. and another young man of around the same age called Flynn. Cornelius Crow's younger son, Ernest, was supposed to have made it a foursome, as the recruits were to work in teams of four, with each team having the responsibility for certain sections. But the younger Ernest did all he could to avoid anything that resembled farm work, including faking an occasional dizzy spell. He was a frail sort was Ernest—not at all robust like his older brother and father. Mostly, he took to reading and studying. It mattered not that it was summertime; reading and studying was what Ernest enjoyed, and the influenza epidemic caused farming to get in the way of his intellectual pursuits.

Despite the summer of '09, being that as it was, a time of crisis, Ernest invented all sorts of excuses to retreat to his books. When he *did* bother to join his team in body, he usually did more talking than working, and would ramble on and on about anything, as long as it had nothing to do with farm work. Pablo found his leaps from the philosophy of Schopenhauer, to passages from Dickens refreshing and a terrific source of amusement, and that his constant jabbering made the day pass with an air of pleasantness. However, Flynn didn't see it that way. In fact, there wasn't much that Flynn *did* find amusing, including Pablo and Cornelius's occasional attempts at polite humor. Flynn would stare contemptuously at them whenever they shared an impromptu gag, or a light hearted moment, then he would return to the task at hand as though begrudging the world for its own sake.

"Not a real friendly sort, is he?" Pablo whispered to young Cornelius.

"His daddy's got a farm about ten miles to the north," said Cornelius, "and he's madder than a pile of cow puckies that he got sent here for the summer. Acts like he's in prison, he does."

"You'd think he'd be glad to get away and have the opportunity to earn some money," said Pablo.

"You'd think," agreed Cornelius. "But he sure don't see it that way."

Flynn spat on the ground to demonstrate his contempt for Ernest's latest jabbering. Then he glared at Pablo and young Cornelius for encouraging the antics of the younger boy.

"No need to be so sour," said Pablo. "Ernest is just trying to keep things on the lighter side. He means no harm."

"Yeah, well maybe you should mind your own damn business, Mister!" snapped Flynn. "I don't need to be takin' advice from no Mexicans!"

Pablo stepped in front of young Cornelius, who was about to rise up against the foul tempered Flynn.

"It's alright, son," he said, trying to defuse the situation. "A fellow's entitled to blow off a little steam every now and again." Turning toward Flynn, he added, "I have a seven-year-old daughter all the way down in Texas. And believe me, there's not a minute of the day when I'm not missing her. But that's alright, because I'm sure there's more than a few of us that are here not because we want to be. But since we *are* here, we may as well try and make the most of it."

Pablo figured that if Flynn was made aware of how duty separated him from Martina, he might not act so foul tempered. But Flynn glared right back at Pablo with those same contemptuous eyes. Being the man that he was, Pablo reached down deep to try and find empathy for a young man whom he figured must be troubled and therefore was acting out. But the young and sour Mr. Flynn surely didn't make it easy.

There was still three weeks to go before the first sorghum harvest when Pablo was preparing to leave Crow's Farm.

"Not that I wish anyone poor health, but it sure was nice having you around," a most grateful Gabriel told Pablo.

"Yeah, I sure hate to see ya go," said the senior Cornelius Crow. Pablo complimented Cornelius Crow on his "two fine sons," then thanked him and Gabriel for the opportunity to work on a farm that he had heard about since arriving in Madisonville, Texas as a frightened young man with a broken heart. Before he went on his way, he made one final peace offering to Flynn, but the sour young man would have none of it.

Flynn notwithstanding, Pablo enjoyed working with young Cornelius and would miss Ernest's shenanigans, but he was glad to be heading back to Texas and Martina. Little did he know, twenty-one years later he would return to Crow's Farm with his granddaughter.

With still plenty of time until the sorghum harvest, Pablo figured it was a good opportunity to drop in on the Crandalls and Hutchinsons. *Betsy will surely get a real charge when she learns where I just came from,* he thought. But upon his arrival at Madisonville, it was Pablo who received the surprise, when learning that Doc Crandall was hospitalized.

"They say I got a bum ticker," grumbled Doc. "But what the hell do these doctors know, anyhow? You'll see, I'll be as good as new in a couple of days."

Pablo looked over at Alice Crandall, whose eyes clearly didn't share Doc's optimism. It was a fact that she tried to conceal, though without success.

"Enough with all the gloomy faces," said Doc. "I'm too damned stubborn to kick the bucket just yet."

With still plenty of time until the harvest, Pablo elected to stay on with Alice until Doc was home and resting comfortably. Once there, Doc grumbled to Pablo, as though somehow Martina could have slipped his mind, "Hey, don't you have a daughter to get home to?" Before Pablo could answer, Doc further grumbled, "Well then, what are you waiting for. Lord knows I have enough babysitters in this ding blasted town! And speaking of this town, where's Ben and Betsy? I thought there'd be a blueberry pie waiting for me in the kitchen."

"You have to watch your diet from now on," Alice Crandall reminded the disgruntled doctor.

"Oh, fiddlesticks," grumbled Doc.

Pablo almost made it to the door before Doc yelled, "Just make sure you and that little lady of yours are back here for Christmas!"

Pablo did an about-face, saluted Doc, and then headed back to Trudeau's Farm and Martina.

Upon his return, Pablo first stopped at the main house, but no one was answering the door; nor could he hear a single strain of melody coming from Laura's piano. It was an unusual scene that he stumbled upon after winding his way down the pathway to the bunk house. Big George was sitting on a bench, but with his back to the table. His shoulders were moving in their familiar manner, but Pablo had a hunch that this time Big George wasn't laughing. By this time of day, Tex Billingsly and Pawtucket Jim were on their way home, but for whatever reason both had chose to remain. The two appeared pensive and were pacing in front of Big George. Laura was there, too, holding onto Golda's hand. Pablo sensed that he hadn't returned to the same place that a month ago he had left—that things at Trudeau's Farm changed and not necessarily for the better.

Laura was looking quite grim, Pablo could tell. Golda, for whatever reason, appeared to be shouldering the responsibility for whatever was causing the collective grimness. As Pablo came closer, he could only recognize Martina by her sorrowful cries, as her slight figure was eclipsed by Big George's massive frame. Martina held tight to Big George's arm and together they wept openly. Pablo ran to their side.

"What's the matter?" he cried. Then he looked up at the grim faces of the others and hung his head. He quick rose to his feet and made his way to Miss Lillie and Big George's place. He pushed opened the door, fearful of what he suspected would be discovered. There lay Miss Lillie, with Edgar, Leila, and Mick gathered around and looking on as though they never believed the day would come.

"She was the closest thing I had to a mom," said Mick, whose memory of his own mother was vague at best, and what he did remember wasn't particularly pleasant.

"It seems forever that she's been this farm's matriarch," said Edgar. "I can't remember the world without her and I can't begin to count the ways that we're all gonna miss her."

While Edgar and Mick paid tribute to Miss Lillie by recalling their childhood, Pablo stared down at her coal black, bony hands—the very hands that reared Martina. He bent down and kissed them. "The most beautiful hands in the world," he softly uttered. "May God welcome them into Heaven."

Edgar excused himself, leaving Leila, Mick, and Pablo with Miss Lillie. He went and placed a comforting hand on Big George's shoulder and said, "Don't worry, my dear old friend, I'll make all the arrangements." He started off for the main house, but only went a few paces before he
144

stopped. Turning toward the grim gathering he said, "Right now I'm feeling ashamed." The odd remark gained everyone's attention. He then added, sounding a bit bewildered, "I have no idea how old our Miss Lillie was." He looked over at Big George, who looked no less bewildered. Then a faint and humble voice was heard saying, "Seventy-seven." For a moment it seemed that everyone stopped breathing. Then they all looked over at Golda, who, with as much poise as she could summon repeated, "Our Miss Lillie was seventy-seven."

By the time Pablo exited the cabin, Big George and Martina had gone and wandered off into the cornfield. There they spoke not of death and how their lives would change, but of their respective tasks when the sun would rise on the following morning.

"I'll be up bright and early milking the cows," said Martina.

"And I'll be out there bright an' early in the fields," said Big George. "An' 'fore ya know it, we'll have *sweet* sorghum, we will!"

"And I can make the biscuits," boasted Martina. "I watched Miss Lillie a thousand times."

"Oh, I know ya can my sweet child," said Big George. "I surely know ya can." Then he reached down and lifted Martina so that they were face to face. At first Martina began humming. Then together they sang: *Joshua fit the battle of Jericho, Jericho, Jericho. Joshua fit the battle of Jericho, and the walls came tumblin' down.*

Chapter Six
The Art of Entitlement

"What's that, Grandfather?" asked Anna Maria, as she and Pablo were coming upon the Holy Ghost Mission when strolling from the train station in Saint Louis.

"It's a soup kitchen," Pablo told his young traveling companion. Then he explained, "When folks fall on hard times, they can come to places like the Holy Ghost Mission for something to eat." Pablo shook his head sadly when he noticed on the front windows of the Holy Ghost Mission, large cursive letters that read *Reilly's Saloon*. On the door, with much less artistic presentation, were the printed words, *Reilly's Café*; no doubt a slight alteration owing to Prohibition. The 18st amendment effectively killed the saloon, whereas the café in all likelihood was evidence of another Depression casualty. Now it was a haven—a soup kitchen. Pablo stopped and peered through the window. He imagined in a town as musically sophisticated as Saint Louis, in its heyday Reilly's Saloon had a gentleman barkeeper very much like Sam Ott to dole out its spirits, while musicians with the skills of Miles Gordon displayed their virtuosity. As for what might have gone on upstairs, he didn't bother to speculate.

"Too many of us will need places like this before long," Pablo muttered as he began to walk away.

It was uncharacteristic for Pablo to express such negativity in front of Anna Maria. He believed it his duty to shield his granddaughter from any sort of unpleasantness the world had to offer. He was angry for his momentary lapse.

Anna Maria didn't know whether to look into the eyes of those downtrodden souls waiting in line to enter the mission or to look away. She felt herself being pulled along and rather abruptly.

"What's wrong, Grandfather?" she cried.

Anna Maria had to trot along in order to keep up with Pablo. Pablo had turned his back on the Holy Ghost Mission and was walking as though he couldn't get far enough away from the place.

"Nothing," was Pablo's whispered cry, but Anna Maria could sense that her grandfather was in distress.

It was thirty years ago that Lefty Carson said goodbye to Mick and the bonfire gang in favor of his Uncle Lou's cement company in Saint Louis, Missouri. Every so often letters and photographs of children would come floating down from Saint Louis to Brownsville, but Pablo hadn't seen Lefty in person...until today.

Like Anna Maria, Pablo didn't know whether to look or to avert his eyes when he passed by the slumping figures lined up to enter the Holy Ghost Mission. It was only out of the corner of his eye that he was able to spot his old friend. But there was no mistake; even after all these years he knew at once that it was Lefty Carson.

"I'm fine now," said Pablo; though it was a struggle for him to regain his composure. "I just thought I saw an old friend standing in line waiting to enter the mission. But I realize now that I must've been mistaken. After all, what would an old friend from Brownsville be doing standing in front of a mission in Saint Louis? I don't know what I could've been thinking. Well, come now my sweet Cheerianna, we've got a train to catch."

Anna Maria was no more fooled by Pablo's attempt to convince himself otherwise of the truth than was Pablo. Nevertheless, she elected not to press her grandfather on the issue, and allowed herself to be pulled along toward the station.

"Uh oh," said Anna Maria after they boarded the train. She directed Pablo's attention to the woman with the absurd hat, who was already seated and awaiting the train's departure.

"Uh oh, is right," said Pablo. "I was hoping that Saint Louis was her final destination."

"Wouldn't it be funny if she was going to Crow's Farm, too?" Anna Maria giggled at the improbable irony.

"Oh, that would be funny, alright." Pablo raised a brow to imply that his granddaughter's sense of humor was becoming a bit warped. "However," he added, "if I was a gambling man, I'd be willing to wager the contents of my bag that woman has never set foot on a farm."

In a blatant display, the woman with the absurd hat turned up her nose at Pablo and Anna Maria as they walked down the aisle of the train to their seats. The woman's actions prompted Pablo to squeeze Anna Maria's hand—a not so subtle reminder for her to suppress the giggle that was no doubt forming in the back of her throat. As they made for their seats, a whole new set of passengers, minus the woman with the absurd hat, looked on with fascination at Anna Maria's striking mane of cinnamon hair, exotic Mayan features, and complexion that was much fairer than the man presumed her guardian.

"What's Crow's Farm like, Grandfather?" she asked. No sooner Anna Maria had gotten the words out, Pablo got that look that comes over him whenever he was about to regale his granddaughter with one of his more fanciful tales.

"I've visited many places throughout my days and travels," he said, "and I can say with certainty there's nothing more beautiful than summer in Kentucky. And there's no better place to see the summer unfolding day after day, week after week, than on Crow's Farm. The smell of fresh strawberries just as they ripen—peaches so big and juicy they bend down the branches so that they dangle right under your nose when you walk by…"

On and on Pablo gushed. As the train chugged its way through Missouri, he made a promise to himself that, if and when he was able to secure a position at Crow's Farm, he would return to Saint Louis and the Holy Ghost Mission and find his old friend, Lefty Carson.

****

Pablo was anxious to return to life in Brownsville. It was once again time for a home of his own and to see Martina off to school. Despite the sound reasons for at last wanting to make his departure from Trudeau's Farm, he made a promise to Big George that he would stay on until the very last stalk of sorghum was fed through the press.

Before leaving, Mick had warned Pablo that during his absence the town of Brownsville underwent some changes, particularly after an incident known as The Brownsville Raid. Following the attack of a white woman, soldiers from companies B, C, and D of the black Twenty-fifth United State infantry, some of whom had returned to Fort Brown from duty in the Philippines, were met with racial discrimination by local businessmen.

Afterward, they were accused of a brief shooting spree that killed one and maimed another. Pablo remembered hearing about the incident, but didn't consider how it could affect his return, or reshape the town for the worse. The raid in combination with the influx of white protestants, who were reluctant to assimilate, helped create racial and ethnic divisions that before hadn't existed.

"So I won't be able to live on the same street as before," Pablo said with a shrug to both Mick and Smokey Bones. He seemed untroubled by the news, that come what may, nothing could dissuade him from returning to Brownsville.

After finding a suitable home, getting Martina situated in school, and returning to his old job, where he was enthusiastically reunited with the old bonfire gang, next on Pablo's *to do* list was a visit to Abercrombie's Drugstore to stock up on his favorite hard candy. He wasn't all the way through the door, though, when a young woman, in an exaggerated display of affection, threw her arms around him.

"Thank you!" she repeated over and over again.

Pablo, out of politeness, returned the young woman's eager embrace. "You're welcome," he said as many times, minus the vivacity. He had no idea why he was being thanked and hugged with such zeal.

"It's me, remember?" the young woman cried. "Marcie…Marcie Cooper!"

"Oh, right, of course," said Pablo. He tried to match Marcie's exuberance, but was still overwhelmed from the ambush. "You look so…different," he added, while gesturing to Marcie's conservative attire.

"Well, I gotta dress according to my job…ya know what I mean," she whispered. Then she winked at Pablo—a subtle gesture to indicate that no one in Brownsville was yet aware of her past employment. Pablo returned Marcie's wink with one of his own to let her know that she should have every confidence that her secret shall remain just *that*…a secret.

"Oh, and look!" she exclaimed. She first struck a pose, then held out her left hand to show Pablo the sparkling gem that adorned her finger. "I'm engaged to be married! Can you believe it! This is the life I used to dream of!"

On the night Pablo walked away from The Inn, he figured there was about a one in ten chance that Marcie Cooper would do the right thing and *take the money and run,* as they say. Most in her dubious position would back down from the challenge of a new life and stay with what they know—spinning their wheels year after year until they're all used up…or worse.

"Well, I guess congratulations are in order," said Pablo, though he was congratulating Marcie Cooper more for a brave and wise decision, instead of her impending marriage. This Marcie had no way of knowing, and moreover, she didn't care, as she was too busy beaming over the fiery gem that was so well displayed on her finger. She invited Pablo to give the precious stone a closer examination. After complying, Pablo looked beyond Marcie Cooper over to Mr. Abercrombie, who he hoped would soon come to his rescue.

"He's a real nice fella, too," said Marcie. "He stopped in here a couple years ago and bought a one pound bag of hard candy. He said it was for a good friend of his, who was away working on some farm."

"*Really?*" said Pablo.

Pablo's gaze broke away from Mr. Abercrombie. He no longer wanted to be rescued. His ears picked up and his interest swelled. He was prepared to give Marcie Cooper his undivided attention.

"Yes sir," said Marcie. "And do you know what happened next?

"I can't imagine," said Pablo.

Pablo couldn't resist the droll reply, though his wryness had gotten lost on the former prostitute, but not on Mr. Abercrombie, who chuckled accordingly.

"Well, he came back the very next day wantin' another one pound bag," said Marcie. "He said his friend really likes hard candy—eats it like it's goin' outa style. Well, I was gonna ask him why he just didn't buy a two pound bag when he was in the day before. But I figured it wasn't just the hard candy that he was wantin' to come back for."

"Well, I guess you figured right," said Pablo. Then he looked over at Mr. Abercrombie and winked.

"Yep, I guess so," said Marcie, who couldn't stop beaming. Then she added excitedly, "Well, one thing led to another, and now I'm gonna be a married woman!" Once again she displayed the fiery gem.

"Again, congratulations," said Pablo. He then agilely slipped around the exuberant woman on his way to see Mr. Abercrombie.

Martina was very patient while her father and Mr. Abercrombie took the time to get reacquainted. She stayed behind and had allowed herself to get roped into admiring Marcie Cooper's ring. It wasn't a grasshopper in an open field, or a critter in the woods; nor was it a cornfield, or Beethoven as played by Laura Trudeau—things that stirred young Martina Cordero. Despite not knowing what to make of the fiery gem, to Marcie Cooper's delight, Martina managed to display a fair amount of interest.

150

"Here," said Mr. Abercrombie, "it's on the house." He handed Pablo a copy of *The Brownsville Herald.*

"Gee, Mister, it was real nice seein' ya," said Marcie. "Stop in again real soon."

"Oh, don't you worry, I will," said Pablo with a wry smile. "We'll be seeing plenty of each other… believe me." Just as he was about to open the door, he turned and added, "By the way; that friend whose been away working on a farm? Tell that cheapskate future husband of yours that he's all out of hard candy." Mr. Abercrombie erupted with laughter. Then Pablo exited the drugstore. When doing so, he left behind a very perplexed Marcie Cooper.

So what if Mick is twice the age of a girl who once tried to convince me that she was twenty-one years old and named Juliet, thought Pablo. Despite the odd match, Pablo had to acknowledge that Marcie Cooper was far better off working for Mr. Abercrombie and marrying the undisputed leader of the old bonfire gang, than had she remained at The Inn.

Just as they had every night since arriving in Brownsville, when leaving Abercrombie's Drugstore, Pablo and Martina strolled hand in hand through the quiet town. As they went about their way, Pablo relived his past.

Martina especially enjoyed watching the lamplighters, though they soon would become obsolete, as a plan for electric lighting was to begin within the year. She also enjoyed taking ferry rides to Matamoros. Martina listened with interest as Pablo spoke volumes about the many structures on which he worked, especially the boardwalk, which upon her insistence was included in their nightly strolls. Martina giggled when first learning the names of Pablo's friends—minus of course, Fat Fuck McGinn, whom Pablo wisely omitted. And where Martina was concerned, the Saint Louis bound Lefty Carson was simply another lefthander. With already having such colorful characters as Frankie "The Prick" Donato, Dirty Jack Doyle, and Smokey Bones with which to amuse his daughter, there was no need to mention Lefty's overachieving testicle.

What Martina had little or no appreciation for when on their nightly strolls, was Pablo's melancholy—the bittersweet expressions that came over him, when word for word he repeated romantic utterances spoken during a time before she was born, and in the very places where they were exchanged. Even at age seven, Martina was astute enough to understand that getting dragged all over town for the purpose of her father reenacting his first date with the mother she never knew, was a strange and morbid exercise. Once, when she thought for sure her feet

151

couldn't take another step, she was dragged to the Blessed Juan Diego de Guadalupe Roman Catholic Church. There, she was told to sit in the very pew where Pablo first gazed upon and then allowed his mind to wonder about Anna Maria. For her father's sake, Martina tried to understand the purpose of these nightly charades, in which she at first was willing, but then later begrudgingly was a participant. With each passing day, though, her own identity was slowly and unmistakably supplanted with her father's hyper-romantic memories of her deceased mother.

"Are you alright?" Pablo asked, when noticing Martina's lifeless gaze one night when they rode the ferry back from Matamoros.

"I cry every night for Miss Lillie," she told him. "And I miss Laura and Big George."

Right before Pablo's eyes, all the life drained from Martina's slight figure. With her limp body and sallow eyes, she looked more worn than a child ever should. Since arriving in Brownsville, gone was the girl who woke with the cockcrow and attacked each day with vigor. Gone was the girl who milked cows, churned butter, and with fire and spirit ran through open fields. It mattered not how many splendorous moonlit nights Pablo saw shining down on the Rio Grande from the ferry or the boardwalk; they would never again possess the same magic they once had when with Anna Maria. At last, it occurred to him that he was perpetrating seven years of delayed grief on the delicate shoulders of Martina, and all for the sake of keeping the memory Anna Maria alive, or to achieve some sense of closure—he wasn't sure which. This he did, while wrongly ignoring the fact that, Martina had been ripped away from loved ones during a time when she was trying to come to terms with her own grief. For her sake, this self-serving fantasy, or dark charade, as it became, had to end.

"Miss Lillie truly was an amazing woman," said Pablo. "I miss her, too. And I promise, starting from this very moment, all this lunacy will come to an end." Then he took Martina into his arms and lifted her up so that they were face to face. He nuzzled her nose just as he often did when she was a toddler.

"It's nice to see your smile again," he said. "I miss that." Then he carried Martina from the ferry across the boardwalk and onto the street. There he set her down. When he did, her spirit was once again light—her feet nimble.

"Let's walk all night long!" she clamored. Pablo grew misty eyed when hearing the excitement returned to his daughter's voice. Not since their departure for Trudeau's Farm had he seen anything but sorrow in her eyes.

152

"Yes, let's!" he cried, matching her youthful enthusiasm. "And together we'll pretend to see everything for the first time!"

****

It was the Christmas of '09, that Pablo Cordero last saw Doc Crandall alive. It took some effort on the part of the old Pennsylvania Dutchman, who lived most of his adult life in Madisonville, Texas, but Doc Crandall was as sharp and jovial as ever. And despite the medication, which he took under Alice Crandall's supervision—or "duress," as he liked put it, he hit the punchbowl with his usual regularity. Doc wasn't particularly thirsty, nor strived for impairment; instead, it was his way of proving to Alice that his *so-called* "bum ticker" as he came to refer to his failing organ, was all "a bunch of poppycock."

That was Doc, always making light of his health for Alice's benefit.

"I'm seventy-four years old, for cryin' out loud! How much longer can I live?" he bellowed, before throwing back his last swallow of punch. Then he firmly brought down his glass on the table as though it was the exclamation point to his remarks. He then added with a chuckle, while pointing skyward, "Besides, it's high time the man upstairs got rid of me and made room for someone else."

Earlier on when regarding his health, Doc Crandall had gone from denial to cantankerous. Lately he has bypassed acceptance on the way to humorous.

"I had a damn good life," he said. "And I surely don't need to be hanging around until I have to eat mush or can no longer recognize my beautiful bride. If this was to be my last supper, it'd be fine by me."

Doc fought off fatigue in order to have one last merry Christmas with his loved ones and dear friends of Madisonville, Texas. "Come on Pastor," he had playfully urged earlier on when mixing the punch bowl, "give my elbow another good hit!" As always, Somerset Evans obliged.

Later on during dessert, Martina patted Pablo on his belly after he shoveled the last forkful of blueberry pie from his plate into his mouth. "Are you trying to tell me something?" he asked, feigning indignation. Doc's smile was one of warmth and affection when he listened to the lighthearted banter exchanged between father and daughter regarding the plump middle that of late was growing on Pablo.

"He tries to tell me that it's all muscle," said Martina for Doc's benefit. Despite Doc's effort to laugh at the youngster's droll remark, Pablo could clearly read the fatigue in the old doctor's eyes. He gazed across the table at Doc and nodded. Doc nodded in return. That's the way it was with Doc and Pablo—their more meaningful exchanges were usually silent. It may have been God's will that Dolci Cordero reached the town of Madisonville before succumbing, but it was Doc Crandall, who from there took matters into his own hands. Pablo could never look at Doc without gratitude in his eyes, and Doc's warm smile always meant, *you're welcome, son.* Today, while sitting across from one another, with good cheer and holiday festivity ringing in their ears, Doc Crandall and Pablo Cordero said goodbye.

It was in the spring of 1910, when Doc Crandall made his departure from the world. His funeral ended up a marathon—a celebration of a life well lived, as darn near everyone in town eulogized the good doctor.

"What a blessing for us all to have had a man like Doc Crandall in our midst," said Ben Hutchinson.

****

Back in April of 1909, after the concrete foundation was poured and steel spans were constructed by the Wisconsin Bridge and Iron Company of Milwaukee, a local construction crew that included Dirty Jack Doyle, Frankie "The Prick" Donato, Fat Fuck McGinn, Smokey Bones, and Mick began erecting the Brownsville/Matamoros Bridge. It would become the first permanent structure spanning the Rio Grande.

Shortly after the sorghum harvest, Pablo joined the work force. When he did, he was quick to discover that Frankie "The Prick" Donato and Fat Fuck McGinn hadn't lost their touch; their singing was just as atrocious as he remembered. He also learned that the criticism that followed a given number was no less sharp. Smokey Bones was the most creative of the bunch when it came to critiquing the dubious crooners, and he brought his A-game every day.

"Good God a mighty!" he shrieked, once Donato and McGinn finished crooning "By the Light of the Silvery Moon". "If I ate a hill of beans, I coulda farted the son-of-a-bitchin' thing better!"

By then the duo had grown accustomed to the insults and expletives their crooning produced, and so remained impervious to whatever Smokey believed he could accomplish following the consumption of beans. The duo continued serenading the construction crew with the day's popular tunes.

154

The one thing that still rang true of the old bonfire gang was all the hilarity and banter that came as part of the package, and it helped the work days to pass quickly. However, Pablo didn't wish for the days to pass so speedily. He would have preferred that the days linger to the point of exhausting him into an early slumber. That way he would never have to face the lonely evening and ache for his loss. At times the days and nights provided an unbearable contrast.

Following the farce of dragging Martina all over town for the purpose of reenacting his days with Anna Maria, Pablo's effort to acclimate to this new stage of his life came with unexpected hollowness. The town of Brownsville no longer held for him the lure that it once had. All that he had hoped to feel after seven years of pondering his return was shattered. His hollowness left him to brood over whether returning to a place considered a home and haven from his migratory beginnings was a mistake. Just as toiling away on the acres of Trudeau's Farm became his salvation, so, too, did the construction of the Brownsville/Matamoros Bridge.

After observing and then assisting Miss Lillie with the making of countless meals, Martina assumed the responsibility of making sure that the food got cooked and served. The second she arrived home from school, she took the money on the table that Pablo laid out for her in the morning and headed straight for the grocery store. Every night without fail, Pablo returned home to a set table and hot meal.

At Trudeau's Farm, mealtimes were like events with plenty of lively chatter and laughter. Never did breakfast or supper pass without an colorful tale from Tex Billingsly and Pawtucket Jim, a broad grin and hardy laugh from Big George, or thoughtful utterance from Miss Lillie, whose age and wisdom was always appreciated. It wasn't unusual that, from the moment everyone sat down, to the sighing that always followed a meal, all three of these delights had occurred.

Every day at Trudeau's Farm was a celebration of life, land, and the human spirit. Even with Miss Lillie gone, the first and last sorghum harvests were not in any want of spirit. And with a little help from Big George, Martina came up with a fine tasting biscuit over which to pour the thick, sweet syrup.

Presently the Corderos' supper time was a pensive time of day. With the day behind them, Pablo and Martina were feeling like two displaced souls, each having one foot in the past, the other in the present, and no sense of belonging. Life on Trudeau's Farm was the only life that Martina had ever known: The songs that she and Miss Lillie sang together, the broad smile of a gentle giant called Big George, the adventures with Laura, and of course the work...always the work.

Altogether it was a beautiful glowing ember from which grew and spread into something known as her life's fire. Indeed, Trudeau's Farm was the milk of Martina Cordero's young life, and Pablo found it difficult to spark conversation without bringing up the past seven years. To do so led to an evening of melancholy, and not just for Martina. With the working and living arrangements being as they were at Trudeau's Farm, Pablo was never without adult company. Now there existed only work and Martina. Even the nightly strolls, which for awhile provided a spark, became a chore. Everywhere Pablo looked, there was a void which couldn't be filled. He recalled Corina LaSalle's written words: *There are holes so deep and so terribly empty that they cannot possibly be filled. I will pray that you have better luck than I.* For Pablo, the transition back to Brownsville wasn't what he had hoped. Where Martina was concerned, life going forward after only knowing Trudeau's Farm was at least as grim. So there they sat across from one another at supper, with Martina feeling lonely and Pablo alone, each searching for some commonality and happiness after losing those so well loved.

****

In spring of 1910, not long after Doc Crandall's passing, Mick and Marcie were wed. Martina was thrilled to be reunited with Edgar and Big George. They were in the wedding party, and Leila and Laura were expected, so Martina had counted the days until the arrival of the happy occasion.

For years now, Pablo had been an avid letter writer. He often wrote the Crandalls, Hutchinsons, and Carsons. Since returning to Brownsville, his output included frequent corresponding with Edgar and Big George.

"Don't forget to tell Big George how much I miss him," Martina would clamor. It took some doing, but someone found a tuxedo large enough to fit Big George.

Since arriving in Brownsville, aside from Mick and Mr. Abercrombie, Marcie Cooper had yet to reach out and acquire any lasting friendships. Much of her socializing came when fraternizing with patrons of the drugstore, but Mick was the only real social life she knew. Sometimes she would bump into patrons of the drugstore. The exchanges were friendly, for Marcie was one with an inviting disposition, but these exchanges never resulted in anything more than small talk. So when it came time for choosing her bridesmaids, rather than digging up old friends from her former life, who would have made her nervous and jittery on what should be her happiest day, she chose Mr. Abercrombie's daughter, Veronica, with whom she often spoke, but only in passing, and Martina, with whom she felt the most comfortable. It should be duly noted in regards to the wedding party: Before any mismatched duo that eventually went on to enjoy a fair amount of celebrity, such as Bud Fisher's tinhorns, Mutt and Jeff, there was Big George and Martina Cordero, proudly walking side by side down the center aisle of a church.

Their appearance brought about broad smiles from all who attended, but none broader than that of Big George himself. One sad note, though, especially where Martina was concerned; Laura Trudeau was committed to a piano recital, so she and Leila were unable to attend the joyful union.

Martina may have been well past the days of playing hide and seek in the cornfield, but she sure had Big George up and dancing most of the day—if you can call having been lifted three feet off the ground in order to rest her head on one of Big George's massive shoulders, dancing. And as one would suspect, Big George brought along plenty of his special potion with which much toasting was done.

"Here's to the oldest bachelor in town…a bachelor no more!" cheered Smokey Bones.

Mick and Marcie departed for their honeymoon, but not without first having been serenaded by Frankie "The Prick" Donato and Fat Fuck McGinn singing "Let Me Call You Sweetheart."

"Gee, sounds like you boys have been practicing," said Dirty Jack Doyle, as he winked and poked Smokey Bones with his elbow.

"Yeah, wonders never cease," said Smokey Bones. "I could actually recognize it."

At the end of the day a tearful Martina grudgingly let go of Big George's massive arm, allowing Edgar and him to return to the farm, where tomorrow plenty of work awaited them.

"We'll be sure to give Laura your regards," said Edgar.

****

On the day of December 12, 1910, the Brownsville/Matamoros bridge was completed. At day's end, Dirty Jack Doyle, Frankie "The Prick" Donato, Fat Fuck McGinn, Smokey Bones, Mick, and Pablo walked across the bridge into Matamoros and then went on to Bagdad

Beach, where, equipped with an ample supply of Big George's moonshine, they built themselves roaring a bonfire.

The 227 foot expansion came with an elaborate set of tolls, which *The Brownsville Herald* published. Pablo read: *Five cents for walkers, ten cents for equestrians, twenty cents for automobiles. Livestock and trade goods will be taxed.*

"Trade goods?" mused Mick with a curious chuckle. "What if you're a prostitute walking across the bridge? Would you have to pay five cents plus the tax?"

"Depends on whether or not she's aimin' to work the other side of the bridge, I suppose," said Frankie "The Prick" Donato.

"It was only a joke, Frankie, you dumb bastard," bellowed Dirty Jack Doyle.

Pablo cringed, but then managed to force a chuckle. He knew it would require a remarkably keen eye for anyone to recognize even a vestige of *Juliet* after she transitioned into *plain old* Marcie Cooper. After a big swallow of Big George's potion, he realized the likelihood was little to nonexistent. The secret was safe.

"What's that ya say? Twenty cents for automobiles?" said Smokey Bones. "What a rip!"

"Why don't we all pipe down for a minute and let the man finish reading the article," said Mick.

"Twenty cents plus an additional five cents for each passenger," Pablo read as he continued combing through the article.

"There, ya see; it only matters if you own an automobile…which you don't," Frankie "The Prick" Donato reminded Smokey Bones.

"Yeah," chimed in Fat Fucker McGinn.

"Yeah, well, you don't own one either," Smokey Bones shot back.

"When they make 'em big enough, I'll buy one," said Fat Fuck McGinn, slapping his ample belly.

"I don't know about you fellas," said Dirty Jack Doyle, before taking an angry swallow of moonshine, "but I'll swim across that damn river before I pay to cross a bridge that I helped build."

Everyone stopped for a thoughtful pause, before Fat Fuck McGinn cried, "Well, what are ya all lookin' at me for? Jack's the one who said it…Oh, I get now," he added with indignation. "You bastards don't think I can swim, is that it? Well, I'll show you fuckers some buoyancy. You all just stand back and watch the fat man swim!"

Fat Fuck McGinn ripped off his shirt, and with all the agility that his rotundness would allow, he ran yelling like a berserker and dove head first into the Gulf of Mexico.

"Now that's what you call some serious fucking displacement," said Mick.

"Displacement?" said Smokey Bones. "When'd you become a damn scientist?"

One by one they all ripped off their shirts and joined their hefty friend for a drunken swim. After a long and well earned romp, which included everyone having a turn climbing up Fat Fuck McGinn and cannonball diving off his shoulders, and then dunking poor Smokey Bones, they emerged sober. Mick then poked the fire and freshened up everyone's cup.

"A toast," he said. "Here's to building bridges and a job well done."

Afterward Mick took a moment to reflect on their old friend, Lucky Kaminski, before ending the toast on a happy note, by announcing the birth of Lefty and Linda Carson's new baby boy. After each last swallow, one by one the constructors of the Brownsville/Matamoros Bridge laid down, allowing their weary bodies to sink into the soft, cool sand. With The Gulf of Mexico in their ears, they slept peacefully until sunrise.

While the boys were romping about and making merry on the beach, Martina spent the night with Marcie. Before Martina closed her eyes, Marcie knew everything there was to know about Laura, Big George, and Miss Lillie, along with every virtue, big and small, of living on Trudeau's Farm. She gushed until her mouth went dry and was too exhausted to utter another word. Conversely, Marcie had very little to offer in the way of her own life. She spoke mostly in the present and of the hope of having children and growing old with Mick. Little was mentioned of her past. As far as Marcie was concerned, *Juliet* died the night she met Pablo, and Marcie Cooper was born the day she came to Brownsville and set foot in Abercrombie's Drugstore. Somewhere along the way a soul was searched in an effort to discover just who *was* this person who fell into enough money to buy herself a new life.

Mick never bothered asking too much if anything of Marcie's past. He figured, at her tender age, what was there to know? At first Marcie found it worrisome and presumed that Mick didn't care, or hadn't the interest.

"Mick's curiosity isn't a hive you oughta go poking," Pablo had warned. Still, it bothered Marcie that Mick wasn't curious enough to wonder about her past.

"What does he really know about me?" was the concern she raised to Pablo.

"You can't have it both ways," Pablo told her. "And why interpret his lack of curiosity as not caring? Why not look at it that he has every confidence that he at long last has found the girl of his dreams and only wants to look forward to a happy life together? You know, Mick has been a bachelor for a long time, but not for any lack of opportunity."

So where Mick was concerned, and also for the sake of Martina, Marcie Cooper was a child, perhaps age two or three, when she lost both her parents. She was raised by an aunt with whom she no longer kept contact, and eventually turned up at Abercrombie's Drugstore. She figured there might come a day when she would have to fill in some of the blanks, but for the time being, she took Pablo's advice and enjoyed life going forward.

"Do you remember your mother?" asked Martina.

"No," was Marcie's sad reply. She forged ahead with what she thought should be the expected response and result of a life lived with no clear memory of someone so important as a mother. She spoke of having vague images in her mind's eye of a woman—images that came to her only in silhouette, along with a familiar scent, and that was all she had to offer.

"I never knew my mother, either," said Martina. "My father told me that she was an angel sent down from Heaven just to give birth to me. Then right after I was born, God took her back to Heaven. Up until I was six, I use to believe it. For my father's sake, I still pretend."

"Sometimes we have to do a bit of pretending to protect the ones we love," said Marcie.

"I think it would break his heart if he ever found out that I no longer believed his story," said Martina. "He used to whisper it in my ear every night before I fell asleep. The funny thing is, I think he truly believes it."

"Sometimes we have to play tricks on ourselves to believe that things are a certain way…the way we want 'em to be," said Marcie. "Like when I was a young girl, I use to pretend that my birthday and Christmas didn't mean nothing because I never got as much as the other girls. When ya tell yourself something enough times, you get to where ya start believin' it."

"Yeah," said Martina with a trace of sullenness, "like my father believes that I'm happy here in Brownsville. Well, I don't care much for my birthday or Christmas. All I want is to go back to the farm."

****

"Something sure smells good," swooned Marcie—her eyes all a flutter.

After the beach slumber party, Pablo came wandering home with hot, just out of the oven cornbread.

160

"Here," he said to Marcie, "take half home to your husband."

"If I don't eat it on the way," Marcie said, smiling.

After Marcie departed with a watering mouth, Martina picked at her cornbread, but showed little interest.

"Aren't you hungry?" Pablo asked.

Martina replied with an indecisive shrug.

"But I thought you liked cornbread," he said.

"I like it just fine…with sweet sorghum poured over it." She followed up the ill-tempered words with a hard glare in the event the words by themselves had fallen short of making her point.

"I could run out and get some if you like," chirped Pablo, hoping the offer would sway Martina's disagreeable mood.

"It would hardly be the same," was her sharp return.

"No, I suppose it wouldn't," said Pablo, sounding much like a defeated man.

Rising to her feet, Martina became as imposing as her slight figure would allow, then reminded Pablo of a promise he made. "You said that in the summer we could go back to the farm for a visit. It's already December!"

Pablo reminded Martina of the bridge and how important it was to the town. But hearing the word *Brownsville* prompted her to scream, "I hate it here!"

"But this is your home," said Pablo.

"No, it's *your* home!" Martina shot back. "I have no home! Not anymore!"

Pablo recognized it wasn't a childish tantrum that he had the task of defusing, but was dealing with a young woman with much on her mind. "What about school? And your friends?" he asked. He was grasping at anything…any virtue their current existence was providing that Martina might perceive as worthwhile.

"I don't have friends!" she cried. "At school they all tell me that I have *'colored expressions'* and that I sing *'nigger songs!'* I try and tell them all about Miss Lillie and how wonderful she was, and all they do is laugh at me. I hate it here! I hate it, I tell you!"

"Don't you even have one friend?" asked Pablo. Before Martina could answer, he hung his head.

"I have no one," she said. Then she glared up at Pablo in a manner that suggested, *not even you,* then went storming off. Pablo didn't try to stop her, but instead sat in silence and stared at his cold cornbread. He knew that he had been fooling himself regarding Martina's happiness. Martina wasn't entirely truthful, though; she did have *one* friend, and that was where she was headed when she went storming off.

****

"Grandfather, Marylou Kendry will help Mama, won't she?" asked Anna Maria.

"Marylou was always a true friend to your mother; especially during the difficult times," Pablo told his anxious traveling companion. "In fact, as a young girl in school, when your mother was having difficulty, Marylou was very helpful. It wasn't easy, you know, adjusting from life on a farm to everyday society. Of course, I didn't always approve of Marylou's decisions and the influence that she had over your mother; but she was a loyal friend."

"What do you mean?" asked Anna Maria. "What decisions didn't you like?"

"Well, you see my sweet Cheerianna, for a while times had gotten tough," Pablo went on. "I told your mother there was no need to worry, that we would be fine. But Marylou convinced her to leave school. The two of them went to work—at first in a factory, then cleaning houses for the some of the well-to-do Protestants across town. Of course, they never bothered consulting me, and I didn't find out about the new arrangement until after I returned from a trip to Trudeau's Farm."

"You were making moonshine?" asked Anna Maria; though the directness of her words implied a factual statement, not a question.

"Moonshine? Of course not!" cried Pablo as though outraged by the accusation. "W-why th-that's illegal." The flustered grandfather stammered through his defense, and while doing so he tried to convince his accuser that he was a man of too high a moral standing to break the law. This he did with the understanding that Anna Maria wouldn't have known that the making, distributing, and drinking of alcohol was perfectly legal at the time of which he was referring.

"Grandfather, it isn't any big secret, you know," said Anna Maria. Then she chuckled as if to make light of his criminal activity.

"Really?" said Pablo, as though he was unable to imagine that the purpose for his many clandestine treks out to Trudeau's Farm hadn't gone as undetected as was once believed. "B-but how did you find out?" he wondered.

"Mama always knew," said Anna Maria. "Whenever you would leave, she'd say, 'There goes Papa, off to make moonshine.' Then we'd have a good laugh thinking how you truly believed that you were getting away with something."

Pablo's bellowing laughter startled the lady with the absurd hat. Glaring over at Pablo as though his outburst was an egregious offense that oughtn't be tolerated, she reached up, and with emphasis adjusted her hat.

"Is that so?" inquired Pablo, while ignoring the woman *and* her absurd hat. "You and Mama had a good laugh at my expense, did you?" Getting back to Martina and Marylou, he added, "Once those two started working, they became a bit too independent for my liking. But I guess it was my fault; I should've spent more time at home."

"What do you mean by *too independent*, Grandfather?" asked Anna Maria. "I thought that being independent was a good thing."

"Perhaps we should leave that story for another day," said Pablo, already regretting having introduced a scenario that was far too complex for his young traveling companion. He prayed Anna Maria would forget to ask, as Martina and Marylou Kendry's independent ways were not a subject he cared to revisit, or share with his granddaughter...ever.

Pablo closed his eyes as the train chugged its way through southern Indiana. He began to regret not having approached Lefty Carson. He felt like a coward and prayed that there would soon come a day for a second chance.

****

"Guess what?" cried Marylou Kendry, who not for another second was able to sit on the news that was prompting her excitement. "I got us another job! In fact I already started last night!"

"Last night?" asked Martina. "Who wants their house cleaned on Friday night? And why didn't you come for me?"

"Oh, I wasn't cleaning anyone's house. That's for darn sure," said Marylou.

"Then what?" wondered Martina.

"Well, if you put down that silly old mop of yours for a minute, I'll tell you," said Marylou.

The two girls sat facing one another on the Richardsons' kitchen floor with their mops resting by their sides. Then Marylou Kendry went on to describe her first night as a cocktail waitress at *The Rio Grande Tavern*, beginning with the friendliness of the patrons and the fine view of the river from the deck.

"It sounds great," said Martina, "but you know my father; he would never approve of me working where men are liable to get drunk and carry on."

"These days he's away more than he's home. He doesn't ever have to find out," said Marylou. "Beside, for all we know, your daddy is sellin' moonshine to Mr. Riggs." (Mr. Riggs was the owner of The Rio Grande Tavern.) "Now look here," she added. "I ain't sayin' no one got drunk last night, but there wasn't no fightin' or nothin'. The place is crawlin' with GIs that just came home, I tell ya. Hell, it's the safest place in town!"

"Still," said Martina, "I don't think I could feel right about doing something I know Papa wouldn't approve of."

"Not even for this?" asked Marylou. With a bit of flair she unveiled the wad of cash that was hidden away in her purse.

"Holy-moly!" cried Martina. "You made all that just last night!" Though she became suspicious that so much could be earned by prancing about with trays of drinks at a popular tavern.

The Great War, as World War I was then called, was drawling to a close. The Rio Grande Tavern had become quite the hotspot among the unwed of Brownsville and Matamoros and for GIs returning from abroad. With their impeccable posture and well creased uniforms, the proud GIs would gather on the outdoor deck of the tavern, which overlooked the Rio Grande River. Mr. Riggs decided that these defenders of country, who "bravely engaged in combat overseas" should have certain entitlements, and that for a modest price he would be the provider—the gateway to such privilege.

Mr. Riggs recruited the prettiest girls he could find—women who were willing to pay a little extra attention to soldiers whom he sold as "combat weary" and therefore were "deserving" —many of whom had "returned home only to find out the news that their impatient sweethearts had moved on." Indeed, Mr. Riggs' sales pitch was quite persuasive. Fortunately or not, depending on one's perspective, he had no trouble finding enough gullible young girls to do anything for a soldier who was "willing to lay down his life for his country." Riggs knew his scheme would be a short lived phenomenon, but at the moment, he had difficulty stocking the shelves with enough liquor.

"You actually did it for money?" cried Martina.

"Well, you don't have to look so appalled," cried Marylou. "Those fellas just want a pretty girl to tell their war stories to… Well, for cryin' out loud, it's only a damn blowjob! It's not like you're giving yourself up! Mr. Riggs don't expect us to do that. In fact, he told us just to be nice to the GIs and not to encourage them such that we end up on your backs. He ain't such a bad fella, this Mr. Riggs."

The mere idea of Marylou's latest escapade caused Martina to cringe.

"You've never even went down on a fella, have you?" asked Marylou.

Martina blushed and followed that with a shrug which was a clear indication that she hadn't.

"Well, I only did it one time before last night," Marylou admitted. "One night my dopey brother came home drunk as a skunk and wantin' me to do it. I mean, can you imagine…my own brother? He woke me up out of a sound sleep, he did, and like a damn fool was waving his nasty little wiener it in my face. I told him that he was crazy, and to go to hell, and that if he as much as touched me with it 'I'll go and get Mama's carvin' knife.' He knew I wasn't foolin', neither. Well, the threat of me takin' a knife to his wiener sure straightened him up.

"Yep, I'd say he got sober in a real hurry; but I was so hoppin' mad, the next day I went and done it to his best friend and made damn sure he knew about it. I can't say I liked it, 'cause his best friend sure ain't the handsomest fella around, but I kept thinkin' 'bout how mad I was at that idiot brother of mine. Well, his best friend may have got himself a freebee, but my brother sure learned his lesson. I told him next time he comes in my room drunk with any bright ideas, I'll save his friend's *you know what* and spit it in his damn eye."

Martina couldn't help but to look shocked by Marylou's boldness and the episode as it was described.

"It's ain't so bad, ya know," Marylou continued. "And if the fella isn't real handsome, you just have to pretend that he's one of them pretty boys we use to like back when we were in school. You remember, the ones we always tried to get to notice us? It helps, too, if you roll you eyes. You know, like you're really enjoyin' it. They like it when you do that, and the best part is, it makes 'em cum faster." Then Mary Lou took the handle end of her mop into her mouth and gave a thorough demonstration. The vulgar display caused Martina to look away and further blush.

"Hey, do I have to remind you?" said Marylou, and she took her wad of cash and waved it under Martina's nose. "In a few months we could be driving a nice car just like all these uppity folks we've been cleanin' for. Now that ain't too hard to take, is it?"

****

Lieutenants' Lee and Caldwell were sipping their second mug of Shiners, a popular local brew, when Lieutenant Callahan came waltzing onto the deck of *The Rio Grande* Tavern. One might acknowledge Lieutenant Callahan's prominent jaw and clear blue eyes as handsome features. However, both attributes, if seen as such, were overshadowed by his arrogance—a trait which he was unable to resist flashing whenever entering a room. It oozed from every pore and superior glance. Upon meeting Callahan, one's first impression was dislike, though it bothered him not, for he relished the role of *bad guy*. Weak men avoided him, whereas strong men pretended he wasn't a threat to their manhood and that he lacked relevance. Women feared him—at the very least he made them wary. He was mindful of his effect, was Callahan, and that, too, he relished.

Lieutenants Caldwell and Lee had invited Lieutenant Callahan to come along tonight, but did so with the hope that he wouldn't show. That's the way it was with Callahan—he got invited, but usually with the hope that he wouldn't show. He was a good soldier, though—there was no denying it; therefore his objectionable character, although not overlooked, was deemed pardonable by fellow soldiers, who despite it paining them to do so, extended the courtesy of an invitation.

In every instance, Callahan managed to let his smugness spoil any chance for camaraderie with his fellow soldiers. "Gentleman," he would call to the others whenever entering a club, tavern, or anyplace where men gather socially. *Gentlemen* was not a term that Callahan used affectionately, but instead with condescension, and to alert all others that the *superior one*—the *alpha male* has arrived and is about to grace mere plebeians with his presence. Thereafter began the game of *let's see who can withstand the strain*. Tonight was no different, as disaffection seemed a specialty of Callahan's. He also had a condescending manner of posing questions to which he already knew the answers. It pained his fellow soldiers when having to admit they agreed with him.

"Welcome home, fellas," said Mr. Riggs, as he delivered a proper army salute.

"Good to *be* home," chirped Lieutenant Caldwell.

"I'll second that," said Lieutenant Lee.

"Some think we shoulda never gone over there in the first place," remarked Callahan, who began to rehash President Wilson's position of neutrality and slogan: *Too proud to fight*. Callahan glared up at Mr. Riggs. He began his examination of the tavern owner's face, as if trying to determine whether he was the sort of man who shared the president's position.

"How 'bout a cold mug of Shiners," suggested Mr. Riggs, attempting to restore the celebratory mood.

Initially, Callahan allowed Mr. Riggs' transparence to pass unchallenged by replying, "I'd say a cold mug of Shiners sounds just fine about now." But after he was presented with the cold brew, he went back to his point. "Imagine them sons-a-bitchin' krauts," he uttered with a sneer, "goin' behind our backs and tellin' Mexico that if they joined them as allies against *us*, they'd help 'em get back part of Texas. Why, if that ain't reason enough to go to war, I don't know what *is*. Wouldn't you agree, Mr. Riggs?"

"Why, sure," was Mr. Riggs' reply, as he in no way wanted to dispute Callahan on the justifications of war.

"Don't forget New Mexico and Arizona," Lieutenant Lee chimed in to further validate the United States' entry into the war.

"Yeah, let us not," said Callahan; though his manner was clearly suggesting that the loss of territory in Texas would have far outweighed that of New Mexico and Arizona. But that was vintage Callahan; echoing a point, when in reality he was disparaging a colleague. He was a master at using subtext to mock, or to bully a fellow. "Imagine," he then added, again with a sneer, "comin' home from a war only to end up a damn Mexican. Now that don't seem very polite...does it? What do *you* think, Mr. Riggs?"

"Of course not," agreed Mr. Riggs. But what else could the tavern owner say?

"Mmm," tastes just as good as I remember," said Callahan, referring to the Shiners. He then gave Mr. Riggs a mock salute, as if the tavern owner had a hand in creating the taste. "The worst thing to have come out of this damn war," he continued, "was our government granting citizenship to all those Puerto Ricans the minute they got drafted. Just what *were* our well intending legislators tryin' to tell us? That if you can point a gun in the right direction, you can get the right kinda papers? As it is, we're already overrun with niggers."

"I fought beside some of them fellas," Lieutenant Lee said with a hint of pride. "They were fine soldiers."

"Why, Lieutenant Caldwell, I *do* believe that our boy here has gone and turned spic lover on us," said Callahan. "What do *you* think, Mr. Riggs? Has our *boy* here gone and turned spic lover?"

"I really wouldn't know," said Mr. Riggs, who began fumbling through his pocket for his handkerchief, which he used to dab the perspiration that had appeared on his brow.

"You're no spic lover, are you Mr. Riggs?" wondered the smirking Callahan. "Ya see, boys," he added, before Mr. Riggs had the chance to answer, "our friend Mr. Riggs here ain't no spic lover."

"There were over 36,000 United States soldiers killed in the war," said Mr. Riggs in an effort to better assert himself in the conversation. "Those fortunate enough to make it home should be grateful. So enjoy yourselves, fellas."

"Touché Mr. Riggs," said Callahan. "Touché."

As Mr. Riggs began to walk away, Callahan called, "Oh, Mr. Riggs…speaking of Puerto Ricans…although I *do* believe in this case my keen eye is tellin' me Mexican; I'm thinkin' dark an' lovely over there is lookin' mighty fine tonight." Callahan gestured in the direction of the girl identified as a Mexican, with the notion that Mr. Riggs should scurry off and retrieve the young woman before she got away.

"You like?" asked Mr. Riggs.

"Wouldn't mind givin' it a whirl," replied Callahan.

"It?" said Mr. Riggs.

"That's right, Mr. Tavern Owner," replied Callahan. "*It.* Is *that* a problem?"

"No problem," replied Mr. Riggs.

Mr. Riggs recruited young, pretty cocktail waitresses to amuse the troops. Admittedly, it was an unorthodox, yet, profitable business maneuver, which thus far had gone well. But as Mr. Riggs gazed into Callahan's icy blue eyes, he wished the idea had never entered his mind.

"She'll be waiting for you upstairs," Mr. Riggs told Callahan. "First door on your right."

Mr. Riggs tried to avoid a hostile tone, but failed. His failure produced a satisfied grin from Callahan, who perceived a flustered Mr. Riggs as a victory.

"Smug son of a bitch," Mr. Riggs muttered under his breath as he walked away.

"Gentleman," Callahan called to Lieutenants Caldwell and Lee, "looks like I'm gonna have me some salsa tonight—a real hot tamale, I'd say. I'll let ya know how spicy it was when I get back. You'll sit tight now."

For a brief moment, Lieutenants Caldwell and Lee stared down at Callahan's unfinished mug of Shiners as though the remaining liquid may have contained some lingering influence of their arrogant colleague. When moving on, the two resumed their earlier conversation. Not that they so much cared to do so, or necessarily found it all that interesting, but it was a means of proving to one another that Callahan hadn't gotten to them—

168

that he had rolled off their shoulders. Of course, they each had wanted to say, *he's a real son of a bitch, isn't he?* But to give such credence to their arrogant colleague could have been perceived as weakness; therefore neither elected to move in that direction. They carried on their conversation with each half listening. They were strong men attempting to pretend that Callahan was irrelevant.

Martina sat waiting and not knowing who among the soldiers would at any second walk through the door. The customary procedure was, once a girl was chosen, she would sit with the uniformed clad man for a session of small talk and complimentary flirtation. Once the two had reached the point of being at ease with one another, they would slip away, making for the room atop the tavern. But Mr. Riggs knew the point of being *at ease* was unachievable with the likes of Callahan. After getting a healthy dose of the smug man wielding his superiority among his colleagues, Mr. Riggs had no desire to witness the arrogant Lieutenant Callahan conquering an unsuspecting young woman. To unleash such a man on Martina would be all the worse. Callahan would cleverly disguise derogatory comments regarding Martina's ethnicity by dressing them up in backhanded compliments. No doubt, he would belittle her, and do so with the notion that he was providing entertainment for his two colleagues.

Mr. Riggs liked Martina; he believed her to be a decent young woman who wasn't cut out for *The Rio Grande Tavern* and couldn't imagine why she allowed the much bolder Marylou Kendry to persuade her into taking such a job. He wished that he had relied on his instincts and informed Martina that he already recruited enough girls, but that he would call on her if needed. After reading the concern that registered on Mr. Riggs's face, Martina made for the room atop the tavern, but not without a fair amount of trepidation.

"Of all the girls for that son of a bitch to pick," Mr. Riggs muttered to himself. But Mr. Riggs knew that he couldn't change the rules just because he didn't like the way the game was going. He also knew that it was a little late in the game for an attack of conscience.

The few minutes that Martina sat alone waiting was more than ample time to become overwrought with shame for what she was about to do. The other day when she walked away from the Richardson home with Marylou Kendry, it was fun and games. She even managed to fool herself into believing that a romantic encounter with a brave soldier awaited her. Being a *good girl*, she saw only the *best* possible scenario. Tonight, jumping out the window into the Rio Grande River and swimming to Matamoros seemed not only a viable, but a more comforting option.

As Martina stared down at the river, her mind drifted back to a time when her days were filled with milking cows, churning butter, and losing herself in Big George's cornfield. She longed for the exhilarating sense of freedom she felt when running freely through the open field beyond the tall stalks of sorghum. *"Child, you's just as pretty as anyone, an' prettier than most, I'd say,"* was what Miss Lillie once told her.

She turned away from the view of the river and settled into a chair where, she envisioned Laura Trudeau in an elegant gown seated at a grand piano before a captive audience, while alone she shuddered, waiting to become prey as Mr. Riggs' troubled expression suggested. At that very moment she hated her father, and had he been present, she would have told him so, or at least tried. She wanted to dash for the window and cry out, but the air in the room, which pressed on her throat, caused her to become sickened and to lose strength. She sank further into the chair and tried not to weep. How she longed for her childhood: To once again be a child back on the farm where everything made sense, or back in school where she was shy and penniless—any place other than *this* room above *this* tavern, where the very walls themselves were stripping away her soul.

"Dear God in heaven," she prayed, "please don't let Miss Lillie see this. Please, not tonight. See that she doesn't watch over me tonight."

Martina rose from the chair and again faced the river—the ever constant and steady river—a river that, come what may, no matter the abuses it must absorb, never falters—never loses strength. Its will was unwavering and it always carried on. Tonight, Martina Cordero would become akin to the river…or die trying.

****

"That about'll do it for tonight," said Big George. "We'll make the last batch t'morrow."

"You know, I've been drinking this stuff since I was fifteen-years-old," said Pablo.

"It sure ain't hurt ya none, has it?" asked Big George with his customary laugh.

"No sir, it surely has not. Not one a bit," said Pablo. "And I can still remember my very first sip, or *swig*, as Mick called it."

"You ever tell Mick the secret?" asked Big George.

"There *is* no secret," replied Pablo.

"That be the whole point," said Big George.

"After all these years poor Mick would be crushed to find out that there was nothing to it," said Pablo. "Best to let him go on wondering. Besides, your legend still has room to grow."

170

"Legends have been built on lots a things, I imagine, but I don't think none's ever been built on homemade yeast and rainwater," said Big George. He then sat to wipe the sweat from his brow. When he did, his massive shoulders slumped.

"What's wrong, my friend?" asked Pablo.

"This ol' farm…it ain't what it once was," said Big George. "Ain't got the same life to it no more."

"Things are changing, my friend," said Pablo. "Everything around us is getting older and we're getting older right along with it."

"I suppose," sighed Big George. "But when Mr. Trudeau was still livin' and we were all young, there was times when this farm could be the happiest place on earth, it could. My, we use to have some times back in them days. But after he died, everything changed. Then, like a godsend, Martina comes along, and soon every acre of this here farm had her spirit in it. Sometimes I swear I can still hear her gigglin' in that cornfield. And I'll never forget that day she an' lil' Miss Laura come strollin' down the pathway holdin' Mama's hand. We had a few good years together, Mama and me…'fore she went off to see Miss Lillie." Then he added reflectively, "I ain't never had no family of my own. But them years Martina was here, it was kinda like havin' a family."

"A day doesn't go by that she doesn't mention your name," said Pablo. "And at night when she says her prayers, she talks to Miss Lillie." He became somber when adding, "She remembers every day that she spent on this farm. It's been ten years, and still, she hasn't forgiven me for taking her away."

"It'd sure be nice to see her all growed up," said Big George. "I'll bet she's as pretty as can be."

"And you would be right," Pablo said with a proud grin. "But she sure has a mind of her own."

"Boy, don't I know it," agreed Big George. "She sure gave Miss Lillie a run for her money. But she made her last years some of the sweetest. Ain't no doubt about that."

Pablo and Big George sat under the stars, sampling the fruit of their labor and reminiscing about old times at Trudeau's Farm and Martina's childhood. Soon Edgar joined them.

****

Martina recoiled when she heard the door pushed open.

"I didn't mean to startle you none," said Callahan. In regard to Martina's defensive posture he added, "No need to be afraid of ol' Callahan, here. He ain't gonna hurt ya none. After all, who'd wanna hurt a pretty little thing like you?"

Martina let her arms fall to her sides, though Callahan's icy blue eyes did nothing to ensure confidence that she needn't *be afraid.*

"Why, you surely are a lovely creature, aren't you." Callahan brushed away a lock of hair that had fallen in front of Martina's face. "And I heard you got you a real pretty smile, too, dark an' lovely. So don't you be afraid to use it now." His request was added in a taunting manner, and it prompted Martina to refold her arms in front of her chest.

"I *do* apologize if I offended you," said Callahan. "I know dark an' lovely mustn't be your name. After a momentary pause, followed by a supercilious smirk, he added, "You're not gonna make me try and guess, now, are ya? 'Cause ol' Callahan, here, he ain't too good at guessin' names, ya see, and we could be here all night."

"M-My name is...M-Martina. Martina C-Cordero."

Martina tried to sound proud, but she squeezed out the two words as if pacifying Callahan pained her to the point of having revulsion for the sound of her own name.

"Why, that's a lovely name," said Callahan. "And a lovely girl oughta have a lovely name. Don't you agree?"

"I suppose," was Martina's reply; though her words were weak and filled with resignation, not agreement. She then sank to her knees, wanting to put a swift end to the wretched encounter. Giving Callahan a performance, rather than having to withstand even another second of his condescending tone, seemed the lesser of two evils. Though, to Martina's surprise, no sooner had her knees touched the floor, she discovered Callahan kneeling beside her. He lifted up her chin and said, "Not so fast, there, girly. Ya see, I can get that any time—from the dime whores under the bridge if I wanted...if that *was,* in fact, what I wanted. But a fine lookin' thing like you don't come 'round but every so often." He added with what had become a familiar smirk, "Come now, you can give ol' Callahan here a smile, can't ya?"

With the back of his hand, he stroked Martina's cheek. She stiffened. "My word," he said with soaring interest. "Could it be that I done caught me a virgin? Is that right, dark an' lovely; do I have me a virgin here in my mitts?"

With a rigid jaw and downcast eyes, Martina remained silent throughout Callahan's taunting.

"Looks like I get to pluck me a tender flower that's hardly even blossomed," he said. "No one's even gotten so close as to smell your lovely scent, have they? Ya know, when I woke up this morning, I had a feeling this was gonna be my lucky day. Ever wake up feeling that way…like it was your lucky day? Maybe it's *our* lucky day. What do *you* think, dark an' lovely? Is this *our* lucky day?"

At that point, Martina could no longer hear Callahan's voice, nor was she able to feel his touch.

****

"I'm all finished with my chores," cried Martina. She danced around Miss Lillie as though she would surely burst if not right away dismissed in favor of the glorious summer day.

"You fed the chickens?" asked Miss Lillie. She eyeballed Martina as though skeptical of the youngster's claim.

"Yes ma'am," was Martina's emphatic reply.

"Milked the cows?" asked Miss Lillie.

"Yes ma'am," replied Martina, again with vigor.

"You churned the butter, too?" asked Miss Lillie, continuing to grill the excitable child.

"Butter's all churned," Martina proudly chirped.

"Well, alright then," said Miss Lillie, "but don't think I won't rein in your lil' behind if I see that anything's undone."

"Everything is ship-shape!" Martina declared with supreme confidence.

"Well, you best wait 'til our lil' Miss Laura's all through with her practicin' 'fore you go chargin' on up to the house and bangin' on the door," said Miss Lillie.

"I will," promised Martina. Then off she dashed, to go and do precisely what she was instructed not to do.

That was Big George's favorite part of the day…watching Martina burn up all her surplus energy. He couldn't help a broad grin whenever he would see her little feet tearing about the farm's acres and beyond on a delightful summer's day.

"She does more to keep these ol' bones of mine young than that corn whiskey you's so proud of, that's for darn sure," Miss Lillie would often tell Big George.

Transported far away from any present day reality—before ever hearing of a place called Brownsville or *The Rio Grande Tavern*, Martina lay on the floor beneath Laura Trudeau's grand piano, her little body gathering all the vibrations as Laura sent clusters of notes showering downward and drowning out Lieutenant Callahan's terrible moans.

"Don't stop playing, Laura! Please, don't stop!" cried Martina. "And don't play that ugly chord this time, okay!"

Loud and with fury, Laura Trudeau played music that for years had been irrevocably etched in Martina Cordero's memory. As Martina listened and felt the vibrations, in her mind's eye, she watched as Laura and she ran stride for stride through the wide open field beyond the tall stalks of sorghum. Their bodies surged when greeted by the wide open space. "Don't be frightened," she called to Golda, just as they neared the rim where the field meets the woods. "We're gonna save your mama," she called back to Big George, as if on that momentous day the gentle giant had been within an earshot. "You'll see. You'll all see. We're gonna bring Golda home and we'll all be together and we'll be happy forever!"

"You just gonna lie there not sayin' a word," asked Callahan, as he had gotten to his feet and began dressing. "You *do* realize we're all through, don't you?" He offered Martina a cigarette, but she didn't respond. She lay there not moving, her mouth creased into what appeared to be a smile, which Callahan mistook for afterglow. "I see the cat must have our tongue," he taunted. "But that's alright, you don't have to talk to ol' Callahan if you don't want." Then he blew a cloud of smoke in Martina's direction. Before leaving, he knelt down beside her. With a fingertip he traced the length of her beautifully curved figure. "I'll be sure and tell Mr. Riggs that you were just fine, dark an' lovely. Just fine, indeed."

****

Martina sat quietly, occasionally nibbling, but with little interest in the dinner that she had prepared and placed before her and Pablo. When she did bother to glance across the table, it wasn't Pablo's attempt at conversation that sparked her interest, but the silver strands running through his hair—strands that until then had gone unnoticed.

"You don't seem much like yourself tonight," Pablo remarked.

"I'm fine, Papa," Martina told him. It was clear that she didn't want to be pressed on the issue of her wellbeing. Ignoring her tone, Pablo further observed, "You seem preoccupied. Is everything alright?"

Martina allowed her utensil to slip through her fingers. "How can you tell that I'm preoccupied!" she snapped. "You're hardly ever here! How is it possible for you tell that I'm any different than on any other night! Can you please answer me *that*?"

Martina stormed away from the table and made for the window. Pablo gave her a moment to compose herself before venturing to her side, though he did so with trepidation. Once there he placed what he hoped would be a comforting hand on her shoulder.

"Things are starting to pick up again," he told her. His tone was cautiously optimistic. "It looks like I'll be working here in Brownsville for the next several months, maybe even longer. We'll be able to spend more time together"

"That's good, Papa. I'm glad for you that there's work and that you'll be around." Martina made an attempt to sound sincere, but her words at best were detached.

Pablo let his hand fall at his side. He didn't know whether to remain in the throes of Martina's misery or dismiss himself. He moped about until he heard her say, "I dreamed of Golda last week...or maybe it was last month...I'm really not sure. I can remember that day in the field like it was yesterday. But it didn't occur to me until just recently how truly frightened she must have been." Then she muttered to herself, "If only *I* could've been so brave."

"It was God's will that Big George and Golda reunite," said Pablo. "You did God's work. You were very brave that day in the field and Big George will always be grateful."

"I wish we could've stayed longer and had gotten to know Golda better," said Martina. "She was just starting to get comfortable and was opening up just as we were preparing to leave."

With downcast eyes, Pablo acknowledged Martina's words with a nod, then turned away. Amid her current gloom, their departure from Trudeau's Farm was not an issue that he was in favor of revisiting.

"Come Papa," she urged, "you should eat and then rest up. Tomorrow will be a long day for you."

As Martina began making her way back to the table, Pablo reached for her. "I'm a very lucky man to have such a thoughtful daughter," he said. "Some days I wonder if I'm so deserving, but I think not."

"Why would you say such a thing, Papa?" wondered Martina.

"I know it hasn't always been easy for you." Pablo waved his hand and was gesturing at their surroundings. "Sometimes I wonder if I did the right thing—if I made the right decision."

"We're fine, Papa," Martina reassured him. "You did what you thought was right at the time. That's all anyone can do."

"Sure," agreed Pablo, though lacking was any degree of conviction. He knew Martina was magnanimous by nature and was making a sincere attempt to absolved him of any blame—that she was at last allowing him to come down from the proverbial hook from which he all along had been dangling. Despite Martina's gesture, when he looked back over the years, Pablo realized that his motives for leaving Trudeau's Farm were far more self-serving than having anything to do with the best interest of his seven-year-old daughter. Though to be fair, Pablo had seven years in which convince himself otherwise.

"What is it that you keep staring at?" Pablo wondered.

"What are these?" asked Martina, as she playfully tousled her father's graying hair.

"I guess I'm getting old," he said with a chuckle.

Martina smiled at the admission; though she could feel changes happening within her own body—changes that, for the time being were subtle, but far more significant than black hair turning silver. She was fairly certain of the reason and it frightened her.

****

Marylou Kendry went and placed a cold mug of Shiners in front of Lieutenant Callahan. Tonight the lieutenant sat alone without any colleagues for whom to act superior. The manner in which he sat and with his icy blue eyes surveyed the room, told one all they needed to know about Callahan.

"Looks like you drew the short straw tonight," the other cocktail waitresses had teased Marylou Kendry, as Callahan seated himself in the area for which she was responsible. To avoid an exchange with the arrogant man, Marylou tried to appear hurried. Before she could get away, Callahan alertly grabbed her arm.

"Where you runnin' off to so fast?" he wondered.

Callahan enjoyed Marylou's feistiness. The other girls would cower under his taunts and smugness, whereas Marylou didn't hesitate to give it right back to him, and in spades, as they say. Glaring down her nose at Callahan's aggressive paw, she said with mock regret, "Why, Lieutenant, haven't you heard; we're no longer that sort of establishment. I guess this ain't your lucky night."

Mr. Riggs decided that his cocktail waitresses should return to being just that…cocktail waitresses. In addition to Callahan, who figured into the decision, it was also civilian demand for military perks, including a drunken lesbian, who recently made quite a stir. It was never Mr. Riggs' intention that his popular tavern transform into a whorehouse, but that's precisely where it was headed when he pulled the plug on his latest business scheme.

"So where has that dark an' lovely been keepin' herself?" wondered Callahan. "You know, that fine little Mexican creature? She is a friend of yours, Miss Kendry, is she not? Strange, that I never see her around anymore. Could it be that I keep comin' on the wrong nights? Is ol'

176

Callahan, here, just unlucky?"

"First off," said Marylou, "her name is Martina. I'm sure a smart soldier like you can remember a name like Martina, can't he?"

"Very well, Miss Kendry. *Martina* it is," said Callahan. "So where has *Martina* been keepin' her pretty little self these days?"

"Home, if it's any of your business," was Marylou's sharp reply. Then she tried to break free from Callahan's grip.

"Why, please *do* elaborate Miss Kendry," said Callahan. The lieutenant guided Marylou to the empty chair beside him.

"She's home, as in, kept under lock and key by her crazy old man," said Marylou.

"Now why, I wonder, would her old man wanna do a thing like that?" asked Callahan.

"Well, you see now, *Lieutenant*," said Mary Lou, attempting to match Callahan's supercilious tone, "it turns out that someone wasn't satisfied with just a blowjob. That's right. It appears that one of you big, strong army men done broke the rules and now the evidence is growin' inside my friend right now as we speak. Now you wouldn't happen to know who that someone was, would you, *Lieutenant?*"

"I tell you what, Miss Kendry," said Callahan. "You tell me where I can find *Martina* and I'll be sure to do whatever I can to find out who among my brethren *done broke the rules*."

"Oh, I'll bet you will," said Marylou as she stood up to leave.

"Oh, Miss Kendry? One more thing. I don't want you to think that I forgot all about you, if you know what I mean," Callahan said with a devious wink. "I surely wouldn't mind waitin' around 'til the end of your shift."

"You better be careful there, soldier," said Marylou. "Haven't you heard? I got some sharp teeth in this mouth of mine, and I been known to take home a souvenir every now and again."

"Touché, Miss Kendry," said Callahan. "Touché."

****

Callahan planted himself directly across the street from the Cordero residence and waited until Pablo appeared. When Pablo did appear, he gave the unfamiliar fellow a polite nod before going on his way. Callahan's eyes followed the unsuspecting Pablo until clear out of sight, then made for the door.

Pablo wasn't a fool; he knew full well that the anger and sullenness he displayed toward Martina, in combination with the punishment he levied, was unsustainable. Still, he needed time to process the sudden change in his life—to work through the sort of dilemma that, just because he willed it to do so, wouldn't conveniently disappear. He struggled mightily over what to say to Mick and the rest of the bonfire gang. *My daughter is with child and there's no father in the picture* aren't words that flow easily from a father's lips. They were words that Pablo couldn't regurgitate, nor swallow, but had remained stuck in his throat, where they twisted themselves into coarse knots that grew more jagged and bitter by the day. The worst would come with having to tell Big George. The gentle giant had lofty illusions when he imagined the kind of woman Martina was becoming. The news, Pablo knew, would surely break Big George's heart.

As he had so often in the past, Pablo took refuge in his daily labor. Lately the laborious days were randomly punctuated with a lilted, though off-key rendition of *Me and My Gal,* crooned by none other than Frankie "The Prick" Donato and Fat Fuck McGinn.

The bells are ringing...for me and my gal. The birds are singing...for me and my gal.

It's been awhile since Pablo heard the bells and the birds, but he remembered them well. He had hoped that whenever it came time for Martina, she would hear them loud and clear and with all their storybook tradition.

Martina paused, at first experiencing no trace of recognition when she examined Lieutenant Callahan's civilian attire. She recoiled, though, when his icy blue eyes looked down at her with all their superiority.

"Well, now, ain't you gonna invite me in?" he asked.

"Why are you here?" Martina's words were shaky and served to reveal to Callahan how uneasy he made her. Although she loathed the arrogant man and was wishing him to disappear, she knew he could overpower her—so she stepped aside and allowed him to pass.

"Now, is that any way to greet a friend?" he asked.

"I didn't realize we were friends," said Martina.

The remark fell far short of the firmness that she intended. Nevertheless, Callahan responded in his usual taunting manner. "Aw, are you tryin' to hurt ol' Callahan's feelings? Is that it? Well, a mutual *friend* of ours told me that you got you a condition. Is that true, dark an' lovely? Do you *done* got you a condition? Because if that's the case, then maybe I gotta right to be here. So why don't we tell ol' Callahan, here, the truth. Does he gotta right to be here? Or is he just out of line?"

Callahan began smirking and strutting about as though he owned the place. His behavior served to make the mother-to-be feel uncomfortable and a stranger in her own home. His overconfident posture, which in the past had overwhelmed far greater spaces, became unbearable amid such modesty. It mocked Martina's tenuous rank. She had the awful sense of once again being trapped inside the room atop The Rio Grande Tavern. She wished to flee from her home, to be anywhere other than in Callahan's presence. She turned her back to him—a gesture which the lieutenant chose to understand as weakness rather than defiance, though Martina herself was uncertain.

"I'll take your silence as a yes," said Callahan, "that I, in fact, *do* have a right to be here."

"You should leave," Martina told him. "My father will be back any minute, and he wouldn't like finding a strange man in his home."

"Funny, but I just watched your father leavin' on his merry way to work," said Callahan. "A hard workin' man like that; I'm guessin' it'll be hours until he returns. By then I'll have gotten what I came for. What do *you* think there, girly? Will ol' Callahan, here, have gotten what he came for?"

Not without an effort, Martina managed to pry her feet loose from the floor and went lunging toward the kitchen. Like a drowning man desperately trying to reach the surface, she made for the other room. She hadn't much time to compose herself, though; not a single unhurried breath had she drawn before hearing Callahan's slow, deliberate footsteps coming toward the kitchen—footsteps which possessed every bit of arrogance and superiority that were contained in his icy blue eyes.

"My, my, where *are* our manners?" asked Callahan. "I've already been here five minutes and you've yet to offer me a chair or a cup of tea. Just what kinda woman is it that carries my child?"

Martina gestured to a chair before busying herself with the task of making tea. She figured the faster she made tea, the sooner Callahan would leave.

"Now, you listen here, girly, so that we understand one another," he said. "And we *do* aim to understand one another…do we not?" Not waiting for a reply, he added, "Ya see, I didn't come by on a whim. I done my homework. And I know the last thing that you'd want to have happen is for that old man of yours to find out where you were workin' and what you were doin' when you done got yourself knocked up. Just imagine the disgrace your poor father would suffer if ever his employers found out about what kinda daughter he was raisin'. And I'm guessin', too, that, all those uppity folks you and Marylou work for might raise an eyebrow when discoverin' what kinda woman they've been invitin' into their homes. Now, am I lyin', or am I tellin' the truth? So don't you go getting' any ideas about who's in charge. You catchin' my drift?"

Martina lowered her eyes in defeat as Callahan sipped his tea. He sipped slowly and noisily—an agonizing reminder for Martina, that it was *he* who was being waited on and *she* who was doing the waiting. After his last sip, he set down his cup and strutted over to Martina. She had remained standing and with downcast eyes.

"Well," he said, as he placed his hands firmly on her shoulders. "Looks like your gonna get the chance to do what you tried to do that night at the Rio Grande."

Callahan pushed down on Martina's shoulders until her knees reached the floor, and she submitted. When he was all through, he strutted about like a peacock, circling Martina, who remained kneeling on the floor. He glanced proudly at his semen glistening on her cheeks. Then he took a few bills from his fold and unceremoniously tossed them on the floor.

"An expectant mother'll need a few things…or so I'm told," he said. He then added with his usual smugness, "Ya know, I think I'm gonna like our little arrangement. In fact, it's already startin' to grow on me. How 'bout you, girly? Has it grown on you, yet? I'll take your silence as a yes." Then he squatted beside Martina, who was still kneeling on the floor with downcast eyes. "I be comin' by every now and again. In the meantime, try not to miss me too much, ya hear?"

Martina held herself perfectly still and listened as Callahan's footsteps got further and further away. She hung on until hearing the door close, then she burst into tears. "I'm sorry, Miss Lillie," she sobbed. "I don't mean to be so weak! I'm sorry to let you down like this!"

She staggered into her bedroom. Looking in the mirror, she wiped the remnants of Callahan from her cheeks. In her heart, she knew that working at *The Rio Grande Tavern* had proven to be a mistake, but the wad of cash that Marylou waved under nose was too tempting. She wondered if it was a mistake that she would ever outrun.

PART THREE: ANNA MARIA

Chapter Seven
The Child Stays

It was said of young Johnny Crow, "*He must take after his Uncle Ernest.*" This accurate assessment of the youth's character wasn't for the purpose of disparaging him, but was simply an observation. For as was the case with Ernest, Johnny Crow was no huge lover of farm work. Not to suggest that he jabbered on incessantly about anything *but* the task at hand, or faked the an occasional dizzy spell, as Ernest had—Johnny wasn't one for those sorts of antics; nor was he heard quoting Schopenhauer or Dickens, as his interests didn't stretch into the world of philosophy or literature. Instead, he often shirked his responsibilities altogether by hiding up in the hayloft in the barn. On one Sunday morning, when he was told to milk the cows and feed the chickens, Johnny broke into his father's shed and made off with an old bucket of white paint and a brush.

"Johnny, where's you off to so early with that old bucket of paint?" wondered Gabriel.

"I-I'm ah...I'm gonna paint the barn," he stammered.

"Paintin' the barn, are we?" chuckled Gabriel, not wanting to overwhelm the lad with suspicion in the event that he had honest intentions. He looked off into the distance at the size of the barn, then regarded the meager amount of paint with which Johnny proposed tackling such an edifice.

"Well, ya better not lay her on too thick," he advised, playing along with the charade, "or ya won't get much further than them barn doors. And that's old paint, so ya best give it a good stir."

"Yes sir," said Johnny. Then Gabriel tipped his hat to the youngster and each went on his respective way to apply his industry.

Gabriel couldn't imagine what Johnny had in mind. He knew with certainty that Cornelius hadn't put his son up to such a task. What's more, he couldn't imagine Johnny taking the initiative, especially with a project so ambitious as painting a barn the size of which in the past had taken four men the better part of a week to complete. Besides, if anything on Crow's Farm needing painting, Gabriel would have known and he would delegate the assignment. Had Cornelius set before his son such a task, Gabriel knew with certainty not to expect a freshly painted barn when he returned in the afternoon.

Johnny dipped the brush into the old bucket of paint. On one of the barn doors he proceeded to paint a vertical rectangle, beginning at the level of his knees and ending at his chest and approximately fifteen inches wide. Afterward, he stepped off what he calculated to be 60` 6``. He took hold of the baseball that his Grandpa Cornelius had given him before he passed. He moved the treasure around in his hand, feeling for the stitches and making certain that he had the right grip. Then he glared down his nose at the barn door and fired the baseball at the freshly painted target. Johnny Crow was a young farm boy with big dreams.

"What in the blazes is making all that racket!" barked Cornelius Crow.

Cornelius's angry tone prompted Irma to abandon the stove and make for the window. "It's just our son," she said with a proud smile. "He's making good use of that baseball his grandpa gave him."

"For cryin' out loud," grumbled Cornelius, "if that's his idea of making good use out of something, we're all in trouble! Ernest only talked everyone to death. This'll never go over."

"A boy is entitled to his dreams," said Irma. "Even if those dreams are loud."

Unlike his son and younger brother, Cornelius wasn't a dreamer—he was never caught wandering about with his head in the clouds, inspired only by fanciful pursuits he had little chance of attaining. He was much more like his father and Gabriel—a rise and shine with his nose to the grindstone sort. He didn't have a dream in his head until he caught his first glimpse of Irma.

Practicing with the hope of one day becoming a major league baseball pitcher was just one way that Johnny Crow managed to duck his duties, but it was by far his most industrious. Often he would disappear to the hayloft of the barn, where he'd spend hours lazing about while imagining that he was Carl Hubbell, or Lefty Grove striking out the games most feared sluggers. In his mind's eye, he'd watch pitch after pitch

183

whizzing by the menacing bats of Mel Ott, Jimmy Foxx, and Babe Ruth. After the final out of the World Series, his teammates would rush to the mound and hoist him high atop their shoulders in victory.

When he was through with his daydreams, Johnny would go fishing into his pockets for his baseball cards. He would spend a great deal of time examining each card. He cherished them all, but the one he treasured the most was the Pete Browning card that his Grandpa Cornelius had come by many years ago with the purchase of a pack of Old Judge Cigarettes. It was some forty years ago that the Senior Cornelius Crow had acquire that card. Eventually, the treasure got passed on to young Cornelius, as Ernest had no interest in baseball, then found its way into Johnny's ever growing stack.

When he was finished with his cards and daydreams, Johnny would bury himself under the hay. With an interest that was equal and often times surpassed that of his lofty ambition, he did what many boys his age are wont to do: He examined his penis. It was during a recent examination that Johnny discovered the thrill of masturbation. Today while buried under the hay in the loft, he heard his mother call, "Corneeeelius." Irma Crow usually stood on the porch and called out to Johnny's father, always drawing out the second syllable and making it sound as if she was singing his name. Johnny had to hurry. He knew it must be supper time and that any second he, too, would receive a singing summons. *Oh Johhhhneeee.*

****

Last stop, Louisville, Kentucky!" barked the conductor. "Last stop, Louisville, Kentucky!"

Pablo and Anna Maria muffled their laughter when they observed other passengers and the exaggerated manner in which they needed to contort themselves around the lady with the absurd hat. At the station, waiting for the lady was an older gentleman. *Too old to be a husband,* Pablo thought, *but one never knows.* The lady rushed to the gentleman's side where she collapsed in his arms and wept like a child.

"*Do* tell me she didn't suffer much, father," she cried. "I shouldn't like to hear that Mama suffered."

"That was surely unexpected," said Pablo.

"I'll say," agreed Anna Maria.

"I assumed she was a snooty old hen, when here all along she was in mourning," said Pablo. "I guess we were a bit hasty in our judgment of the poor woman."

"I guess so," agreed Anna Maria, whose mood suddenly shifted. Watching the poor woman sob over the loss of her mother caused Anna Maria's heart to ache for her own mother. The shift in temperament was overwhelming and Anna Maria began to wilt alongside Pablo, whose pace suggested the desire to be free from the enveloping crowd. He felt the burden of her weight as he dragged her along. She repeatedly glanced back at the weeping woman until her eyes could no longer dissect the crowd.

"Well, Crow's Farm is in that direction," said Pablo with near certainty. "Back in '09, Cornelius sent Gabriel to pick up me and the others who came in at the station. I'll bet nowadays there's a bus that runs out that way; but it's such a nice day, and it isn't more than a couple of miles, as I remember. What do you say, my sweet Cheerianna? It would be just like our Sunday strolls in Brownsville, only this time we'll get to explore a new land."

"Sure," replied Anna Maria, though she was still in the throes of her gloom and didn't know to what she was answering. Sensing his granddaughter's preoccupation, Pablo rambled on with delight about Kentucky and the summer of '09, with the hope of lifting the spirit of his young traveling companion. He chuckled when he recalled Ernest's constant jabbering and faking of dizzy spells, and the education he received on Schopenhauer and Dickens. Then, in the midst of all his own jabbering, in the not too far distance he spotted their destination.

"My sweet Cheerianna." Pablo's tone was devoid of the lighthearted rambling that he demonstrated throughout their hike from the station. "It's been a long journey and I know you're tired. But our lives have changed and now we must have the strength to change with them. Many times as a younger man, I had to summon whatever strength I had in order to change…in order to survive. Now you must do the same."

For the first time in her young life, Anna Maria Cordero understood that all the fanciful tales that Pablo told, and which she eagerly looked forward to hearing when together on their Sunday strolls, were just that…tales. Loosely based on reality, perhaps, though tales, nonetheless.

"You must be brave like your mother," Pablo told her. "Then one day, if it is God's will, we'll all be together again."

"I'll try, Grandfather," said Anna Maria. "I promise, I'll try."

When first he arrived at Crow's Farm, with only a glimmer of familiarity, Pablo observed a man clad in the tradition of a farm worker, but appeared too old for such labors. His advanced years caused him to lurch with a slight tilt at the waist, but still there remained a hop to his gait. The man returned Pablo's gaze, and when doing so had a similar glimmer.

Only for a moment, though, did he regard Pablo and his young traveling companion. After which, he appeared to narrow his gaze to the brown, suede satchel that hung at Pablo's side—the very same satchel that rarely left his side throughout the summer of '09.

"Can I help you folks?" the fellow called out. As he spoke, he made his way toward Pablo and Anna Maria. Pablo wasn't sure if the man was thoughtful enough to meet them halfway, or was heading them off, preferring that those taken for strangers not advance any further.

"I've come a long way hoping to see Cornelius Crow," Pablo called back to the man. "I worked for him many years ago. I'm sure he'll remember."

"Oh, *that* Cornelius Crow," the man said. "Well, I'm sorry to say, he ain't around no more. Died a few years ago, he did. I guess word didn't reach wherever it is you're from."

"I guess not," said Pablo, who was seized with the sort of misgiving that usually follows when a man has heard that his very last bit of hope has been crushed. In recent years, Pablo had lost touch with the folks from Madisonville, many of whom had passed. The news of Cornelius Crow, as the man suggested, never reached him. Not wanting Anna Maria to sense his dismay, Pablo managed to maintain his poise. It was desperate times, though, and he was a desperate man. This was a fact that he wanted the man to understand, but not at the cost of upsetting his granddaughter.

"But his son took over the farm," the man added, brightly. "Oh, not Ernest. That boy couldn't get away from here fast enough. Took off for college and that was the end of him. He's up in the big city, he is. He's one of them 'intellectuals', if you know what I mean. 'Course he does come back to visit on holidays; drives a real fancy car, too. Never did like the farm, that boy. But young Cornelius filled his daddy's shoes just fine, he did. 'Course he ain't so young himself anymore."

Pablo sighed when remembering how well he and young Cornelius worked together back in the summer of '09.

"When did you say you worked here?" the man asked.

"The summer of '09," replied Pablo.

"The summer of '09? Why, that was the summer the flu done hit us," the man said. "You're Pablo, aren't ya? Pablo Cordero from Texas! Now I recognize you!"

"Gabriel?" said Pablo.

"Looks like we both put on a few years," chuckled Gabriel. Then he doffed his hat, revealing a place where hair once grew, then pointing to a back that has labored more days than most. Pablo, in turn, reached for a head that's now exclusively home to silver strands.

186

"That was some summer, '09 was," said Gabriel. "Looked like we were done for, for sure. But by the grace of God, and with the help of friends, by the time it was all over it turned out to be the best summer we ever had. Cornelius never forgot you, ya know. He always said what a good worker you were…and smart, too."

"Well, I've come all the way from Texas in need of work," said Pablo.

"I'm not surprised," said Gabriel. "Times are hard and they're only gonna get worse. Folks have been shiftin' all over the place and combin' the countryside tryin' to find work. But I'm sure Cornelius'll find something for you. By the way," he added. "Who's your lil' travelin' companion?"

"This is my granddaughter, Anna Maria," replied Pablo. "But I call her Cheerianna."

"She's not lookin' too cheery," said Gabriel. The remark came with a friendly wink and with the hope of coaxing a smile from Anna Maria, who by then was looking well spent.

"We've had a long journey," said Pablo.

"I don't doubt it," said Gabriel.

A man will go through many more changes in the course of twenty-one years, when beginning at age fifteen, rather than let's say…thirty—which was the respective ages of Pablo and Cornelius in 1909. However, Pablo was no more recognizable to Cornelius, than Cornelius was to Pablo.

"It was often that my father talked about the summer of '09," said Cornelius Crow. "And when he did, he never failed to mention your name. In fact, he called Edgar Trudeau that very next summer to see if you wouldn't mind trekkin' on up here to Kentucky. He was disappointed to find out that you moved on."

"It's sure nice to be so well thought of," said Pablo.

"Well, just like back in the summer of '09, if there's one thing that still rings true twenty-one years later, that is, there's always plenty of work to be done here at Crow's Farm," said Cornelius. "Hell, there's days it seems that if I brought in the army it still wouldn't be enough."

"Cornelius, you're soundin' more and more like your daddy every day, may he rest in peace," said Gabriel.

"Corneeeelius," called Irma Crow from the front porch. With loveliness and clarity her voice rang out across the acreage.

"Mmm, must be lunchtime," said Cornelius. "You two must be good and hungry after your long journey."

"We'd be lying if we said we weren't," replied Pablo.

"So just who is this beautiful young traveling companion of yours?" asked Cornelius.

"My granddaughter, Anna Maria," replied Pablo. "But I call her Cheerianna."

"She's not looking too cheery about now," remarked Cornelius.

"So she's been told," said Pablo.

As if handed a cue, the tired and droopy eyed Anna Maria let out a yawn. Just as they all turned and went marching toward the house, she felt something tugging at her arm.

"Shhh," whispered Johnny Crow. He put a finger to his lips after stealthily coming up from behind her. He gave a wave of his hand to indicate that she should follow him. At first Anna Maria recoiled. Her eyes went in search of Pablo, who along with Cornelius and Gabriel, were well on their way to the house. She looked back at Johnny and right away was able to size up the fresh faced farm boy and determine that he was anything but a threat. Again Johnny reached for Anna Maria's arm. "Come on," he urged, pulling her along. "I wanna show you something."

Despite not knowing the prospect, Anna Maria chose the bright, clear eyes of the farm boy over her growling stomach. This wasn't a decision driven by any measure of curiosity, but rather, after listening to three men drone on about the summer of '09, she was delighted to discover someone her own age. It mattered not that Johnny, with more force than she would have liked, was whisking her away to an unknown destination. She figured that he was a good person to know.

As the men were approaching the house, Pablo watched the workers march out of the fields. "Well, I'll be darned," he said. He would have recognized the contemptuous eyes of Flynn anywhere—even after a *hundred* and twenty-one years. Everything else about the man may have changed, but the burning disdain he seemed to harbor for the world was still ingrained in his eyes. Pablo followed those eyes. They were fixed in the direction of the porch, where stood the lovely Irma Crow. The sweet way in which Irma called out for Cornelius seemed to agitate Flynn. *Cornelius either chose to ignore the hateful way in which Flynn glared at his wife, or didn't notice,* Pablo thought. He had no way of knowing which.

"Yeah, he's still with us," said Cornelius. "And the miserable bastard hasn't changed a bit."

"Why do you keep him on?" wondered Pablo.

"His old man lost their farm a few years back," said Cornelius. "Rumor had it, it was gambling debts, but no one knows for sure. When a fella loses his farm, all sorts of stories start floatin' around. Anyway, the
188

poor bastard ended up drinking himself to death. I guess in a way I felt sorry for Flynn; although, I don't know why; he was no less sour at fifteen and then he had no cause."

"Some folks don't need a cause to be sour," said Gabriel. "It's just the way there are, always mad at the world. And if ya ever troubled yourself to go askin, I'm bettin' they couldn't even tell you why."

"I recon you're right," said Cornelius. "But I have to admit, it took a lot for ol' Flynn to come here with his hat in his hand asking for work. I suppose I didn't have the heart to turn him away."

Pablo looked up at Irma Crow and thought, *who couldn't fall in love with that smile? Cornelius Crow was a lucky man.*

Before Pablo made Irma's acquaintance, he glanced back once more at Flynn. Flynn's father gambled away the family farm, or so it was rumored. Cornelius inherited the family farm, paving the way to a good life and the *lovely smile* that awaited him on the porch. Pablo didn't need anyone to draw him a picture to understand Flynn's resentment. But, as Gabriel so accurately pointed out, "Some folks don't need a cause to be sour." Lord knows, Flynn didn't need a cause, but he sure had one. Irma Crow's lovely smile and sweet voice calling out her husband's name were daily reminders for Flynn, of all that Cornelius Crow had and what he himself lacked. What others saw as delightful feminine charm from a wholesome and good woman, for the sour man, was a blunt instrument that every day managed to find its way to his head. Pablo would have been wary of Flynn no matter, but now wondered how long before the tightly wound and sour man cracked up altogether.

Pablo watched, as not without a terrific effort, the tightly coiled screen door which led to the porch was being pushed open. The effort it took by whoever was trying to gain the porch reminded Pablo of the first time he saw Miss Lillie's boney figure emerging from her cottage.

"Either I'm getting older or this door's getting heavier," the woman grumbled. "I don't know which it is, but neither is any good."

It was the very same door through which everyday Johnny Crow would explode, and with baseball in hand would make for the barn. He kept forgetting to hold the handle; the tightly coiled door would snap back, producing an awful banging against the jamb. By the time Cornelius and Irma's ears recovered and they had finished yelling to Johnny, "Please, next time won't you try and remember to hold the handle," the youngster was well out of range.

"Either the door goes or the boy goes," Cornelius would grumble in jest, as if leaning in favor of ousting the boy. "One of these days I'll be shaving when he runs outa here and you'll find me dead on the bathroom floor with my throat slit."

"If it's peace you were after, you should have wished harder for a girl," Irma would tell him. Then she'd follow with, "When that door stops slamming, you'll love the man, but you'll miss the boy. Oh, how you'll miss the boy." Her thoughtful words always warmed Cornelius's heart.

Pablo launched himself up the steps and onto the porch. He whizzed right on by Irma, whose acquaintance he had yet to make. This he did in order to embrace the woman who had just finished fighting her way through the screen door. Cornelius looked on with bemusement at the impromptu display of affection. Then he uttered, "I forgot that you two know each other."

"Only as long as you've been alive, my dear nephew," said Betsy Hutchinson, who then stepped back to examine Pablo, as though making certain that it was really him.

Pablo Cordero and Betsy Hutchinson hadn't but a moment to reminisce. Along with Cornelius, Irma, and Gabriel, the two old friends gasped, when somewhere off in the distance there came a thud, followed by a loud, shrill scream.

"Good lord, what was that?" cried Irma.

"I don't know," was Cornelius's wary reply, "but it sounded like it came from somewhere over near the barn."

"Whatever it was, it can't be good," said Gabriel. "We better get on over there."

They all took off in the direction of the barn. Cornelius led the way, while the older legs of Gabriel and Betsy Hutchinson lagged behind. It wasn't until then that Pablo realized that Anna Maria was no longer at his side.

"For cryin' out loud, Johnny," hollered Cornelius, as he tried to catch his breath, "what in the blazes do you think you're doing!"

"I wanted to practice my pitching with a real live batter up there, that's all," cried Johnny. "Honest, I didn't mean no harm."

"A real live batter!" shrieked Cornelius. "That's your idea of a real live batter—a terrified young girl!" He gestured to Anna Maria, who was still somewhat startled. "For cryin' out loud, Johnny, you could've killed her."

"But Dad, I had her stand two feet away from the plate and I threw a perfect strike right down the middle," Johnny proudly claimed.

"It's alright, sir," Anna Maria told Cornelius. "I wasn't expecting him to throw it so hard, that's all. I won't scream next time."

"Next time?" said Cornelius, as to clearly suggest that there wouldn't be a *next time.*

"My great nephew is practicing to be a professional baseball pitcher," Betsy Hutchinson told Pablo. Betsy's raised eyebrow told Pablo all he needed to know about what his dear old friend from Madisonville, Texas thought about her great nephew's fanciful pursuits.

"If anyone is still interested, lunch is ready and waiting to be eaten," said Irma Crow.

Not only did lunch include good, wholesome food, but bashful glances and curious exchanges between Johnny and Anna Maria. It also included the expected examination by the adults at the table, as they regarded Anna Maria's rare and exotic combination of fair skin, Mayan eyes, and cinnamon hair.

The work day ended, followed by supper, after which Pablo and Betsy slipped away for a quiet sunset-turned-dusky stroll of the farm's many acres. "I like a quiet walk, especially on the warm, humid evenings," said Betsy Hutchinson. "You can really smell the peaches and strawberries."

"I remember," said Pablo. "Aside from the antics of Ernest, that's my best memory of this place." After a thoughtful pause he added, "It's funny, but you don't notice these things when you're working…the smells, that is. But when the day is all done and everything becomes calm and quiet, and it's just past that time when the sun has disappeared, all the senses seem to come alive."

Betsy reached over and took hold of Pablo's arm. Despite her advanced age, she didn't need any assistance with walking. Rather, it was a gesture of affectionate over a shared sensibility. They went about the remainder of their stroll with their arms locked together.

"I'm surprised, but delighted to see you here," said Betsy.

"And I, you," said Pablo. "I never imagined you'd leave Madisonville."

"Well, when Doc Crandall passed, it was as if he took half the town's spirit with him," said Betsy. "Whenever anyone came up with an idea, before they'd dare breathe a word of it to anyone else, they'd always say, 'I'd better go and see what Doc thinks.' Then off they'd dash. Nothing ever got decided in Madisonville without first being run by Doc. He was the town's brain, trust, and counselor to all. Anyway, as you remember, Alice hung on a few years, but she was gone by '15. The town lost its matriarch and I lost my best friend. Then came the war and a few of our boys went off to fight. They all came home but one. It kinda gets you thinking…why *one?* And why *that* one? Instead of being thankful for the ones who made it home, all we could do was grieve for the one that didn't. I guess in a small town you learn to count your losses as much if not more than your blessings. Then came the winter of 1922. Of course that was when the good Lord went and pointed His finger at my Ben. It was at his funeral that I last saw you. Now, here I am, come home to roost at the place of my childhood.

"Cornelius and I had a few good years to reminisce our childhood before he passed on. We'd sit on the porch after supper in the fall and spring, sipping our tea and gazing up at the stars. On the warm summer nights we'd stroll arm in arm, just like we're doing tonight. He truly was a sweet man, my dear younger brother. I know Gabriel misses him something terrible. He was fond of saying, 'Gabriel and me have been together for so long we're starting to look alike.' It was always good for a laugh, especially with Gabriel being a colored man and Cornelius being so fair. And now with my dear brother gone, my nephew is grateful for every day that the good Lord keeps Gabriel around, because no one understands the soil we walk on better than him. But now it's your turn. I'm fairly certain that you weren't just in the neighborhood or were passing by. So what was it that brought you all the way up here to Kentucky?"

"You might say that my life in Brownsville ran its course," said Pablo. "It was time to move on."

"Oh?" said Betsy, with a note of skepticism that clearly suggested there must be a good deal more to the story than perhaps Pablo might have planned on revealing.

"I'm here at the behest of my daughter," he told her.

"And how is Martina?" wondered Betsy. "What a lovely child she was. And please do forgive me for not asking earlier."

"She's been better," said Pablo regrettably. "It was Martina that insisted I leave Brownsville. She pleaded with me to take her daughter, my sweet Cheerianna, away. She was of the notion that should Anna Maria discover her father's identity, which came close to happening, it would ruin her life. I must say, I'm inclined to agree. This Callahan character that Martina got mixed up with; he's a bad apple for sure—a real devil. You work your heart out for your family, always trying to do what's best, but it doesn't seem that the world can allow even *one* error in judgment. Anyway, my granddaughter should never come to know such a reality. But even so…"

"But even nothing," Betsy interjected. "Sometimes it's just best to trust a mother's instincts."

"Maybe so," said Pablo. "But I feel like a coward running off as I did."

"I've known you to be many things, Pablo Cordero, but never a coward," said Betsy. "Learn to trust Martina. *She's a tough little farm girl with a strong spirit.* Those were your exact words many Christmases ago, remember? And as I recall, Doc and Ben agreed because they were able to recognize her strength of character. I'm sure whatever troubles exist in Brownsville, they'll blow over. Meanwhile, you and Anna Maria can have a home here in Kentucky. Ahh, the strawberries, can you smell them?"

"*And* the peaches," said Pablo. "I'd almost forgotten just how big this place is."

"Incidentally, every so often I get a letter from Somerset Evans," said Betsy.

"And how is the good pastor getting along these days?" wondered Pablo.

"You know how it is with us old folks," said Betsy, as she playfully poked Pablo with her elbow, "we're never talking about life going forward, only of the *old days*. But he's fine, our good pastor. He always remembers to ask for you and wonders if you're alright and if I ever hear from you. He always did worry about you, as did we all. It was hard to imagine anyone so lovely as your Anna Maria leaving the world at such a young age."

"The good pastor worries about me, no doubt, but it has nothing to do with me grieving for Anna Maria," said Pablo.

"What makes you say such a thing?" wondered Betsy.

"The year I came for Christmas with Anna Maria, sometime between dinner and dessert I was counseled by our friend the pastor," said Pablo.

"Oh?" said Betsy, wary of what might follow.

"I needed counseling," said Pablo.

"This is beginning to sound strangely like a confession," said Betsy. Before she had the chance to brace herself, Pablo stepped in front of her.

"I killed a man, Betsy," he said. "Right before my mother died— just days before we met, in fact. I killed a man, and I did it with this."

Pablo reached into his brown, suede satchel and unveiled the beautifully hilted knife given to him by Josiah Walton. Betsy tried not to look too alarmed when staring at the shiny blade and remarkably crafted handle. Despite its beauty and fine workmanship, she wondered why on earth Pablo held onto an instrument used for such a deed.

"You must have had a good reason, right?" she asked, urging Pablo to inform her that was the case. "After all, Pastor Evans forgave you. Didn't he?"

"The man's name was Jed Wright," said Pablo. "He owned a farm on the Texas/Oklahoma border. He was my mother's rapist. I saw it happening right before my own eyes. First, he tried to pressure me into selling her. Imagine, thinking a son would sell his own mother. Well, what he couldn't buy, he decided to take by force. I knew it was coming."

"I'm so sorry you had to see such a thing," said Betsy.

"He was going to tell the other migrants that the only thing standing in the way of a little extra coin in their pay was the sale of a woman," said Pablo. "He was putting me in an impossible position. He rigged the game so that it came down to him or me. I had to make a choice. I should've taken Mama and ran off before things got so far. Maybe I didn't want to believe that it could really happen—that he was *that* evil, so I stayed. Then I killed him."

"I don't claim to be anything other than the wife of a baker and an old picker form Kentucky," said Betsy Hutchinson. "But I'd say you made the right choice. Lord only knows what Ben would have done in your shoes; bludgeoned the man with whatever was handy, I suppose. But I'm curious. It happened decades ago. You were only fourteen-years-old—still a boy, in fact. Why confess now after all these years?"

"Because you were always warm and kind and treated me like family," replied Pablo. "And now here you are, offering me the bosom of your home as a haven. At the very least I owe you the knowledge of how I came to turn up in Madisonville all those years ago. And yes, I made my peace with God and maybe even with myself, but I still wanted you to know."

Pablo regretted not telling Doc Crandall years ago when he had the chance. Then Alice Crandall died, followed by Ben Hutchinson. It was Pablo's belief that by telling Betsy, in spirit, he was telling them as well.

"Okay, that's fair enough," said Betsy. "But now let us think of more pleasant things, like the smell of ripening strawberries and peaches, and of blueberry pie, and that sometime between lunch and dinner I readied Ernest's old room for you and that beautiful granddaughter. Lord knows he won't be using it anytime soon."

"I'm afraid neither will I," said Pablo.

"But I don't understand," said Betsy.

"Times are tough and men are desperate," explained Pablo. "It wouldn't look good for someone to show up out of the blue and right away be granted certain privileges. The other workers might get resentful, leaving Cornelius to explain what? I certainly couldn't pass for a relative. So I had better make myself comfortable in one of those bunkhouses."

"I see your point," said Betsy. "Especially when I think of that Flynn character. He's got the disposition of a rhinoceros with a thorn in its ass; pardon my expression. I don't know why Cornelius keeps him on."

"I'll be grateful for anything that you can do for my grand-daughter," said Pablo. "But from sunup to sundown I'll be just another worker here on Crow's Farm. Although, I certainly wouldn't mind a few more of these evening strolls."

"Nor would I," said Betsy. "And furthermore, I'd consider it a terrible slight if from time to time you didn't sneak off for a slice of my blueberry pie. I make it almost as good as Ben used to."

"I will make it my solemn duty to do just that," vowed Pablo.

Before Pablo made for the bunkhouse to get acquainted with the men, he went and tucked Anna Maria into her new bed. It had been a long and exhausting trip from Brownsville to Louisville and she had no trouble collapsing despite her unfamiliar surroundings. Pablo gazed at her long cinnamon hair tossed atop a white pillowcase, where it appeared more striking than he remembered.

"Soon I'll write a letter to Mick and Marcie, and also to Marylou. I'll tell them where we are and why they need to look after your mother from time to time," said Pablo. "They'll understand."

"I'm sorry, Grandfather," said Anna Maria.

"My sweet Cheerianna, you mustn't blame yourself. It's not because of you that we had to leave," said Pablo. "You see, sometimes when we're young and foolish we make mistakes. And sometimes a mistake can catch up with us. When it does, it can become a complicated web in which even our children can get caught. That's why your mother sent us away. She wants her mistake to begin and end with her, so that you can have a good life and be happy. One day things will return to the way they were. You believe me, don't you?"

"Of course, Grandfather," was Anna Maria's weak reply.

Pablo wasn't sure whether Anna Maria's exhaustion was the cause for the weakness of her words, or if she was unable to provide, or perhaps *fake* conviction that was otherwise lacking. He made it as far as the bedroom door, when Anna Maria added brightly, "There's lots of nice people here. Gabriel makes me laugh and Johnny reminds me of Maxwell."

"Maxwell?" said Pablo.

"You remember, the boy from the train," said Anna Maria.

"Of course," replied Pablo.

"Oh, and guess what, Grandfather?" asked Anna Maria, moving from bright to perky and was now sitting up. "I hit the ball! I only tipped it, and it traveled only a few feet, but I still hit it. Johnny said the only reason that I was able to hit it was because his arm was getting tired. Then Cornelius came by. I thought he was gonna let Johnny have it. But when he saw how determined I was, he stopped. I'll bet tomorrow I'm really gonna sock one."

"I have no doubt that you will, my sweet Cheerianna," said Pablo. "I have no doubt at all."

Pablo walked away feeling a little lighter in his heart now that Anna Maria seemed in good spirits. However, as he made for the bunkhouses, it occurred to him that he had a dilemma. There was a choice to be made, though the odds were in his favor, as there were four bunkhouses and only one Flynn.

To Pablo's delight, not only was Crow's Farm still around, but so too were Gabriel and Cornelius, both of whom he was fond. Gabriel *was* and remained the chief overseer of this vast land called Crow's Farm, and after twenty-one years, without hesitation, Cornelius welcomed Pablo aboard. He would gladly labor for these two men. But the clincher was Betsy Hutchinson, who had "come home to roost" and was there to welcome him and Anna Maria with open arms. Pablo Cordero was once again the most fortunate unfortunate man in the world.

But as the saying goes: *A man can only stand so much good fortune.* Those were words Pablo recalled Mick utter many years ago during a bonfire night. The words rang true, as there was still the sour Mr. Flynn to consider.

Pablo gave a friendly wave to those well mannered enough to look his way when he entered the arbitrarily chosen bunkhouse. Four men were seated at a table and were playing a hand of gin rummy. Two of the men took the trouble of tipping their hats when he entered. Away from the table another was telling a story he apparently believed was hilarious, for he couldn't talk without laughing. The fellow who was the primary recipient of the story was laughing right along, though mostly out of politeness. He diverted his attention when Pablo entered the bunkhouse. The fellow was quick to return Pablo's friendly wave and had hoped that a stranger's entrance would shift the room's dynamics in a way that would put a swift end to the drawn out anecdote he was thus far forced to suffer through.

196

Unfortunately for the fellow and his burdened ear, that wouldn't be the case.

Sitting off in a corner, alone, excluded from the card game *and* story, was a man they all called Sauceman Sal. Salvatore Mascagni was an Italian immigrant who spoke little English, but whom Cornelius granted a small piece of land on which to plant plum tomatoes. From those tomatoes he made gravy for all the workers at Crow's Farm.

"If he ever thought to jar this stuff and sell it, he'd make a fortune," Cornelius often said.

Sauceman Sal's eyes brightened when he took notice of Pablo's dark complexion and ethnic features. Immediately, he felt less foreign and alone. Though, no sooner had Pablo made Sauceman Sal's acquaintance, another figure, which until then Pablo had yet to notice, stirred, then sat up in his cot.

"Well, what do ya know fellas; it looks like the varsity just showed up," said the sneering Flynn. "Now we got ourselves a genuine Mexican come to show us how to *really* work hard. Ain't we the lucky ones?"

"For God's sake, Flynn, let the poor guy get all the way through the damn door before you start grinding 'im up," barked Owen Hoyt.

Owen Hoyt was the only one in the bunch ever to stand up to Flynn. Not to suggest that he had ever gone after Flynn, but he would remind the sour man that he wasn't the only one in the room with an ample supply of testosterone. And although Owen Hoyt's remark indicated his disapproval, the sharp tone in which it was delivered had as much to do with the dismal hand of cards he was just dealt, than the derisive and reproachful manner in which Flynn regarded the newcomer's ethnicity.

"I meant no disrespect, fellas," Flynn announced to the room, avoiding Owen Hoyt's eyes. Flynn didn't want to give the impression that he was apologizing directly to Owen Hoyt. "We had us a Mexican come through here back in '09. If I'm not mistaken, I believe that was the year of the flu epidemic. Had a brown, suede satchel, he did. It looked just like the one this *here* fella is carrying. He was a devout sort and even read the Bible."

"You've got a good memory," remarked Pablo.

"You bet I do, Poco," were Flynn's menacing words.

Ignoring Flynn, Pablo claimed one of the two remaining cots. It wasn't until his body made contact with the inadequate mattress that he understood the depth his exhaustion. He cast his droopy eyes in the direction of the last remaining vacancy, but determined its suitability to be the same. The sadness over leaving Martina—the constant effort of keeping up his granddaughter's spirits—the long journey—it had all caught up with him. He could feel himself spiraling.

As he did, he heard the hateful Flynn muttering on about the depression, and that "decent white men are desperate for work" and how wrong it was for Cornelius to "hire a damn Mexican."

Silence followed the coarse remarks. Pablo wondered if the others chose to ignore Flynn or had *nodded* their agreement. At last, he decided that he was too old and tired to care. Spiraling further, he saw the faces from the train parading by in every which direction. The faces became a multitude, blending with those once familiar, who many years ago on Sunday mornings marched upon the Blessed Juan Diego de Guadalupe Roman Catholic Church. *What a shame for the poor lady with the absurd hat to have lost her mother,* he thought. It seemed a stray thought, though unlike the many that ran through his mind and were cast adrift, the thought of a dying mother lingered, as it brought about images of Dolci—some lovely—some disturbing. His eyes grew heavier, just as they had after lying down at the end of a bonfire night when plenty of Big George's moonshine had been present. As he continued to spiral, he imagined that he heard the crooning of Frankie "The Prick" Donato and Fat Fuck McGinn. Remembering his old friends brought a smile to his face, or so he imagined.

He had the sensation that he was dreaming, and yet, was still aware enough to wonder whether his smile was apparent to the others and what they would make of it. *I'd like to see Flynn try and tangle with the old bonfire gang,* he thought. The crooning of his old friends gave way to Miles Gordon's virtuosity, as Pablo discovered himself standing in the lounge of Serendipity, where he waited to be summoned by a woman whom he believed was, and turned out to be his grandmother. Poor Corina, who escaped atrocity, survived the foul men of the marketplace, but ended up a prostitute. Poor Dolci, to whom the world was so unkind. Poor Josiah Walton, who lost everything a man can lose, except his soul. *Where is God?* he wondered. *Where is God?* At last, he felt a tender and familiar warmth on his shoulder—the likes of which he hadn't felt in years. He cried for the sheer joy of a simple touch, then tossed aside *The Brownsville Herald* and leapt to his feet.

"You win, as always!" he cried out with great joy.

Anna Maria looked radiant with child—a true angel. Pablo fell to his knees and wrapped his arms around her. "How different it all would've been had you lived," he cried. "I've come to know too much of the world without you."

198

"You're almost home, my darling husband," Anna Maria told him. "It won't be much longer."

****

Kentucky was a border state, to which President Lincoln had declared, "I hope to have God on my side, but I must have Kentucky." The president eventually got his wish when Kentucky petitioned for its acceptance into the union.

Monte Crow, a Kentuckian, became a colonel in General Grant's army. Following the Civil War, he was granted forty acres of what ended up rich, fertile Kentucky land. The other two hundred and sixty acres that now make up the remainder of Crow's Farm, Monte himself purchased. Asked Lorelei, his wife, and the youngest granddaughter of one of the Sons of Liberty, who boasted knowing James Otis and Samuel Adams personally, "Is there anything left to the county or have we purchased it all?"

It could not be said of Monte Crow that he was a crackerjack farmer. Much of what he learned was *on the fly,* as some in the county had put it. In the early years much of the farm's acreage remained undeveloped; only wheat and hemp were grown and some livestock was raised. Once Betsy and Cornelius were old enough to work and the farm began turning a sizable profit, the growing was expanded to corn, hay, and berries. Livestock, which until then had been cattle, went on to include horses and poultry. By the time Betsy had become Mrs. Hutchinson, and Cornelius had taken over the reins, apple and peach orchards were added. After Cornelius died, his son, at Gabriel's suggestion, dropped hemp in favor of tobacco and also added soybeans.

Crow's Farm, from the view of the porch, was a vast expanse of land that went on for as far as the eye can see. This morning, as she did every morning since becoming Mrs. Cornelius Crow, Irma stood on the porch at the earliest sign of daylight. Leaning against the railing, she stretched out her arms and breathed deeply, as if trying to inhale all three hundred acres of the county's largest farm. From the dewdrops on the berries, to the sweetness of the orchards—even the residue from the threshers and mills she tried to draw to her nostrils. And just as the earthy combination of smells filled her with delight, Gabriel came strolling up the path and calling, "Mornin', Miss Irma."

No matter how early Irma woke, Gabriel was always up first. "The sun wouldn't dare show itself until certain Gabriel was up to greet it. Heaven help us if he ever oversleeps," the senior Cornelius Crow had said. It was a remark that Young Cornelius grew up hearing and would later adopt, and to which Irma would reply, "I believe it is *he* who hangs out the sun for all the world to see."

Gabriel became separated from his folks during a post Civil War riot in Tennessee. He traveled about in search of them, surviving by any means necessary. He wandered into Kentucky, where Monte Crow found the fourteen-year-old alone on the streets of Louisville. Gabriel worked side by side with Betsy and Cornelius and was put up in the main house. Monte believed that he was too young to be exposed to the roughneck manners of the hired hands and workers who lived in the bunkhouses. It took a few years, but Gabriel saved darn near every cent Monte paid him and was able to buy a place of his own.

"Coffee is inside waiting for you," said Irma.

"And I heard it a perkin' from down the road, I did," said the broad grinning Gabriel, whose exchanges with Irma were as affectionate as they were genuine.

Gabriel had watched Cornelius grow up as closely as he had watched his own two sons. He took every inch of every acre of Crow's Farm personally and was glad when Cornelius decided to follow in his father's and grandfather's footsteps. He had once said to the senior Cornelius when they approached the end of a difficult season, "The land is the land and will always be the land; it's only us that's gettin' old and tired." Then one day the junior Cornelius brought Irma home to meet the family. It was instant rejuvenation, as Irma was like a beacon of light in a tired old place that had gotten to where it could stand a few changes.

Other than his wife of forty years, who passed away back in '25, Irma Crow was the only woman on earth who without trying could make Gabriel smile. She was akin to the sunshine, and in her presence, everything seemed happier and more alive. *Every day is a gift,* is a phrase one hears a thousand times during one's life, but for most it's just words. But there exist those few who truly understand the gift of a new day, and Irma Crow was one such person. A late winter sunset setting ablaze the earliest signs of spring is one example of the many simplicities that stirred her inner being. Then one day the woman who gave Crow's Farm a renewed spirit, delivered a new life. Irma watched with amusement as that *new life*, which ordinarily came to the breakfast table and plopped in his chair with droopy eyes, stirred with fascination when he set his sights on the girl with the cinnamon hair and Mayan eyes.

Anna Maria Cordero awakened something in Johnny Crow that Irma thus far hadn't seen. It caused Irma's eyes to twinkle and she laughed. When the less observant Cornelius asked that his wife explain her laughter,

200

she did so with a subtle wink and nod. The result produced hardier laughter from Cornelius. Anna Maria and Johnny remained otherwise occupied, as each was enraptured by the other's charms. Both were oblivious to the fact that they were amusing the adults in the room…Gabriel included.

When breakfast concluded, Johnny and Anna Maria were dismissed to a litany of chores. Ordinarily this would have given Johnny cause to groan with displeasure. This morning, though, he let only a *small* groan escape before realizing that he could effectively use his chores as a means of showing Anna Maria just how important a figure he was at Crow's Farm. And by golly that's just what Johnny did.

Johnny rose to his feet and sprang into action, leaving behind Irma and Cornelius to wonder, "Who has stolen our son's body?" Johnny Crow made throwing feed into a coop sound as complicated as physics, and a task only someone with a golden right arm that would one day land them on a major league roster was capable of tackling. Since Anna Maria's arrival, Johnny had already reminded her six times of his future as a major league pitcher. Though, to be honest, she wasn't counting. For all she knew it could have been a hundred and six times—it didn't matter; where she was concerned, Johnny Crow was a friendly voice after a long journey, much of which had been made with a heavy heart.

"Ya see, it's all in the wrist," said Johnny. He rolled his wrist such, that he scattered the feed evenly throughout the coop.

Next it was off to milk the cows. It's quite possible that every dairy producing animal in all of Jefferson County could have been milked by the time Johnny finished with his dissertation on the art of yanking teats.

"Ya see, it's all in the technique," he said, a point he made ad-nauseam. When Anna Maria asked for a try, Johnny insisted that she first spend the next few days observing. She shrugged at the suggestion, as it didn't appear to her that secreting milk from cows was a daunting task and required only a slightly higher degree of skill than throwing feed into a coop. Nevertheless, she figured it prudent to allow Johnny his self-aggrandizing.

Next they grabbed baskets and set off into the fields under a warm June sun for a session of berry picking. Not even Johnny could complicate berry picking, though in the beginning he made an effort to do just that. It didn't take him long, though, to realize how ridiculous he was beginning to sound. At last, the tutorial on chores too simple for words came to an end. All that remained were two young people trying to see who could fill their basket the fastest, and Anna Maria won in a landslide. Though, it should be noted that she wasn't as distracted as Johnny.

The bright June sun in Anna Maria's long mane of cinnamon hair was the most thrilling display of brilliance that Johnny Crow had even seen—even more so than any afternoon sun he saw shining down on a golden wheat field with a gentle breeze blowing through it and making the stalks appear as if dancing. More brilliant than a sunset in an orchard following a late afternoon shower. These were things in which Irma Crow found beauty and was always pointing out to her son. But the play of sunlight in a young girl's beautiful mane of hair was a new thrill for Johnny, and he wanted to dive into its loveliness. His dream of one day becoming a major league pitcher took on a new dimension. Anna Maria sat in the stands and was wringing her hands amid the thousands anxiously awaiting their hero to strike out what they prayed would be the final batter of the World Series. The drama was building with each pitch. Then Johnny found Anna Maria's exotic eyes in the crowd. This allowed him to reach back for a little extra. The ball rolled off his fingertips, and in an instant went blazing past the batter. The umpire stood and with emphasis called "*strike three!*" Jubilation followed. Indeed, Johnny Crow was a young boy with a big dream. Though it occurred to him after his rapture, if for some reason the major leagues didn't come calling, he could end up the happiest farmer in all of Kentucky if Anna Maria Cordero became a fixture at Crow's Farm.

Johnny smiled sheepishly when Anna Maria began to help fill his basket. They went and unloaded their harvest before making two more trips into the field. Afterward they headed for the barn.

The barn was the place where Johnny escaped with his baseball cards and dreams. Lately he had been burying himself under the hay in the loft when dreaming of things that weren't related to baseball. At last, he could now apply a specific name and face to those dreams, and it would heighten the sensation in ways he never imagined.

"You can milk the cows next time," Johnny told Anna Maria. "I should've let you try it today."

"That's okay, Johnny," she said.

"And you can toss that feed into the coop any old way you want," her further confessed. "They're gonna eat it up, no matter."

"I know," said Anna Maria. "But I still learned a lot today, thanks to you."

The remark made Johnny smile.

"What are those?" she asked after Johnny reached into his pocket.

"My baseball cards," he replied. "Wanna look at 'em?"

"Sure," said Anna Maria.

The names and faces on the cards couldn't have been more unfamiliar. Nevertheless, Anna Maria listened attentively, as card after card, and with painstaking detail, Johnny took her through the entire stack. It didn't take her long to wish she hadn't said *"sure,"* but she hung in there just the same.

"I like that card!" she called out, as suddenly her interest peaked. "He's wearing a nice suit and I like his mustache."

"It's called a uniform," said Johnny. "And all the players back in his day had mustaches."

"The card looks much older than the others," Anna Maria acknowledged.

"It is," said Johnny. "It's over forty years old and it belonged to my grandfather. He said he saw all the great ones play: Honus Wagner, Tris Speaker...even Babe Ruth! 'But no one could hit like Pete Browning,' he used to say. Just think how great he must've been to get a nickname like *"The Louisville Slugger."* I mean, he would've had to have been the best. Right?"

"Of course," agreed Anna Maria. She allowed herself to slip into Johnny's world, a place where boyhood heroes and pipedreams of becoming just like those heroes were paramount.

"It's been since forever that we had a major league team here in Louisville," said Johnny. "We have minor league teams, though, but anytime we want to see a major league game, we have to take the train all the way to Saint Louis. But I don't mind. I like riding the train."

"Corneeeelius," Irma called from the porch. Her lovely voice rang out beautifully across the acres. It reminded Anna Maria of when Martina would call out, *"Anna-Mareeeeahhhh."*

"It must be lunch time," said Johnny.

"Good, I'm starving," said Anna Maria."

Anna Maria departed the barn knowing more about baseball than she ever cared to. Johnny departed wishing he could somehow grow a mustache. As they made for the house, the men were coming out of the fields. Many, like Owen Hoyt, had been at Crow's Farm for years and Johnny had known them since he was a toddler. The rest were victims of the depression, desperate for work...any kind of work. Johnny waved hello to those he knew and all but one bothered to return his friendly gesture. It was *that one* that managed to garner Anna Maria's attention.

"What's wrong?" asked Johnny.

"Nothing," lied Anna Maria, but Johnny clearly saw his new friend shudder, and her exotic eyes, which since her arrival had stirred the young dreamer, registered fear.

Anna Maria didn't recognize the man's face, nor any other discernible traits...except his eyes; she knew his eyes and would have known them anywhere. Those eyes ruined many a day and often invaded a peaceful slumber. Her rational mind told her that it couldn't be possible for Callahan to have turned up in Kentucky. But rationality supplanted by fear is common enough among adults, never mind young girls. That night, when Pablo went to tuck in his granddaughter, he had to do *some* tap dance in order to convince her that Flynn wasn't Callahan.

"My darling Cheerianna, surely you must know that it isn't possible," said Pablo.

"I know, Grandfather," she said. "But his eyes!"

"Look, I'm not saying Flynn is a good man, because he isn't," said Pablo. "In fact, he's miserable and rotten, and you'd do best to try and stay away from him. But he's not Callahan...not in body *or* spirit. You believe me, don't you?"

"Of course I believe you, Grandfather," replied Anna Maria. "I know you would never try and convince me of something unless it was the truth." After an exchange of warm smiles and a comfortable silence, she added, "You look tired, Grandfather."

"I'm getting old," he said with a smile.

"Do you *want* me to disagree with you, so that we can argue?" she asked, glaring up from her pillow.

"I would like that very much," said Pablo with a chuckle. "But it won't change a thing. The truth will still be the truth."

"You have that look again, Grandfather," said Anna Maria.

"And just what look might that be?" asked Pablo brightly. He always swelled with curiosity whenever his granddaughter was about to reveal any notions that stemmed from her own intuition.

"The look you get whenever you've been thinking about my grandmother," replied Anna Maria.

"Ahh, my sweet Cheerianna, your beauty is only equaled by your perceptiveness," said Pablo. "And you would be right; I dreamed of your grandmother last night, in fact. She's been on my mind all day. And when I talk to her, I tell her all about you. She's very proud."

"I talk to her as well," said Anna Maria. "And I tell her all about *you.*"

"Oh?" said Pablo.

"Yes, Grandfather," she said. "I tell her all about your mischievous ways."

"My what!" cried Pablo, feigning indignation.

"She knows all about your moonshining," said Anna Maria.

"I don't doubt it," said Pablo. Then he collapsed in bed beside his granddaughter and they laughed until their sides hurt.

****

One laborious day passed after another. As expected, the temperature began rising when the calendar neared July. In the morning hours, Johnny and Anna Maria worked on their chores. In the afternoons they were free to be children in summer. Johnny worked on his pitching, while Anna Maria stood at the plate watching pitch after pitch pound against the barn door. Occasionally, she would take a swing, producing only a foul tip or dribbler that stopped rolling a few feet in front of the plate. Johnny was always handy with an excuse whenever Anna Maria was able to get wood on the ball, either claiming that his arm was getting tired, or that he was trying out a new pitch that he had yet to perfect. Afterward, they would go and cool off in the barn, but as soon as Johnny went reaching for his baseball cards, Anna Maria would beg to go and watch the men thresh wheat or husk corn. Sometimes she would clamor to go off into the fields to watch the combines in action. The machinery fascinated her; she could sit in the sun all afternoon watching each piece of equipment perform its specific function. She wanted to learn all about the inner workings of each machine, and like her mother as a child at Trudeau's Farm, she asked a million questions. Unlike Martina, though, who at age five was only out to charm grown men, Anna Maria's interest was genuine, as evidenced by the astuteness of her questions, which were answered accordingly.

On the contrary, Johnny couldn't have cared less. He found the machinery an endless drone of humdrum, and their purpose for their implementation his life's albatross. The way Johnny figured, if God was *just*, He would have given human beings the ability to digest tree bark and gravel so that he wouldn't have had to grow up a farm boy.

So that's how it was with Johnny and Anna Maria in the summer of 1930: She would pretend to have a keen interest in baseball, while he agonized through lesson after lesson on the inner workings of farm equipment. Their fascination was with one another, though, not one another's interests; but since they only had one another for company, for the time being both baseball and machinery were tolerated. Then one day it happened; Anna Maria Cordero got her timing down, and in a big way. The result sent Johnny home looking sulkier than his mother had ever seen him. Irma was busy that day and for a while pretended not to notice her son's gloom.

When she finally bothered to asked, Johnny cried, "How am I ever gonna become a major league pitcher, when I can't even throw a ball by a girl? She's hitting every darn thing I throw up here!"

At first, Irma thought that her son must be exaggerating. But that wasn't the case; Anna Maria *had* sent pitch after pitch sailing over Johnny's head. After each time Johnny retrieved the ball, he would return to the mound, then rear back and throw it harder. But the harder he threw it, the further Anna Maria hit it. She found the sound that the bat made when it squarely met the ball, satisfying. The last straw, as such occurrences are often referred to, came when she sent one sailing clear into the cornfield. Johnny threw down his glove in disgust and went storming off in the direction of his house.

"Right now, you and Anna Maria are the same size," Irma explained to the sulking young man, who was convinced that his dream was coming apart at the seams. "But over the next few years, you'll grow and become much stronger...you'll see. And when you throw that ball it'll be like a blur. No one will be able to hit it."

Johnny Crow was too conflicted and was only half-listening to Irma's encouraging words. The very girl, who time and again caused him to sneak off to the barn and bury himself in the hayloft, was killing his dream. For Johnny, as would have been the case for most young boys, this was unfamiliar territory.

Anna Maria picked up Johnny's glove, dusted it off and went looking for Gabriel. One thing about ol' Gabriel, along with his many other qualities, he never acted put upon, or too busy for a chat— especially when sought out by a youngster. Anna Maria never approached Gabriel for the purpose of idle chatter, and today was no different. Though this wouldn't be a conversation about farming, or the inner workings of machinery, but something much more rudimentary—or, complicated, depending on how one perceives the many dilemmas men and women have created for one another. It was Anna Maria's belief that Johnny should be proud of her newly found batting skills—that she was beginning to excel at the one thing he talked volumes about from sunup until sundown. Pablo and Martina had taught Anna Maria many things, but they hadn't gotten around to the manipulation of the male ego. This sly art form she would learn from an old farmer, who was in possession of more than his share of age, wisdom, and experience.

Anna Maria spent the remainder of the afternoon acting as an extra pair of hands, while in the grip of Gabriel's life experiences, which she found delightful. And as folks of a certain age are wont to, Gabriel doled out his experiences in generous portions. The well seasoned farmer and the young girl talked, laughed and shared, until Irma's lovely voice rang out beautifully from the porch.

"Must be time for supper," said Gabriel.

"Gabriel, do you miss your wife?" asked Anna Maria.

"Oh, every day, I do," he told her. "Sometimes I think I'm just here countin' the days until the good Lord finally points his finger and tells me it's time to come home. Some days I wonder what's takin' Him so long, 'cause I know my sweet Marybeth is up there waitin' on me. And between you and me, she was never the most patient woman. But other days are fine, like today for instance, when I'm talkin' to you. But you better get along, now. Don't wanna keep Miss Irma waitin'." As Anna Maria turned and prepared to go sprinting off, Gabriel added, "Now don't forget what we talked about: Johnny may be boy in his heart, but when he's around you, he wants to feel like a man...he wants to feel heroic."

As Anna Maria was making for the house, she stopped and watched the men coming from the fields. Some, like Gabriel, were locals and would head for home, only to return bright and early the next day. Most, though, headed wearily for the bunkhouses for the most basic of meals and a cot. Anna Maria's eyes managed to find Flynn's, whose contemptuous glare made her shudder. She turned away. Flynn's laugh was menacing and victorious when he saw the effect that he had on the young girl.

When she dared to once again look his way, she thought it odd to see Owen Hoyt and Sauce-man Sal break away from the pack and head for the house. The two appeared grim and troubled, and yet were resolute in their march. Their unwillingness to look Anna Maria's way gave her a paralyzing sense of foreboding. With her feet fixed to the ground, her eyes traveled from Owen Hoyt and Sauce-man Sal to the miserable Flynn, and then back again. Finally, every last man had come from the fields, with one lone exception. Anna Maria took off running into the fields, screaming for her grandfather.

****

"You're looking kinda sallow there, Pablo," Owen Hoyt had cared to mention. "Everything alright?"

"I'll be fine," was Pablo's reply. "There's not much left to the day."

"Why no you relax, Senior Cordero," said Sauce-man Sal. "*We* finish up."

"Is everything alright? Relax, Senior Cordero? What is this, a damn country club!" barked Flynn.

"For cryin' out loud, Flynn!" Owen Hoyt hollered in return—imploring the rigid Flynn for an ounce of compassion. "Clearly you can see the man's not well. And what in the hell has he ever done to you, anyway? You been up his ass from the minute he got here. Why don't you give it a rest already."

"Twenty-one years ago when Cornelius' old man was in trouble, I came and helped him out," said Flynn. "I didn't want to, but I did. But when *my* father was in trouble and losing his farm, no one offered a hand! No one lifted a damn finger for *him*. I had to come here with my hat in my hand and *beg* for a damn job. And now we got niggers tellin' us how to farm and Mexicans workin' right alongside us! The whole fucking world is upside-down!"

"Anziano!" cried Sauce-man Sal, as the distressed Pablo Cordero collapsed to one knee and tried to speak.

"Just let 'em be," said Flynn. "We got work to do."

"Fuck you, Flynn," shouted Owen Hoyt.

Owen Hoyt abandoned his task and ran to Pablo's side. He put an ear to Pablo's mouth to try and catch his faint words. Owen cradled the slumping man and gently lowered him to the ground. No sooner was his head resting on the ground, the life of Pablo Cordero had expired.

****

Cornelius arranged for a decent Christian burial, after which, Johnny and Anna Maria remained hidden away in the barn. The two sat atop the hayloft with their legs dangling and talked about anything that would draw their minds away from the fact that, in the kitchen, Anna Maria's fate was being decided.

"So what are we gonna do about the girl?" asked Cornelius.

"*The girl* will stay here with us, of course," said Betsy Hutchinson. She then glared disapprovingly at her nephew for not being respectful enough to refer to Anna Maria by name.

"With us?" said Cornelius, as though such a prospect had yet to cross his mind.

"Pablo Cordero was a dear friend of mine and I loved him," said Betsy. "I also promised to look after his granddaughter and that's just what I aim to do."

"But Aunt Betsy, she's a human being," said Cornelius. "You can't just possess her as though she were some trinket you came by at the marketplace. Surely the poor girl must have *some* family *somewhere* who can be responsible for her."

"For now, she has only us." Betsy's firmness indicated to her nephew that, in the matter of Anna Maria Cordero, she had no intention of yielding.

"Cornelius, surely you wouldn't put her out in the street…would you?" Irma chimed in.

"Nephew, you are the head of this household—I've never for a second disputed it—I never once undermined your authority," said Betsy. "But this is *our* house, and I must insist that the child stay."

"She's a lovely girl, Cornelius," said Irma. "And it would break Johnny's heart it she were sent away."

"She knows all the equipment—every piece of machinery like the back of her hand," Gabriel told Cornelius. "And she's taken quite an interest of all the goings on around here, and she's a real fast learner, too. It won't be long 'fore she's a real asset to the farm. I can vouch for her as sure as I'm standin' here."

"Well, I guess that settles it, then," said the shrugging Cornelius, as Gabriel's reasoning put an end to the matter. But before they moved on, Betsy Hutchinson cleared her throat with emphasis. It was a signal to remind Gabriel of the one remaining issue yet to be discussed.

"While we're all here," said Gabriel, "just yesterday, Owen Hoyt happened to pass along Pablo's dying words."

Cornelius and Irma turned an eager ear toward Gabriel; Betsy, too, as she was pretending to hear the words for the first time.

"He said at last he was finally goin' home to his Anna Maria," Gabriel went on. "But before that, he mentioned some fella named Lefty Carson. Said he was livin' in some mission over in Saint Louis and that he needed help."

"Well, that settles it," said Irma. "We can't deny a man his last dying wish."

"Of course not," said Betsy.

"I suppose one of us should go to Saint Louis and try to find this Lefty Carson and see what we can do for him," said Irma.

"*One* of us? *We?* For crying out loud," grumbled Cornelius.

"My, haven't we become a couple of manipulative old coots?" a smiling Betsy Hutchinson whispered to Gabriel, once Cornelius and Irma had left the room.

"We didn't do anything your daddy wouldn't have done if he were still here," Gabriel whispered in return. "He and Miss Lorelei were the two kindest folks I ever knew."

"How true," said Betsy.

During the time in which Cornelius had gone in search of Lefty Carson, more or less, Anna Maria had become Gabriel's apprentice. Not only was it a constructive way of channeling her grief, but Gabriel also provided her a window, albeit a small one, into her grandfather's past. From the summer of '09, a decade before Anna Maria was born, grew the unlikeliest of friendships…an eleven-year-old girl and an aging farmer. Day after day the two bonded over a month that occurred twenty-one years ago. Soon they were no longer a child and an old man, but two people, who more than anything looked forward to spending time together. Anna Maria still ran through the morning chores with Johnny. The chores were mindless and she had outgrown them, though she still enjoyed the berry picking.

Cornelius and Irma had started Johnny out with the simplest of chores with the hope that his interest would grow and that one day he would discover farming *an invaluable labor and honorable profession*, as Dutch Kirby use to say. Though it wasn't long before Cornelius realized that his son would walk a path similar to that of his brother Ernest. So much for trying. But who can blame Cornelius? After all, every man wants to die knowing that his life was worthwhile and that his son was proud of him; and what better validation then a son wanting to walk in his father's footsteps.

After lunch, Anna Maria would take the time to mollify Johnny by standing at the plate in front of the barn door, where she unsuccessfully flailed away at pitch after pitch. So that her ineptness appeared plausible, she occasionally tapped a little dribbler that stopped rolling a few feet in front of Johnny. She cited that Johnny "must be throwing harder" and that the day that she sent his pitches soaring over head and into the cornfield must have been "dumb luck."

"Okay, last pitch," she called. "Gabriel is waiting for me."

Johnny leaned back and fired a perfect strike right in the center of the faded white rectangle that he painted on the barn door last summer.

"Wow, Johnny! That was so fast, I could hardly see it!" said Anna Maria. Then she laid down her bat and was off to see Gabriel. While still within an earshot, she turned and called to Johnny, "Why don't you come along? Gabriel is so interesting to talk to."

"That's okay," said Johnny. He halfheartedly waved at Anna Maria and walked dejectedly to the barn. One minute Anna Maria had his spirits to where they were soaring sky high. The next, they were plummeting back to earth. He wanted to go and ask his mother what it means when a girl can do that sort of thing, but Irma would only be reaffirming what in his heart Johnny already knew.

Johnny wasn't troubled that he was traded in for Gabriel; he liked Gabriel as much as anyone. What troubled him was the reason. Johnny saw Anna Maria's willingness to want to learn about machinery, equipment, and farming, as her crossing over to the other side and into the world of adults. Johnny wanted to remain young and live in his little dream world and was overjoyed whenever Anna Maria joined him in that world. Now he feared that after only a short summer, she had outgrown him.

Johnny closed the barn door, leaving behind the world of adults and their endless drone of work, in favor of his baseball cards, boyhood dreams, and dreams of another sort. Despite his solitude, which brought about scattered moments of unbearable loneliness, the afternoon seemed to pass swiftly. No sooner had he cooled down, or so it had seemed, Irma's lovely voice could be heard ringing out over the acres. Johnny, who by then was buried beneath the hay, knew that he needed to hurry.

The barn, which all along provided a sanctuary from the harsh summer elements, seemed to bear in on Johnny with the strength of a midday sun. His legs had grown tense to where he couldn't have moved them had he wished. His breathing, although scarcely audible, became frenetic—the heat from his body, a force-field that would have wilted anything had it ventured too near. He was on fire, as there he laid, a conflicting entity simmering in the cool, still barn. In his feverish mind, he desired to be realized by Anna Maria—to understand the danger and thrill of being discovered—a discovery that would cause him to gush to Anna Maria, that he was powerless against her exotic beauty, which time and again had brought him to this point. Only in this altered state could he relish such desire, or even allow it as a thought.

It was only moments later that Johnny froze; he didn't dare to move a muscle. From his dubious position of buried beneath the hay in the loft, he saw sunlight flooding in by way of the barn door, which was being pushed open. He figured that since he hadn't responded to the call for supper, Irma must have sent Anna Maria out to search for him, and *she* knew where to look. Johnny stopped breathing altogether, though, when it was Irma whom he spied slipping into the barn.

Lord knows, the last thing a boy would ever want to have happen is for his mother to catch him with his pants down. Not that Johnny would be any less embarrassed were Anna Maria to stumble upon his current predicament, especially when no longer in the throes of his altered state and having gone limp. Either scenario was unfavorable; though in no way was Irma a religious fanatic, who would tell her poor compromised son that he had sinned and that he should be wary of a lightning strike. If ever the happenstance should arise, Irma would smile warmly and tell Johnny that he was a normal, healthy boy. Then later during an opportune moment, she would laugh like hell when relaying the news to Cornelius of their son growing up and the embarrassment it caused. However, Johnny had no way of knowing, as family time had yet to include the discussing of such things as adolescence and masturbation. With Anna Maria present, it's unlikely that it ever would. Cornelius would have to take Johnny aside and explain the changes in his body and the urges that would follow. Irma would have do the same with Anna Maria.

"I know you're in here, Johnny Crow, so there's no use in hiding," said Irma.

Johnny tried to will his mother to perform an about-face and exit the barn. During this effort he was also trying to concoct a story that would account for his whereabouts. Claiming to have been with Anna Maria and Gabriel wouldn't work. Even had he the time to collaborate on such a lie with Anna Maria, she would have requested an explanation, which at best would have been agonizing and awkward. Moreover, claiming to have been working with one of the hired hands would not only have been a bold-faced lie, but given Johnny's position on farm work, an implausible one at that.

Irma placed a foot on the first rung of the ladder as if preparing to climb up into the loft, or perhaps she intended only to peer over the edge. But that was as far as she got before her head jerked around and she stepped away from the ladder. Johnny was far too engrossed with his mother and his own precarious situation to realize that another party had entered the barn.

"Why Mr. Flynn, what brings you out here to the barn at this time of day?" asked Irma. Johnny peered through the hay over Irma's shoulder at Flynn, who was standing inside the barn door. It was a simple enough question that Irma had posed and was pleasant in its delivery, but Johnny had a clear sense that Flynn made his mother anxious.

"I'm surprised with as hard as you work you're not starving about now," added Irma, as though she was willing Flynn to leave the barn in favor of supper. She ended her remark with a contrived chuckle, which served to reveal just how wary she was of Flynn.

"What the hell would you know about hard work?" snapped Flynn. His tone carried an abundance of disdain toward Irma and what he perceived as her lofty and comfortable station.

Like Cornelius, Flynn believed the family farm, a place which for many years he coveted, would one day be passed on to him. He harbored plenty of bitterness toward Cornelius, and looked for reasons to harbor contempt for that which he loved. He saw Irma as the kind of wife he might have had…genteel, sweet, and pretty. It made him bitter, and over time his bitterness turned to hatred. He saw whatever privilege Irma enjoyed as coming at the hands of his long laborious days. And although Irma was certainly no stranger to hard work, she thought it prudent not to challenge Flynn on his perception of her, especially on the heels of his belligerent tone.

"I suppose I don't know very much about hard work," she humored him.

"You *suppose?*" scolded Flynn. "If you don't know about hard work, then maybe it's best to keep your mouth shut!" He followed his coarse remark by delivering a backhand that landed on Irma's cheek and sent her sprawling to the ground.

It was now apparent to Irma why Flynn turned up in the barn "at this time of day." He had been waiting for this opportunity ever since he arrived at Crow's Farm begging for a job. How many times had he heard Irma's lovely voice ringing out across the acres? *Corneeeelius.* And how many times had he seen the love in Cornelius' eyes when he was summoned by the sweetness of her voice. With each passing day, Flynn was pushed nearer and nearer to a place known as one's limits.

Flynn was a foul tempered youth whose disposition had only worsened with age. Now, all his wretchedness and misery, which was almost too much for a single human soul to possess, even for one so distorted as Flynn's, was about to become unleashed on Irma. He raised her from the floor by her hair, then brutally bent her over a bundled stack of hay. "Let me hear you call Cornelius, now, you dirty little cunt," he taunted.

At first, Irma wanted to scream with the slim hope that Gabriel and the others might hear her and come running. What stopped her, though, was Johnny. It was when Flynn slammed her delicate figure onto the bundled stack and lifted up her dress that she discovered Johnny's terrified eyes peeking out from under the hay.

Johnny's presence, no matter how ineffectual had it been known to Flynn, was of great comfort to Irma. His eyes, which Irma could have picked out of a crowd of thousands, were beacons of hope and reminders of all that was still good in the world. Despite the vileness of her tormenter, she smiled.

At first, Irma's idyllic expression confused Johnny. Then, as if struck, he understood. He understood as though he was right inside Irma's head reading from her very thoughts. The warmth of Irma's smile—the loveliness that blossomed from her eyes and soul—for the first time Johnny understood how much a part of it he was. *I can take all that the world can throw my way, as long as I have my dear, sweet boy by my side. So lie still, my son. Lie perfectly still and don't make a sound, for I want you to grow big and strong, and to chase your dreams. I want to embrace everything that is you, and one day we'll walk arm in arm under a beautiful sunset. We'll feel the warm rays on our face, and together we'll understand that the world is good. So you lie still and don't make a sound, and soon the bad man will be gone.*

Next came what both Johnny and Irma believed was an explosion. After which, in a strange and perplexing moment, Irma could sense the life leaving Flynn's body. She couldn't yet comprehend what the booming sound had to do with the odd sensation, but she knew they were related. Unsure of whether to sigh with gratitude, or fear for her own life *and* Johnny's, she turned about, but with trepidation. Her eyes then traveled to the ground, where sure enough, Flynn's lifeless body was discovered in a heap. Johnny rose up from under the hay and made the same discovery.

He and his mother braced themselves for a second explosion they sensed could follow, but it never came. When they removed their eyes from Flynn and looked up, they saw Anna Maria Cordero standing just inside the barn door. Dangling at her side and in her right hand was a smoking Colt Revolver—the very same single action 1873 model once owned by Theodore Roosevelt, Buffalo Bill Cody, Wyatt Earp, Billy The Kid, and of course, the ill-fated Jed Wright. Somewhere lodged inside Flynn's brain was a bullet that had been resting inside the gun's chamber for the past thirty-six years.

It was seldom that Pablo Cordero removed the Colt Revolver from his brown, suede satchel in order to admire its workmanship. He only did so when he thought no one else was nearby. Martina never knew of its existence. But not even a wily old grandfather could take into account the quiet little feet and spying eyes of a curious granddaughter.

214

"My sweet Cheerianna," Pablo had said, "this is no toy. It's dangerous and should never be taken from its hiding place. Do you understand?"

"Yes Grandfather. But why do you have it if it's so dangerous?" asked six-year-old Anna Maria.

"It was a gift from a prince," Pablo had told her. "And it isn't good to refuse a gift from someone so important as a prince."

Unlike Irma and Johnny Crow, who were both frozen in place and unable to speak, Anna Maria didn't look all too surprised by her actions *or* accuracy. She glared down at Flynn, as if possessing the desire to deposit another bullet into his body to make certain of his deadness. Irma finally managed to take hold of her senses and called over to Anna Maria. A moment later she pried her feet loose from the ground and went to her side. Again she called out her name, but Anna Maria didn't respond. Johnny remained perched in the hayloft. Still too frightened to move or speak, he permitted his eyes to travel from the hole in Flynn's head to Anna Maria's empty eyes. For years those empty eyes would haunt Johnny. At last, Anna Maria turned to Irma and said, "I fixed it."

Moments later, Gabriel, Owen Hoyt, and Sauceman Sal arrived. First, they glanced into the barn at Flynn's dead body sprawled out on the ground, then over at Anna Maria, who had already begun her slow march toward the house with the Colt Revolver dangling at her side. Gabriel suspected what must have occurred and cried that someone so foul as Flynn had violated Irma. He walked away, but shortly afterward returned with a gas can.

"Been awhile since we had a barn razin'," he said. "I recon we're overdue."

Gabriel spilled the gasoline around Flynn's body then struck a match. "I hope your soul is burnin' in hell the way your body is gonna burn in this here barn," he said. It was only minutes before the entire barn was consumed with flames.

"That's some helluva bonfire," said Owen Hoyt.

"I don't recon we'll be losin' much sleep over why we'll be needin' to build a new barn," said Gabriel.

"I recon you're right," said Owen Hoyt.

Flynn got drunk, torched the barn, and ran off. No one has seen him since, and the police can't find him anywhere. That was the story that was told to Cornelius when he returned from Saint Louis. It could be said that Cornelius was mildly skeptical of the story. However, it could also be said that Cornelius wasn't too disappointed that Flynn was gone. The following day a letter came addressed to Crow's Farm from Brownsville, Texas.

Dear Pablo,

  You'll never believe who just came back to town. You guessed it. Our old friend Lefty Carson! Like a lot of folks these days, he and Linda have fallen on hard times. They were too proud to take from their children, so they moved in with Marcie and me. I'd like to be able to say that work is steady, but we're doing the best we can. Mostly Lefty and me sit around nights remembering the old bonfire days with Big George's moonshine. It sure would be nice to have one more go around with whoever's left of us. Take care, my friend. And don't you worry. We'll all doing the best we can to look after Martina.

       Your friend, Mick

Well, thought Cornelius, a*t least it was a pleasant train ride.*

Chapter Eight
Reunions

Dearest Cheers, (Cheers became Johnny's pet name for Anna Maria. He though it was a nice way to remind her of her beloved grandfather)

I guess by now you've heard all about the invasion. No doubt the whole world has. You can't imagine what it's like here. I can't imagine it myself and I'm right here caught up in the thick of it. Growing up on a farm, I always imagined a beach to be a tranquil place, where all that's heard are the gulls flying above and the roar of the ocean. I imagine not too long ago this place was just like that, and hopefully will be again. Right now I'm sitting beside my friend, Hank, from England. He's resting now, but when awake, he goes on and on about this pub back home and a particular ale that he and his "chums" are fond of drinking. Tanner's Jack, I believe he calls it. Like the rest of us, Hank longs to be back home. When caught up in such a place, one finds themselves longing for the simplest of things—things that most often are taken too much for granted. But in a place like this, even those things which are simple are too much to ask for. I'm afraid my English friend won't make it through the night, though I'll be praying very hard for him.

I've been to so many places and have seen so many things since leaving the farm it's hard to sort them all. But there's this one vision that's always in my mind. I can't seem to shake it, nor do I want to. The vision is of you sitting high atop that horse you love so much. Becky, I believe you call her. Remembering the way you looked when high in her saddle with your cinnamon hair waving under your riding cap, is a picture of beauty and magnificence that is unmatched anywhere, and that I know for sure. I don't know why we drifted apart these past few years, especially after getting so close. Now that I'm thousands of miles away, I find myself wondering if it's possible to revisit that moment in time when "we" almost happened. Even if the possibility is only remote or if it's just a fanciful dream that'll never come true, it's the one thing that keeps me going.

Love, Johnny

My darling Johnny,

I have so much to tell you. Your father and I have decided to finance Sauceman Sal in a spaghetti sauce venture. Owen Hoyt came up with the name "Mr. Mascagni's Magnificent Marinara." Pretty catchy, don't you think? It's already in grocery stores all over Louisville, and I'm betting, soon the whole state. And from there, who knows!

Your father has rebounded from that dreadful flu, thank goodness. He's looking well and claims to feel stronger every day, though I've managed to convince him to delegate more responsibility. At first, as you'd expect, he made a big fuss. You Crow men are so predictable. But my stubbornness finally prevailed.

Your mother slips away every night to walk in the fields at sunset. She always did love walking at that time. In the past, she enjoyed having company, but lately she wants to be alone with her thoughts. I guess it helps her to cope with you being gone. When we're all together at the end of the day, we always end up talking about Aunt Betsy and Gabriel and how fond we were of them and how much we miss them. It's true, of course, we miss both of them terribly. But talking about them has become our not so clever way of avoiding talking about you. I think we're each afraid to mention the war for fear it will set off a chain reaction of worried looks that would only lead to tears.

My grandfather taught me many things as a child, and two of them being: War is ugly, and life is short. It was strange growing up in a household with someone with whom you shared romantic feelings. I still remember our prom night; we had one eyes on our dates and the other was glued to one another. But I suppose it was me who was afraid of failure and who first backed away. But that was another time. As far as revisiting the moment when "we" almost happened? I'm already there, Johnny. I'm there waiting and praying every day for your return.

Love, Cheers

****

Following the bombing of Pearl Harbor, as did tens of thousands of other young men throughout the country, Johnny Crow enlisted in the United States Army. It couldn't be said that it was a particularly popular decision at Crow's Farm. Upon hearing the news, Irma left the room to go and cry in private. Cornelius was conflicted. He understood perfectly the honor and duty one should possess for one's country, but still found his son's decision troubling; therefore he did what he usually did whenever things were too heavy on his mind: He went outside to lose himself in work. As for Anna Maria? She erupted.

"You're your father's only son! You have no right to do this!" she protested.

"I have every right," Johnny declared. "It's my life—at least it was the last time I checked."

"There are other ways to help the war effort, if that's what you're aiming to do," cried Anna Maria, "and it won't come at the cost of your own life. Besides, you're needed *here*!"

"No, Cheers, *you're* needed here!" snapped Johnny. "You're practically running the damn show these days. No one will even know that I'm gone!"

"So you've decided to choose a war as a means of feeling worthwhile?" said Anna Maria. "Why?"

"Because I watched my own mother being raped!" screamed Johnny. "Because I laid there like a little cunt while you shot Flynn—that's fucking why! And because since the very day that you arrived, I have ardently loved and admired you, and have always wished that it was the other way around!"

"You don't have to prove anything to me, Johnny," cried Anna Maria. "You never did. It's all in your own head. It's always been in your own head."

"That's exactly right, Cheers; it's not about you. It's about me," said Johnny. "I have to prove myself to me."

In Johnny's eyes, Anna Maria had been a woman since the day that she arrived at Crow's Farm. Johnny, on the other hand, had spent the last eleven years trying to figure out how to become a man, and in his own estimation always came up short. The big blowup over Johnny's enlistment was the last time Anna Maria and Johnny spoke in person. Anna Maria refused to see Johnny off. However, it didn't take her long to regret the decision. Her letter of apology was in Johnny's hand before he finished basic training. For awhile their letters were merely cordial. Later they became more friendly, but without necessarily being warm or loving.

Everything changed after the Normandy Invasion.

****

Gabriel knew every pebble on every acre of Crow's Farm. He knew how to give to the earth and how to get her to give back. For years, Anna Maria was right there at his elbow taking in all the elder's wisdom and experience. By her second summer at Crow's Farm, she knew how to operate all the equipment and machinery. By her fourth summer, she knew how to repair them. These days, as she sat high atop Becky, with her cinnamon hair waving under her riding cap, she commanded respect like no other. None who went before her—not Gabriel, not Cornelius, not even the Senior Cornelius Crow commanded such respect. Among the workers still around from the old regime, there existed great respect, whereas the newbies feared her. After all, legend had it that she once killed a man. "Stared 'im down, then shot 'im right between the eyes in cold blood," Owen Hoyt would tell them.

Owen Hoyt and Sauceman Sal did all they could to further Anna Maria's legend. Her reputation was such that, if you looked at her cross-eyed, you were likely to end up staring down the barrel of a Colt. "A real gunslinger, she is," Owen Hoyt was fond of saying. "Once saw her pick a fly off a horse's tail from a hundred feet away, and the dang thing was still wavin' when she did it, and the horse never even flinched. Now that's some dang shootin'."

There were some who chose to doubt the two men's claims. But when they beheld Anna Maria Cordero's statuesque figure sitting regally atop Becky, as her Mayan eyes keenly gazed out upon the landscape, something told them that she was no one with whom to trifle. The way the men regarded Anna Maria was a real head-scratcher for Cornelius, who years ago became resigned to the untruth that Flynn torched the barn, ran off, and was never again seen. Though, more and more, he too found himself yielding to her will.

****

"Anna Mareeeeahhhh," called Irma from the porch.

Anna Maria glanced down at her wristwatch. *That's odd,* she thought, for it was only three o'clock in the afternoon. Nevertheless, she climbed up onto Becky and rode straight away to the house.

"You have a guest waiting for you inside," said Irma.

"A guest?" said Anna Maria, unable to imagine who would be calling on her in the middle of a work day. She jumped down from Becky and went tearing up the steps, thinking it might be Johnny. But before she managed to fling open the door, she though, *Johnny isn't a guest. And besides, if he were here, he'd have come looking for me.*

"That's an interesting smile," said Anna Maria, as she began to regard Irma with suspicion. "I don't believe I've ever seen *that* one before."

"Stop trying so hard to figure things out and just go inside," said Irma. "You have a guest waiting."

Still wary of Irma's peculiar smile, Anna Maria slowly backed her way into the house, where inside sat a woman. She looked older than her years might suggest, as the past hadn't been particularly kind, and for this she was embarrassed. She sat with her back to anyone who might enter the room. Although it was her wish to be discovered, examined, then hopefully but not regrettably recognized, her head was posed with a downward tilt.

Who is this poor humble creature, wondered Anna Maria. When she called "*hello,*" the woman turned slightly, exposing very little of her face. At last, the woman's curiosity got the better of her, and she stood and faced Anna Maria with as much poise as she was able to summon. In a matter of seconds, years of languishment and hopefulness came pouring out of her—it seemed to gush from everywhere. Her weary eyes widened and at once recaptured the old fire they had when riding high atop one of Big George's massive shoulders after being discovered in the cornfield. Martina Cordero's journey had been long and hard, but it had reached its glorious end.

****

My darling Johnny,

    I have wonderful news. Mama has come to stay with us! She came only for a visit, but your mother insisted that she stay. We gave her Aunt Betsy's old room. I hope you don't mind, Johnny, because it gives me great joy to at last be reunited with her. I realize that over the years I spoke very little of Mama. Just wondering about her at times was too painful. She refuses to speak of the past several years, but only wishes to talk about me and our lives going forward. I've chosen to honor her wish. I can tell you, though, she's an old farm girl from way back, and I can't remember seeing her happier. Some days, she helps your mother and others she spends working in the fields. She's acclimated herself quickly and has become quite valuable. At suppertime, your mother enjoys listening to all her stories about Miss Lillie and Big George. They're folks that Mama knew from her childhood. She's been teaching us all the songs that Miss Lillie taught her, and after supper we sometimes sing. Your father especially enjoys listening to all the stories from all the Thanksgivings and Christmases that Mama spent in Madisonville with Aunt Betsy and her husband, Ben. Oh, Johnny, I do wish you could be here.

But for now, just know that you are in my heart and that I'm counting the days until your return.

Love,
Your dearest Cheers.

Dearest Cheers,

The going had been slow for the longest time. We were going at a snail's pace, only picking up 1,000 yards a day. But now, in a very short time, we managed to travel forty miles. The Germans have pulled out of Normandy, and Paris has been liberated. Still, there's a ways to go, but at last there's a light at the end of the tunnel.

That's wonderful news about your mother. The old farm is sounding more and more like a place a fellow can't wait to get back to. But honestly, Cheers, it seems that I've seen enough men die, or narrowly escape with their lives to fill the town of Louisville. And I know this is too selfish even to think, less write down on paper, but I believe that God is keeping me alive for you. I believe it's in His plan for us to be together. But you know me; I've always been a bit of a dreamer. But I can tell you that, no matter how many planes I've seen roaring overhead—no matter how much gunfire, or how many explosions have rung in my ear—at night when I close my eyes it's only you that I see—it's only your voice that I hear in my head, and for a while the war doesn't exist. That has to mean something. At least that's what I'm choosing to believe.

Goodbye for now my dearest Cheers.

Love, Johnny

****

"You were quiet tonight at dinner," remarked Anna Maria, after rapping gently on Martina's door. "Is everything alright?"

Anna Maria went and lay down beside her mother.

"Everything is just fine," said Martina. "I'm very happy here."

Anna Maria sounded worried when suggesting, "But you look tired, Mama. Irma thinks that you should rest and take a few days to yourself, and I agree. After all, Mama, you've been going at it very hard."

"I'll be fine," said Martina. She then gave her daughter a dismissive wave to suggest that she needn't be fussed over. "Besides, it's the end of the day; I should be tired. If I wasn't tired by now, it would mean that I hadn't done enough."

"I can plainly see where I get all my stubbornness," said Anna Maria.

"Well, after all, my sweet child, we don't take after strangers," Martina drolly pointed out. Then she reached up and put a gentle hand to Anna Maria's cheek.

"What are you grinning at, Mama?" Anna Maria wondered, as she leaned down and playfully nuzzled Martina's nose.

"What else, but you," replied Martina with a hint of pride.

"I make you grin?" Anna Maria asked.

"What makes me grin, dear child, is laying here and wondering how it's possible that anyone can be so beautiful. That's what makes me grin. I'm finally beginning to understand why your grandfather was so captivated by my mother."

"Ah, but like you said, Mama, we don't take after strangers," said Anna Maria.

The remark made Martina smile. The two lay together, enjoying one another's warmth and a comfortable silence. When Anna Maria sensed that Martina was nodding off, she got up to leave. She hadn't made it as far as the door, though, when Martina stirred and said, "He must be a fine young man, your soldier. I see the way his letters make you smile and warm your heart."

"He is, Mama," said Anna Maria. "He truly is a fine man."

"I only wish that your grandfather could be here for the wedding," said Martina, as though a wedding was a foregone conclusion. "He would be so proud."

"Johnny hasn't asked me to marry him, yet," said Anna Maria; though her voice swelled with the notion that a proposal was inevitable soon after Johnny's return. "But you're right, Mama, Grandfather would be proud...of both of us." Again she went and lay down next to Martina. "As a young girl, I always had the sense that my grandmother was watching over me—that she was always close by. And now that she and Grandfather are together, I can feel them both. I can feel them both right here in this very room, and they're smiling, Mama. They're smiling because we have peace and happiness, and because we love each other just as much as they love us."

"*Somebody* has surely inherited their grandfather's romantic way of looking at the world," said Martina. "But I guess some of it must have even rubbed off on me as well, because I don't believe they ever parted. I believe that, when your grandmother died, she and your grandfather each broke off a piece of their soul and gave it to one another for safekeeping, and to make sure that their bond, no matter what, would never break."

"What a lovely thought," said Anna Maria.

"The world still has much loveliness, my child," said Martina. "And I shall be most anxious to meet your soldier."

****

My darling Johnny,

Good news! Mr. Mascagni's Magnificent Marinara is flying off shelves in grocery stores all over Louisville! It won't be long before it's in stores all over Kentucky! Oh, and Johnny, I must remind you of your father's birthday. He turns fifty next month and we're planning a big celebration. It's a real milestone, you know, so please don't forget to write. Your mother and I get an abundance of letters to read, but seldom, if ever, do you write your father. And even though he'd never say so, I think he feels slighted. So please do remember to write and to make a great fuss over his birthday. Trust me, to do so is not "unmanly."

Mama seems very tired these days. I'm afraid she isn't well. Though, when I dare to suggest such a thing and plead with her to rest, she dismisses me as being silly, and that I shouldn't waste my time making a fuss over her. I suppose she has a stubborn streak, just like everyone else around here. But I worry about Mama, just as I worry about you. I know you've told me time and again not to worry, and now I'm getting more of the same from her. Maybe it's just me, but it seems the more fervent someone is when trying to convince you not to worry, the more there is to worry about. Anyway, lately that's the way I'm finding things. I don't mean to ramble on like this, Johnny, and I certainly don't want to bore you with such drivel. I suppose I should end this letter before I go so far as to convince you that, the love to which you soon shall return, has gone and made herself into an old worrywart. Take care, my love.

Love, your dearest Cheers

Dearest Cheers,

We were on our way to Germany when we ran out of gasoline and other critical supplies. It's unclear how long it will take before we can get moving again. It boggles the mind to think of how much pounding this poor continent has taken. God only knows how long it'll take to clean her all up and then rebuild her. It surely won't be as simple as running a combine over a field. What I wouldn't give to be back home doing just that.

Tonight we all went to a Catholic Church in Belgium. It's much different than our Protestant church back home. It must be centuries old, but it makes you feel good when you're inside. Maybe it's the architecture, or trying to imagine the lives of folks who came here to pray in the 1500s. Either way, it sure felt nice—like we were transported back in time and for awhile were insulated from the war. But the best part was watching colored and white soldiers kneeling down and praying together. I guess war is a great equalizer. It doesn't matter who you were before you put on the combat fatigues, because once they're on, you're just a small part of a large band of brothers. Maybe after this is all over and done with, some of it will carry over. It sure would be nice.

War can sure change the way a fella looks at the world. I spent my whole life dreaming of ways to get away from the farm, and now that I'm finally gone, I can't wait to get back. How's that old saying go? Be careful what you wish for. If I could talk to your mother, I would tell her, if I had been smarter and listened to your daughter, tonight she and I would be holding hands on a moonlit stroll after seeing a picture show in Louisville. But I'm thousands of miles away, and instead of her warm hand, all I have to hold is her last letter and my rifle. So maybe you should listen when she says to rest and not work so hard.

There's something that's been on my mind, Cheers, and I can't seem to let it go. For months, now, I've wanted to tell you that I love you, but I wanted to wait until we were face to face, so that I could look into your eyes when saying it. I'm sorry, Cheers, but I just can't wait any longer. I love you. I love you with all my heart.

Love, Johnny

"I love you too, Johnny," said Anna Maria. Then she pressed her lips where Johnny had signed his name and placed the letter on her nightstand.

****

Anna Maria and Martina sat side by side, enraptured, as Brahms' Piano Concerto No. II, in all its splendor, filled Louisville's Memorial Auditorium. Like most farm girls, aside from the day's popular songs, Anna Maria wasn't a music aficionado. Seldom did the music of such composers as Brahms reach her ears; though, she did find the concerto's fiery second movement, known as the *allegro appassionato,* stirring. Meanwhile, Martina zeroed in on the pianist, whose energy and virtuosity sent her spirit soaring to a place where men like Callahan cannot exist, and where cancer cannot unsuspectingly creep into one's body.

Martina didn't heed her daughter and Irma's advice to rest and not work so hard. She ignored the warning signs her body had given. When asked to stay on at Crow's Farm, Martina made it her mission to do whatever she could to unburden Irma and Anna Maria. Now her days were dwindling.

It was early November during breakfast, and Irma was already planning the Thanksgiving menu and was asking for dessert suggestions, when Anna Maria leapt from her seat and went tearing through the house. Up the stairs she rumbled with newspaper in hand. It had been her custom to rap lightly on Martina's door before opening it just enough to slip through. On this particular morning, though, she went blasting into the bedroom like a raging bull. Dashing to the bedside, she placed the section of the paper that she had been reading on Martina's chest.

"Is this *her,* Mama?" she asked, excitedly. "The girl you used to tell me about?"

Not without some effort, Martina sat up in her bed. With hands that shook, she held up what Anna Maria wanted her to see. She read in silence: *This Friday and Saturday at Louisville's Memorial Auditorium, the Louisville Philharmonic will perform Brahms' Piano Concerto No.2 with guest soloist, Laura Trudeau...* Without touching another morsel of breakfast, Anna Maria raced over to the box office in Louisville.

There was no trembling or pain of any kind in Martina, as she allowed herself to become enveloped by the cyclonic storm that raged from Laura Trudeau's fingertips. It was difficult to imagine that this woman, who asserted herself with such verve, was the same delicate creature Martina remembered from her childhood. She closed her eyes hoping that somehow the years could melt away, and that when she opened them, she would discover seated at the grand piano a young girl with barrel curls who used to send notes raining down on her as she lay on the hardwood floor gathering the vibrations. Martina smiled when remembering the loud, dissonant chords Laura used to play that always ruined her repose. Laura always laughed at the way the terrible sound sent Martina lurching upward. Aside from the amusement Laura got from playing those harsh chords, it was her way of saying that she was tired of playing and in want of fresh air and sunshine. Martina needed no arm twisting whenever fresh air and sunshine were suggested. The mere mention of each prompted her to take Laura by the hand and pull her along. "Come on, Laura, let's run through the fields!" she would cry, unable to contain her excitement. Laura allowed herself to be pulled along, but always threatened to thwart the adventure should Martina pick up any bugs.

Trudeau's Farm and its surrounding fields were Martina Cordero's playground—her heaven on earth. There, every meal was a celebration of life and the year's first and last sorghum harvests were joyous occasions. For awhile, Pablo managed to convince himself after that morning he returned from Bagdad Beach with hot cornbread—the very same morning Martina spoke her peace that the ill-feelings over leaving Trudeau's Farm were at last behind them. Although Martina seldom intimated so, she never forgave her father for taking her away.

As the years went by, Martina's mind embellished those early years on the farm, making Brownsville, in her view, all the more bleak, and a place where, even if she tried, happiness couldn't be found. It wasn't until she discovered herself walking up the road to Crow's Farm, a place of which Pablo spoke fondly and, of which during holiday dinners in Madisonville, Betsy Hutchinson told engaging stories, that she felt anything resembling her childhood happiness. At last, she was free from Callahan—free from everything.

"You're just an old farm girl at heart, aren't you Mama?" remarked Anna Maria.

"We are what we are," said Laura, as though suggesting that an old farm girl was a fine thing to be.

Anna Maria set down a tray with a pitcher of water and two glasses on Martina's nightstand, then left the room. Laura smiled sweetly when looking up at her. When Anna Maria had gone, Laura turned to Martina and said, "She's beautiful. Beautiful just like her mama."

"I'm *some* beauty," said Martina.

"There are some things that your illness can't take away," said Laura. "That fire that burned in you as a child; it's still there. I can see it."

"It makes me happy that you remember me," said Martina.

"You'd be the very last person on this earth that I'd ever forget," said Laura. Then she went and sat on the edge of the bed. "So many things have come and gone in my life since our days together back at the farm—half of which I couldn't recall if I tried. But I remember every day we spent together." Martina hoisted herself up so that she was resting on her elbows and closer to Laura. She wanted to try, or to better understand why this magnificent pianist, who has spent years playing to packed concert halls all over the country, as much as anything valued their shared childhood.

"You changed my life that day in the field," said Laura. "I was always so fragile and cautious…afraid of everything. But it all changed for me that day. I can still see the determination in your eyes when you took off after Golda. And just as if it was yesterday, I can feel the compassion that came pouring out of you once you caught up with her. You restored a human soul. You brought Golda back to life, and in doing so, you changed mine. No one else could've done what you did that day. And to this very day, I've never admired anyone so much as I admired you on that sunny afternoon in the field. It was like a miracle.

"For years, whenever I walked up on stage and felt those butterflies in my stomach, I would remember how brave and fearless you were. My whole life, my hero has been a seven-year-old girl and I always hoped there'd come a day when I would get the chance to thank her."

"It's not nice to make a sick woman cry," said Martina. She looked away, for had she met Laura's gaze she would have burst into tears.

"Don't be silly," said Laura. "I'll bet you can still run faster than me."

"That's a nice thought," said Martina, "but I'm afraid my running days are over." Then she looked up at Laura and smiled like an angel. "I'll bet the world has got some wonderful views—from mountain tops, tall buildings, and bridges; but seeing that old farm from atop Big George's shoulders gave me the best view of all."

"I'm thinking you're right," said Laura.

"Strange, but I can still remember Miss Lillie's hands—the way they felt," said Martina. "And lately at night when I close my eyes, I've been feeling her hands on me real gentle-like. It's as if, because she took care of me right after I came into this world, she's gonna take care of me leaving."

"It'd be just like her to do that," said Laura.

"It sure would," said Martina. "I think that's why I'm not afraid."

"She was the best," said Laura.

Martina reached up and wiped away the teardrop that was rolling down Laura's cheek. "We *are* still talking about Miss Lillie, aren't we?" she asked. "Because I don't want any tears shed over *me*."

"Of course we are," said Laura as she burst into tears.

Martina brought Laura down to her chest and held her. "You were magnificent tonight," she said. "I've never known anyone to have such abilities. And I thank God for keeping me around long enough to hear you play in front of all those people. But now I have a small favor to ask if you don't mind."

"Anything," cried Laura.

"My running days truly are over," said Martina. "But I surely wouldn't mind a stroll through the field in the night air with my dear old friend."

"No bugs?" asked Laura, managing a smile.

"No bugs," said Martina as their tears turned to laughter.

On the following morning, Anna Maria brought a tray with eggs and hot biscuits with syrup to Martina's room. "Rise and shine, Mama," she whispered in her ear. "It's time for breakfast."

"Miss Lillie told me not to go wandering off too far," said Martina, "so I best be getting back."

"Mama, you're dreaming," said Anna Maria.

"Look, child," said Martina, "I can see her waving me in, telling me that it's time to come home. Soon Big George, Papa, and the others will be coming out of the fields, so I best be getting along. Miss Lillie needs me to help with supper."

"Mama, do you see Miss Lillie?" asked Anna Maria.

"I can see her reaching for me, child," said Martina.

"Then we should sing, Mama," cried Anna Maria. "Let's sing."

Joshua fit the battle of Jericho, Jericho, Jericho. Joshua fit the battle of Jericho…

"Come on, Mama, sing with me," pleaded Anna Maria. "You remember?"

And the walls came a tumblin' down.

****

My darling Johnny,

Sadly, things have changed here at home. Although, I guess you won't notice any difference because you never got the chance to meet Mama. In a way, it makes my heart ache like never before. She so looked forward to meeting you and always remarked how your letters brightened my day. In the past, I've lost Grandfather, Aunt Betsy, and Gabriel, and as much as I mourned their losses, I didn't feel that they were cheated out of any years or that God owed them anything other than Heaven and to be at peace. But now that I've lost Mama, it seems death is something that I just found out about—like all along it was some big secret that everybody else knew about but me. Your mother and father, God bless them, have been kind as always, but lately I've retreated to my grandfather's Bible.

I'm not sure what I'm looking for or what I should hope to find, but in my search my thoughts always turn to you. God knows how many hundreds and maybe thousands of young men you've seen die. It's awful to think, but somehow it helps to reconcile losing Mama. She was one old farm girl against thousands, who for better or worse, will never get to experience life beyond this terrible war. Then it suddenly occurs to me that you're one of those young men over there fighting for our country and praying for life beyond the war. My heart breaks for Mama, but I can't breathe for thinking of what could happen to you. I don't dare say a word to your mother, less show her how upset I get at times, as it's always been me that has tried to kept up her spirits. So I climb up on Becky and ride her hard. I ride through the farm, the wide open spaces beyond, and then out onto the country roads. The winter wind blows through my hair and beats against my face until it becomes numb. After awhile I can't feel a thing, but it isn't until miles later that I climb down from my beautiful mare. From the cold and the thrill of the ride I begin to tingle all over, and for awhile everything seems right with the world. But the feeling doesn't last for very long. I've tried to convince myself that, the longer I ride, the longer the feeling will last, but it doesn't seem to work that way. So I climb back up on Becky and trot on home, hoping for a different result tomorrow. Along the way I'll recall something Gabriel once told me. "Dying is the easy part," he would say. "It's the living that's hard. But the good Lord gives us just enough joy to make it all seem worthwhile."

I guess that's the one question I never got around to asking Mama; did the past year that she spent with us make it all worthwhile? I'm trying to imagine that had I thought enough to ask, that she'd have said yes. I'm here Johnny, waiting for you to come home and to put joy back into my life.

Love, your dearest Cheers

Dearest Cheers,

It's Christmas Eve. At least I think it still is. A while back some of us were deployed to Bastogne, a town in Belgium. It's got to be the coldest place on earth. Earlier we came under attack, but were reinforced by the 101ˢᵗ Airborne and 10ᵗʰ Armored divisions. We ended up surrounded and the Germans asked for a surrender, but our General told them, "Nuts."

Can you imagine? Anyway, the next day the weather cleared and much needed supplies were parachuted in. Now we're in much better standing. But now I must ask a favor of you, Cheers. If ever you hear me dreaming about being anything other than a farmer from Kentucky, search the area for the biggest thing that you can find and then beat me over the head with it until you're fully convinced that any remaining foolishness is gone and shall never return. My, what I wouldn't give for a slice of homemade blueberry pie and some Kentucky sunshine!

I truly am sorry to hear about Mama. But if you really want to know if her life, no matter how hard, was worthwhile, all you need to do is look in the mirror. It shouldn't take too long to figure it out. You are a testament, a living breathing monument to how worthwhile her life truly was, and every day from my knees I will thank her and pray for her eternal soul.

Love, Johnny

Chapter Nine
The Secret of Cheerianna

"For cryin' out loud, what in the blazes is all that racket out there?" complained Johnny. "And at this hour of the morning!"

"That *racket*, dear husband, is our son," replied Anna Maria.

"I don't give a hoot and a half whose son it is," growled Johnny, "I'll still have 'im arrested for disturbing my peace."

"You know, they say the apple doesn't fall vey far from the tree," remarked Anna Maria.

"Yeah, well, I guess in my case it fell straight down and landed no more than an inch or so from the darn truck and then stuck there," grumbled Johnny. Then with a huff, he pulled the bedspread over his head. Not that he expected the bedding to adequately filter out the dreadful banging and allow him to return to his peaceful slumber.

Anna Maria made for the window, where she stood and watched eight-year-old Johnny Crow Junior standing in the same spot that his father had stood back in the summer of 1930. The youngster went into his wind-up, and with a fair amount of velocity, he fired a baseball toward a barn door on which a white rectangle had recently been painted. The ball sounded as if it exploded when it found the target. Like his father before him, Johnny Crow Junior was a young farm boy with big dreams.

Two months after Johnny came home from the war, he and Anna Maria were married. Within a year of the wedding, Johnny Junior was born.

"I'd like you to meet your new boss," Cornelius had said to Johnny upon his returning from overseas. Then he pointed to Anna Maria. By then, not only was Anna Maria running the farm; she was also overseeing Sauceman Sal's pasta sauce venture.

232

"We all work for *her*, now," said Cornelius. "She's got a better head for business then any of us."

"Gee, what a surprise," was Johnny's droll reply.

At the wedding reception, Johnny stood up and delivered a moving tribute to Martina and his new bride. In the days that followed, he spoke of the places he had been and the friends he made along the way, but never of the war. Anna Maria brought Johnny up to speed with everything that had been going on at the farm and in Louisville. What they never spoke of, though, was their big blow-up over Johnny enlisting in the army. Once Anna Maria penned her apology for not seeing Johnny off, the matter was closed and was never revisited.

During their blow-up the name *Flynn* got mentioned. Not before that day, nor since, had either mentioned his name. And aside from their blow-up, what happened in the old barn in the summer of 1930 was never mentioned. Besides, Gabriel forbade such talk. And where Irma was concerned, for the sake of Cornelius who was never told the truth of what happened that day, some secrets were best to remain just that…secrets. That was fine by Johnny and Anna Maria, as neither cared to revisit that day. But what Johnny didn't know, nor ever would, for Anna Maria would take the secret to her grave, was that Flynn wasn't the first man that she had shot and killed.

As she always had, Martina pleaded with Anna Maria to leave when Callahan showed up. Grudgingly Anna Maria made for the door, but not before glaring back at Callahan. Once outside and about to walk away, through the open window she heard her mother refuse Callahan. Anna Maria froze before she dared to take another step. It was the first time that Martina openly defied her tormenter, and Anna Maria was fearful of the outcome.

"Do allow me explain, so that maybe you'll understand once and for all," said Callahan. "Ya see, girly, this here is my game. And *because* it's my game, I get to be in charge—and the person in charge gets make the rules. That's how things generally work in the world. Am I makin' myself clear? 'Cause if not, I'll try and explain it to you different. But you don't want me to have to keep explaining things, do you? Because if ol' Callahan here has to keep explaining things, neither of us is gonna be happy."

Anna Maria seethed when hearing Callahan's condescending tone. She was certain that her mother would wilt and exhibit the downcast eyes and obedient posture that always brought forth Callahan's victorious grin. How she hated that grin; it crept into her thoughts at night and ruined many a slumber. But Martina didn't wilt as expected. This time, Callahan's mocking tone and lecherous behavior brought forth a more vehement refusal.

It was always Anna Maria's belief that Callahan was an evil man—a distortion of a human being. As a younger child, she found him frightening. She often wondered why her mother allowed such a man to enter their home, especially when she, a mere child, could plainly see that her mother was also frightened by the terrible man. With a child's timetable being what it is, after a day or so, Callahan's visits were all but forgotten. It seemed like ages had gone by before he returned. As time went by and Anna Maria got older, his visits seemed more frequent, although that wasn't the case. Another effect of her getting older, was that her fear of Callahan was replaced with rage. She managed to keep herself under control, where upon Martina's rebuff of the terrible man, he became violent.

Anna Maria looked on as Callahan took fistfuls of Martina's hair and dragged her down the hall to her bedroom. Still, she remained under control. Without making a sound, she reentered the house. In the bedroom, she could hear Callahan raging and Martina struggling. Still she remained under control. She knew exactly where Pablo kept his brown, suede satchel. Swiftly, she crept for its hiding place. When she unbuckled the satchel, she found resting just below the holy Bible, the beautifully hilted knife, and a surprising amount of cash, the famous 1873 single action Colt Revolver—the same one owned by Theodore Roosevelt, Buffalo Bill Cody, Wyatt Earp, and Billy The Kid—the same one that she was told was "not a toy" and was "a gift from a prince" and was made to promise that under no circumstances was she to touch.

Anna Maria took the revolver and began her slow march toward her mother's bedroom. She stood in the open doorway and saw her mother's naked body forcibly bent over the foot of the bed. Callahan had a powerful hand resting on Martina's head and was pushing it into the mattress in order to muffle her screams. Anna Maria raised her right arm. Callahan turned just in time to see the barrel of the revolver pointed directly at his head.

Anna Maria had no recollection of returning the revolver to its hiding place; nor did she remember taking a stick and prying loose a stone with which to scratch out the words *I fixed it* in the hard clay just outside the house after her concerned grandfather asked, *what happened?* What she *did* remember, however, years later and with some degree of satisfaction, was the mixture of surprise and terror that registered on Callahan's face when he turned his head. The surprise came about when he realized Anna

234

Maria was able to sneak up on him. The terror came about *not* from the gun, but from having just enough time to look into Anna Maria's Mayan eyes and to recognize their grim determination. Callahan was the sort of man who knew the difference between someone who brought a gun to the party to show it off, and someone who came prepared to shoot. It took him only a fraction of a second to make this determination. A fraction was all he had before the bullet entered his skull.

Sometime after Johnny came home from the war, and before Anna Maria and he were to be wed, she had intended to divulge the reason for her and Pablo's abrupt departure from Brownsville. She didn't want Johnny to enter into something as important as a marriage without first being made aware of an event of such significance. But the right time never came, nor could she find the right words. Furthermore, had she told him of Callahan and her reason for taking his life, it would have placed them right back in the old barn in the summer of 1930—a place and a moment in time which neither cared to revisit. Finally, like Irma in the case of Flynn, Anna Maria decided that some secrets should remain just that…secrets. She was able to rationalize her decision with the fact that Johnny had shielded her from the atrocities of war. She didn't dare ask how many people he killed, and Johnny certainly didn't offer any such information. Admittedly it was a weak rationale, but she was reaching for any sort of justification that would allow her to make peace with herself.

"Good lord," grumbled Johnny, "did *I* make that much racket?" Johnny held his ears after the baseball once again came pounding on the barn door.

"Oh, no," replied Anna Maria, "your son throws much harder than you used to."

"Really?" asked Johnny, not knowing whether to act proud or slighted. Johnny made his way to the window to see for himself his son's golden arm.

You go right ahead and dream, my son, Anna Maria thought to herself. *Dream all you want, because Mama is going to be here. Your mama is always going to be here for you; and I'll share your dreams, big or small, and together we'll embrace them.*

"A real chip off the old block, I see," said Johnny. Then he placed his hand on Anna Maria's stomach. "Does it feel like a girl?" he asked.

"Your mother seems to think so," replied Anna Maria.

"Perfect," said Johnny. "The world is perfect."

****

"Look at all the roses, Grandfather!" exclaimed Anna Maria, as the train chugged its way into Kentucky. "Aren't they beautiful?"

"Indeed they are, my sweet Cheerianna," replied Pablo. "And it's said that Kentucky roses are among the *most* beautiful. But is it the roses themselves that possess such beauty, or does their true beauty lie in how they make us feel when gazing upon them?"

"What do you mean, Grandfather?" wondered Anna Maria.

"No doubt, the stem of a rose is graceful—its petals soft as a whisper," said Pablo. "The rose is like a delicate creature in a harsh and hostile world, and whose existence depends wholly upon us. It is our own inner beauty that allows for the rose. It is our willingness to tend to that which is weak that's so beautiful."

"I like that, Grandfather," said Anna Maria. "And one day I will say those very same words to *my* granddaughter."

"And for that I will pray," said Pablo.

Afterward

Down through the years there have been many novels involving, or directly tied to The Civil War and World War II. Despite their status as monumental human events, it was much of what occurred in between those epic battles that came to define America. The days of Reconstruction, the great railroad boom, the early popularization of a game that would become a national pastime, The Guilded Age, and immigration were all events that helped turn a land called The United States into a lofty idea known as America. It was during this time that America was up for grabs, and that a young man of the likes of Pablo Cordero could rise from the ashes and gain society. It was a thrill to write this novel of hope, to walk in Pablo's shoes, and to discover a truly golden age of America's fantastic past.

About the Author

Michael De Stefano is from Philadelphia and makes his home in Cinnaminson, New Jersey. He is the author of *The Prodigy of Saint Pete's*—the story of Andy Trumaine, an orphaned boy whose gift to others as he journeys through life is his good sense of the world; and *In the Time of Their Restlessness*—a tumultuous coming of age story in urban America in the 1970s.